THE
LEGEND
OF
HOOPMAN

MICHAEL T. GREGORY

REPUB

The Legend of Hoopman
Copyright © 2023 by Michael T. Gregory

ISBN
978-1-961879-22-5 (Paperback)
978-1-961879-23-2 (eBook)

"I would like to think Ryan Reeves for having faith in me. Appreciate you brother!

I would like to thank Evan Trumeter for his hard work and support. You have a tremendous future in front of you and I hope you get to use your writing talent for a very long time.

Special thank you to Kyle Ross at Blueprint Press. Thanks to you and your team, this book has come to fruition.

Finally, thank you to Lori and the girls for all their support. I couldn't write without you! All my love!"

TABLE OF CONTENTS

Chapter One 1

Chapter Two 6

Chapter Three 28

Chapter Four 50

Chapter Five 66

Chapter Six 86

Chapter Seven 97

Chapter Eight 122

Chapter Nine 139

Chapter Ten 164

Chapter Eleven 190

Chapter Twelve 207

Chapter Thirteen 219

Chapter Fourteen 244

Chapter Fifteen 268

Chapter Sixteen 292

Chapter Seventeen 308

Chapter Eighteen 329

Chapter Nineteen 354

Chapter Twenty 372

Chapter Twenty-One 398

Chapter Twenty-Two 417

Epilogue 427

CHAPTER ONE

The crowd had assembled in a tree covered patio behind the Alamo. An appropriate sight for a military retirement. Sergeant Major Nathan Hawkins stepped to the podium and said, "Ladies and Gentlemen, please stand and help me recognize one of the finest soldiers our nation has to offer. Or should I say, 'HAD' to offer? The former Chief Warrant Officer Four, now retired, Charlton 'Chuck' Hayes." The assembled crowd of fifty guests and fellow soldiers jumped to their feet and gave "Mister" Hayes a standing ovation. Chuck Hayes had just finished twenty years of an illustrious career as a cyber intelligence analyst in the United States Army.

Twenty years of constant travel across the United States of America and in dozens of foreign lands. Twenty years of blood, sweat, and tears that included a hundred emotional highs matched by an equal number of depressing lows. Twenty years of ordinary, selfless military service.

Yet, Chuck Hayes was no ordinary man. There were more than a few things that Chuck was good at. At 39 years old, he still maintained a physique that made men half his age envious. On one hand, he was trained in martial arts and hand-to-hand weapons. Chuck felt the training made his hands quicker. On the other hand, he was skilled at the use of computers, integrating computer hardware, using multiple software programs and cyber telecommunications. The latter specialties were indicative of his "kinder, gentler" side. Chuck Hayes was the epitome of the techno-warrior. The Army had taken twenty years to make him what he was. He was a man whose time to leave had come.

There was one other thing Chuck Hayes could do exceptionally well. It was the one thing that made Chuck somewhat of a legend. That one thing was play basketball. For over thirty years, it was the only constant in his life. Chuck had played hoop in four continents, thirty-two states, and at last count, twenty-three countries including Cuba, Korea, six in Africa, and all of Europe except Lichtenstein.

Chuck Hayes could handle the ball, throw every kind of pass, and shoot from anywhere with either hand. On the court, he always covered the other team's best defender and usually departed the floor with great respect from the men he had played against. No longer the jumper he once was, Chucks' technique for defense and rebounding was based solely on position and tenacity. On the basketball court, Chuck was relentless.

Chuck's military career was not without downfalls. Through the constant moves and ever-changing duty assignments, Chuck had only two regrets. First, he felt he didn't have the courage to make his marriage work, and secondly, he never finished getting his college degree. Chuck had managed to complete his Associates Degree in Cyber Security through Army night courses. But he wanted more. It was not that he felt he was required to have a degree to prove he was equal to anyone else. After working with thousands of men and women with and without degrees, he understood a piece of paper didn't guarantee intelligence or character. Having that piece of paper indicated something positive about the person. It was a sign of personal accomplishment.

Now that Chuck Hayes was retired, getting a degree was one of the top goals in his life. Now he would have the time to do it. He had done everything he had ever wanted to do in the Army. For his country and for his soldiers. It was time to do something for Chuck Hayes.

Chuck's best friend was Sergeant Major, retired, Nathaniel "Hawk" Hawkins. Hawk was a former Military Policeman and a damn good one. Hawk had gotten Chuck out of a bad situation when he was a young sergeant. For that act of pity the MP had extended to the young drunk, Hawk had gained a friend for life. Chuck would have given his life for Hawk because he had saved Chuck from the stockade. Nate Hawkins was proud of the man that Chuck had become. In Hawk's eyes, Chuck had been a tremendous asset not only to the Army, but to his country. Chuck had done things that would never be talked about, never known to the public and surely overlooked by a country that was focused on social media singers, "dot-com bubbles", and bitcoin.

For Hawk, it was an honor to lead the retirement ceremony for Chuck. Chuck had done the same thing for Hawk just five months prior at his own ceremony. Hawk set Chuck up for his retirement speech with an innocent enough question. "What are you gonna do now, Mister Hayes? Besides gives us a good-bye speech," smiled the Sergeant Major.

Chuck looked at the crowd that had grown quiet. Chuck knew were waiting for him to speak. He coughed to clear his throat and began, "First, let me say thank you all for coming. I didn't know I had this many friends. Did the Hawk pay y'all to come or what?" He waited for the chuckling to stop, then said, "I have really enjoyed my time in the military. It hasn't always been a lot of fun," he shook his head. He continued with a smile, "But it has been exciting." Those in the crowd that knew Chuck laughed and nodded.

Chuck suddenly changed his tone. He became serious. "I have lived more, and done more, than thousands of men my age. I look back with nothing but fond memories of my friends, and the United States Army. However, there is one thing I haven't done yet. That is complete my education. I want to learn more. I want to take as many classes as I can. I've been accepted right here in San Antonio at St. Michael's University. I'm gonna be a college student!"

The crowd was shocked silent. A twenty-year military veteran going back to college? What was he thinking? With his experience he could easily get a job making 100 thousand dollars a year anywhere in Texas. Probably more if he wanted to move. But college?

Chuck left it to the Hawk to lighten mood. "Going to college, eh? You're gonna be the oldest freshman in the country!" The crowd laughed at the Sergeant Major's comment, but for the most part remained stunned. Hawk leaned into the microphone to add, "You're just going to school to chase skirts again! Same thing you warned all those soldiers about, right!?" That remark even got a smile out of Chuck Hayes. Then the Hawk really let go. "Hell, you might as well go out for the hoop team, Chuck. Cause them boys stunk last year!" The comment brought nods from the assembled crowd, as well as some boisterous yells from people that had played hoop with Chuck and obviously agreed with the Hawk.

Chuck Hayes' smile faded. He looked at his old friend and said, "They do need another guard, don't they?!" The room erupted in laughter. Chuck Hayes couldn't possibly be serious about playing college basketball, could he?

Chuck looked at the Hawk and said, "I've got a new life now. A life where I can afford to take chances and nobody but me gets hurt. Let me see how classes go, and if I can find the time, I might give the team a chance to hoop with me."

The Hawk's smile faded, and he pulled Chuck close. "Man, you ain't been on the All-Army team in ten years. Those last three post Championships don't mean shit to those college boys! Look at you, man! A 39-year-old man who can't jump anymore! No, wait! Never could jump. You can't be serious?"

Chuck smiled at his mentor and said, "It's a time thing, Hawk. Not an age thing. I have the time to devote to getting my degree and playing ball. You know the desire has always been there. St. Michael's is a great fit for me." Chuck didn't say what he really thought. His opinion was that the team sucked and desperately needed a guard. "At this time in my life, I owe it to myself to give this my best shot." He shook his head and said, "I can play there, Hawk."

Hawk did not disagree. A slight grunt came out of the Sergeant Major, and he said, "You know something, my friend?"

The huge smile returned, "You're right. If anybody can pull this off, it would be you."

"Well, now that I've convinced you, suppose you convince me!" laughed Chuck. For the last twenty years, Chuck Hayes had always been good at planning. It was another thing the Army had taught him to do well. He'd run this plan through his mind for the last two years. While stationed at Ft. Sam Houston, he had managed to catch at least six games a year at the St. Michael's campus. He knew their game, how they played, where their weaknesses and their strengths were. Deep down, he thought he could help the team win some basketball games.

There was a small doubt in the back of his mind that other people would think he was too old to play. Chuck knew better. He knew he "had game". The doubt was never a question of age on the court, but a question of communication off the court. After all was said and done, the college kids were "civilians". Not only were they civilians, but they would also be University students. Kids half his age. That was what he felt most uncomfortable with. It would be his ability, or lack thereof, to communicate with his new peer group which might jeopardize his dream of playing college ball.

God had a plan for Chuck. But it was too late to turn back. He didn't exactly have a job anymore. He said his good-byes. He thanked his guest and told Hawk he'd be seeing him next week, then walked out to his pickup. His plan was in motion, and the only thing that could stop him was Charlton Hayes.

CHAPTER TWO

How he hated baseball season. Football was bad enough, but football just didn't afford anybody the chance to make money. Saturdays and Sundays were the only days when the real bets were made. Years ago, dice and poker had been Steve James' obsession. It wasn't long before he found out how to make money, you needed to bet every day. That's why Steve James loved basketball season. Steve could bet every day on basketball games. Pro ball, college ball, or even a pick-up game, it was all easy money for him. Point spreads and parlays were his life. As a routine, he prayed to the god of chance, the god of odds, or the god of luck. He had forgotten about Father Tony's lecture on false gods. That was the one lecture the young Catholic schoolboy should have taken to heart. Now, every moment of his life he was reminded how his prayers had been answered.

Steve walked behind the seemingly endless row of computers. His limp slowed his pace, and the pain was a little stronger today than normal. He thought that maybe the island would get some rain. His knee usually forecast the weather better than the weather app. He walked around the mainframe and into the control room. His assistant, Jeffrey Roberts said, "Slow night tonight, boss. We'll probably only take in about three-fifty, maybe three-hundred sixty thousand."

"As long as we don't have any big losers," said Steve. He hoped for his clients' sakes, nobody lost too big. It was baseball season. Nobody scored big during baseball season. Baseball was boring. If a client lost on a baseball game and couldn't pay, they deserved it. Finally feeling the pain, he reached down and rubbed his knee. Steve had learned his lesson about losing. Did they treat the big losers worse now than they treated them five years ago? He'd only heard the rumors. He continued to rub his knee to see if maybe this time he could make the throbbing go away. It was useless. He exhaled loudly and focused on his job. He looked at the computer screen and said to Jeff Roberts, "Just baseball. Who gives a shit?"

Four months to go. Steve couldn't wait until basketball season. He had a plan for this year. This was to be the season of payback. His season to make everything that was wrong, turn right again. November couldn't come soon enough. Then it would be Steve's turn to stick it to that bastard in Vegas.

The pretty young girl with braces smiled at Chuck and said, "Welcome to St. Michael's! Are you looking for your son or daughter?"

Chuck sheepishly answered "Uh, no. I'm here to register."

The young girl instantly turned red. "Oh, I'm so sorry, Sir! I thought maybe you were a parent!"

"I am a parent." Chuck laughed to try and relieve her embarrassment. "Just not of any student that's here," he said with a smile. "I guess you could say, I'm a transfer. They gave me credit for 44 hours, so I suppose I'm a sophomore."

The girl blushed and said, "I'm sorry. If you go right over there, all new student registrations begin in that line."

"All right. Now we're getting somewhere," he said with a grin. "Thank you." He grabbed his paperwork and headed to the line. His first exchange with a fellow college student seemed to go just about as he had expected. The age thing came up but wasn't a problem. This college thing was going to be a great experience.

Four hours later, he was headed to his assigned room. Just a bit tired from never ending lines of confused people and the process of controlled chaos that comes with class registration. His room was a small apartment that he would share with one other person.

Campus housing was set up so upper classmen and transfers got newer housing, more space and only two people per apartment. When he got to the room, he found that his new roommate hadn't moved in yet. He went out to his truck and started bringing in boxes. He was glad that he had not accumulated too much 'stuff' after 20 years of military service. His ex-wife had all the "good stuff" with her in North Carolina. He only brought clothes, his laptop, the old stereo complete with 56 albums and 58 compact discs, and, of course, his two basketballs. One ball for indoors and one for outdoors. The rest of his personal stuff including some furniture, boxes of memorabilia, and the other 178 albums and 212 CD's, were locked in a storage shed about five miles from campus. He was tempted to bring his karate workout gear, but like the small arsenal of weapons he owned, those too stayed locked up. This was college, and Chuck was positive there was no need for any of that here.

Chuck was opening a box and putting albums on a shelf when the door popped open. Chuck looked up to see a stack of boxes walking through the door. "You want a hand with that?"

A muffled voice came from somewhere behind the boxes, "No, thanks! I got it! I got it!" The boxes continued to enter the room as if on their own. "Just . . . just let me know where there's a good place to put them down."

"Well, right about where you're standing is good for now," said Chuck smiling at his roommate's predicament. "Here! Let me help you set them down." He stepped closer, grabbed the top two boxes, and set them on the floor.

As his new roommate looked up, the beaming smile immediately disappeared and was replaced with a look of confusion. "Ah . . . hello, Sir. Ah . . . my name is Marshall. Marshall Wright." The confused look was replaced with the smile again. Marshall Wright was five foot ten, wore glasses, brand new blue jeans, and he had a pony-tail tied behind his head. "I guess I'm your son's new roommate!" he beamed as he stuck out his hand.

Chuck took the hand and said, "I don't have a son." He let the words sink in and continued, "I'm your new roommate."

"Ah . . . You're my new roommate?!" said Marshall. After a slight delay, the smile returned. "Great. Cool. I was just expecting . . ."

"I know. I know. Somebody a lot younger!" said Chuck. "The name is Charlton Hayes, but I'm used to everyone calling me Chuck.. I'll only get upset if you call me Mr. Hayes!" Chuck smiled again. That put Marshall Wright much more at ease. "Well, why don't I help you bring your stuff in, and you can tell me a little bit about yourself."

The two men stepped out of the air-conditioned apartment and began hauling in Marshall Wrights' belongings. During the hauling, Marshall explained he was a transfer from Midland Community College, a junior, majoring in Chemical Engineering and "probably going to work on a minor in Physics". His family, back home in Odessa, didn't have enough money to send him to one of those "good schools", so St. Michael's was all he could afford.

Chuck couldn't help but notice the CD's. It was a collection of Matchbox 20, something called Phish, the Goo Goo Dolls, Paramore and other groups he'd never heard of. He also noticed Marshall only had a little boom box to play his music on. This gave Chuck an idea that might make him a better roommate. "Hey, Marshall, if you want, you could use my stereo to play some of your music."

Marshall was taken back by the offer. He looked at the stack of stereo equipment and said, "Really? You think it'd be okay if I played my tunes on your stereo? That would be great, Mister . . . I mean, Chuck!"

"I would also say you can play my CD's if you want to. If you take care of them and don't leave them laying around. Agreed?" asked Chuck.

Marshall picked up one of the CD's in Chuck's collection. After a couple seconds Marshall cocked his head to one side and frowned, "Sorry, Chuck, I don't think that'll be a problem. I haven't heard of any of these guys!" Marshall fingered the CD's. Then he nodded and a smile appeared. He said, "I've heard of the Beatles, but . . ." The smile faded. "Boston. Cars. George . . . Thorogood." Marshall continued looking through the music collection and said, "Van Halen! I've heard of that guy!"

Chuck shook his head and smiled, "Van Halen is not . . . 'a guy'. It's four guys and two are brothers."

Before he could say anything else Marshall said, "Parliament? Is this some kind of British band or something?"

Chuck replied, "Ah, no. No, they aren't British." Chuck was immediately taken back in time. The stereo was always blasting Parliament when he played pick-up games at the park. The CD's continuously played rap music. The park was where you got the best competition. He started to try and explain the unique funk-disco shock rock style of George Clinton, but it only left his roommate confused. "Look! I'll play some for you later."

Marshall wasn't interested. "Chuck, that probably won't be necessary. I plan on being a totally dedicated student," explained Marshall Wright. "I don't think I'll have a lot of time for stuff like that." Chuck nodded his understanding. It hurt him a little thinking he had missed an opportunity to connect to his roommate. To think that Marshall wasn't willing to try something that he had recommended offended Chuck. He shook off the thought. Marshall still seemed like a nice kid. Chuck didn't have the right to preach. The communication cycle is comprised of receivers as well as transmitters. He shrugged off Marshall's comment and continued helping his new roommate set up the apartment.

By the time they finished, it was eight o'clock. Marshall looked wiped out. It was apparent that the young, thin twenty-year-old was not in the best shape. After the last piece of clothing was tucked in its drawer, Marshall collapsed on the couch. "Man am I beat! You wanna watch some TV?"

Chuck came out of his bedroom dressed in gym shorts, a T-shirt and high-top Converse basketball shoes. He was passing his outdoor basketball slowly from his left hand to his right. "Come on, man! Let's go shoot some hoop!"

Marshall was amazed. "No way! I can't believe you're going out to play basketball!"

"I'm going! Come on. There's a little court at the end of the block. We'll just shoot around for an hour or so. What do ya say?" Chuck tried not to beg.

Marshall looked over at Chuck and said, "What are you? Some kind of Hoopman or something?"

"Hoopman?" Chuck smiled at the comment. "No. Not really." Then it hit home. It had a certain ring to it. He liked the way it sounded. It sounded better coming from Marshall than "Old Man". He grinned at his roommate and said, "Now that you mention it. Yeah, I guess I am Hoopman!"

"You must be! Going to play ball after all this. I can't even walk," said Marshall. "You are definitely the Hoopman!"

"Well, you wanna play some ball with Hoopman?" asked Chuck. For a second it appeared Chuck might have convinced Marshall to join him.

Marshall moved on the couch, but it was only to grab the remote. "I don't think so. I'm just going to stay here and go over some of the books I got today. You go ahead."

"All right, Marsh. Suit yourself." Out the door he went. The new nickname, "Hoopman", was actually quite appropriate in Chucks' eyes. For as long as he could remember, he had played hoop. Now that he was older, he certainly couldn't be called Hoopboy! The new name worked, and it was by no means derogatory. He filed his new callsign away and started down the street for the court.

As he dribbled the ball, just hearing the rhythm put Chuck at ease. It was a familiar sound. It was a sound that offered comfort in unfamiliar surroundings. Right hand followed by the left. Then twice with each hand. Chuck worked his way up to five dribbles with each hand, then all the way down to singles again. Then he would spin around in the road as if a defender were in front of him. Then he made some behind the back dribbles. When he got to the court the sun was setting and the temperature was still a muggy ninety degrees. The Texas heat made the court an additional ten degrees hotter. The sweat had already started to darken Chuck's shirt.

The university apartment complex court had glass backboards, a rubber coated surface, a ten-foot chain link fence all the way around the court and painted lines showing the lane and the three-point line. Everything Chuck needed to work on. It was a Monday night, so that meant three pointers. Chuck's usual routine consisted of three pointers on Mondays, Wednesdays, and Fridays. Tuesdays, Thursdays, and Saturdays meant fifteen footers. Everyday included 100s of lay-ups with both hands and 100 free throws.

This night, the court was empty because the students had not moved in yet. That was fine with Chuck. The solitude offered him a chance to relax. With both ends of the court open, it also offered him a chance to get some running in.

First, he focused on form shooting. He didn't feel strong enough to crank three pointers all night, so he settled for fifteen minutes of threes. Chuck would use visualization to concentrate his form when he shot. He would see himself swishing three-pointers from everywhere. He was deliberate in his movements as he placed the ball on his fingers; cock the wrist back, jump as high as possible and focus on the front of the rim as he shot. Then, BANG! Snap the wrist and follow through. He would watch the target and listen for net to answer his question. Something about the rip of the net always made him smile. Hearing the ball swish through the net was a prayer answered. Practice was a spiritual event. It was the way Chuck found peace in his life. Instead of gaining heaven through the "Pearly Gates", he gained his entrance by putting a ball through the rim. The better the shot, the more at peace Chuck would become. Basketball was Heaven, the court was his Eden, and he was in Paradise.

Chuck's paradise was interrupted by another mortal. A white late model Jeep Cherokee floated past the ball court. The windows were down as the driver slowly studied the man on the court. The Jeep stopped and the driver watched Hayes shoot free throws. George Strait was playing on the radio. A young man got out of the Jeep and slowly walked to the light pole.

Click went the light switch. The solitude that Chuck was enjoying was broken by the sound of the fluorescent lights coming to life with a loud "HUUMMMM". Chuck hadn't even realized how dark it had gotten. Slowly, the court grew brighter, and the darkness was chased away. The young man pulled an old, beat-up plastic basketball from the Jeep. He moved through the gate and onto the court, dribbling the whole time. Chuck turned back to his basket and continued shooting. Between retrieving shots, just as every player does, Chuck would glance to see how good the young man was.

The first thing he noticed was the flaming red hair. He didn't look old enough to drive much less be alone in the Jeep. Chuck guessed he may have been barely eighteen. The next thing Chuck noticed was the boy could shoot. The ball was draining through the net on nearly every stroke. After the left hand snapped, the net would pop. The form on his jump shot was tremendous. His jumper was an effortless stroke of pure beauty, rarely seen on a playground. From what Chuck had seen, the kid was the real deal.

Then he saw something he didn't believe. The kid, barely over six feet, red hair and freckles, stood flatfooted under the basket, and effortlessly dunked the ball. Chuck stopped dribbling and held his ball. The rim was still shaking. The kid ran over to the fence where his ball was bouncing and scooped it up. He dribbled a couple times then WHAM! Another slam. Chuck smiled. He had to see if this young man was a player or a hack.

"Hey! How are you doing? I was wondering if you wanted to shoot around a little. I get bored running up to the net after each one of my shots. You see, they seem to go in all the time," said Chuck with just a touch of trash.

"Sure, Man. My end or yours?" said the kid. The slow Texas accent rolled heavy in his voice.

"I'll come on down there. I wore out the net down here," Chuck said.

"All right. How 'bout we use your ball then?"

Chuck tossed his ball to the freckled youth. "Cool. This one works good. Besides, it looks like your ball is about broke. You thought about retiring that thing?"

"This old thing! I couldn't retire her. We been playing together since I was five," smiled the kid. He looked at the new ball, spun it on his finger, then tossed it up in the air towards the corner. He hustled to the corner, grabbed the ball, quickly turned to the basket, set and fired. The form was natural and in control. New ball, same results. Swish! Damn, thought Chuck. It was time to see if he was for real. "Let's play a little horse."

The kid agreed to the game and Chuck gave him first shot. Big mistake. They matched each other, shot for shot, for five minutes. Finally, Chuck missed a three pointer. Five more minutes went by until the kid missed a bank shot.

Chuck smiled and worked methodically. Shot for shot the two players matched each other's best. Fifteen feet, twenty feet, left-handed bank shots, and three pointers. Soon enough, an hour had passed, and the kid was down to his last letter. Chuck eyed him cautiously. They had spoken only in two-word sentences since the game started. A "Nice shot" here or an "off glass" there was all they said to each other. They were waging a battle of physical skill and mental warfare which equaled the challenge of any chess match or street fight. The combatants engaged in a type of psychological warfare. Testing each other's will. Testing each other's manhood.

Chuck dribbled quickly to the top of the key and looked at the kid. "What time is it?"

The kid wasn't wearing a watch but said, "Gotta be 'bout ten-thirty."

Chuck stepped back about ten feet from the top of the key and said, "I guess it's about time for me to go home!" Then he launched. Nothing but net.

The kid grabbed the ball and went to the spot. He was smiling and shaking his head. He sized up the shot, looked at Chuck and said, "I think you might be right. I can't even see from this far out." With a deep breath, he fired. The ball came off his left hand cleanly with a perfect backspin. It hit the front of the rim and bounced straight up. For an instant, Chuck thought he might be playing for another few minutes. Instead, the ball hit the rim again and bounced off. "DANG!" said the kid. But Chuck noticed he was still smiling.

That showed him two things. The kid was a good ball player who was finally tired after an hour of shooting horse. And secondly, he didn't have the killer instinct. He was probably just some frat kid ready to go hit the beer circuit after a little sweat. Even if he was some frat kid, he had given Chuck a real good game for nearly an hour. No doubt about it, he was a great shooter.

Chuck dropped the cocky attitude and became Charlton Hayes. He ran over to the bench and got his towel. He held out his water bottle to the kid. "My name is Charlton Hayes. I just moved in. What's your name, young man?" For an instant, he felt every day of his thirty-nine years when he called the kid "young man".

The kid took the bottle of water and smiled. It was an honest, genuine smile and Chuck could see his crooked teeth. "Thanks, man." The kid drank heartily and wiped his face with an extra T-shirt he had brought. "My name is Clayton. Clayton Dyer. But I guess you might as well call me 'Pepper'. Everybody else does."

Chuck knew where the name came from. Pepper must have had a million freckles. He threw his soaked shirt on the ground and put on the dry one, then stuck out his hand to shake. "I'm a freshman here. I live over on the main campus. They told me this would be a good place to shoot around." He nodded and looked at Chuck. "They didn't tell me anyone would be here who can shoot like you."

Chuck laughed and said, "I have a few more years of experience than you at shootin', right? I should shoot better."

Pepper laughed, "You got that right!"

Chuck decided to dig a little deeper. "A freshman, eh. You gonna play ball here?"

Pepper Dyer sighed and said, "I don't think so, Mr. Hayes."

"Please. Just call me Chuck!"

He smiled and lowered his head. His freckled skin turning crimson red as he hid his face. "I'm sorry. Chuck!" The red went away. "I don't think I can play ball here. My folks are only gonna let me stay here if I keep my grades up. I'm not exactly a rocket scientist."

Chuck Hayes laughed. "Sure you are!" He could see Clayton Dyer's look of confusion and decided not to tease him. He grabbed his ball and went out to the foul line extended so he was about 45 degrees off the backboard. "You know where the ball needs to hit on the glass to bank it in from here, right?"

"Yeah, sure! About a 45-degree angle!" said Pepper.

Chuck fired the ball neatly off the glass and through the net. "Trajectory mastered. Rocket Science!"

Pepper laughed at Chuck, shook his head and his crooked teeth showed again. "Okay, man. I'll take your word for it!" His smile faded a little. "I just barely got in here. I'm a little worried about keeping my grades up. My Daddy works day and night to have enough money for me to get here. I owe it to my folks to keep my grades up."

"Yeah. I suppose you're right. But as good as you shoot, you should at least try out." Chuck decided to change the subject. "What are you going to major in?"

"I'm thinking about being a veterinarian." With that, Clayton Dyers' smile reappeared.

"And what about hoop?" asked Chuck. "I mean, did you play ball in high school?"

"Oh, yeah! A little school called Madisonville in east Texas. I played for four years there."

Even if it was a little town in east Texas, playing four years meant you could hoop. "Four years in high school?"

"Yeah, I didn't start as a freshman, but I got to play a lot. Our school was so small, I would play the jayvee game, then play some varsity right after that. My brothers convinced the coach to let me play sometimes when I was a freshman."

"Your brothers?" asked Chuck who was becoming interested in the story.

"Yeah. Daryl and Harlan were both on varsity when I was a freshman. I got to play with Heath and Mickey when I was a Senior."

Chuck had visions of twenty people sitting around a huge table eating hominy grits and chitterlings. He quickly dismissed the image. "So where did you learn to jump like that? I know you only weigh about a hundred pounds, soaking wet, but damn!"

"Well. Daddy hung a basket on the barn," explained Pepper. "It could only hang on one spot that was solid enough to hold the rim. Turns out, that made the rim about four inches higher than normal. For us to dunk, we always had to jump a little higher."

"All your brothers jump like you?" asked Chuck.

"No. Heath can't jump. He's kind of fat. He weighs about 180. He mostly plays baseball. One scout said he could probably pitch some minor league ball next year if he gets better control of his curve. He's only got a 90 mile per hour fast ball," said Pepper as if everybody could throw that fast. "I'll be darned if I'd get in the batter's box against him!"

Chuck laughed and said, "I have to ask. How many points a game did you get?"

"My senior year, I guess it was about 25 a game. Two college scouts checked me out, but said my grades weren't strong enough, and the competition we played against was too weak. I just play for the heck of it now," said Pepper.

"You can shoot with anybody. With a shot like yours, you could play ball here." Chuck tapped him on the shoulder and got his ball to leave. "Well, my man, I look forward to playing hoop with you this year," said Chuck. He turned and felt the stiffness starting to set in. He couldn't get his Motrin fast enough.

"I hear the best games are at the gym just after four on weekdays or at nine on Saturdays. I figure I'll check it out on Saturday," said Pepper Dyer.

Chuck smiled, "You willin' to play with an old man like me?"

"Shoot, Man! I reckon you and me together ought to be able to run all day!" said Pepper.

Chuck felt the tightness in his back and winced, "Yeah, run all day! By the way, how old are you?"

"I'll be eighteen next month," he answered.

"Old enough to vote, eh? You are gonna register to vote right?" asked Chuck.

"Nah. All them politicians are the same, man. I'll see ya here in the evenings and on Saturday at the gym, right, Chuck?"

"Yeah. Nine o'clock sharp!" Chuck waved and headed to his new apartment.

A warm shower, a Motrin and seven hours of sleep would be just what the doctor ordered. He was happy with the way he shot the ball. What pleased him most was the fact that he communicated with a college kid. Even if the language was basketball, it was a start.

Chuck spent the rest of the week getting books for his classes and learning the campus. He timed his walks, so he knew how early he had to leave to make it to class on time. He found the library and wandered through it. He went to the school store and bought a couple of obligatory St. Michael's T-shirts and gym shorts. He found the dining facility food to be surprisingly good and thought that if he hadn't been working out so much, he would easily have gained a few pounds. At night he would run, shoot, and lift weights at the campus gym. Chuck was taking full advantage of not having classes. He was using the time to get his body into a routine.

On Thursday night he shot ball with Pepper. A couple of metal heads shooting around wanted to play two on two. Not one to turn down any competition, Chuck made Pepper play, and they promptly smoked the two tattooed warriors 15-5 and 12-3 before the competition said they had to leave. After the easy wins, Chuck and Pepper shot for another hour. For the last fifteen minutes of the evening, they ran wind sprints. Chuck was impressed that Pepper wanted to run as hard as he did. It also impressed him that the kid kept up with him for the duration. He was in surprisingly good shape for an eighteen-year-old.

In addition to Chuck being given only enough credits to qualify as a sophomore, he also found out he had to make up some classes that St. Michael's refused to count. He didn't want to take Intro to Psychology in his first semester of "real college" but figured the challenge of getting it out of the way would get his mind right about school. He also took Texas History, Telecommunications in America, Public Speaking, Anatomy and Physiology, and Political Science. Courses in his major of Computer Science could wait until next semester. Naturally he was the most "senior" student in every class. He figured of his six classes Anatomy and Physiology would be the toughest. To his surprise, his Political Science class had the most demanding syllabus.

The good thing about the Poly Sci class was the professor was gorgeous. The first day of class Miss Gracelyn Winters wore a medium length skirt with a matching jacket and looked beautiful. She was about 35, a brunette, perfect skin, and a beautiful smile.

From the first moment he saw her, Chuck knew he would have problems focusing during her class.

The other classes all had what Chuck would term traditional professors. Forty- to fifty-year-old men, all well-established, or "comfortable" in their classroom. The kids all seemed to be what he expected. He immediately saw class involved casual clothes, usually T-shirts and shorts in loud colors, and hair styles that could never be duplicated. Never the same tattoo. Generation Next was in tune with individuality.

After twenty years in the military, where any semblance of individuality is crushed, it would take a while to get used to life on campus. Getting older didn't stop the changes or make them any easier. Chuck had learned acceptance shouldn't foster reluctance when he had his first overseas tour. It was in Korea that he learned everything in life is what the individual makes of it. If you were certain you would have a bad duty tour, chances were good you would. But if you thought positive things, enjoyed the tour, and made the best of it, you would have an enjoyable experience. That was exactly what he intended to do at St. Michael's. Even if it meant he had to change to do it.

Saturday morning Chuck Hayes was at the door when the gym opened. As the janitor let him in with four others, he noticed when Pepper Dyer came jogging up. The redhead had a sheepish grin on his face as he waved hello. Pepper came up next to him. "Hey there, Chuck!" Chuck got a ball and they headed to the court.

Chuck smiled and said, "Hey there, yourself!" Not quite mocking the young man as much as teasing. He smacked the lad playfully and said, "You ready to run?"

"You and me, Old Man. All day!"

Chuck cocked his head sideways and gave Pepper a glance. "Old Man?!"

"Sorry!" said Pepper as he turned red. Chuck could tell the younger man was embarrassed again.

"I'll tell you what. We win every game we play, and you can call me . . . 'Hoopman'!" He could see the name register with Pepper.

Pepper nodded and said, "Hoopman will work!"

Chuck smiled and said, "Just don't call me Old Man!"

Pepper headed to the basket, obviously glad to be out of the conversation. Chuck threw him a perfect lead pass. Pepper caught it on the fly, stopped, popped and listened for the swish. It was a sign of things to come.

By ten o'clock the gym was coming to life. At least thirty people showed up and two full court games were in progress. Chuck Hayes managed to get the first game started and picked the team he wanted. First, a chubby black kid about six-foot four who didn't say too much when Chuck picked his first pick. Next, he took Pepper. He could tell Pepper was hurt when he wasn't the first guy Chuck picked, but intuition told Chuck the other guy picking teams wasn't going to take the skinny, freckled, redheaded kid. Chuck picked up another younger kid that looked all of sixteen and an older guy about 25. In his mind Chuck named them Doogie Houser and the Gradman, guessing the older guy was a graduate student.

The first game was a wash. Chuck barely worked up a sweat. Pepper was hot and hit about seven of the twelve points. Chubby was a very good rebounder and defender with a soft touch on his ten-footer. Doogie was more mouth than ball player, but he had energy to run on the break and play defense. Chuck guessed that he spent too much time watching the NBA and not enough time in the gym. Gradman was the weak link. He tired quickly and usually needed help on defense.

Game two was a little tougher. The other team had a couple of guys who had obviously played together. They rarely gave the ball to anybody else. After they took a nine to five lead, Chuck gave Pepper a look which indicated he wanted the redhead to shoot the ball. Next, he mentioned to Doogie that he was getting his butt kicked. The kid rolled his eyes but didn't say a word because Chuck was telling him the truth. Chuck pulled Chubby to the side and told him he was coming to help out on the big guy. Gradman was told to set picks for Pepper and tighten up his 'D'. That was all it took. Chuck's doubling up on the post player took him out of his game. The other side didn't score the rest of the way. They finished it off after Chuck drove the lane, drew three guys to him, then dished out a bounce pass to Pepper in the corner. Pepper said a barely audible "Money", as he hit the shot from the three point line.

The other team's big man came unglued by his teammate's play. His buddy had been "faced" by the skinny redhead. "DAMN, TOOLLY! I told you to D-up on Opie!"

"SCREW YOU, MAN! You get your sorry ass shot to fall in the basket at crunch time and we'd still be playin'!" said the other half of the two-man team.

Chuck was wiping off with a towel and his teammates were standing around him shaking hands and congratulating each other. Chuck nodded toward the opponents and said to his team, "It's a five-man game. Everybody plays together and everybody wins together. Dig?" He smiled at Pepper and hit his fist with a clenched fist of his own.

"I dig it!" said Pepper with a huge grin. His crooked teeth were showing as he smiled.

Chuck hit all his other teammates knuckle to knuckle. Then he got to Gradman. "That includes you, Gradman."

"I thought they had us that time." He was still sucking wind. "My name is James Quinlin. What's your name?" asked Quinlin.

"My name is . . ." Chuck didn't get a chance to answer.

"Hoopman!" interrupted Pepper.

"Excuse me! We haven't run enough yet for you to call me that." He turned to James and said, "My name is Chuck Hayes, but you can call me," he looked back at Pepper and said, "He can call me, Hoopman! Not you. Get your sorry outta shape butt on the floor. Skinny, red-headed, non-shootin' Gomer!" He was laughing when he said it. Pepper turned red and tried to remove his embarrassment with a towel.

The moment was broken by a holler from across the gym, "Let's run, Old Man!" Chuck smiled at the comment and looked at James Quinlin. "He must be talking to you!?"

Chuck recognized the guy making the call instantly. He was the best player on the St. MU team. He was a 6-foot two inch speedster named Charles Holmes. He usually played shooting guard but was an exceptionally good ball handler for a man his size. He came with three other guys, and they had obviously stacked the team with another taller player who was six foot five and two other speedsters.

Luckily, the other taller man had no game and Chubby ate him up. The youngster, Doogie, had gotten into the flow of the "team" concept was hustling his butt off. Gradman was holding the two guard with solid defense which gave Chuck the feeling they could actually win. Pepper continued to impress Chuck with great shooting and, more importantly, an ability to play help side defense. Chuck took Charles Holmes one on one.

Chuck's boys came out on fire taking a five to one lead. Holmes's game was obviously off. He and his running buddies looked out of shape. But they constantly talked about what they were going to do, how bad they would beat Chuck's team and how great Charles Holmes was. Chuck was surprised to see Charles was covering him on defense. Was it out of respect? Chuck didn't think so. He thought Charles intended to cover Chuck to rest on defense. Chuck decided to do what Chuck did best. Run.

Chubby was hitting the boards like a mad man. Every rebound seemed to come off into his hands. Chuck was nearly demanding the outlet pass every time. He constantly pushed the ball down the floor. The move worked for a while. But it took its toll on Chuck's teammates too. Ten minutes later it was ten to ten.

The talking had stopped at that point. The other team had to work just to get back into the game. The cockiness was gone, replaced by an air of intensity rarely found in a pick-up game.

Chuck could see Chubby was getting great position inside. On the next possession he held it up outside and let the big man get established. He dumped the ball inside and ran hard to the basket. Holmes couldn't keep up. As Chuck blew by, Chubby dumped him the ball in the lane. Chubby's man switched, frantically trying to prevent Chuck from getting a lay-up. Chubby read it and rolled to the basket. Chuck bounced a pass behind the defender and Chubby hit the lay-up in stride.

Going back on defense, Chuck said to Doogie, "If Holmes tries to dribble to his left, you take off!" The kid looked confused. "You're the only one with legs left to sprint, so take off and I'll hit you!" The kid nodded, still not believing Chuck would do what he said.

Charles Holmes tried to dribble Chuck Hayes back into the lane. Chuck got position on the quicker man, as he tried to go right and drive for a lay-up. When Charles spun backwards and tried to dribble left into the lane, Chuck was ready for the move. He timed his reach perfectly. Doogie took off down the court. Coming from behind the unsuspecting guard, Chuck reached with his left hand and stole the ball cleanly from Charles. With one dribble, Chuck turned and heaved the ball. Doogie caught it under the basket and laid it in. Game.

Charles Holmes was stunned. "Yo, man! What was that?"

"That . . . was game," smiled Chuck as he walked off the court.

Holmes was still fuming. Struggling to figure out what to do next. "Hey, man! You fouled me!"

Chuck stopped. He turned and looked at Charles. 'You really want to call that a foul?'

"Yeah, man! You were all over my arm," said Charles meekly.

Chuck looked at the rest of his teammates, then at Charles' teammates. "You want to lose again?" He walked back on the court and right up to Charles. He got close to Charles and said quietly, "All right. You want to play a little longer, so we'll play." He smiled and looked into Charles Holmes' eyes. "You're still gonna lose."

Charles frowned and yelled, "LET'S GO!" Pepper was shakin' his head and Chubby gave him a confused look. Chuck wanted to send a message to Charles. As the other team put the ball in play, they immediately threw it in to Holmes. Charles backed Chuck down into the lane. He faked left and turned right and tried a jumper from ten feet.

Defensively, Chuck was all over the shot. He timed his jump perfectly and got a piece of the ball as it left Charles' hand. It came up two feet short and Chubby smothered the rebound.

Coming down the court, Pepper ran by and said to Chuck, "You need a pick?"

"Naw, man, thanks. I'm all over it!" said Chuck.

As Chuck pulled up at the top of the key, Charles looked like he was ready to kill somebody. Chuck pushed hard to the left with two dribbles, pulled up and launched. Charles was a step late and smacked Chuck's wrist too late to have an effect. The shot was away cleanly and in the basket. Ball game.

"Thanks for the game, Charles," said Chuck quietly.

"Man, I fouled you. You guys take it out!" said Charles loudly.

Even his own teammates were walking off the court. Chuck just headed for his towel. The hand hurt, but he refused to rub it in front of Holmes. He looked over his shoulder and said, "Nice game, fellas!"

Gradman came up smiling, "Man, that was the most fun I've had playin' ball in years. I honestly enjoyed that."

"That's what it's all about, right? Having fun," smiled Chuck. "You got one more left in you?"

"NO WAY! I'm wiped. You gonna keep running?" he asked.

"Got nothing else to do today. Couple more. You know, experience and wisdom will beat youth and enthusiasm any day!" said Chuck.

The graduate student smiled a broad grin and shook his head. "I gotta go. Thanks, Chuck. Um, I mean, Hoopman!" said James Quinlin. "Next week? Same time?"

"Yeah, James. Same time," smiled Chuck. "By the way. Are you a graduate student here?"

"Yes, part time I am," smiled James Quinlin. "In my real life, I work as an assistant district attorney."

"You're gonna be a DA, huh?" asked Chuck. He filed the information away for some reason. He wasn't sure why, but it seemed like a prudent thing to do.

"Someday," answered Quinlin with a smile.

"I hope I never need to see you for that purpose. Nice game and we'll see you next week," said Chuck.

A couple minutes later Charles Holmes came over. "Nice game, Man." Chuck nodded and shook hands with the St. Michael's star. "I see you lost a man. Can I run in his place?"

Chuck thought about it. He could see his teammates were listening. He looked around the packed gym. There were dozens of players sitting on the sideline waiting to play. Chuck smiled at Charles. "Well, you just finished losing and there's guys who have been waiting to play for thirty minutes. I think we should let somebody else run with us. Somebody fresher."

Charles was stunned. "SAY WHAT?!" Holmes stuttered as he searched for words to express his outrage. He was the best player on campus, and he knew it. Yet this old man did not want to pick him up to play ball. Charles anger overcame him and he yelled, "Y'ALL GONNA GET YOUR ASSES KICKED NEXT GAME!" He turned and stomped off. What else could he do?

Chubby looked over at Chuck and said, "You know, if we picked him up, we'd run all day."

"Guess we'll have to run all day without him," smiled Chuck. He went over to the sign-up board, went to the second team down and hollered out, "C J, you wanna run with us?"

CJ turned out to be a Sophomore that ran track and had a pretty good game. They won again and Doogie had to leave for lunch. They picked up another big man who Chubby really appreciated. His feet were starting to get sore. Two more games and the bigger player headed out to get some lunch. Pepper and Hoopman won four more games and called it a day.

The Saturday games would become routine. Whenever Chuck would see Chubby, whose Saturday morning dedication matched Chuck and Pepper's, he made it a point to try to get on the same team as the bigger player. Once in a while, James Quinlin even got to play with them.

The one constant was playing with Pepper. Every Saturday Pepper would be there right on time. The friendship continued to grow, and Chuck started to consider the freckled young man a confidant. They would meet on the playground outside the dorms and shoot after dark. They would meet at the gym at night and shoot until the janitor kicked them out. They would meet at the dining hall and talk about basketball. A generation apart, from vastly different backgrounds, they had literally nothing in common except for their love of basketball.

CHAPTER THREE

"Hey there, Charles! How you doin'?" said the voice in the phone.

Charles Holmes slowly answered the question, "Um, I'm doin' good. Real good."

"You lookin' forward to this season? I tell ya' I can't wait," said the voice. There was an eerie silence as Holmes waited for more words to come. Finally, the caller got down to why he was calling. "Are you, ah, still in this year?"

More silence. Homes said flatly, "Uh, yeah. Yeah, I'm in."

"Oh that's great news, my man. Great news. We can do even better this year. You'll be a star this year."

"Um, yeah. A star," said Charles. "Look, I gotta go. I got some studying to do."

"Studying, eh? Great, Charles. A student athlete, too! The papers are gonna love you! I'll be seein' ya'!" Without waiting for a response, the phone went dead.

Still holding the phone, Charles Holmes looked out the window and said to no one, "Yeah. They're all gonna love me." He slowly put the phone down. Realizing the tears were starting, he quickly walked to his bedroom. If his roommate saw him, he wouldn't understand why Charles had tears in his eyes and started to shake uncontrollably.

"Mr. Hayes? Perhaps you would care to share some of your thoughts on the Kennedy Administration?" asked Miss Grace Winters.

Chuck was glad she had called his name first, so he knew she was going to ask him the question. "Sure! Contrary to popular belief among some in this class, I was not old enough to vote for the man!" The class, those that were still paying attention, laughed. "The sixties were a difficult time for the country. There were foreign policy issues with Russia, Cuba and Vietnam. But President Kennedy did a remarkable job at handling those issues. The country was suffering internal problems with race and inequality, riots in large cities, and we struggled to get along. Politically we could not determine the role of the United States in Southeast Asia. Kennedy had vision through all the turmoil. He was a youthful, dynamic personality who could be described as a true leader at a time when our Nation needed one."

A student behind Chuck said, "I was sixteen before I knew what the President did!"

Chuck smiled and shook his head, "My grandfather would talk to my brothers and I every evening about the country. The changes that were happening. Mostly, the good things. And some of the bad." Chuck paused and looked around. "My grandfather cried when the President of the United States was assassinated. I didn't remember the significance of the event at the time. It was traumatic for all people, all races, and all political beliefs. I know to my grandfather; it was very significant." Chuck nodded to no one, then said, "Kennedy was good for the country, and he was good for the equal rights movement. To see how Blacks in the sixties cried over the death of a white man, I knew he must have been a special man." Chuck took a deep breath. "Now if he were President today, I'm sure the tabloids, Entertainment Tonight and every other sensationalist magazine wouldn't give the man any peace. I think that back in the sixties, there was more respect in our nation. Respect for the position of the Presidency, not necessarily the President. And don't take me wrong, but I think there was more respect for the elderly in the nation then too."

The same kid sitting behind Chuck said, "We respect you!"

Chuck gave him a dirty look and said, "You gonna respect the foot I put up your butt, too?" The class erupted in laughter. Ms. Winters couldn't help but smile at the remark. Chuck went back to the discussion. "I also feel the best thing Kennedy may have done was to unite the nation by using the space race to get us to the moon. As a nation, we were proud of the fact we had put men on the moon. It was good to see how our country came together over that effort." Chuck let that sink in. "I think the closest we come to being together as a country now, is through sports. Especially, the Olympics. I consider athletes that represent the USA in any capacity as modern-day heroes. Not as important as the President. But Kennedy probably transcended the presidency in his role as an American Hero." Chuck looked at Ms. Winters and asked, "Did that make any sense?"

Ms. Winters looked around the class and saw the smiles and nods that Chuck got from his classmates. "Yes, Mr. Hayes. An excellent assessment." She started to ask another question, but looked at her watch and said, "That's enough for today. I want you to be ready for a quiz next week and bring me your outlines for your "American Politician of the Century" papers by Friday." There were groans from the students as they grabbed their books and started out of the classroom.

Chuck went up to Grace Winters' desk and handed her his two-page outline on Ronald Reagan. Ms. Winters looked at the outline and asked, "Reagan? I would have expected JFK after your last few comments."

Chuck said, "He was cool, but Reagan turned the country around. Got it on its feet through some tough times. He was a leader who probably doesn't get as much respect as he deserves." He started to leave, then Grace Winters stopped him.

Grace stepped from behind her desk and watched as the last of her students left the room. "Reagan is probably as good a choice as anyone else. Lots to cover on him." She sat on the corner of the desk. Chuck watched her as she sat down. Suddenly his eyes noticed something unusual on her arm. He wasn't quite sure, but he thought it might be makeup. Grace noticed he saw the mark. She covered it quickly with her hand. It took a second, but he realized the mark she was trying to cover up was a bruise. Grace Winters got up from the desk and walked behind it. Chuck noticed her face went flush.

"A person has a right to feel the way they feel about anything," he said and smiled. He tried to lighten the mood by adding, "Even Presidents!" His immediate thought was to ask her about the bruise but settled for something not so inquisitive. Before he could stop himself, the words came out. "I guess you can't go to dinner with a student, but would a movie be out of the question?"

Grace didn't totally blow Chuck out of the water. "I don't think that would be appropriate, Mr. Hayes."

Chuck nodded and said, "I guess you're seeing someone then?" Chuck started to walk away. "I noticed you weren't wearing a ring, so I just supposed you were . . . available."

Grace said, "No. I don't wear a wedding ring." She suddenly looked uncomfortable. "I'm . . . I'm not really going out with anyone. It's just that I don't . . ." She struggled to find the proper words, "I'm not looking for a man in my life right now."

Chuck shook his head and said, "Me neither! So we have something in common." He smiled, hoping she took the comment as the joke he intended. Unfortunately, she didn't catch the humor. Chuck turned to leave.

"You seem nice enough," said Grace.

Chuck smiled at what he assumed was a compliment. "Thank you, Ms. Winters." He caught one more glance at the bruise on her arm. "I gotta get to my next class." He turned and started to leave.

"Mr. Hayes!" Grace yelled to catch him. Chuck stopped and turned around. "You were in the military, weren't you?"

Chuck wasn't sure what brought the question on, but he had an idea what prompted the question. "Yes, I was, Ms. Winters."

He started walking backwards slowly, unsure exactly where the question and his answer were heading.

"You saw the mark on my arm, didn't you?" asked Grace.

The comment made Chuck stop in his tracks. He couldn't lie. He nodded, then his eyes met hers.

"I . . . I just worry that you . . .," she struggled for words.

Chuck had an idea what she was worried about. It was a guess on his part but someone, probably a man, had physically put the bruise there. Grace Winters was associating Chuck's military past with violence. She was afraid that Chuck was as violent as the man who had left the mark on her arm. "Ms. Winters. Yes. I was in the Army." He walked back towards her and looked around. They were alone. "Yes, I've seen more than my share of violence, and yes, I caused some of it. It's violence that is associated with purpose. It's not anything I'm proud of. I'm by no means ashamed of anything that I've done in the past. Could I hurt people in the future, is that what you're worried about? More specifically," he met her eyes again, "could I hurt you?" He dropped his chin down and smiled. "I've never hurt a woman in my life." He showed her his hands and said, "Not with these, at least. Maybe with a big mouth or a stupid comment." He tilted his head to look at the bruise and the smile went away. He looked at her beautiful eyes again and said, "I could never do somethin' like that."

Chuck let the comment set in before asking, "Do you need any help, Miss Winters? Not that I could ever do anything to help you out. But, if you were in a situation, you know, a difficult situation," he looked at the bruise again before adding, "I have a lot of friends who can work . . . issues like this."

"I bet you do," she said. Her smile faded as she thought of a good answer. Finally, the words came. "My issue, as you call it, is over. He is gone and out of my life. When this happened," she pointed to her arm, "it was the last time anything like that will ever happen to me again."

Chuck nodded and smiled. "That's good for you, Miss Winters." Chuck started walking backwards slowly. "So let me try this again. Now that we have that cleared up, would you like to go to a movie sometime, Miss Winters? Not a real date or anything. Maybe you could show me how dates with civilian women are supposed to be?"

"Maybe, Mr. Hayes," she smiled back at him, but Chuck could tell she was thinking about her bruised arm. Even in despair, she was still beautiful.

Chuck stopped at the doorway. "I'd like that, Ms. Winters. I'd like that a lot." He turned and quickly walked away. He really liked this woman. He was certain there were rules about professors dating their students. His military mind had negative visions of getting hauled before Dean Crowell and getting kicked out of school for fraternizing with his professor. He made mental notes to himself. Find out if Grace Winters had been married or was involved with someone. Then, check out the rules on dating your professor. She might even be worth breaking the rules for.

It was time for his weekly call to Becky. His conversation with Grace Winters still fresh in his mind, he dialed the phone. His thoughts of the opposite sex quickly faded when Master Sergeant Darren Sutherland answered the phone. "Hi, Darren. It's Chuck. Is Becky there?" He could tell Darren Sutherland was none too excited at the prospect of his wife talking to her ex-husband.

"Yeah. Sure, Chuck. She's right here," said Darren.

Chuck started to engage in small talk but decided he really didn't have the desire to fake the conversation and stayed quiet as he waited. Finally, there was a voice on the other end. "Chuck, is that you?"

"Yeah, Becky. How are you?" asked Chuck sincerely.

"We're all doing really good on this end," answered Becky. Chuck could tell exactly what she meant by answering "we're" doing good. It meant that Anna was doing good. "Darren is going TDY next week to Germany and I think Momma is gonna come over."

Chuck knew how much Becky hated it when he was assigned temporary duty in some far away land, and he could tell from her voice she wasn't happy about Darren's trip either. The thought crossed his mind that temporary duty was one of the contributing factors that broke up their marriage. He quickly dismissed the notion and got back to the conversation with his ex-wife. "That's too bad about Darren havin' to take off again. Say 'Hi' to your mother for me and tell her all is well. School is fun and I'm falling into a nice routine. She'd be proud of me."

"Chuck, she was always proud of you," said Becky. She was quiet for a moment then added, "I'll get Anna. She's in the driveway shooting. Hold on."

Chuck waited anxiously waiting until Anna's voice came on the other end. "Hi, Daddy!"

"Hi, Baby! How are you? I heard you were out shootin'?" said Chuck.

"Yeah, mostly jumpers from the top of the key. The driveway isn't wide enough to work on the baseline shots too much." she said.

"I hope most of them are going in?" laughed Chuck.

"Of course. I finally got permission to take the car to the gym on base. On Saturday, I'm going in to try and play ball. I wanted Darren to go with me but he's going to be getting ready to go to Europe for something." Chuck could hear the dejected tone in her voice. He felt deep down that it should be him giving her the car to go to the gym. Just as he felt he should be there to shoot with her in the driveway.

"You're old enough to know the deal, Anna," said Chuck.

"Yeah, I know. When duty calls and all that," said Anna. Anna was all too familiar with the military and what it required. It had cost her a father and was now costing her a stepfather. To her credit she changed the subject and the happy tone reappeared in her voice. "So how's college, Daddy? Are you the oldest guy in your class?"

Chuck laughed at her teasing tone. "I'm having a lot of fun. The age thing hasn't even come up. Not once," he lied. They continued to talk about college, her grades, driving and some of the other things that Chuck was missing in her life. He wanted to apologize again but was certain she was getting tired of it. Too soon, it was time to hang up. "Well, I better go, Honey. I've got some studying to do. And I'm sure you do too. Remember . . ."

She cut him off and said, "I know, I know. You can't play ball if your grades aren't good."

"That's right." Chuck sighed. Then added, "I love you."

"I love you too, Daddy. I'll talk to you next week," she said.

"Until then, Baby. Bye-bye." He waited until she hung up the phone. He hated to be the first one to put the phone down. Sometimes he wished he was closer to them. Then he would remember the fights and the arguing. The distance was probably a good thing for him and Becky. Chuck was certain it was a bad thing for Anna.

"How's things goin' out in cactus land, Petey?" said the voice on the phone.

"Oh, as good as can be expected, Mr. Grant," answered Peter Henderson. Henderson was the Assistant Coach of the St. Michael's Armadillo basketball team. "There really aren't any cactus plants around here, Mr. Grant. You should come out and see it some time." Henderson believed for an instant that Grant would leave Las Vegas for San Antonio.

"I don't need to come to Texas, Coach Henderson. That's what I have my boys down in San Antonio for. I have everything I need right here in Vegas. I'm pretty sure the ladies in Bum-scum, Texas, don't come close to the beauties here!" said Jackson Grant. "If I did come to Texas, I'd go to Houston where there's some night life and something close to a real basketball team. Tommy Clark said UT is gonna bring in seven digits this year between football and basketball alone."

"Last I knew, Tommy didn't have anybody on the payroll like we do," said Pete Henderson.

"That's exactly what I wanted to hear, Petey!" said Jackson Grant. "Exactly why I called."

"I can't say we'll pull in as much as UT, but if we get half the performance we got last year, we'll make you some money, Mr. Grant," said Henderson.

"Good, Petey. Real good. Just keep on top of things there, okay?" The tone was more like a demand than a request.

Pete Henderson quickly responded, "Sure. Sure thing, Mr. Grant. No problems here." At that moment, he honestly felt he was telling the truth.

Chuck was at the gym shooting his last few free throws. Pepper had just left. It had only been a month and the young red headed boy was starting to fill out. Chuck thought the heavy calorie diet the University provided was sitting well on his protégé. The food worked just the opposite on Chuck. He needed to cut down on the calories to maintain his lean physique. It was pretty good "chow" compared to some of the other meals he had eaten. An Army MRE, meal, ready-to-eat, was terrific when you were hungry, but not anything you would go out of your way for.

Chuck was shooting baskets when he noticed an older man at the other end of the gym watching him. He couldn't tell who it was at first. The gray-haired man was about five-ten, had a belly roll hanging over his belt, and was dressed in blue jeans and a T-shirt. The man quietly came across the court and stopped to watch Chuck shoot. It was then that Chuck noticed who the man was. The older man with a soda can in one hand and the other in his pants pocket was one of the most popular men on campus. Sixty-four-year-old Darrell Round was the Coach of the St. Michael's Armadillo basketball team.

Chuck continued to shoot. Coach Round moved under the basket and started rebounding. After the tenth shot went through the net he said, "We gotta close up here in a few minutes." Chuck kept shooting. "You, ah . . . you gonna miss any time soon?" laughed the coach.

Chuck smiled and said, "I probably will now because you broke my concentration." Chuck dribbled twice, shot, and swished it.

"What's your name?" asked the smiling Coach.

"Charlton Hayes, Coach. But you can call me Chuck." Chuck took the ball, rolled it in his hands and shot again. Swish.

"You work on campus? Or are you a graduate student here?" asked Round with a chuckle.

"I'm just a plain old everyday student!" laughed Chuck. He dribbled again, stepped back, and swished a fade away. Coach Round threw the ball back to Chuck. "Actually, I'm a transfer." The Coach gave Chuck a look that said he didn't know whether to believe him or not. Chuck picked up on it and tried to explain. "I was in the Army, and I just retired last summer."

Coach Round burst out laughing. "You're . . . retired? Dang, son. I'm 64 years old and I ain't retired!"

"Yes, sir. I put my twenty years in and decided I needed to finish my education." The shots kept falling. "I have an associate degree, but most of my course credits didn't count. So, they are carrying me as a sophomore."

"You're not the oldest Sophomore I've ever seen. But you're probably the best shooter I've seen your age who isn't playing somewhere else," said the Coach.

"Well, I have managed to play a few years of ball here and there. A jump shot in Korea isn't any different than one in Texas," said Chuck.

"Something tells me you're probably in pretty good shape. The Army keep you from getting a gut like mine." Round patted his belly.

Chuck stopped and looked at the Coach. Then looked at the man's 'spare tire'. He shook his head and said, "The taxpayers paid me to expand my mind, not my mid-section!" They both had a good laugh at that one. "I guess I'm in okay shape. I could always do better." Chuck dribbled to the top of the key. He turned and fired a three pointer. The ball swished through the net.

Coach Round caught the ball and suddenly looked serious. "You think you're in good enough shape to run with kids half your age?"

It was Chuck's turn to get serious. The ball came back to him crisply. He caught it and looked at the Coach. "No problem, sir!"

Round smiled and nodded. "Good deal, Chuck. I expect to see you at tryouts. I'll give you the same chance I give everybody else. Your experience as you call it, could really help my team. Probably as much as that jumper," said the Coach.

"I'll be there, sir. And I'll try not to embarrass any of your superstars," laughed Chuck.

Round laughed. "I gotta go now. I'd love to stay here and waste my time rebounding for you, but I gotta get home. And one other thing!" said the Coach as he started walking away. "Don't call me 'sir'. You make me feel older than I really am!" He chuckled, walked away and yelled over his shoulder. "Get out of my gym, Chuck!"

"I can do that, Coach!" Chuck took one last long shot and retrieved the ball. He quickly ran up to the Coach. He had one more question to ask. "Um, Coach. Would it be okay if I looked at your game films from last year? I was hoping to look at some of your players' tendencies and how some of your opponent's play. If that's okay with you?"

The Coach stopped walking and looked at Chuck. "Stop by my office tomorrow. I think I can set you up."

"Thank you, sir. I mean . . . Coach!" smiled Chuck. "That'll take me some time to get used to."

"You damn well better get used to it quick, 'cause that's a habit I ain't used to! See you tomorrow, Chuck." Without a second thought, Coach Darrell Round knew Chuck would be there the next day.

Round knew right away that Chuck Hayes was different from anyone the man had ever met. He was honest, polite and one helluva shooter. If the rumors going around campus were any indication, this man might prove to be one of the keys to a successful season. It would be nice to go out with a winning record.

Round sat down behind his desk and looked at his calendar. The start of the season wasn't that far off. Then he noticed the red circle that reminded him of the doctor's appointment which was scheduled for the next Thursday. He didn't need to see the doctor to know what was going on in his body. He was getting old, plain and simple. Time was a luxury he didn't have anymore.

Round's hope was the same as coaches across the country every year. This year was different for him. He just wanted one last winning season. Round thought about the shooting display he had just seen and wondered if it was real. He looked at the trophies in the cabinet across the room. He hadn't won a trophy in over a decade. Chuck Hayes was the real deal. He could feel it in his bones. Those were the same sore aching bones that were causing him so much trouble. Yet, they were strong enough for one more season. He would get the tapes ready first thing in the morning. Chuck Hayes probably didn't even need the game videos. Round wondered if it could be Chuck Hayes that could make St. Michael's a winner again.

Charles Holmes was in the gym working on his jump shot when Pete Henderson walked under the basket. "Hello, Charles!" He grabbed the rebound and threw it out to the point where Charles Holmes was standing.

"Hello, Coach Henderson." Charles caught the ball, dribbled twice, and shot.

The ball hit the front of the rim hard and bounced back to where it came from. "That was a brick, Charles. We can't have shots like that this year," said the coach.

"The shot will be there, Coach. Don't you worry about that," said the player. Charles shot again and nearly missed everything.

The Coach grabbed the missed shot and walked it out to Holmes. "Seems like your concentration is off. I was watching you from the box and it looks like your concentration has been off all afternoon. You havin' some kind of problem I should know about?" He stuck the ball out for the guard to grab. When Charles tried to grab it, Henderson pulled it away and hissed, "'Cause if you got a problem, it's my problem too!"

Charles stepped back and put his hands on his hips. He looked away, sighed heavily and then looked at his coach. "I don't think I can do it."

"WHAT?" hissed Henderson.

Holmes stepped back. "I said . . ."

"I know what the hell you said," said Henderson, "and you're not thinking clearly at all! What's goin' through that beady little mind of yours, hmm?"

Charles slowly said, "I think we got a chance to win this year. We got a chance to win the conference and . . ."

Henderson threw the ball to the other end of the court and got in Charles Holmes' face. "WE GOT NO CHANCE! WE WON'T WIN A THING!" Slowly, the Coach got his composure and stepped back from the player. "The only chance we got, my good man, is to make some money! The easiest money you ever made. Right?"

Charles followed the ball as it rolled against the wall. "Yeah, right. Easy money."

Henderson walked over to Holmes and put his hand on his back. "No time to get cold feet now. We're in this thing together. I got your back. Trust me, nobody will know."

Charles nodded. He knew there was no way the assistant coach could help him with anything. "Sure. Nobody will know."

"That's right. Another solid season," said Henderson. "Just a few games." The coach stepped back and said, "Look, I gotta go.

You need to work on that shot. You're shooting like you did when you were a freshman. Get some confidence! It'll fall."

Charles Holmes just nodded and watched as the coach walked away. It wasn't confidence in his shot that was gone. Charles had lost confidence in himself. As much as he wanted to be a man, to do what was right, he had no answer for his problem. He was smart enough to know that Henderson didn't have the answers either. Charles was in deep, and he couldn't take it much longer. Something had to give.

Pepper, Marshall and Chuck were watching videotapes from last year's St. Michael's basketball games. They were watching the final five minutes of the St. Michael's game against Baylor.

Marshall told Pepper, "I'm thinking about being the mascot this year."

Pepper looked at Marshall and said, "The mascot? You gotta be kiddin' me!"

"Yeah, the mascot! I heard the spot is open. Nobody wants to do it!" said Marshall.

"That's because the mascot sucks!" said Pepper. "I saw a game on TV last year and the dude was weak. His costume had holes in it."

Chuck suddenly sat up on the couch and grabbed the remote. He played the video back and ran it again. Marshall and Pepper were surprised when Chuck practically yelled, "What is he doin'?"

"What's up?" asked Pepper.

"I can't believe what I just saw!" said Chuck. He ran the tape again. "Look at this."

"Yeah, I see it. Holmes throws a pass out of bounds! He did that a lot last year. So what?" said Marshall.

"Watch this," said Chuck. He rewound the tape again. "He's bringing the ball up the court, see. Here he looks right at the other guard as he breaks to the basket, then Holmes looks away. The guy is moving right towards the basket, then Holmes turns and throws the ball to where the other guard was."

Marshall and Pepper looked at each other confused. Pepper said, "Yeah? So? He isn't known for his passing." Chuck got a real quizzical look on his face.

"You say he did this a lot?" asked Chuck.

"Yeah, I saw about four games on TV last year, and in three of them, he had at least ten turnovers," said Pepper.

Chuck rewound the video and played it again. He could tell Charles Holmes had looked at the other guard and knew he was moving. Charles threw the pass into the sidelines at the precise spot the guard had moved from. Chuck forwarded and caught the score. Baylor, undoubtedly a heavy favorite, was winning 67-62 with four and a half minutes left in the game. About a minute later, David Parnell, the Armadillo forward, made a great rebound of a terrible Holmes' shot and stuffed it home. St. Michaels was down by three with two minutes left. Then Chuck saw another curious act by Holmes that convinced him something was up. Chuck noticed during the timeout, Charles didn't even go shake David Parnell's hand or congratulate him. Something stunk. Chuck fast-forwarded the video and got out a notepad and wrote down the score. Baylor hit another shot after the timeout and went up by five. Charles ran the ball up the court, then drove the lane and threw a pass to Parnell while the forward was double-teamed. David Parnell was stripped by a Baylor player who was immediately fouled by Parnell as he tried to stop the clock. Baylor made their free throws the rest of the way, finally winning by ten. Chuck wrote down the final score and went to his room to make a phone call.

The man rolled his wheelchair over to answer the phone. He knew the voice on the other end of the phone instantly. "Hey, Chuck! Or should I say, 'Hoopman'! How the hell are you? What's up? You never call; you never write! I only see you at the gym, what, once a month!" said Edward Newton. Eddie was a high school All State basketball player from San Antonio. He joined the Army right out of high school hoping to get GI Bill education benefits. He had hoped to serve four years, get out, go to college, and maybe play college basketball. That dream was cut short by an IED. Eddie somehow managed to survive. After months of therapy, everyday life is a struggle for normalcy. Edward Newton was a survivor. He had taught Chuck Holmes many things, not just about computers and network warfare, but about trust and faith. Eddie was Chuck's inspiration.

"I'm sorry about that, Eddie. I see you heard about the 'Hoopman' thing," said Chuck.

"I heard about some old man tearing it up at the gym on the StMU campus and knew it was you! Man, I hear about everything when it comes to basketball. You know that!" said Eddie.

"I know I don't get back to you as much as I should, but I'm a college dude now, ya' know!" said Chuck. He went quiet for moment as he got down to the reason for his earlier call. "I got a little . . . situation I think you can help me with." Chuck knew about Eddie's history. After his basketball career ended, Eddie Newton became one of the best cyber security analysts in America.

Ed Newton had known Chuck a long time but had never heard the tone he had used on the phone. He could tell his friend was serious. Ed said, "Sure, buddy. What can I do for you?"

"I need you to do a little research for me," said Chuck. "I need you to check out points spreads of basketball games St. Michael's played last year."

"Last year, eh. I got a few minutes to hop on the box and check it out," said Ed Newton. "What hoop games?"

"All of them. I need to know the point spreads and results of last year's St. Michael's games. I have some film I'd like you to see, as well," said Chuck.

"I gotta check on my hometown clowns, eh?" asked Ed. Chuck hesitated on the other end of the phone. Finally, Ed said, "You gonna give me a little bit more, or do I just stumble through this on my own?"

"I'm gonna let you stumble for now, Eddie. If my hunch is right, and mind you, it's just a hunch, you'll see what I saw and know where I'm headed," said Chuck.

"If you can get me the film, I think I can have this for you by next Thursday. Will you be able to make it to the gym?" asked Ed.

"You got it, Ed. I'll see you there," said Chuck. "And one more thing, Eddie. Thank you. Again!"

"No sweat, Hoopman. Anything for you. It's the least I can do. You're the best rebounder I got. See you Thursday. Ciao!" said Ed Newton.

After the call, Chuck continued to watch videotapes late into the night. He took some notes and wrote down the scores of the games he saw. He continued to watch Charles Holmes' play and counted multiple incidents in nearly every game where Charles would throw terrible passes or lose control of his dribble without any defensive pressure. Chuck had played with Charles and had watched him play in the gym. Holmes was a much better player than the guy he watched in the videotapes. It would be interesting to see what Ed would find out.

Chuck found himself waiting till the other students left before getting his book bag and heading towards Grace Winters' desk. Without a doubt, Political Science was his favorite class. Not because the subject interested him that much, just that Grace Winters made it interesting. Plus, she was usually in a good mood. Chuck noticed that about college life in general. People were a lot happier in school than they were in the Army. He remembered having good times in his military career, but never for a period as long as the last month. He too had found himself in much better spirits because of his surroundings. College was what good times and happiness was all about. Regardless of how old a student was.

"Mr. Hayes, you seem to be way too happy for a student about to go through midterm examinations," smiled Ms. Winters.

"Well, Ms. Winters, I'm pretty excited about those midterms. It'll be a good test of what this education is doing for me. A good challenge," smiled Chuck.

She cocked her head and looked at Chuck quizzically, "You really are enjoying this, aren't you?"

"I'd pay twice the tuition just for the opportunity to be here," said Chuck.

"I wish all students felt that way," said Grace.

Chuck said, "Most of them are so young they don't really understand what they're doing here. I've seen so many young people their age, who don't even know how to read, much less comprehend it and form an opinion."

"No wonder you enjoy it here so much!" said the professor. She gathered her bags and started for the door.

Chuck moved with her and thought he had an opening. "I was wondering if maybe some time, I could come by your office and discuss that paper you want us to write."

"I don't know, Mr. Hayes. Do you think you can get away from the gym long enough?" she asked.

"How'd you hear about that?" replied Chuck.

"Oh, it's all over campus. There's even talk that some 'old man' might make the basketball team this season. I've seen you in the gym shooting, and you're pretty good. I usually run after work," she said.

"I don't know if I can make the team, but I might give it a try," he said.

She stopped at the door and said, "You should probably come by Friday afternoon. If you can find time in your busy schedule, Mr. Hoopman?"

Chuck was shocked. He wasn't sure if it was because she called him Hoopman or because she told him to come by her office on Friday. "Um. Friday, yeah. That would be great! I'll do that."

She nodded, "I think my schedule will still be open."

"Great. Great. Well, I guess I'll see you then," said Chuck. He turned and walked away. He felt like a jerk. Just like a kid on a first date. But then it started to sink in. She said 'Yes'. It was true that college was the best time of a person's life. Regardless of one's age.

Chuck was leaving his public speaking class when one of his fellow students tapped him on the shoulder. He stopped and turned around. He had to take a step back because the student that tapped his shoulder was huge.

"Are you the guy they call Hoopman?" questioned the mountain.

Chuck closed his mouth so that he didn't look too stupid. "Yeah, I guess you could call me that." His smile finally returned to his face as he became accustomed to the student's height.

"My name is Jose Rivera-Torres. I'm thinking about going out for the basketball team. I played a little in high school, but I didn't think I could play here. Some of my friends told me to come and talk to you," said Jose.

"Can you walk with me? I don't want to be late for my next class," said Chuck.

"Sure. My friends saw you playin' ball, and they told me you were pretty laid back. And you win," said Jose.

Chuck didn't quite know what to say. "I win some. But I lose sometimes too." He looked at the large young man for a reaction and got a sort of puzzled look. "I guess I win more than I lose. As for laid back, I suppose I have more patience than most people."

Jose Rivera-Torres said, "I didn't go out for basketball here for a few reasons. First of all, I can't shoot worth a damn. My hands are so big, the ball isn't that comfortable when I shoot it. Next, I don't like people too much, so I have a temper. And third, I think those black dudes on the team are a bunch of jerks."

Chuck didn't know what to say. He thought about blowing the kid off and going on to class. He knew that wasn't the right thing to do so he walked off the sidewalk into the grass and motioned for Jose to follow him. "First of all. The hands are no big deal. No pun intended! Shooting is not just practice. It's focus, repetition and concentration. It's mostly a mental exercise. Second, if your temper was that bad, you would be in jail now instead of college. Thirdly," Chuck stopped and looked into Jose's eyes. "Are those black guys on the team jerks, or are they jerks because they're black?"

Jose looked around as he thought of his answer. "I think they're jerks. It doesn't matter that they're black."

"That's okay then, Jose. I can play hoop with jerks. I won't play ball with a racist," said Chuck. His familiar smile had faded. "If you're a racist, I don't have time for you." He searched for a reaction in Jose Rivera's face.

"I'm no racist," said Jose.

"Jerks are everywhere. It's a fact of life. If you're gonna be around some, you might as well be playin' hoop with them. Comprendez?" said Chuck.

Jose smiled, "Si." He changed the subject. "I hear you been playin' almost every night. Would it be all right if I came and played ball with you? I'm not in very good shape."

Chuck looked down at the large gut Jose had on his waistline and said, "Forgive me for saying this, but you're fat! I don't care how big you are; if you can't get up and down the floor, you won't even play on an intramural team, Jose. This is NCAA Division II college ball we're talkin' about trying to play. There are guys who are gonna run my old ass into the ground, and I like to think I'm in good shape! If you come to the gym, we won't be playin' ball. We'll be running, shootin' and runnin' some more!"

"I think I'm ready. I need a challenge in my life, or I'm gonna eat my way to a heart attack," said Jose. The sadness in his voice was obvious. He looked around again to see if anyone else had heard him. To Chuck, it was becoming painfully obvious this giant was more child than man.

"Are you a man of faith, Jose?" asked Chuck.

"Yes, definitely! That's how my Momma raised me," said Jose.

"OK. Because you are going to need to have faith that God above has a plan for you. That he wants you to play basketball." Chuck let the comment sink in. "I can tell you honestly, your faith is going to be tested."

Jose nodded. "I know it. I believe that somewhere inside me, I'm supposed to play basketball."

"We'll work into it slow. We got about a month before tryouts. If you keep showing up, I can't promise you'll make the team. But you will be in probably the best shape you can be in to make it," said Chuck. He looked at his watch and said, "I gotta get going. One question," he said as he turned to go. "How big are you, Jose?"

"Last time they checked, I was six-foot nine and over 350," his head dropped when he said it as if embarrassed. "They didn't have a scale that went over 350."

"We need to get you down to playin' weight if you're gonna have any kind of chance to play at the college level, okay? That means you're gonna work harder than you ever thought about workin'. I'll help you, but you gotta help yourself," said Chuck.

"I ain't afraid to work hard. If you think I can make the team," said Jose.

"Let me take a look at you on the court and we'll see. I'll be honest with you. If I don't think you can make it, I'll tell you," said Chuck. "Keep the faith in yourself, whatever happens."

"Fair enough," answered Jose.

"All right then, big man! I'll know you're serious if I see you tonight," said Chuck.

As Chuck hurried to class, he started thinking about the St. Michael's basketball team. They didn't really have a center. They had played the previous year with one tall kid that could barely catch the ball, Parnell at power forward and three guards. If they could get a big man, any big man, that would be worth ten rebounds and a little bit of defensive presence, they could win a few ball games. Whether or not that big man was going to be Jose Rivera-Torres was yet to be seen. Jose would have to work extremely hard to make the team. Chuck wasn't sure if the huge young man would put out the effort. This year's Armadillo team had some real potential, and there was no need to have those hopes diminished by someone who wasn't going to give it his best. Chuck knew his faith was going to be tested.

As Chuck headed to class his thoughts switched from team potential to Charles Holmes. He couldn't help but think what a great asset Charles would be if he were focused. He hoped that he was wrong, and that Charles hadn't been shaving points in the games he had reviewed. There was only one person who could tell Chuck if his thoughts were correct or not. That was Charles Holmes.

CHAPTER FOUR

"Hi, again, Mr. Grant," said Steve James into the phone. "What the hell do you want?" snarled Jackson Grant. "I got places to go."

Steve James bit his tongue. Grant was not only a ruthless crook; he was the King of the Jerks. "I just wanted to see if you had considered purchasing those security implementors I emailed you about," said Steve.

Grant grunted into the phone. "You and your security measures. Security implementors. I don't even trust you, you schmuck!" hissed Grant.

"Mr. Grant, we could have multiple people used to secure the system if that's what you want. Two or three people required to provide fingerprints or use a retinal scan to gain access," said Steve. "That would help make the system safer." He didn't want to sound like he was begging. Steve knew if Grant didn't put the protection in place that would just make it easier for him later on.

"We haven't had any problems, so there's no reason to get too overly cautious about security at this point," said Grant. There was a hesitation, then Grant added, "Just keep the system workin', and I'll worry about security when I need to."

Steve James had learned quite a while ago when to quit when it came to Jackson Grant. "Okay, Mr. Grant. That's your call."

"Now switch off, geek!" Grant slammed the phone down.

Steve placed the receiver down and rubbed his knee. What could he do? He tried to suggest to protect his boss' business. Grant was obviously worried about Steve's past. Grant assumed a reformed gambler wasn't to be trusted. Especially if that reformed gambler had received a number three drill bit just behind his knee cap. Not just outside the knee. You would think once was enough. But with a second "entry point" from the opposite side, Steve could only beg for it to stop. He would still jump awake some nights in a cold sweat. Screaming, begging Grant to make the bad man with the drill stop. For his begging, Steve got what he wanted. Grant finally stopped his torturer before he went to the other knee. Then Jackson Grant asked a question that probably saved Steve's second knee. "What can you do for me to get my hundred grand back?"

Steve immediately spilled his guts about on-line gambling. Systems integration, information management, the security of accounts in offshore banks, satellite link ups and digital communications. Everything he knew about the cyber gambling business of the 21st Century, Steve screamed to keep the bad man with the wicked tool from entering the soft flesh behind his left knee. He managed to save not only one knee that day, but probably his life as well.

It didn't take him long to determine his new "boss", Jackson Grant, was an idiot. Within a month, Steve started developing a plan to pay his boss back for what he had done. He made the first hundred grand back for Grant in 43 days. Over the course of his employment, Steve had made Grant a millionaire many times over. Soon it would be time to take it all away. By not upgrading the company's security to Steve's specific desires Grant had merely played into Steve's plan. Without the upgrades, it wouldn't be nearly as hard to get revenge.

Chuck had been at the gym for twenty minutes just shooting jumpers with Pepper. Everything seemed normal. Pick-up games were going on at the far end of the court. Suddenly, the gym grew quiet. Pepper noticed the eerie silence at the far end of the court and looked over towards the now silent crowd. He saw the huge man walking onto the court and said, "Holy cow, would you look at the size of that guy!"

Chuck looked across the gym and saw Jose Rivera-Torres walking through the crowded floor. It looked like Moses parting the sea as people on the court moved away to let the man through. Chuck said, "This guy is gonna come play with us for a while. That okay with you, partner?"

As if he could say no, Pepper responded, "I got no problem with that." Then he dribbled toward the basket and said, "As long as you cover him!"

Chuck smiled at Pepper and said, "Let's see how out of shape this guy is." He turned towards Jose and yelled, "Hola, Amigo! You ready to play some ball?" Chuck clapped his hands toward Pepper indicating he wanted the ball. Pepper obliged and tossed the ball to Chuck. Chuck caught it and said, "Howdy, Jose!"

Jose was at the top of the key when Chuck sent him a pass aimed at his face. Jose caught it more out of self-defense than a desire to catch it. He took two dribbles and headed down the lane. He tried to shoot a lay-up but pounded the ball off the backboard completely missing the rim. One word popped into Chucks mind: Project. On the plus side, he caught the ball, he knew how to dribble, and he did intend to shoot a lay-up. On the negative side, he looked uncoordinated, unathletic and uncomfortable with the game. He watched intently as Jose got the ball under the basket and shot a couple of shots in close. Jose hit a couple of shots inside the lane, but it was obvious he couldn't jump.

They just tossed the ball around, feeling each other out. Pepper shot jumpers, Jose rebounded, and Hoopman passed to both as he constantly moved. After twenty minutes, Jose was already winded. Chuck said, "Come on, fellas, let's get a drink." They walked over to the water fountain. "You feel okay enough to run up and down the floor some?" Chuck asked Jose.

"I'll give it a try. I'm already tired, but I won't get any better unless I play, right?" said Jose.

"Exactly. We're gonna go play one game of five on five, just to see how well you get up and down the floor. Just one game Jose, so play hard," said Chuck.

Chuck jogged to the other end of the floor and found seven more guys to run a quick game. Just for a little test, Chuck decided the game would be played to 21. Chuck spent most of the game watching Jose, seeing how he moved, how he set his body, and picked his spots at different areas of the floor both offensively and defensively. By the time the score was 11-8, Chuck could already see the big man's positioning was slowing. He wasn't getting to places on the floor that he previously was getting to. The other team was double and triple teaming him.

After having the ball stripped a couple times by the other team's guards, Chuck had seen enough. He went up to Jose and quietly whispered in his ear, "If you pull that ball down under your chin one more time where their guard can slap it, I'm gonna kick you in the butt!" Then gave him a look that showed he was dead serious.

Jose stopped running and looked at Chuck as if he had already been kicked. Chuck turned up court to go play defense then looked back over his shoulder and said, "And if you don't get back and play defense, I won't throw you the ball!" For a moment, Chuck thought he had pushed the big man too far. To Jose's credit, he inhaled deeply and ran back on defense. The rest of the game went off without a hitch and Hoopman's team won 21 to 15.

They walked over to the water fountain in silence. Chuck said thanks to all the other players and informed them that they wouldn't be playing any more. He smacked Jose on the arm and said, "Come on over to the basket and shoot some more!"

Jose sarcastically answered, "Or what? You gonna kick my ass?"

Chuck stopped dead in his tracks. "Wait a minute. I said, 'In the butt'. I didn't say I was gonna "kick YOUR ass!" He tilted his head and asked, "Is that what it takes to get you motivated? A few words get you angry?"

"NO, MAN!" said Jose. "You don't gotta talk to me like that! My father doesn't even talk to me like that!"

"I told you this was gonna be a lot of work. I told you shooting is more mental than physical. I haven't told you how bad I hate losing," said Chuck. "If you don't want to win, you might as well leave the gym right now." Chuck was quiet for moment as he let the comment sink in.

Chuck softened his tone as he finished his turn at the fountain. "You have a lot of work to do. Let's go shoot some more and I'll talk, you can listen." Chuck turned and headed to the far basket. Over his shoulder he said, "If you don't come, I'll know you got no guts. No heart. And no chance to make the team."

Pepper was already shooting. He was barely sweating after the game in which he hit seven shots. "Hoopman, he ain't that bad a ball player. He's just really, really out of shape."

"It's not just the fact that he is out of shape. If he doesn't have it in his heart, he won't have it on the court, Pepper." Chuck looked over his shoulder and saw the big man getting more water. He shook his head and said, "How many people you know would give anything, I mean anything, to have his size? I played with guys six foot-four that can dunk on him. He wants to play on the team here. I don't even think he can play for a high school team right now."

Pepper shook his head and said, "I think just because of his size he could make the team."

"And do what, Pepper? Sit the bench? Come in at the end of the game for fifteen seconds of playin' time? I'm gonna push him. I want to know if he wants to not just make the team but contribute. Because if I make the team, I want to play. I want to play hard, and I want to win. I want the guys around me to be the same way!" Chuck stepped back to the top of the key and shot. The ball swished through the net. "Because that's what it's all about!"

Pepper got the rebound and stopped. He nodded toward the other end of the gym and said, "I think he's coming back. Maybe he does want to play."

Jose came up to Chuck and said, "What now? You want to run me till I puke, right?"

"No, Jose. I don't want you to do anything. That is, anything you don't want me to do!" Chuck stopped dribbling and walked up to the mountain and said, "It's all up to you. I am just a tool and I have faith in the lord. It is He that gives me faith. I will share that faith with you. I can help you get in shape. I can help you improve your game. I can help you feel better about yourself when you look in the mirror at night. But I can't get into your heart and give you the love you need to play the game. Or the desire it takes to play the game at the level you want. That's for you, Jose. You need to find faith young man. You can do that." Hoopman dribbled the ball to the basket and hit a lay-up, smacking the backboard with his hand after the shot.

Jose mumbled something. Chuck heard the mumble but misinterpreted what he heard. He turned and hollered, "DID YOU SAY SOMETHING, JOSE?" Chuck walked over and looked up at Jose and said, "Did you say something?" Pepper stepped closer to try and get between the two men.

Jose bit his lip, then quietly said, "I said, I can do this."

"That's not what you said the first time. I may be old, but I can hear whining from a mile away. If you're gonna whine, take it somewhere else." Chuck grabbed the ball and threw it to the big man. "If you're gonna play ball, let's do it!"

Jose caught the ball and nodded. He took a deep breath and dribbled toward the basket. This time he was concentrating. Jose didn't jump too high, but the basketball went off the backboard and through the basket. Chuck smiled. Jose Rivera-Torres had a different look on his face. It was a look of seriousness. A look of determination that had not been there an hour ago. In Chuck's eyes, he looked like he wanted to win. A sense of faith appeared.

They played for another hour running, shooting and getting to know each other. The gym was about to close when Chuck yelled, "GET DOWN AND KNOCK 'EM OUT!" Pepper dove for the floor and started doing pushups. Chuck joined him. Jose was clueless at first. He slowly got down and tried to do a push up. Chuck talked as he knocked out pushups. "Come on now, big man! Last thing we do. You don't need a weight room. You got all the weight you need to push around on your gut. Come on! Push up!"

Slowly, Jose got his body into position. He dropped down towards the floor. With every ounce of energy, he pushed up. Slowly, he repeated the act. His arms started trembling. After ten seconds, he crumpled to the ground. Two push-ups. Chuck looked at Pepper and hollered, "Recover!" Both got up and went over to Jose.

"You okay, man?" asked Pepper.

Jose's face was beet red. He was breathing heavily. He finally rolled over onto his back. "I think I'm gonna die."

"You did two, right, big guy? I didn't do many more than that when we started. You get used to it!" said Pepper. He ran over and grabbed a towel and tossed it to Jose.

"You gotta start somewhere, Jose. You made a good start tonight," said Chuck. He put his hand on the large man's shoulder. "Let me tell you the positives. You got good hands. When you were fresh, you got great position. You can rebound and you can pass pretty darn well. Now the bad news. If I was to try and describe the kind of shape you were in, I would have to say . . . pear shape." Pepper laughed out loud and caught a look of anger from Jose.

Chuck continued, "You are so far out of shape, you might not have enough time to get into shape before the season starts. Next, you shoot like you want to hurt the rim. Treat the rim nice and she'll treat you nice right back. And finally, you got to get more aggressive. You are the biggest guy on the court, and yet little guys were slappin' the ball away from you." Jose nodded and a small smile showed up. "You noticed after I told you to keep the ball up, they never got it from you again, right?" Again, he nodded. "If you listen to me, I can help your game."

Jose tried to push himself up. Chuck extended his hand to the big man, and he eagerly accepted. As he got to his feet he said, "Just one question. Would you really have kicked me in the butt if I lost another ball?"

Chuck avoided the answer. "Look, Jose. I told you I don't like to lose. If you're doing all this to just make the team, do it on your own time. I'm gonna make the team and I'm gonna win. Whatever it takes to win, within reality, I'll do. I pray that I play well enough to win. All the time. I wouldn't kick your butt unless you needed it. Okay?" Jose nodded again and smiled. "Now it's up to you to keep it from being necessary." He threw Pepper the ball and ran to the top of the key. Pepper threw the ball to Hoopman; he caught it, shot and said, "AT THE BUZZER!" Swish. "I gotta go, fellas! See you tomorrow, Pepper!" Then he turned to Jose and asked, "How 'bout it big man? See you here tomorrow night?"

Jose nodded. "I'll be here. I'll be sore, but I'll be here."

Chuck smiled and ran out of the gym. Pepper looked at Jose and said, "I think he likes you, man!"

"How can you tell? I thought he really was gonna hurt me when we were playing. He had this look on his face that told me he was mad," said Jose.

"I can tell he likes you! He gets angry at some people he plays with, but I've never seen him get on any one person before. That's how I can tell he likes you. He cares and wants to see you do good," said Pepper.

Jose nodded and started for the door. "I'm gonna be so sore tomorrow, I probably won't make it to class," said Jose.

"You'll make it, big guy. 'Cause if you don't make your grades, Hoopman really will kick your butt!" said Pepper playfully punching Jose in the arm.

"Ow, man! Don't do that! I told you I'm sore," said Jose with a smile. The two new friends headed out of the gym. "You really think he likes me?"

"I know he does," said Pepper. He stopped and looked up at Jose. "You know you got a whole lot of work to do to make the team."

"So do you, ya little red-headed stick boy!" said Jose. He started to chase Pepper out of the gym, but he could hardly move. "Man, if I could catch you, I'd smack that little red head of yours!"

Pepper stopped at the gym door and said, "You got a long way to go before you catch me, big man!" Out the door he went, laughing as he ran down the hallway.

Jose Rivera-Torres limped to the door. He looked over his shoulder at the courts. The lights clicked off and the gym went dark. For the first time in a long time Jose had enjoyed himself. Being on the basketball court again, playing hoop and meeting people that weren't intimidated by his size. Pepper was such a good shooter that he made the game fun. And Hoopman. He was the first person to take an interest in Jose in years. He told it like it was. Jose knew he had problems; his weight and his shyness were the most evident, but all the people he hung around with just treated him like a big child. Deep inside, that was what bothered him most. He wanted to be treated like a man. Not a giant kid. Chuck Hayes was treating him like a man. Despite his self-perceived flaws, Hoopman cared and wanted Jose to rise to the challenge the game presented.

As Jose limped out of the gym into the steamy Texas night, he made a vow. He was going to work his butt off. Not just because of Hoopman. Hoopman would have told him to pack it up if he wasn't capable of playing for St. Michael's. Jose wanted to play basketball to show everyone he wasn't just another fat Mexican-American kid with a bad attitude. He was going to show everyone Jose Rivera-Torres was worthy of respect, on and off the court. There was just one thing missing. For the first time in years, Jose said a prayer.

It was Thursday night and as had become Chuck's custom, once a month he would go to the Ft. Sam Houston gym to shoot baskets with some of the local ball players with disabilities. He looked forward to these get togethers, because it offered him a chance to get away from the trivialities of everyday life and be with people who weren't as fortunate as Chuck Hayes. Most were paraplegics in wheelchairs from accidents or war, like Eddie Newton. Since he'd retired, he had only been able to come to the gym twice. He missed the warm reception he received when he would show up. Usually the players would roll up, holler his name, hug him, and hold his hands like a long-lost friend. This night, something was different.

It didn't take long to figure out that Eddie had already talked to the players. "HOOPMAN! HOOPMAN!" came the calls from across the gym. The players mobbed Chuck as soon as he came through the door. He let the new name go on, as the reception was wild.

"WHOA, NOW! Hold up, now! Somebody's gonna get smushed!" Chuck slowly got the group headed back to the floor and playing basketball. He would take a ball, show them some ball handling drills, and then go through routine passes. Chest passes, bounces passes and occasionally, a fancy behind the back pass to watch the younger players eyes light up. After a half hour with the group, Chuck headed to the other end of the gym to shoot around with a group of older guys, almost all military veterans in wheelchairs. He was looking forward to this evening because Eddie was there. Eddie would have some answers for him.

"Hoopman! About time you got down here. We thought you were gonna shoot with those kids all night. It's been such a long time; we thought you had forgotten about us," said the longhaired man in a custom-made wheelchair.

Chuck immediately went to the man and extended his hand. "Hi, Eddie! How could I ever forget about you?" He looked over Ed Newton's shoulder and said, "Howdy, fellas!" The other seven wheelchair players nodded and waved. "You guys up for a little hoop or what?" The players were more than ready. They already had teams picked and were just waiting on Chuck to get them started. Chuck acted as an official and general peacekeeper throughout the game. Of the eight players, five were veterans, two were victims of accidents and the last individual had been born a paraplegic.

Chuck was not really 'needed' per se, merely an acceptable neutral party to insure equality in the game. He would help chase down loose balls, keep the game fair, and keep some of the players with tempers "focused" on exercising. This prevented individuals or sometimes teammates from monopolizing the game or becoming too antagonistic to make the play enjoyable. With Chuck around, there was only enjoyable games between eight guys all playing hard to win. For just a short time, the combatants were equal to everyone else on the planet. They were basketball players like any other players who strapped on sneakers.

After 45 minutes, the wheelchair pickup games were over. The teams shook hands, and verbal exchanges of 'Thanks', and 'see you next time' were passed. The score didn't matter. It was kept, but not for the purpose of determining who won or who lost. Merely as a minor formality, more like record keeping. A requirement to show the game was being played. In these games, there was never a loser.

Most everyone else had left the gym. Only Eddie Newton, his best friend and shadow Chris Crowley, and Chuck remained. They talked about the game a little and some of the plays. Before too long, Eddie got down to business. He was always one to get to the point. "So, what did you want me to check on those scores for?"

Chuck looked at Chris, then back to Ed. "I'd rather not say unless we discuss it in private."

Ed looked at Chris and said, "If you're gonna ask me what I think you're gonna ask me, it's better if Chris stays."

"What do you think I'm gonna ask you, Eddie?" said Chuck more seriously than he intended.

Eddie looked at Chris and back towards Chuck. "From what little info you gave me, I'm bettin' you want to know about point spreads to determine if somebody may or may not have been shavin' points?" Chuck smiled just a bit. Then he looked at Chris. Eddie said, "Chris knows more about gamblin' than anybody I know. In fact," he looked at Chris and said, "If I may be so bold!" Chris smiled and looked back at Chuck. "He knows more about gambling in Texas than the Texas Rangers do! That would be the law officers, not the baseball team!"

Chuck nodded. "All right." He looked at Chris. "I'm not sure about anything, so I'd appreciate it if you kept this conversation . . . just between us."

Chris said, "No problem, man. Eddie says you're a straight up dude. What's said here, stays between us."

Chuck smiled his agreement and said, "Last year's Baylor-St. Michael's game was the first place I saw something weird. I was watching the video and saw some things that looked . . . questionable."

Chris was first to respond, "Something that you think may have been point shaving?"

Chuck nodded. "Baylor won by ten."

Eddie pulled out a piece of paper from a notebook beneath his towel. "Was it the home game?"

"Yeah. Yeah, it was at St. Michael's Auditorium. The Dillo Hole," answered Chuck.

Eddie looked at the sheet, smiled and handed it to Chris. "St. Michael's was getting nine points. Imagine that."

"So if they lost by ten . . ." said Chuck.

Chris answered, "They didn't cover the spread. At home, there is no reason they shouldn't have covered the spread against Baylor. Baylor wasn't ranked and sat two starter early in the season with injuries."

"That's what I was afraid of," said Chuck.

Ed asked the question Chuck didn't want to answer. "What did you see on the tapes that made you think something was wrong?"

Chuck coughed a fake cough. He didn't want to rat out Charles Holmes. Suppose he was wrong. But there was no other way to explain it. He took a deep breath and began, "With about five minutes left in the game, I noticed . . . one of the players throw a really, stupid pass. I mean, to me it was obvious he intended to miss his target. He threw it to where the man was, not where he was moving to."

Chris said, "Let me guess. Charles Holmes, right?"

Chuck nodded. "How'd you know? Did you see it too?"

"There's been a bunch of rumors about Holmes coming up with loads of cash. He doesn't work and the scholarship doesn't cover all the things he's bought," said Chris. "He wasn't receiving any NIL money. Charles Holmes wasn't getting NIL money from anything we could find."

Chuck asked, "NIL money? What's that?"

Eddie answered, "Name, Image, and Likeness. It's a way that college athletes can get paid big bucks. Endorsements, stuff like that. NCAA had to allow it. It's been overdue. But hasn't really showed up in Division II athletics. Yet."

Chuck nodded, "That's good to know." The comment sunk in and he continued, "Two minutes later he drives the lane, dishes to Parnell, who happens to be double covered. I mean, my daughter knows better than making that pass." Chris and Eddie nodded. "But I also noticed something else. After Parnell made a tough basket off Charles's wild miss, he didn't even give his teammate the time of day. Who doesn't shake hands or high five his teammate when he makes one heckuva shot? Holmes' mind was not on beating Baylor, but what the score was. That basket moved St. Michael's to within five."

"There's been a lot of talk about it, but no proof. We have the spreads written down." Eddie handed the sheet of paper to Chuck. "Chris helped me look 'em up. I'm willing to bet, most of the time, St. Michael's didn't cover the spread."

Chris added, "There were at least three games last year St. Michael's lost when they were favored."

Chuck rubbed his chin, "And if you know the spread and know who's betting which side, you can make some money, can't you?"

Chris said, "A bunch of money. Maybe, five or six digits worth of money over the course of the season." Chuck nodded silently. He was thinking about what to do next.

"Is there anything else we can do for you, Chuck?" asked Eddie. His tone let Chuck know he and Chris wanted to help but didn't know what they could do.

"For right now, fellas. This is it," said Chuck. "I don't know what I'm gonna do. I need to check some other scores and see how they played against other schools."

Eddie said, "Chris, get those other notes we took." Chris grabbed a notebook from his gym bag. He pulled a handful of paperwork from the notebook and gave it to Chuck. Eddie said, "We checked the scores versus the point spread for the entire season. They failed to cover over seventy-five percent of the games and outright lost five they were favored to win. You can look them up for yourself. We put the references at the bottom of each game, but these figures won't lie. If someone were betting for St. Michael's with the points, odds are they lost. If you knew they weren't going to cover and bet on the other team, you could make a killing. Somebody made a lot of money off St. Michael's not playing up to expectations."

"And if somebody had a player, say the All-Conference guard, on the payroll. That would certainly make good insurance for those bets to turn out the right way," said Chuck. Chris and Eddie nodded solemnly. "All right then. Let me go look at some more videos and see what I see. I don't want to accuse Charles Holmes of this unless I'm absolutely positive he did it."

Eddie grabbed Chuck's arm and said, "If there is anything we can do. I mean anything, all you have to do is ask, okay?"

Chuck thought for a minute. Chuck and Eddie had worked some special projects while Chuck was on active duty. Eddie was the best cyber analyst he knew. He didn't know about Chris Crowley but he had an idea. "Chris, what do you do?"

"I'm a computer programmer," answered the man. "I write code."

Chuck smiled. "How did I know that?" From Chris's statement, a tiny seed was planted in Chuck's mind. Perhaps the seed would grow later. After all, if the St. Michael's program was controlled by gamblers, he would be up against some serious competition. Perhaps out of his league. The seeds of another team sprang up in Chucks' mind. Hoopman was not one to turn down an assist from friends. Old friends, new friends, cyber security analysts, computer programmers, or assistant DAs. Friends are a wonderful asset.

"If you're in Chris, we need to keep it between us for now," said Chuck. Chris smiled a huge smile and agreed. "All right then. This is what I need you two to do. Get as much information as you can on college betting. Find out the who, what, where and why for me. I'm sure there is a ton of information on the net, and that's just up your alley. I'll give you a call next week. That'll give me time to look at some more video. From there, I'll decide what to do. I guess I'll be talking to Charles Holmes. It might be interesting to see what he has to say about all this."

"Chuck, you might take it easy on Holmes. Chances are good, somebody else is pulling his strings," said Chris.

"You mean Coach Round?" asked Chuck.

Chris said, "I don't think it's Round. He drives a 2003 Ford pickup truck. You want to find out who's pulling the strings, look for the money."

Chuck nodded. He shook hands and headed out the door. The conversation had left him feeling curious. Who could be working Charles? Was Holmes the only one on the team who was shaving points? And worst of all, if he shaved points last year, was he going to shave points this season too?

Chuck hurried into his apartment. The clock told him it was a little after eleven. He'd already missed SPORTSCENTER, so he popped in a St. Michael's game from last season. Three hours later, he had seen enough. One telling factor was an away game against Northeast Louisiana. According to the point spread St. Michael's was supposed to lose to University of Northern Louisiana by seven. Charles Holmes played like a man possessed. He scored 24, had twelve rebounds, eight assists and five steals. St. Michael's won by a dozen. In that game, he wasn't shaving points. Perhaps he had been given incentives for a big win. There was no way to tell without questioning Charles. Only educated guesses and knowledge of players and the game.

The next game, he was not the same player. He had at least ten turnovers, only eight points and didn't seem to have the fire he had against UNL. In fact, he very well could have been a different player. The jersey number was the only thing that indicated the player was Charles Holmes.

Chuck looked at the clock on the wall. It was late and he didn't want to watch anymore. It seemed obvious to him Holmes was cheating, but the only way he could be sure was to confront him. Basketball season started in less than three weeks. He knew that Charles Holmes was a talented basketball player, but the videos didn't lie. How could Holmes be so good in one game, then play so terribly the next? He hoped that he was wrong, yet deep down he knew Charles Holmes had shaved points last year. What Chuck didn't know, was if Charles Holmes was going to repeat his pattern this season? Chuck wanted to get this situation cleared up, one way or another, before the season started. Chuck decided it was time to pay a visit to the so-called "best D II guard in America".

CHAPTER FIVE

It wasn't too hard to find Charles Holmes. Everyone on campus knew where he lived. He was the closest thing to a superstar the St. Michael's campus would ever have. A couple of questions here and there, a short ride on an elevator and Chuck was at the dorm room of Charles Hilton Holmes.

Chuck wondered what he would say. He didn't even know if Charles would let him in. It was ten-thirty at night; the campus was still alive, but Chuck paid no attention to the activity. He had a flashback to his days in the Army as a non-commissioned officer when he would go into a trooper's room to check on them. He thought for an instant that it was too late to knock on the door, then he heard the music. He expected rap music or hip-hop, but to his surprise it was an Al Green song he heard coming through the door. He took a deep breath and knocked on the door.

Charles answered and his smile quickly faded. "Mind if I come in?" asked Chuck.

Charles didn't quite know what to do. Confused, he asked, "You sure you got the right room?"

Chuck pushed the door open and looked around. Charles seemed to be alone. "If this is a bad time, I guess I could come back later?" The smile finally appeared.

That seemed to loosen Charles Holmes up. He relaxed and said, "Naw. Ain't no time any better than now. Being how you're already in." He moved back from the door and offered Chuck a seat on the couch. "Have a seat. What are you doin' here? You finally lookin' for somebody good to run with, or you still runnin' with chumps?"

Chuck smiled and said, "No. I run with a good crowd. We might not be the best ball players on campus, but we win."

Charles knew the statement was true. After all, they had beat him earlier, and the gym rumor mill said they were getting better. "Yeah, you do. But if you had me runnin' with you, you would never lose," said Charles with a huge smile. "I've seen your game. You run pretty good for an old man."

"Thanks, I think," said Chuck. He looked around and saw the stereo. "I didn't know you younger guys listened to Reverend Green?"

"You listen to Al Green?" asked Charles.

"Ever since I was a teenager. It was all the coach would let us play on the bus if we lost," said Chuck. "That was back in high school, man!" He laughed at the thought of how long it had been.

Charles Holmes brought Chuck back to reality. "What are you doin' here?"

Chuck's smile disappeared. It was time to come clean. "I'm here to ask you a question, and I want an honest answer." Charles Holmes cocked his head and a frown appeared. "I want to know if you shaved points last year?"

Charles jumped up off the couch. "You want to know what!? The answer is, NONE OF YOUR DAMN BUSINESS!"

Chuck was always good at reading people. The look on Charles' face, the indignation and the anger were all he needed. He didn't need to hear Charles admit it. The tone in his voice was the answer. Chuck tried to calm Charles' fears. "I'm the only one who knows." After the statement, Chuck was quiet and let the words hang in the air.

Charles tried to keep up the facade. "Man, you got it all wrong! Who told you I was doin' that?"

Chuck thought he saw Charles' eyes glass over. "Look. Nobody told me anything. I watched some videotapes from last years games." Chuck shook his head and continued, "I don't care about last year. I'm only interested in this year. Because

I'm gonna play this year, and I'm gonna win. So, if you're gonna shave points this year tell me now. Because it's," not wanting to threaten Charles, Chuck looked for the right words. He softened his tone but was adamant, "It's counterproductive to where I'm taking my team."

Charles was in the full defensive mode. "YOUR TEAM! You ain't even made the team yet!"

Chuck still felt Charles' weakness and stayed on the offensive. He laughed, "So it's gonna be your team?" Chuck got off the couch and looked hard at Charles. He decided it was time to display a little attitude of his own. "Listen to me! You had your chance last year, AND YOU SOLD OUT! DIDN'T YOU?" He stepped towards the younger man. "Was it just you or were there others on the team? I wanna know! Were you by yourself in this bullshit? TELL ME!"

Charles walked to the door. "You need to leave. Get your punk ass outta my place! Comin' in here, accusing me of bullshit. Man, you don't know nothin'!"

Chuck shook his head in disgust. He walked towards the door and stopped. It was time for a different approach. He turned to Charles and said, "Whatever it is, I can help you." He looked into his eyes and for just an instant, thought he had reached Charles. "Let me try. Please?"

Charles swallowed hard and turned away. "You can't help me, man. Nobody can."

Chuck wanted to reach out and touch the young man on his shoulder. To get through to him and let him know it wasn't too late. The season hadn't started. He went with the only thing that was left. The game. Basketball was something both men had in common, and basketball might be the answer. Chuck's eyes softened and he said, "Meet me at the gym tomorrow. I know you think we're just a bunch of scrubs but come play ball with us." Chuck smiled and added, "I'll prove to you that we have a serious chance to win some games this year. Have faith."

Playing ball was the answer. It reached Charles Holmes where he lived. It went to his heart. Chuck could tell he had found a crack. Charles said, "We'll play some ball, and you'll stop all this crap about shaving points, right?"

It was a step in the right direction. Chuck agreed. "Sure. Sure, just hoop." He stepped out into the hallway. "I won't bring it up unless you want to talk about it. I'm always available." Chuck looked once more into the young man's eyes and said, "Let me tell you something. I don't mean to threaten you, but I know what will hurt you the most." Chuck looked to see his reaction. "If you do it this year, the only people I'm gonna tell are your teammates." He turned away, walked into the hallway and listened to the door slam closed. He knew instantly that the comment had hit home. If Charles Holmes still cared enough to worry about his teammates' feelings, maybe he cared enough to play straight this season.

Charles was totally confused. Chucks' little visit had caught him off guard. How did Chuck figure it out? If he knew, who else knew? Would he really tell the rest of the team? If Chuck told anyone, the news would be all over campus in no time. The NCAA would find out and he would get kicked out. Then Henderson and his 'friends' would pay him a visit. How the hell was he going to get out of this? Could Henderson help? Charles Holmes thought about asking Henderson for support. He immediately knew the answer to that question was; never. Henderson was making too much money and was in too deep with the gamblers pulling his strings. Maybe Hoopman was the answer? He was smart enough to catch Charles. Could Chuck actually help him? That's when he made the right decision. What choice did he have? He'd go to the gym and play with the man. After that, he would decide if Hoopman could help or not. If it looked like they could win, it would help make the decision that much easier. As for telling Hoopman about Henderson's involvement, that was something he hoped he wouldn't have to explain.

Chuck arrived right at six o'clock. He was surprised to see Jose and Pepper already there and shooting jumpers. He stretched out on the sideline and watched the two players shoot. Then he saw something he couldn't believe. Jose Rivera-Torres shot a sky hook from the lower right side of the lane. The shot hit 'nothin but net'. Chuck continued stretching and watched the big man's footwork. He did the same thing again. Jose pivoted off his left foot and shot the hook as if he was Kareem Abdul-Jabbar. Chuck smiled. If he could hit that consistently, Jose would not only make the team, but he could also be a factor.

Chuck came up and starting shooting. "Hello, fellas. Jose, you want to shoot that sky hook you got for me?" Chuck waited as Jose got to the spot. He threw the ball in low and watched as Jose caught it cleanly, pivoted, and with the ball at the end of his hand, flipped his wrist and watched the swish. Chuck yelled, "Where the heck was that the other night?"

"I don't know, man. I don't use it too much," said Jose with a shrug.

Chuck shook his head and ran to the low post. "Jose, if you get the ball down this low, with that hook you have and the point you release it at, nobody in the world is gonna block it!"

Jose shook his head, "Lots of dudes I play with make fun of me. Sayin' it's old game. That I should be dunkin' everything."

"Let me guess. You quit playin' because you think you gotta dunk everything, and you can't jump high enough to dunk," said Chuck with a smile. Jose nodded. "Man, Jose! That's the best-looking sky hook I've seen in twenty years! You gotta shoot that shot!" He threw the ball to Jose. "Do it again." Jose took the ball and shot the hook. Swish. It was beautiful.

Jose said, "My Dad used to love the Lakers. He would show YouTube video's of Abdul-Jabbar's career. I saw that hook shot and fell in love with it. He was so consistent. Other teams would see it coming, and you knew they couldn't stop it." Jose looked as if he were a million miles away.

Pepper interrupted the exchange with, "Hoopman, I think we're about to have a visitor." He pointed across the gym where Charles Holmes was walking towards them. Chuck nodded to Pepper to throw Holmes the ball. He did and Charles ran to catch it. He dribbled to the top of the key and popped. The shot was short. The rebound came back to Holmes and he shot again. This time it was good.

Chuck jogged over and stuck out his hand. "Hey, man! Thanks for coming out." Charles looked down at the hand with a cocked head. He looked at Chuck, slowly took the hand and said, "No sweat, man." Then he looked over at Jose, who just happened to miss a ten-foot set shot, and said to Chuck, "I've seen Opie with the laser guided jumper, but where'd you get the frijoles eatin' brick layer?"

Chuck frowned at the adjectives Charles used and instantly thought of how Jose had described his rapport with black basketball players. Some saw a big, heavy Hispanic kid and assumed he couldn't play ball. The assumption was usually incorrect. Maybe the man couldn't play an uptempo, run and gun style game. However, in the right system, a slow tempo player can flourish. Chuck wanted to prove this to Charles. "The brick-layer may be outta shape, but he can play some." Chuck took a shot and said, "Let me show you. You feel like runnin' with us?"

Charles Holmes nodded. He seemed surprised that Chuck didn't want to talk, especially when Chuck had been so 'talkative' the night before. "Sure. If it's okay with you that I run with you. I mean I have been here as long as everybody else, right?"

Chuck nodded, "Yes, you have! Let's kick some butt!"

Charles knew another kid on the sideline and Chuck picked him up. The five-some was set and at first glance looked beatable. They appeared to have only two guys who could play. Charles and his friend. Yet to see the skinny redheaded guy, a huge, out of shape Hispanic, and a near 40 year old male round out the team made them look like easy competition.

The first point was Chuck to Charles Holmes on a beautiful back door cut. It was a sign of things to come. Pepper would join in with some terrific picks on the weak side that would free up Holmes for wide-open shots. Charles was a little off for the first few jumpers, but by the second game, Holmes was deadly.

In the third game, Chuck decided to get Jose involved. He knew Jose was getting tired. As he was getting back on defense, he said to Jose, "Next time, get open in the post. I want to see if you can shoot that hook!"

Charles played tough defense on a shooter forcing him to miss a jumper. Hoopman got the rebound and ran it down court himself. He waited for Jose to get set up on the right side low post. As soon as Jose was set, Chuck hit him with a pass. Jose caught it, pivoted and flipped the ball in with the hook. Chuck looked at Charles Holmes and winked. Charles's jaw dropped in disbelief. Meanwhile, Pepper stole the inbounds pass, ran in to five feet away and banked one high off the glass. Game.

That was the last game of the night. The competition had decided enough was enough and studying was probably more fun than getting beat 12-5. There were high fives all around with handshakes for winners as well as losers. Chuck jogged to the far end of the gym with Pepper right behind him. He retrieved a ball and started shooting again. Out of the corner of his eye he saw Jose coming down the floor. Chuck took a glance behind Jose and, to his surprise, Charles Holmes was walking right behind the big man. To his amazement, it looked like the two were talking to each other.

The unlikely foursome stayed for another thirty minutes. Chuck used the cool down period to have a foul shooting contest. Chuck and Jose against Charles and Pepper. As fate would have it, the score was tied when the janitor said it was time to lock up. Chuck put Jose on the line. "No pressure, big man! You miss it, we lose." Jose smiled and he got tense. He missed. Chuck yelled, "GET ON DOWN!" Chuck, Jose and Pepper all dropped and started doing pushups. Charles looked at the three men on the floor and shook his head. But not wanting to be the only one not doing the exercise, Charles dropped and started doing pushups. Jose did six good ones before he started fading. Pepper started laughing as his arms were beginning to shake.

Chuck looked at Charles who was still pushing the gym floor. It became a one-on-one contest. Chuck was silent and showed no emotion. Charles said something under his breath, and his pace began to slow. Chuck kept pushing even though he was beginning to feel the pain. The janitor hollered from across the gym, "CHUCK, YOU GONNA GET OUT OF HERE SOME TIME TONIGHT?"

At that precise instant, Charles fell to the floor exhausted. Chuck bounced up and said to the janitor across the gym, "WE'RE DONE, TOMMY!" He jogged over to his towel and headed out the door with his partners. "Nice work out, fellas! Hey, Jose, you look like you've already lost some weight."

"Maybe a couple of pounds. I do feel a lot better. My arms are tired, but I'm getting stronger. I can tell," said Jose. "I gotta go study, Hoopman. I'll see you tomorrow night."

Pepper joined in with his ever-present smile. "Me too, boss! I got an exam Friday and I'm trying to get ahead of schedule."

"That's cool! I'll see you tomorrow," said Chuck. He was alone with Charles Holmes. They stepped into the night air in silence.

It was Charles Holmes who spoke first. "Where did Jose get that hook shot? Man, that shot is a thing of beauty."

"Jose says he's been shooting it for years. He doesn't shoot it in games because he thinks everyone wants to see him dunk. Problem is, he's too," Chuck hesitated before adding, "large to get up high enough to dunk," said Chuck.

"He is pretty 'large' as you say! But that hook shot is awesome. He looks like a fat version of Kareem," said Charles with a chuckle.

"Jose is self-conscious about his weight. It turns off a lot of people and it makes him shy," said Chuck. "Suppose you carried about 300 on your frame? You'd worry about what other people thought too."

Charles nodded, "And I wouldn't be able to dunk then either! If he drops the weight, he could be a terror inside!"

Chuck stopped and looked at Charles, "It would sure open up the outside for your jumper." Chuck could see a smile come to Charles face. Just as quickly, it faded. "You know. Tonight, was the first time this year I've felt real good on the floor. I had a good time playin'." He took a deep breath and added, "For the first time in a while it was fun."

"It can be like that all the time, Charles," said Chuck. Charles stopped walking. "It was always meant to be a game. It was meant to be fun." Chuck listened but got no response. He knew better than to push it. He threw his towel over his shoulder and said, "I'll see ya'." Chuck turned to walk away.

Charles Holmes coughed a little to clear his throat. He hollered at Chuck, "You got a minute?"

Chuck turned and said, "For you. I got two minutes."

Charles Holmes was sitting on a bench, wiping his face with a towel and talking with a quiet voice. He kept looking around to see if anyone was within listening distance. Chuck stood across from him stretching. He didn't want to sit or he would tighten up into one big 39 year-old knot.

"I was asked to kind of, you know, mess up in a couple games last year," started Charles. "At first, it was no big deal."

"A couple? I saw at least six," said Chuck with a frown.

"All right, it was during most of the season. Sometimes when they needed us to lose by more than the point spread, I'd make sure we did. On the rare occasion we were supposed to win, I'd make sure that we'd win, but that we didn't win by too much. I was told before the game how much we were supposed to win or lose by, and I'd make it happen."

Chuck heard the word "they", but let it slide. "And what about Northeast Louisiana?" asked Chuck.

Charles face lit up. "I had the night off!" He smacked his hands together and said, "I had it goin' on that night! I couldn't miss!"

"Shoulda been like that every game, Charles," said Chuck. "You've got a lot of game, but you aren't using it right. You are literally toying with your talent. For what? To get a few dollars?"

"It's a lot more than a few dollars," said Charles. He looked around again as if someone were listening. "I made over sixteen thousand dollars last year. They told me at the end of last year that I could make twice that this season. If I played ball for them, they'd get theirs and I'd get mine."

"So let me get this straight. For thirty thousand dollars, you'd sell out your team this year?" asked Chuck. Then he added quietly, "You'd sell yourself out for a few thousand dollars? In what might be your only chance in college to be on a winning team? Maybe even a Championship Team?"

"I didn't say I was gonna do it this year," said Charles defensively. Chuck looked at him with a frown. "It's been botherin' me a lot." Holmes appeared to become worried. "I don't think I can do it again. After tonight, shoot! If we can get that big man playin', and Pepper's got game, too. We have a chance to win a lot of games."

"Not unless you're seriously thinking about blowin' off all that money!" said Chuck sarcastically. He shook his head and added, "You know we can win. We haven't even run with Parnell yet. He's a monster!"

"He could make All-Conference this season," said Charles. A big smile came across his face. "Yeah. I ain't gonna run for those guys this year." He looked at Hoopman and said, "I can play clean, and we can sweep the conference." His eyes got big, and a huge smile appeared, "Maybe we can get a spot in the D II tournament!"

At that point Chuck smiled too. "I hadn't thought about that. That would be nice to play for a national championship." Chuck looked up at the night sky. "Shoot. We better come back to earth. I gotta make the team still." He looked at Charles and said, "And I guess you gotta go tell somebody, somewhere, you're not on their payroll this year." Chuck looked at Charles and asked, "Do you want help with that?"

The bright, youthful enthusiasm from moments prior had disappeared. It was replaced by a young man nervous and apprehensive about a ghost he had to face, and he didn't really know how to do it. Somehow, through it all, Charles wanted to face his demons as a man. As he spoke, there was no trace of nervousness, "I can handle it." He looked at Chuck and said, "I don't need any cops either. All right?"

Chuck nodded in agreement. "Okay, no cops." Calling the police was not what Chuck had in mind. Despite Charles's confident tone, Chuck thought Charles Holmes was in too deep. He had no idea it might be deep enough to cost Charles his life.

For a short time, Chuck got a chance to put basketball behind him. He had a real date with a beautiful woman. He was as dressed up as Chuck Hayes could possibly get. Chuck managed to take an hour out of his schedule to slip into a Men's Warehouse store and buy some nice "civilian" clothes. He wanted the evening to be special. To do that, he needed to feel special.

Chuck picked Grace up promptly at six o'clock. Just as he expected, she looked spectacular. As he met her at the door, he stepped back and said, "WHOAA!" She was wearing a knee length black skirt, with a slit up the side. The lightweight black sweater she wore fit tightly over a white lowcut blouse. Chuck noticed her boots but was too focused on the rest of her to say anything except, "You look . . . gorgeous!"

Grace smiled, stepped outside, and said, "Well, thank you, Mr. Hayes!" She closed the door and looked Chuck up and down. "You clean up pretty nice yourself."

Chuck said, "What? These old things? Come on." He followed her as she headed down the walkway. He loved to watch her walk. "What do you feel like? Dinner? A movie? Both?"

She looked over her shoulder and said, "I'm thinking perhaps just dinner. I'm hungry."

"Great! Ladies' choice then," said Chuck still smiling. They got to Chuck's truck and he held the door for her as she got in. Chuck knew right away that Grace was surprised by the act of courtesy.

As they rode, they talked about food and music. Easy, normal topics and good icebreakers that kept the atmosphere light and friendly. She liked country and western music and decided to take Chuck to her favorite barbecue place. The County Line Barbeque was on the north side of the Riverwalk. The evening was cool for October in Texas, so they sat on the deck, watching the sun set. She ordered a glass of Chablis while Chuck started with a Shiner Bock Beer. She chose the ribs and baked potato. Chuck thought about getting ribs, but was worried about getting sauce on his fine, new clothes. He ordered brisket, French fries and a slice of pecan pie for dessert. He was splurging, not just on the meal, but on his calorie consumption too.

Dinner was fantastic. It was the first real night of relaxation he had enjoyed in months. Grace was sitting back watching him as he sat across from her. She picked up her wine and slowly swirled it in the glass. She cocked her head slightly to the side and said, "All right. I give up."

Chuck shook his head and said, "Give up what?"

She sighed, "What's a terrific guy like you doing going to college?" She hesitated as Chuck looked out at the sunset with his smile still beaming. "Shouldn't you be married and getting your kids ready for college? I mean, you are about . . . what? Thirty-eight, thirty-nine?"

"Good guess. I'll be a whopping forty in March," said Chuck.

She waited for more answers. When she saw no more were coming, she leaned over the table and said, "And the married part?" A terrible thought went through her mind, and she suddenly became serious. "Are you still married?"

Chuck was a little shocked by her seriousness. His face became red, and he quickly replied, "Not anymore!" Slowly the red faded, and his smile returned. He could see she wanted to know more. "I wouldn't do anything like that!"

Chuck took a deep breath and started a story that he never liked to tell, but thought it was appropriate with Grace. "I was married. About twenty years ago, I married my high school sweetheart. We waited until I had joined the Army. Had started a "career" so to speak. But the Army and marriage don't always work well together. I mean it takes a real strong woman to put up with everything the military puts a man through. My first couple of tours, I mean jobs, as you civilians call them, were pretty tough! I spent ten out of the first fourteen months away in training. Then when we finally got back together, I signed up for some special assignments. Two months after my daughter was conceived, I was neck deep in a desert in Kuwait. A three-month mission there and another one that took me to Panama, which kept me from seeing my daughter's birth, pretty much did it for my wife. And I don't blame her one bit. I wasn't around when she needed me. About six months after I came home from that mission, I was off for a one-year unaccompanied tour in Korea." Chuck took a sip of beer. "When I came home, she had moved into a friend of a friend's house. I didn't fight it. He was better for her than I was."

"Somehow, I doubt that," said Grace.

"We had an amicable separation and eventually divorced. She remarried to the guy she was living with. And the ironic thing was, the guy she married was also in the Army and gone nearly as much as I was!" said Chuck with a small smile.

"Are you still in touch?" asked Grace.

"Yeah! She stopped asking for money after she finished college and got a job as a paralegal in North Carolina. I still send her some for my daughter. I think she's got about $30,000 saved up for college next year. And I consider her mom and I to be friends," said Chuck.

"Anyone else?" asked Grace.

Chuck laughed. "Uh, no! No one else."

She tilted her head again and said, "So I don't have any competition at all?"

Chuck laughed. "No. No competition whatsoever, Ms. Winters."

"What about college? I mean this is a big change for you, isn't it?" she asked.

"I guess some of my peers are going through the same thing with new cars, new wives and trying new things. I suppose I'm just not as volatile at this point in my life. Or just more in control of this middle age crazy thing than them," he said. "Compared to the changes some of them are going through, I'm relatively calm! Things like, giving up on civilization and heading for the hills, trading in the old Honda for a new Corvette, or leaving a woman you've lived with and loved for twenty years, to be with a woman young enough to be your own daughter. That's just not me. I can't do that."

"I guess college isn't that crazy after all!" she smiled. Then Grace changed the subject. "I've heard a lot about you playing basketball for St. Michael's. You are trying out for the team, aren't you?"

It was Chuck's turn to laugh. "It depends on who you talk to!"

"I've talked to lots of people who know more about basketball than me, and they say you are very good," she said.

"I don't know about all that," Chuck said modestly. "But I have to admit, I'm going to try out for the team."

Grace's mouth dropped and she said, "I heard you were thinking about it. Do you really think you can make the team? At your . . ."

Chuck cut her off. "At my age?" Chuck's smile faded. "Ms. Winters, you shouldn't be talking to people about me." He gave her a mock frown that quickly disappeared. He suddenly became serious. "I can play hoop at the college level. The age is just a thing.

It's a fact. I've accepted that I'm a whole lot older than all the other guys trying out. And I do mean a whole lot older! But it's as much about heart and soul as it is about physical capabilities. Sure, I can't jump as high or run as fast as the younger guys, but I've played so much for so long," his words trailed off. "This is something I believe God has planned for me. He's given me faith in myself." He looked away and searched for what he wanted to say next.

After a moment, he thought he had found the right words and began again, "God has given me talent and now an opportunity to play. I see things on the floor that other people miss. I've got twice as much experience playing the game as college kids. I'm smarter and more patient than them. And most of all, I am more ruthless than them. They've all lived such good lives." He looked back at Grace and continued, "I've seen so much bad in my past that this experience can only be good to me. This chance is a blessing. Even if I don't make it through the first practice, I'll love every minute of it. Even if everybody in the stands laughs at me. If I make the team, I will always take care of my teammates too." Suddenly he found himself thinking about Charles Holmes and he felt worried.

Grace noticed his mood change. "You look like you went away for a second?"

"The Bahamas! I love the Bahamas! That's where I went," said Chuck trying to cover loss of attention.

"I'm a professor, Chuck. I've seen people go to the Bahamas in my classes, and you didn't just go there!" she said.

Chuck decided to tell her the truth. "I was just thinking about one of the kids on the team. Great young man. Real good ball player if he keeps his head on straight."

"This kid. He doesn't have his head on straight right now?" she asked.

Chuck answered, "I think he's getting it that way. There were rumors of gambling and point shaving involving last year's team, and this kid may have been a part of all that mess."

"I haven't heard anything about that," Grace said.

"That's good, because if the word were to get around, the team and the college would be in deep trouble," said Chuck. "Not only with the NCAA, but probably with the law." Chuck finished his beer and looked at Grace. "This young man has assured me he wasn't going to get involved with the gamblers this year. For the team's sake, I hope he doesn't."

Grace thought for a second then said, "What about the gamblers? Do they know this player isn't going to gamble for them this year?"

"He doesn't really gamble for them," said Chuck trying not to correct her. But her point was made. It wasn't one that he had not thought about. But her tone made it sound more ominous than he thought the situation to be. "He works for them. And, no, he hasn't told them yet."

"Are they going to let him quit?" she asked.

Chuck thought about his answer. He looked at her and smiled, "Yeah. Yeah, I'm sure they will." He fiddled with his empty beer bottle and looked at Grace. "They'll have to do without his services this year." Grace nodded and smiled. Chuck said, "Well, I better get you home. Too much more of this and I'll put you to sleep."

"I think you probably know ways to keep me up a while longer," she said with a devious smile. "Perhaps you could try some?"

"HEY, NOW!" laughed Chuck. "If I mess around with you, won't I end up kicked out or something?"

"Or something?" she laughed.

"I mean aren't their laws or some of form of governmental control that prevents me from doing things . . ." his voice trailed off. He raised his eyebrows and said, "Things I want to do!"

She interrupted, "And what would those things be?"

Chuck stood up and grabbed her chair to help her up. Quietly he said, "Only good things, Ms. Winters. Only good things."

Grace Winters smiled but didn't say a word. She just took his hand and walked beside him as they left.

Chuck stopped at the door, looked panicked and said, "Is this gonna affect my grade?"

Grace continued walking and said, "Only if they aren't 'good things', Mr. Hayes."

Chuck hesitated and then yelled, "If you're such a damn good professor, you'll make sure I get an A then!"

Chuck and Grace were so caught up in each other that they failed to notice the car parked across the street from Grace Winters' house. There was a pile of cigarette butts outside the driver side window. The driver was an impatient man, and the fact that the love of his life had abandoned him was not sitting well. He watched in silence as the couple got in his truck and drove away. He quickly jotted down the plate number and followed the vehicle as it drove away. When they got back to Grace's house, he waited until Grace's lights went out before he left. The truck was still there. His anger had only grown. But he knew he needed to leave, or he would do something he would regret.

Chuck was sitting in his bedroom studying when the phone rang. Marshall answered it and immediately came knocking on the door. "It's some guy named Eddie? He sounds strange."

The expression on Marshall's face made Chuck laugh out loud. "Thanks, man. It's okay. He is strange. And he's a really good friend of mine." Marshall nodded, but the confused look remained. He handed over the cordless phone and left.

"Eddie! Talk to me, Goose!" said Chuck.

"Hi, Hoopman. We've been doing a little bit of investigating, and we've come up with a couple of interesting points for you," said Eddie. Eddie covered the phone and said something to someone at his end. Chuck thought he heard Chris's voice. Eddie's voice came on the line again. "First of all, the heavy hitters for Texas university betting, in both football and basketball is an on-line group called Big Casino of Texas. They operate out of Austin. Chris gets the impression they're a bunch of former Dell employees who couldn't play at UT and were probably kicked out of Dell for 'bad habits'."

"Those 'bad habits' being gambling?" asked Chuck. He was so naive.

"Duh, no boss. They were probably tootin' half their paychecks in cocaine. We hear ecstasy and fentanyl are huge up that way, but it still ain't free," explained Ed.

"So we have some online gamblers and potential dopers in Austin . . ." said Chuck.

Ed quickly cut him off with "And they finance these habits by fixin' games throughout the state." He paused to let that sink in. "It seems as though they are into half a dozen or so programs across Texas. Who knows if they're across the state line, but we're guessing they are. Especially into programs in Louisiana and Mississippi because those players tend to need money a little more than average college kids. They fix the games and use the spreads out of organizations from Vegas and Atlantic City, which are probably the overseers for the operation. And they run the operation with on-line betting out of the Caribbean. It's offshore so it's protected from the U.S. government."

"As slow as I am, I think I understand it now!" said Chuck. "By using a group offshore, that money on-line isn't subject to taxes on the income."

"Not to mention, not subject to the rules, laws, and regulations of U.S. gaming practices," added Ed.

"Okay. At least I have an idea of what we may be up against," said Chuck.

"That's not all," said Ed.

"You're killin' me, Eddie. This is enough," said Chuck.

"A little closer to home, it seems a certain Assistant Coach is driving around a 2021 Porsche Panamera."

"I'm no mathematician, and I don't know what kind of money they pay him, but no assistant coach on the planet makes enough to drive a Porsche," said Chuck.

"Chris is trying to find a connection between our new target, St. Michael's Assistant Coach Henderson, and the BCT in Austin. We haven't found anything yet, but it just feels like he's into those clowns up to his eyeballs," said Ed.

"The plot thickens," said Chuck sounding too much like a dime store detective.

"If I was you, Hoopman, I'd watch my back side around Henderson," said Ed.

Chuck agreed and was touched by the true concern in his friend's voice. "I appreciate the information, Eddie. Especially that part about Henderson. Maybe I need to go have a little talk with him. I'll try to do that before tryouts, so that we have . . . an understanding," said Chuck with a chuckle. Then he added, "And thank Chris for me, Eddie. That's some great work on such short notice."

"You have a favorite for the UT, Texas A & M football game? Chris is continuing the investigation by engaging in on-line chats with some employees of BCT. Seems they know something about the UT defensive injuries that isn't on ESPN yet! You want to play? They're giving A & M and seven!" said Ed.

Chuck shook his head in disbelief. "No thanks, Eddie. I couldn't care less about betting on that game. I'm a big enough sinner. I've got more important things to lose my money on. Again, thanks a bunch and I'll see you Thursday." He hung up the phone and lay down on his bed. His military mind took over and he categorized his "adversaries". He was used to planning and working with the military "five paragraph Operations Order". Situation, Mission, Execution, Command and Control, and Signal was a way of life that had become engraved in his mind.

The pieces of an OPORD came together in Chucks mind. The "Situation" was coming clear. His "enemy" may very well become the BCT and their sponsors. His initial "intelligence" report was in, but he needed more in depth reconnaissance. The mission wasn't exactly clear, but after his Afghanistan mission, he was used to that. The seedlings of execution were planted as well. It would just take a little more intelligence, perhaps some up close reconnaissance, and a whole lot of luck to pull off his plan. But there are ways to increase your luck. When it came to improving one's luck, Chuck Hayes knew exactly how to do that.

CHAPTER SIX

It seemed like just another night at the gym. But Hoopman felt something different was happening, and it wasn't good. The usual crowd was there, and after three games of full court, the normal college kids headed their respective ways to do what normal college kids do. Go to the library, back to their dorms, or head to the watering hole for a beverage.

After the games, Hoopman and his "posse", as the group was being nicknamed, headed to the main floor basket for more practice. Chuck was practicing his jumpers with Pepper, Charles, and Charles' friend, Marvin Earl. The group was shooting around, with Jose working on his hook shot, Charles and Pepper concentrating on threes and Chuck working on his form from the baseline. Marvin spent most of his time rebounding and working with Jose. Chuck had spent hours throwing the ball down to the low post, cutting off imaginary picks from teammates who weren't there. His intent was to show Jose what to expect from the other players movements while in the half-court offense. Marvin would sometimes step in to play defense on Jose, so he would have to decide to pass to Chuck as he cut to the basket or shoot the hook. Jose was getting very good at reading his options. It wasn't quite nine o'clock when Charles said he had to leave.

Everyone said their good-byes, but Chuck had the feeling that something wasn't right with Charles. He walked to the door with the younger man and grabbed his elbow softly. "You're leavin' kind of early tonight, aren't you?"

Charles smiled and said, "I got an appointment."

Chuck could tell by the way Charles said it the 'appointment' meant he was meeting someone, probably Henderson, to say he wasn't going to shave points this season. Chuck smiled and said, "About time! I thought you were gonna get this thing out of the way last week. Tryouts are three days away." Charles nodded meekly. "You want me to go with you?" asked Chuck.

"No. That's not necessary. I have it under control," said Charles. "I'm goin' over to the office and..," said Charles realizing he had said too much. "I gotta go."

Chuck nodded. But the word 'office' hung in the air like a noose. He respected the younger man's wishes and let him go alone. As much as he wanted to go with Charles and confront Henderson, he decided against it. "Good luck and let me know if you need anything. Anything at all!" He turned and went back to shooting.

"About time you got here, Charles!" said Henderson. He was sitting behind a large metal desk smoking a cigar and blowing smoke rings. He pointed to the clock on the wall that read 9:07. "I said nine o'clock! You think I got time to sit around and wait for your sorry ass all night? Huh? After all, wasn't it you that called this little get together?"

"Um, yes, I did, Coach. I was working on my jumper. I'm sorry about being late," said Charles Holmes.

"What the hell do you want?" asked Henderson.

Charles exhaled and came right to the point. "I ain't shaving points for ya'll this year. I'm finished. We're gonna have a good team this year and I want . . ."

Henderson jumped up behind the desk. "YOU WANT WHAT?" He began screaming, "YOU WANT WHAT, CHARLES?" He came around and got in Charles Holmes' face. "We already went over this! We got one chance. One chance to make a little bit of money and that's it! This team isn't gonna win shit! And you're gonna make sure of that!"

Charles recovered quickly and stepped forward. The long lacking sense of self-confidence had reappeared. "No. No, I'M NOT!" A cocky smile showed on his face and a bright defiance appeared in his eyes. "I'm playin' ball for the 'Dillos' this year! Not you. Not those chumps you gotta kiss up to!"

Henderson started to crack. He tried the buddy-buddy approach. "Look, Charles! Those so-called 'chumps', they own you. Hell, they even own me!" He let the comment sink in, but he wasn't through with the pitch. "They promised us a lot more money, too! You sure you don't want to rethink this? We can be a great team, you and me. We can go places. I don't plan on staying' in this back water city forever. When I get a big-time coaching job, you can be my assistant. What do you say?"

Charles smiled defiantly. "No way. They may own you, but they don't own me." Charles started to walk out.

Henderson came with the last option in his bag. The threat. "You know, they could hurt you, Charles?" Henderson looked to see if the threat hit home. He added more emphasis. "I mean, I've heard about some of their tactics. Whoa, man! Not pretty. They screw people up bad!"

It didn't work. Charles Holmes was prepared. "Coach, you gotta do what you gotta do. And I gotta do what I gotta do. I'm playing for the team this year. You tell whoever you gotta tell, I'm playing for me this year. Not them!"

Henderson stepped back and walked behind his desk. "I'll tell you what, Charles. I'm gonna let you sit on it for a while. I know you've been working out hard. I've seen you at the gym in the evenings. Somebody has gotten this idea into your head. Is it that old guy? The guy you work out with?"

For the first time, Charles was on the defensive. "Naw. No way, coach. I made this decision on my own."

But Henderson was no fool. He could read between the lines. What was left of Charles Holmes' honesty had just cost him. The lie didn't work. "Let me tell you something, Charles!"

Henderson leaned on the desk. "That old man won't even make the team if I have anything to say about it." That took Charles by surprise. He wasn't aware that Henderson knew that Chuck had planned to try out. "Is that what it's gonna take to bring you around? 'Cause I can make sure he isn't a part of your life." Henderson let the comment hang in the air. "Then you won't have this 'holier than thou', puritan type attitude with me. You'll come back and you'll be on your knees." Charles shook his head in disagreement and turned to leave. Then Henderson stabbed him with words one more time, for good measure. "That is, if you have any knees left."

There was no use in lying. Charles looked over his shoulder from the doorway and said, "Hoopman's got nothing to do with this. This is my decision, okay?"

Henderson just smiled. "Your . . . friend. Hoopman? He won't make the team. After he gets cut, he probably won't even be in school next semester."

Charles shook his head and thought if Henderson went after Hoopman, there was nothing he could do about it. He needed to take care of himself. "Whatever, Coach. But you're gonna make it right with them for me, aren't you?" The courage Charles had when he arrived at Henderson's office was completely gone.

Henderson looked like the cat that ate the canary. "I don't know, Charles? These guys are demanding. You think about it. I don't need an answer right now. I'll give you a couple days to come around. Then we'll see where you stand. Okay, Charles?" He sat back in the chair, put the cigar in his mouth, his feet up on the desk and said, "Now get the hell outta my office!"

Chuck saw Charles enter the gym. Six years of being a non-commissioned officer had taught Chuck how to read people. Their expressions, their moods, the things that made them tick, and the things that motivated them. He could always tell when something was wrong. One look at Charles Holmes and Chuck could tell exactly what it was. Charles knew Henderson had intimidated Charles. The question was, how badly?

Chuck grabbed a ball and dribbled toward the younger man. He stopped about ten feet away and said, "You come back to shoot a little more?" All the time knowing that wasn't the reason. He tossed Charles the ball.

Charles caught it and tried to muster a smile. He couldn't bring himself to do it. "Naw. Naw I ain't gonna shoot anymore tonight." He threw the ball back to Chuck and said, "I just came back to tell you everything is cool." Chuck caught the ball and eyed Charles cautiously. "I'm serious, man. It's cool!"

Hoopman knew it was a lie. But he chose not to confront Charles in the gym. He looked over at Jose, Pepper and Marvin. They were eyeing the pair of men across the gym. Chuck flashed a thumbs up sign to Pepper and the redhead returned to shooting. The others reluctantly joined him. "Great, Charles. I'm glad for you!" Chuck couldn't keep his smile. He could see his friend was wounded. He hadn't returned with the same pride, the same cockiness he had left with. If it was Henderson that young, confident Charles Holmes went to see, that Charles had stayed there. Henderson had sent a different Charles back.

For his part, Charles Holmes felt empty inside. It was bad enough that trying to quit on Henderson hadn't gone well, but now he was lying to a man he trusted. He could take no more. He could feel the tears coming. "Look, man. I gotta go study."

Chuck cocked his head and looked at Charles. The battle was lost. "Sure, Charles. We'll see you tomorrow." Quickly Chuck turned and dribbled away. He listened to see if Charles would call out his name. He would be there if he wanted to tell him the truth. Chuck only heard the door slam as Charles left the gym.

Chuck stayed later than the others that night. He had worked out an agreement with Tommy, the janitor, that allowed him to lock up after he was done shooting. All alone in the gym, Chuck took out his frustration with Charles Holmes on his own body. He dribbled up and down the floor shooting jump shots, getting the rebound and racing to the other end. The lights were only on over the center court. As he ran, something still didn't feel right. It wasn't just Charles' situation. He couldn't put his finger on it, but something else was bothering him. It was nearly ten o'clock when a sound made the hair on the back of his neck stand up.

It wasn't much of a noise. Most people would have thought nothing of it. It was a simple exhale, but there was a little smoker's hack at the end of it. He wasn't alone anymore. Then the smell hit him. It was a foul, nasty smell. Chuck hollered into the darkness. "Tommy?! Is that you?" Maybe it was just the janitor.

Chuck stopped at mid court and held the ball. That's when he recognized the smell of cigar smoke as it hit his nostrils. But it wasn't just a cigar. It was the nasty odor you smell in bars on greasy guys that try too hard to pick up women. It was the smell of a cheap men's cologne that had been splashed on way too thick. If that wasn't enough, Chuck thought Jack Daniels himself was about to pay him a visit. They were smells that didn't belong in a gym. They were the smells of a loser.

Chuck cursed himself for how exposed he was. He felt the same as when he was shooting baskets all alone on the makeshift court in Kuwait. That night had not turned out well. Sure, he made it to his battle position in time to fire back. He was fortunate he hadn't been court-martialed for the incident. "Peacekeepers" weren't supposed to discharge their weapons. Even if those weapons needed to be fired. But this was different. He shouldn't have needed a gun here. Chuck would have felt much better if he had one.

Suddenly, the quiet was broken with a yell, "YOU SHOULDN'T BE IN HERE THIS LATE!" A man stepped out of the darkness and walked onto the corner of the court. Chuck recognized Henderson immediately. "Suppose you were to fall and break your ankle." Henderson put a cigar to his lips and struck a match. He was only 27 or 28 years old and trying to act 40. Chuck was unimpressed. "An older guy like you . . ." He took a drag on the cigar and exhaled the smoke. "You might have a heart attack or something. Hell, nobody would find you until morning!"

The tone of the statement was peaceful enough, but Chuck knew enough to understand the threat behind the statement. He dribbled closer to Henderson and said, "My heart is as strong as any eighteen-year old's heart." He turned to the basket about twenty feet away and let fly. "And it isn't clogged by any of that crap you're smokin'." The shot swished and only the bouncing of the ball broke the silence. For an instant, Chuck wanted to take the cigar out of Henderson's mouth and bury it between Henderson's eyes. It would be his way of telling the pompous bastard that his threats might work on a twenty-year-old, but he'd have to do better to unnerve Chuck. He quickly looked over his shadowy adversary to see if the man was carrying any weapons. He tried to look for a shape under the man's sweat shirt, but Henderson was still too far away in a dark corner. He could make out the cigar in one hand and the other hand had gone into his pants pocket. Seeing Henderson was not an immediate threat Chuck relaxed a little. It was time to find out what this prick wanted.

Chuck found his smile and ran to get the ball. "What brings you in the gym so late at night, Coach Henderson?"

Henderson was taken back by the fact that Chuck knew his name. He was quiet for a moment but quickly recovered. "Just heard the ball and saw the lights. I don't believe we've met? Your name is. . . ?"

"Oh, I'm sorry. We haven't really been introduced." Chuck dribbled over to Henderson and stuck out his hand. "Name is Charlton Hayes. But you can call me Chuck."

Henderson looked at the hand. His face looked as if he was trying to swallow bile. He didn't quite know what to do. After a couple seconds, he took the hand and pulled a weak smile from somewhere, stuck it on his pasty lips and said, "Charmed, Chuck."

He let go and cocked his head off to the side, "Or perhaps I should call you . . . Hoopman?"

Touché thought Chuck. He had already heard of Hoopman. It was obvious that the younger man had no respect for 'Hoopman' or for just plain Chuck. Chuck knew immediately Henderson was the total asshole everyone had told him about. Chuck decided that because they both knew "of" each other they had tried to be coy in their first meeting. But now it was time to take the gloves off. He never was one to kiss ass. In the presence of a pompous, self-important prick like Henderson, now wasn't the time to start. Not just because of what he was doing to Charles Holmes, but the whole attitude he demonstrated. It was taking every ounce of restraint Chuck could muster to keep from grabbing Henderson's throat. "Only my friends call me Hoopman. I don't think I know you well enough to be . . . friends, Coach." Chuck smiled when he said it, but that was the only thing helping him to control his temper. Chuck didn't like the bastard one bit.

Henderson took the jab in stride. "Well, I guess I'll call you Mr. Hayes, then! I mean, you're a lot older than me. Hell, you are actually an old man!" For the first time since their encounter, Henderson was smiling. Yes, the gloves were off. He took a deep drag on the cigar and said, "I hear that you're gonna try out for the basketball team next week. That true?"

Chuck held the ball on his hip and said, "I'm not just gonna 'try out', Coach. I'm gonna play on your team this year."

Henderson laughed out loud. "I don't think so, Mr. Hayes! We have so much talent, I don't think we have room for a . . . novelty player, such as yourself."

A "novelty player"! Chuck nearly lost what little composure he was maintaining. Then it hit him. Henderson was trying to provoke him. Looking for a reason, any reason, to start something. The late-night visit, the rude comments, the pompous demeanor. Henderson had a shit-eating grin that let Chuck know he was in control. It was up to Chuck to figure out how to get out of the gym without putting his fist into Henderson's smiling mug. The anger would have to wait. He took a step back and laughed with Henderson. It was all he could do not to puke. This wasn't the place or the time for a confrontation. A smart man picks his battles on his own ground, at a time of his own choosing. Chuck's time to engage Henderson would come. He needed to be patient.

Then out of the blue Henderson said, "You know an older guy like you could probably set himself up for the future around here." Chuck just stared at the Coach trying not to let his mouth drop open. The jerk was offering him a bribe, while still trying to be coy. Henderson thought about what he had said and realized Chuck may not have known how much money could be made betting on St. Michael's hoops. Henderson decided to take a chance that Chuck was as greedy as the next man. "I know . . . people that can see to it that you have a profitable year while you're here." Henderson let the comment sink in. "What do you say?"

The bribe hung in the air for Chuck to digest. Was Henderson offering money for Chuck not to play? Was it insider information on what games to bet on and when? One thing was certain. He wasn't offering Chuck a spot on the roster. Then the anger started to rise again. Chuck was seconds away from turning loose on Henderson with all the anger he felt. Yet, he knew he couldn't do that. Not if he ever wanted to play meaningful basketball.

Chuck put his anger in a compartment in the back of his mind where he stored ill will. It was the same place he kept all the anger he had from years of hostility. Years of not being able to fight against 'adversaries' that kept poking his country with sticks. Years of watching third world nations blackmail his nation. The last superpower, treated like the world's sucker. Years of seeing his beloved military institution chipped away. Years of so called "peacekeeping" missions that weren't peaceful. Trying to placate cowards like the Taliban and others that use religion as an excuse for hate. Years where America soldiers bore the brunt of slurs and taunts, that led to stones and bricks, and eventually bullets. Now terrorists claiming there was virtue in their cause when they were nothing more than criminals and murderers. That was one of the reasons he retired. Chuck had experienced years of the kind of vile stench that Henderson and his type brought to everything they touched. People who made a living off the weak at heart and weak in mind. People that couldn't find faith in God. Those that looked to evil men for answers. He knew his path.

Chuck was not able to do anything for all the weak people in the world while on active duty, but he was able to do something for St. Michael's University. It was time to clean up the program, and the best way to clean it up was to start with Henderson. If that meant the prick had to go, so be it. This was not the place to do it. Chuck smiled and calmly said, "Oh, I got enough money from my VA retirement benefits, so I'm set."

Henderson was angry that his pitch wasn't even considered. Every man Pete had ever met had a price. What made this Hoopman so high and mighty that he couldn't be bought like the rest of them? Henderson hid his surprise. He was still in control. "You should think about my offer. It won't be on the table after tryouts."

Chuck took the hard right instead of the easy wrong and put his anger away. It was as if they were playing poker; he could see the cards Henderson held and knew he couldn't beat them. It was time to fold. "Hell, Coach! A novelty player or a side-show, I don't much care. I just want a fair shot at playing. I can get a fair shot at making the team, can't I?" He felt like he was going to throw up.

Henderson was still smiling. "Same chance as everybody else, Mr. Hayes." He stepped back and said, "I'd say your chances are slim and none." Henderson turned and said over his shoulder, "And slim just left town, Hoopman! You should ask him for a ride!" Then he burst out laughing and headed out the door.

Chuck pulled the ball back and started to throw it against the wall. His arm was trembling as he fought the urge to hurl the ball at the back of the coach's head just as Henderson slithered out the door. He was angry at himself for not handling the situation with Henderson better. He should have put the Coach on the defensive. He should have asked him if he was blackmailing Charles Holmes. Asked why he was trying to bribe a "novelty player". He should have asked him if he was up to his neck in organized crime. Then he should have taken the smug bastard by the throat and choked the living crap out of him. But he knew better. It needed to be on Chuck's turf, at his time and his place of choosing. Not Henderson's.

It took another thirty minutes of running for Chuck to calm down. He was physically exhausted, so the anger wasn't as powerful as it could have been. He turned off the lights and headed out the door. He threw his towel over his head and started to jog home.

By the time he got home, he felt much better. He drank a huge glass of water and sat down to watch SPORTSCENTER. He tried to put the encounter with Henderson behind him. But the meeting nagged at him. As Chuck sorted through the conversation, he realized that it wasn't really Henderson's attempt to bribe him or his hold over Charles Holmes that was bugging him. There was one comment that stuck in his mind. The "novelty player" line really hit home. He wasn't doing this as some kind of "novelty"! Damn it, he was there to play, to start for St. Michael's, and to win! He knew he could play. Henderson sure as hell wasn't going to stop him. He decided right then there would be another 'meeting' with Henderson. At a time and place that Chuck would decide. Chuck would be better prepared for the next encounter. It would have to wait until he was wearing a St. Michael's uniform.

CHAPTER SEVEN

Speech class was always entertaining. Chuck was amazed how ninety percent of the class was absolutely terrified of getting up in front of a group of people to talk. They can make a video for 30 seconds and let the unknown world see it all but couldn't talk to more than one person at a time. On this particular day, the class was responsible for bringing into class an item of their choice and giving the class a three-to-five-minute speech on the item. There were some interesting items that his classmates brought in.

The most intriguing items included a velvet Elvis painting, a bonsai tree, a "Nine Inch Nails" CD, contraceptive jelly, a bag of M & M's, a Santa Claus tie, a television remote, and a bag of something that the student called "pot". The professor was just a bit nervous, but to his credit, he let the student continue with his anti-pot speech. To Chuck the so-called pot looked like a combination of oregano, Bermuda grass and pencil shavings. He hoped the kid wasn't smoking the stuff in the bag for fear he might get lead poisoning.

Chuck could tell which of the kids had forgotten about the assignment and grabbed something from the snack machine or a friend right before they got in class. Others were obviously more prepared for the assignment. One girl with a huge peacock feather gave a fantastic speech on the history of feather fans from their use to cool pharaohs to their overpriced status at the mall. The next "interesting" presentation came from the student with the M & M's. As he pulled out the candy pieces one by one, he walked around the class discussing the Clinton-Trump presidential campaign of 2016 and the impact on immigration. As he walked, he discussed the candy as if they were people and what would happen to that "person", be they blue, red, yellow, brown, or orange. Chuck thought that was deep stuff for an eighteen-year-old. It seemed extremely insightful, and he would have given the kid an A. The professor didn't think so, and the student ended up with a C. Apparently it was "well presented but lacked depth". His grade was probably lowered when he claimed the red M & M's had a better understanding of immigration than the blue ones.

For his presentation, Chuck naturally brought in a basketball. He started off holding the ball in his hands, initially talking like a military drill sergeant. He said in a loud authoritarian voice, "THIS IS MY BASKETBALL. THERE ARE MANY LIKE IT. BUT THIS ONE IS MINE!" Then he spun the ball on his finger and continued, "Basketball is my life. I have moved from place to place in my lifetime," he said as he moved the rotating ball from fingertip to fingertip. Then he added, "I've been around the world." Then he spun the ball around his arms as they formed a circle in front of his chest. He continued, "I've been up!" He rolled the ball up his arm and held it there. Then he rolled it down his arm behind his back, the length of his left arm and caught it down low by his knee. "I've been down." He looked at the class and frowned, "I've been kicked around." Then he treated the ball like a soccer ball and bounced it back and forth between his feet. "I've been stepped on!" said Chuck. He let the ball drop to the floor and stepped on it without letting it bounce.

He paused for effect. Then he started again, "No matter how down I get," he pushed the ball out about twelve inches in front of his foot with his toe, and then used his foot to kick the ball up in the air. "I always get back up again," he said as he caught it with a smile. Then he started walking around the room and moving the ball as fast as he could in a 360-degree circle around his waist. As he walked, he talked, and he picked up the speed. "My life goes by fast. As I get older, it seems to go faster and faster. But I vow to never let my life get out of control." The speed of the ball was a blur. "If I ever lose control, bad things could happen to me! If I lose control, it will stop!" He threw the ball hard against the wall, then caught it and remained perfectly still for a moment. He went up to the kid with the M & M's and said, "If you lose control," he gently popped the ball on the kid's head and added, "You could hurt somebody!" The class chuckled.

He dribbled on the nicely carpeted floor back to the front center and closed with, "This is my life. I control what happens to it." All the time dribbling, between his legs and behind his back, always looking at his audience. "This is my basketball. There are many like it, but this one is mine. I have had many balls in my lifetime." He caught the ball behind his back. "I take care of them all!" He looked at the crowd, then slammed the ball hard between his legs and caught it about six inches in front of his groin. He stared at a guy in the front row and asked, "Are you taking care of your balls?" The class burst out in applause and starting clapping wildly.

Chuck was satisfied. The professor understood the symbolism and provided an appropriate critique and subsequently gave him a B+. Just for catching the last bounce he probably deserved an A. At least he had fun doing it. Not to mention, he didn't screw up the last part.

Two nights before tryouts, Chuck, Pepper and Jose met for their last shoot around before tryouts. After doing 20 pushups, Jose got on the scale and was down to 318 pounds. For his part, Pepper was up to 169. Clayton Dyer had added nearly ten pounds since he started college, and the weight had gone directly to his shoulders and his legs. He wasn't the stick boy he had been three months previously. They were ready. As ready as they could be to compete against the best talent St. Michael's had to offer. Jose still needed to get in better shape, but he wouldn't have had any chance had he not worked out six nights a week with Chuck.

Chuck was disappointed that Charles had not shown up again. He hadn't seen Charles since that night in the gym when Henderson had appeared. Neither Pepper nor Jose said anything about Charles or asked where he was. Chuck was sure that Pepper had figured out that something was going on, but they never discussed it.

As they were about to wrap it up for the night, a strange creature came running out onto the floor. Jose stopped in his tracks and said, "What the heck is that thing?"

Pepper scratched his head and said, "I'm not rightly sure, but I would guess it's a cross between a rat on steroids and a teenage mutant ninja turtle."

Chuck was laughing out loud. From somewhere inside the seven-foot costume came Marshall Wright's voice, "Hi, guys! It's me, Marshall!" Chuck nearly fell on the floor. "I'm the new 'Dillo mascot!"

"Holy crap, Marshall! You look like a rat with a mushroom on your back!" said Pepper.

"This is all they have. They said I could fix it up any way I wanted, provided it was in good taste," said Marshall.

"Good taste?" laughed Chuck. "You look like roadkill!"

"Man! You're not really gonna wear that thing, are you?" asked Jose. "You've gotta be the bravest guy on campus!"

Marshall was unconsciously scratching underneath the suit. "No big deal. It gives me a chance to contribute." Jose saw him scratching and moved away. "Does the mascot get to travel with the team?"

"Not if he's dressed like that!" said Chuck. He walked over to his friend. The smell nearly knocked him over. "OH, MAN! You gotta get outta that thing and hit the showers! It stinks and I'm guessing you stink now too!"

"I thought this thing was a little bit . . . nasty!" said Marshall. "I better go get cleaned up. I'm outta here, fellas." He turned and headed towards the locker room. The costume didn't allow him any room to spread his legs and run, so Marshall was shuffling his feet to get to the showers.

Chuck hollered after him, "This weekend, I'll hook you up Buddy! I've got a couple of friends that'll square you away!" Marshall kept scooting and didn't look back. Chuck thought he saw a hand wave, but the 'Dillo shell quickly disappeared into the locker room.

Chuck looked at Pepper and Jose and said, "I know a woman who can make him a costume that will rock this place."

"He needs something!" said Pepper. "The fans here can be brutal. We only seat about 9,000, so they call this place 'the Hole'. You know, like where an Armadillo lives."

"Yeah, I know," said Chuck unable to conceal his smile. "I came here for a couple games last year. It was so loud I could barely hear myself. The student fans here are great!" Chuck waved his friends back onto the court. "Let's shoot some, fellas. After this, I gotta get to the library and do some research for a paper."

Jose looked puzzled. "You go to the library after playin' ball?"

"Yeah, man! It's quiet and I can get on the computers without any hassles," said Chuck.

Pepper looked at Jose and asked, "You do know where the library is, don't you?"

Jose started to chase Pepper and couldn't get close. "Man, I'll kick that scrawny little butt of yours! You "Howdy Doody" lookin' punk!" He stopped and looked at Chuck. "Can you catch him for me?"

Chuck shook his head. "Not tonight, amigo!"

They finished shooting and obviously Jose had forgotten about chasing Pepper down. Jose could barely walk. That was all for the night. Chuck got his towel and his water. He looked at Jose and Pepper and said, "I'm gonna take tomorrow off, fellas. I want to let my body rest a day before we attack the tryouts."

Pepper smiled. "I like that! Attack the tryouts." Jose nodded in agreement.

Chuck stuck out his hand and shook with both players. "I've really enjoyed your company and support. I would not have worked nearly as hard if you guys hadn't pushed me. I really feel I'm almost in the best shape of my life."

"I definitely am!" said Pepper.

Jose agreed. "I haven't been this tiny since I was thirteen. None of my clothes fit me!" The guys laughed. "My momma thinks I'm sick!" They all laughed as Jose shook his head, unable to control his laughter.

Chuck smacked Jose on the back playfully. But the atmosphere changed, and they became silent. Their little get togethers in the evening had come to an end. A whole new effort would start. They had been through a lot of hard work to achieve the level of both mental and physical fitness they had reached. Each man was proud of what he had accomplished as an individual and by what they had done together working as a team.

Chuck broke the spell of the moment and headed for the door. "See you in two days, fellas. Then we kick some butt, all right?" They nodded. He got his stuff and ran home to shower.

After he got dressed, Chuck called Grace Winters. "Gracious good evening, Ms. Winters!"

"Uh! Who is this?" answered Grace.

"That was quick! You don't even recognize my voice?" laughed Chuck. "Forgot me already!"

Grace gave in and laughed, "Of course I knew it was you. Caller ID. That and nobody else calls me after ten o'clock at night except my mother!"

Chuck laughed. "I definitely ain't your mother." He grew quiet. "I mostly called to let you know," his voice got softer. "With basketball tryouts tomorrow, I'm probably not going to be able to see you too much the next couple of weeks. I want to give this my best effort and that, unfortunately, is going to take up more of my time. I'm sorry, Grace."

"Well, just use me up and dump me!" said Grace.

"That's not what I'm doing, Grace!" said an embarrassed Chuck.

She laughed. "I know. I was just teasing you. If your other classes are going as well as mine, you should be okay in the grades department too."

"I tried to get them up before the season started in case I couldn't give them as much time as before," explained Chuck.

"Good planning, Mr. Hayes," said Grace.

"Mr. Hayes, eh!?" said Chuck barely hiding his own smile. "My dad was 'Mr. Hayes'. You better keep callin' me Chuck." He quickly changed the subject. "I'm headed to the library right now." Then he added, "I'm gonna miss our time together. There's still class, I guess. I'll try to stop by your office if I can get some extra time."

"You are a terrific guy, Chuck. You do what you have to do. I'll be here for you when you're through," said Grace. "I can wait till after basketball season. I'll be OK without you for awhile." Chuck noticed something in her tone that didn't sit right. He was aware of some of the details about the ugly divorce Grace had gone through. However, she never told him anything about the man that put the bruise on her arm. She continued, "I will say when you get ready to fill that void in my life again, just let me know. Because you are my leading candidate."

"COOL! Of all my roles, leading candidate for 'man in Grace Winters life' is the one I'd really like to play," said Chuck. He exhaled into the phone as he changed the subject. "It's all about timing, Grace."

"Yeah, right. Timing. You and basketball. I got it!" she said.

For just an instant, Grace sounded like Becky. Except Becky was saying "Army", the way Grace had said "basketball". Chuck answered as honestly as he could. "You won't be out of my mind, Grace. I promise you that." That was the best he could come up with. He was never good at sharing his emotions. Particularly with the women in his life. It was getting late. "I gotta go, Grace. I'll see you in class. Good-bye."

"Bye, Chuck. See you in class," said Grace, then she hung up the phone. She really liked Chuck Hayes. He was by far the nicest, kindest man she'd met in years. Plus, he had a way of making her feel good again. She was comfortable around him. It had been a long time since she had felt that way. If it weren't for basketball, she might fall in love with him.

"You really want to do that?" asked Chris Crowley.

"Look at the info we have now. Austin is the place where it leads. I say we go up there, talk to Bobby, and just dig a little deeper," said Ed.

"How long?" asked Chris.

"A week. We go there for a week, get with Bobby. Dig into the inner circle and find out how they work. Come on! You were always the one who wanted to "live on the edge". Now's your chance!" said Ed.

"Is Hoopman gonna be all right with us bringing Bobby in?"

"Bobby is the best programmer I know. And, BONUS! He understands the dark web! If he can help us get in, we should use him. We don't even have to tell Hoopman why," said Eddie grinning broadly.

"All right. But I'm gonna tell him it was all your idea. I don't want him pissed at me. Sometimes he gets that look on his face, and I can tell he killed somebody before," said Chris.

"Hey! Cheap shot. He hasn't killed anybody since . . . at least ten years ago! If we get more info and options for him, Hoopman will love what we've done," Ed winked at his friend. "The BCT doesn't end in Austin. We need to find the source. Are you in?"

Reluctantly, Chris nodded, "I can't let you do this alone."

"GREAT! Tomorrow, we go to Austin!" said Eddie.

Chris wasn't sure what he and Ed could do in Austin that they couldn't do by computer in San Antonio. But Ed wanted to put "eyes on target", whatever the hell that meant. Like they were going hunting. Sometimes that Army lingo confused Chris. Plus, whenever Bobby and Ed got together, they could really get into "projects". It started with simple hacking, but now they were full-fledged white hat hackers. One always tried to one up the other. Chris still had fresh memories of the last time when they almost got caught screwing around with Nellis Air Force Base. Whatever the project was, when Ed and Bobby worked together, Chris felt they always went too far. Chris was absolutely, 100 percent certain it wouldn't be any different this time.

The first tryout practice took place at one minute after midnight. Just like at the big schools. The physicals were already taken but there was paperwork to do. Chuck couldn't help but be a wise ass to Henderson. "On this form it asks, 'last team and last coach's name'. Do you want my military unit or the post team?" The assistant coach eyed the older man curiously because it seemed as if Chuck was talking in a foreign language. Chuck kept poking the puppy. "Plus, we never really kept a scoring average. We kept score, but after you're up by thirty, who cares?" Henderson still carried a blank expression. "I'll just put down Ft. Sam Houston Post Team and 20, is that okay?"

The confused coach answered, "Yeah. Yeah, sure. Your post team and uh, you said twenty points right. Per game?"

"I'm just guessing there. It was probably a little more, but, like I said, we never really kept track," said Chuck. "As for the coach, I guess that would be Captain David Stipes."

The Assistant Coach scratched his head, looked at the man and said, "Yeah, that's fine. Fine." The older man finished the form and handed it in.

"Can I go shoot now?" asked Chuck with a beaming smile.

"Yeah, man. Go ahead," answered the coach. Chuck ran off to get a ball.

Round walked over to Henderson and grabbed the paperwork Hayes turned in. He quickly looked over the sheet. "Twenty points a game?" He looked up and watched as Chuck hit a twenty-footer.

Round looked at Henderson and said, "I think he's underestimating his average."

Henderson just grunted and said, "There's no way to prove these numbers. I'm bettin' this guy is nothing and he'll fold when he gets real competition."

It was Round's turn to grunt. He looked at Henderson and said, "That's the trouble with you, Pete. You don't know when to bet and when to fold! I think this guy's a player. We'll learn the truth soon enough. Besides, I asked him to be here."

Henderson was seething but was smart enough to hide his emotions. He held back his true thoughts. Henderson said to himself, "I know more about betting than you'll ever know, old man!" Anything Henderson could do to keep Chuck from making the team, he would do it. That meant making him look bad in Coach Round's eyes.

After the paperwork, the players lined up, ran ball handling and lay-up drills.

There were over fifty guys trying out. They ranged in height from six foot eleven to five foot five. Jose was by far the 'largest' at 318 pounds and on the light side, was a freshman walk-on who may have weighed 120 pounds fully clothed. Chuck could spot the players from the wannabe's instantly. The good news was there was talent available at St. Michael's. The question was could Coach Round spot it.

After forty-five minutes, at least five wannabees had left the gym. The group was running wind sprints. The drill was called "Five in Thirties". The players lined up on the baseline and ran five times the length of the floor in under thirty seconds. Few of the players could make it. Chuck was usually third behind Holmes and Parnell. After five minutes, Chuck was consistently finishing first; Pepper was second and then came Dexter Thomas. Chuck knew Dexter well from the Saturday morning games. Thomas was the big man Chuck had picked up the first Saturday that he and Pepper had played in the gym. He had nicknamed him Chubby. At the start of the season, Dexter Thomas wasn't Chubby anymore. He had lost nearly thirty pounds and was in outstanding shape.

For his part, Jose wasn't lost in the madness. He was never last in any of the runs. Chuck would find him in the drills and wink or smile at him, to keep his hopes up. The running was hurting Jose, but he never quit.

After fifteen minutes of sprints, and three players puking, the running stopped. Defensive drills started. Feet quickness, movement across the floor and positioning were the keys to success in the drills. Chuck survived by constantly reminding himself to keep his knees bent and his butt low. Occasionally, he would look at Pepper or Dexter Thomas and bend his knees and point to the ground. When it was their turn, they would respond by remaining crouched low throughout the drills.

Chuck was amazed at the number of students who came to see the practice. They had stayed and watched through all the drills. Some had their phones up and were recording the practice. Chuck saw that some had notebooks and were keeping track or scratching notes. For the most part they were quiet. Except when Parnell would slam home a dunk or Holmes would pop a three pointer. Chuck did notice the gym would buzz a little whenever he had the ball. He couldn't make out what the students were saying, but the sense that they were talking about him would not go away. He liked it.

Finally, the moment everyone had been waiting for arrived. Five on five drills half court. Chuck was disappointed he wasn't selected to play on either of the main courts. He sat on the side and watched. He made mental notes of his competition and determined the best way to set up, move around, out position or just plain destroy his opponent. Some would be easy. Others, were quicker, could jump higher and wanted to make the team just as bad. But experience and cunning have a way of winning out over youthful enthusiasm.

After ten minutes of scrimmaging, Round finally got Chuck on the floor. Chuck didn't know anybody on his team but had seen some of the other players at the gym. Henderson was the lone observer from the staff watching his game. Chuck said nothing to the Assistant Coach and Henderson acted as if Chuck didn't exist. He always took the ball out of bounds and rotated through. No plays were being run so the players were forced to improvise or make moves on their own. Within five minutes, Chuck had his team setting picks and breaking to the basket. He seemed to always get the ball to the open man. He only shot twice and was angry with himself when he missed an open fifteen-footer. He wasn't sure, but he thought he saw Henderson smirk when the rebound went to the other team.

The two teams switched ends and added new players. To Chuck's surprise, Dexter Thomas ended up on his team. Coach Round came to Chuck's end. Chuck nodded to the coach and gave him a little smile. The coach responded with a small smile of his own, then turned and said something to Henderson. The assistant coach turned and headed to the other end. Henderson immediately started yelling at one player about having "his head up his ass".

Chuck knew this was his chance. This was the moment he'd been waiting for. He set up at the top of the key and nodded to Thomas. Thomas knew what was coming. Chuck passed the ball in and headed towards the small forward as he posted a smaller player. Chuck set a pick, and Dexter ran hard off it to the corner. The pass came and Thomas hit the shot. Round nodded but said nothing.

The next play, Chuck passed to the off guard and ran away from the play. Dexter Thomas posted low, took the pass, and threw it out. Then he spun quickly to the weak side and set a ferocious pick on Chuck's unsuspecting man knocking him to the floor. Chuck ran untouched to the basket and hit the wide-open lay-up.

Coach Round yelled at the youngster rubbing his hip, "Son, you got to keep your head up on defense or somebody is gonna kill you! The rest of you guys on D better talk to each other! That could've been you on the ground! LET'S GO! COMMUNICATE OUT THERE!"

On the third play, Chuck dribbled right and passed to Thomas in the corner. Then he sprinted toward the foul line. Dexter hit him with a nice pass and Hoopman drove hard to the basket. As he did three guys collapsed to try and stop the lay-up. Thomas knew what was coming and broke from the corner to the basket. Chuck leaped drawing three players into the air with him. Somehow, between the defenders he threw a left-handed behind the back pass that hit Dexter Thomas in stride. Thomas finished the shot off with a two-handed slam that brought the student body sitting in the stands to their feet. Chuck went over and slapped Dexter a high five and gave him a pat on the butt. "Nice lay-up, DT!"

"Nice pass! Keep givin' me the ball! Let's do this, Hoopman," said Dexter with a huge smile. Dexter was caught up in the moment and the feeling was contagious. Chuck looked at Round and saw the smile. Then the Coach turned and went to the other end. Chuck was disappointed that the coach left, but if that was all he had time to see, he was glad it was something good.

Henderson came back and immediately substituted someone in for Chuck. He sat for the rest of the night. Before the practice ended, they had to run more sprints. Chuck had tightened up terribly due to the time he had spent sitting. Henderson didn't fail to let the group know Chuck was not running as fast as before.

"What's the matter there, old man? Can't quite keep up with these young guys now, can ya'?" said Henderson while wearing a cat with the mouse grin. Chuck wasn't breathing hard, but his legs were stiff, and he didn't want to push it and risk pulling a hamstring in the first practice. "We keeping you up too late. Look at all these other guys busting their asses?"

Chuck looked at Pepper and said, "I can think of one ass I'd like to bust!" Pepper smiled but was having a hard time keeping his wind.

Jose was called out to shoot a free throw. He tried but didn't even hit the rim. On the base line again, they took off and ran for another five minutes. Chuck began to loosen up and was in the top five again, but only in front of the others because they were exhausted. As Henderson looked for another victim, Chuck whispered to Pepper, "Here goes nothing!"

"Hey, Coach!" yelled Chuck. Henderson turned with a disgusted look on his face. "I think I can hit five in a row." Chuck heard Pepper groan. The gym grew quiet. Chuck could feel every eye in the building turn toward him.

Henderson cocked his head and said, "I don't think you have it in you." He thought for a moment then said, "I'll tell you what, Hotshot. You take your five shots and for each one you miss the group runs for five minutes." The students remaining in the stands moved closer to hear the conversation between coach and players.

Charles Holmes interrupted, "Let me shoot 'em, coach!"

"No, no, Mr. Holmes. Hotshot here thinks he's gonna save you all from runnin'. You still up to it, Hotshot?" asked the assistant.

Chuck smiled at Henderson. He turned to Pepper and asked, "You ready to go home?"

Pepper was holding his side but still managed a smile and said, "Dang right. Go hit them shots, will ya'?"

Chuck ran out to the foul line. Charles yelled, "You better not miss!"

Dexter Thomas looked at Charles and said, "Shut the hell up." Then he looked at Chuck and said, "Hit these shots, Hoopman. I gotta go study."

The gym had grown quiet. The thirty or so students left moved closer to the floor. Henderson threw Chuck the ball. "Let's see what you got?"

Chuck dribbled a couple times. He looked at all the faces on the line ready to run. Some had smiles on their face, some had frowns, and a few even had a look of fear. Chuck blocked out the faces of his "peers" and looked at Henderson. He was smug as he watched Chuck dribble. He honestly thought Chuck would miss and that would allow him to torture the 40 remaining players for a few more minutes. Chuck took a couple of deep breaths. He focused on the front of the rim and let fly. The shot felt good. It hit the front of the rim, bounced once and then went in. He heard a couple of gasps from the men on the line, but they were soon replaced with handclaps and high fives.

Chuck got the ball back, took a couple dribbles, held his breath and fired. Nothing but net. This time he heard the players go, "Yeah!" and a couple of "nice shot" calls. He repeated the feat on the third shot and the whole group was with him. On the fourth shot, the students who were still there were on their feet and clapping. Again, nothing but net.

Chuck got the ball for his final shot. As he was dribbling, he looked at Henderson, pointed at Jose and said, "That big guy needs his beauty rest, Coach." He caught the ball, looked at the rim, held his breath and shot. Swish. The players went nuts. Chuck got high fives from everybody. The students were hollering and headed out on the floor as if the Armadillos had just won a game.

Henderson couldn't stand it. "ALL RIGHT! WE'RE NOT DONE YET!" The players stopped smiling and looked stunned. "Let's go! We got one more set to do. Then you're done."

Chuck started to say something, but Coach Round had seen enough. He came and took the ball and said in a quiet voice, "That's enough for tonight, boys. Good job by every one of you." He looked at Henderson with a fatherly gaze and cocked his head. He was a good enough coach not to dress down his assistant in front of the team. "The first cuts will be made on Wednesday. I expect to see everybody out here on Monday at six, ready to run. That gives you two days to recover." He walked over to Jose and patted him on the back. "Some of you look like you could use it."

Round walked to the center of the crowd and said, "Bring it in here, fellas." The players did as directed. "This year's motto is going to be 'Dillo Defense'. Kind of corny, I know. But guess what?

You don't have to run and gun to win. You just gotta score one more point than the other team. Fifty to forty-nine or just plain ten to nine. It don't matter if you don't score too much. Just score more than the other team. Remember that." He stuck his hand out and said, "Bring it in here. On three, "DILLOS DEFENSE"! One, two, THREE!"

"DILLO'S DEFENSE!" came the yell.

"Now get outta my gym! We'll see you Monday," said the coach with a big smile. The players headed for the showers. Round looked at Henderson who was still red with anger. All Round could do was shake his head and walk away.

In the locker room, Pepper came up to Chuck with a huge smile on his face. "Nice shootin', Hoopman. I thought we were gonna be out there for another hour," said Pepper.

"Not a problem," said Chuck with a smile. "I didn't feel like being under Henderson's guns anymore." He could see Pepper was confused by the wartime analogy. "I was sick of takin' his crap!" Pepper smiled and nodded in understanding.

Jose came over and sat down heavily next to his friends. "I was nervous all night! I couldn't get anything to fall." He started shaking his head. "I can't believe how bad I played."

Chuck looked up from his locker. "What?" He stood up and looked around. "It's the first night, so don't start callin' yourself out yet. Tonight, was nothing! We got a couple more practices before they start cuts. You just need to relax, Jose."

Jose looked at Chuck and nodded in agreement. It must have sunk in because he smiled. "I have to admit even after all that runnin', I don't feel that bad."

"Save some of that feelin' for Monday, amigo. I think it's only gonna get worse," said Pepper. "We'll see you Monday." Pepper headed for the showers.

Dexter Thomas came over and said, "Hey, old man, you keep throwin' me passes like that, we'll kick the shit outta anybody in our league. No trash talk, just fact!" He stuck out his huge hand. Chuck looked at the big palm and took it. "We can do something this year. I'm with ya, Hoopman!"

"Yeah, Dexter. I'm with you, too," said Chuck. "By the way, nice finish!"

"You throw me passes with the lane that open, I'm downright dangerous," said Dexter with a broad smile. "And by the way, Hoopman. You can call me Dex. Everybody else does."

Chuck nodded. "I'll see you Monday, Dex!" Both men smiled as Dex Thomas headed out of the locker room.

Chuck was finally finished at his locker when he noticed Charles Holmes tying his shoes at his locker. He stopped and looked at Charles. Holmes looked up, started to say something, then looked down and finished tying his shoes. Chuck shook his head and said flatly, "Goodnight, Charles." Chuck quickly turned and left the locker room.

Charles realized he was wrong earlier when Chuck went to shoot the foul shots and he wanted to apologize for his behavior. He started to tell Chuck he was sorry, but when he looked up, the older man was gone. Charles stood up and threw his towel across the room towards the dirty towel basket and missed it by five feet.

A voice spoke behind him. "What the hell is with you, man?" It was David Parnell. Parnell was a Junior co-captain the year before and he had seen Charles at his best. Now he was seeing a different Charles Holmes. This one was not the same carefree free-spirited shooter he had played with the past two years. Charles shook his head and started to try to say something when Parnell cut him off. "Man, you better open your eyes. He may be an older dude, but he can play! If you don't want to accept that, that's your problem. But I'm thinking he's gonna be on this team. And if you keep acting the way you were tonight, he's probably gonna be pushin' your sorry ass for playin' time."

Charles Holmes started to get indignant. He took a step towards Parnell. Parnell, at six foot seven and 225 pounds of sculpted muscle stepped forward and said, "You wanna start some shit with me, too?" Charles backed down. Parnell relaxed a little. "Man, I saw you play sometimes last year when you dominated the game. Then the very next game I saw somebody else in your uniform. I'm here to tell ya', you do that this year, we'll have us a different point guard in. I've seen him at the gym. He worked and worked to get here, and he deserves a shot. If you open that closed mind of yours, you'd be able to see he can play. The one thing he is doin' right now is givin' his best effort." Parnell turned away then said over his shoulder, "You ain't ever given us your best effort. Have you?" David Parnell left before Charles could answer.

Holmes sat on the bench in the locker room alone. For some reason, he expected Henderson to come in and give him grief too. That would be typical of Henderson's style. But there was only silence. As he sat there alone, Charles realized Parnell was right. He knew he played inconsistently last year. There were 'circumstances' that Parnell would never know about. But that was then. This year would be different. Charles Holmes was going show them. He was going to be the best player on the Armadillo roster. This was going to be his year to put it all together.

Monday afternoon's practice rolled around, and it was more of the same. Coach Round let Henderson run the practice, and Round observed from a distance. Chuck expected Round to be more involved. Maybe show just a little more energy. Chuck shook off his feeling and decided that if that was the way Round coached, he would have to deal with it.

After twenty minutes of running which included full court lay-up drills, one on one ball handling the length of the floor and defensive slide drills, the team was separated into two groups. The focus of the practice shifted to defense and the drills were more difficult. Particularly for players who didn't enjoy putting in the effort required to play defense. To Chuck Hayes, it was a time to shine. On one end, Coach Round worked the players on various help defenses from the high post and taught them how to move across the lane and pick up weak side help. Unfortunately for Chuck, Henderson was working his end of the floor. The assistant coach started with the defensive art of drawing charges.

"I want to see the defensive man beat the ball handler to this spot under the basket," said Henderson as he pointed to a position in the lane. "Now let's line up and show me some hustle. I want to see that defensive man get those feet planted and take on the man driving to the basket. Let's go!"

Six or seven players went through the defensive position with none of them performing the task to meet the standard set by Henderson. Most seemed to get to the spot, get both feet planted and take the body blow delivered by the oncoming ball handler, but it was never good enough for the coach. Then it was Chuck's turn.

Hoopman took a deep breath and assumed the position of help side defender, low in the post. The ball handler, who just happened to be six foot five and about 250 pounds, took the ball and dribbled toward the basket. Chuck jumped over and planted his feet and allowed the player to run him over. Both men fell to the ground in a pile.

"OH, COME ON NOW!" yelled Henderson. "What was that?" Henderson walked over and looked down at Chuck. "I don't even think that was close!" Chuck picked himself up and looked at the coach. Henderson cocked his head and hissed, "Let's do that again. Show me some speed!"

The ball handler went back to the start position, got the ball and started for the basket. Chuck jumped over into the lane, set his feet and waited for the crash. The larger man jumped as if to shoot a lay-up and his knee hit Chuck square in the groin. Both men went down in a heap under the basket. Chuck rolled over and grabbed his groin, grimacing from the blow.

Henderson ran over and started hollering, "You were even slower that time!" He looked down at Chuck and said, "Get up and do it again!" Chuck looked up at the coach with one eye open. "I SAID, GET UP!" Chuck took a deep breath and exhaled audibly. Henderson growled, "You want to play ball here or sit up in the bleachers?"

Chuck didn't say a word. He lined up and got ready to go again. Henderson threw the ball to the forward and stood back with a smug grin on his face. The ball handler hesitated. "Let's go! You tryin' to get cut the second practice out, big fella? Start the drill."

The forward shook his head and said to Chuck, "I'm sorry, man."

Chuck inhaled and said with a smile, "No sweat, man. Let's go!"

The player started dribbling and Chuck jumped in front of the man even further away from the basket this time. He planted his feet, put his hands by his side and braced for impact. The extra foot further from the basket prevented the player from getting his knee up. Chuck took the blow before the player was off the ground, went down hard and watched as the ball handler nearly broke his nose on the floor. This time no knee hit his groin, but an errant foot stepped on Chuck's knee.

"GOD DAMN, YOU ARE SLOW!" said Henderson. "Get the hell outta my drill!" Henderson was screaming. "I've seen a bunch of slow people in my basketball career, but you are a sorry excuse for a defender. Go to the end of the line."

Chuck picked up a jog and moved to the end of the line. His knee hurt, his nuts hurt, and his pride hurt. Henderson had sent him a message, and for the first time in his life he started to have doubts about himself and his ability. Emotionally he was torn between wanting to run away or walking over to Henderson, putting his hands around his scrawny neck, and squeezing until the bastard was dead. But he could do neither. Chuck knew what the deal was. He was being tested by God. He closed his eyes and said a little prayer to calm himself. The prayer helped him get control.

The next time he had to do the charging drill, he saw what Henderson's plan was. He bent over, coughed a couple times, and tried to pray the pain in his groin away and gather strength. The pain had faded and he was ready to go again. The second time around, Chuck only had to do the drill once and Henderson could find no fault with it. A little grunt of disgust was all Chuck got for his effort, but at least he didn't have to do it a second time.

The charging drill was merely a sign of things to come. Every time he tried to do something; Henderson was there to prevent any positive results. If he drove to the basket, he wasn't a team player. If he shot a three, he had missed a teammate who was open. If he passed the ball, he passed it to the wrong man. Henderson was spending an exorbitant amount of time trying to press Chuck into quitting at just the second practice. All the 'guidance' being provided by Henderson was in a word, worthless.

Halfway through the practice Chuck was nearly back to one hundred percent pain wise. His resolve to show Henderson he was good enough began to grow. As the criticism and the bitterness grew, so did Chuck's anger. He began to pick up his game a notch.

Towards the end of practice, Chuck got to play in front of Round. Things went much better for Chuck as Henderson's criticism and oversight faded. Within thirty minutes of the change, Chuck's anger was gone, and Hoopman returned. He was smiling again, passing behind his back, and shooting like there was never a problem. The thoughts of Henderson's pettiness were memories.

When practice was over, Chuck started for the locker room. Coach Round called him over. "You had a pretty good practice, young man!" said the smiling Coach.

Chuck looked down and said, "It didn't start too good."

"You must mean that charging drill that Coach Henderson put you through," said Coach Round with a smile. "He does that every year to some poor sap. This year, it happens to be you." Chuck smiled. "I don't know what you did to him, but I'm guessin' he don't like you too much."

"I suppose you're right, Coach," said Chuck. "I guess it's a good thing that this is your team and not his!"

Round chuckled, "You got that right." He smacked Chuck on the back and said, "I'll see you tomorrow, Hayes!"

Chuck smiled and said, "Wouldn't miss it for the world, Coach." Chuck headed to the locker with a big smile on his face. The hell with Henderson. He was gonna make this team. Even if Henderson put him through charging drills every day. If that didn't work, Chuck figured a good ass-kickin' might be in store for his torturer. The thought of doing just that and Coach Round's kind words kept him smiling all the way home.

Chuck jumped up quickly to answer the phone. It was Nate Hawkins on the other end. "How's it going, Bud?"

"Can't complain, Old Fart! What are you doin' calling me?" asked Chuck. It wasn't normal for the Sergeant Major to call so late at night. Not that Chuck minded too much. Doing a speech in class was a heck of a lot easier than writing one.. He was nearly asleep with the book lying on his lap.

"I mostly called to see how basketball practice was goin'?" chuckled Hawkins. "I mean, is your body still in one piece?"

"Screw you, Hawk!" laughed Chuck. The comment woke him up.

"You can tell your roommate . . . wow that sounds funny! Tell your roommate that his costume is ready. My wife finished sewin' and of course I added a couple of 'special' items so Marshall can have a little fun. I suppose you could come over and get it this weekend. If you're not doing anything? Which is typical of a college boy!" said Hawk.

"I don't think I've got anything on my calendar," said Chuck. "I'll check with Marshall and call you tomorrow." Chuck figured he was still at the library, or he would have answered the phone.

"How's practice?" Chuck could tell Hawk was serious.

"It's not so bad. I always was in pretty good running shape. It's the speed of the running that's hurtin' me. I have to admit I'm used to a little slower pace. Sometimes the sheer speed of these kids is amazing. My muscles are getting used to the extra stretching they have to do to keep up. As for the pace, I'm not there yet. But I think in two or three weeks, I'll be just about as quick as anybody on the team," said Chuck trying not to sound too confident.

"That's good, Chuck," said Hawk. "Because I'm looking forward to comin' to your games and watchin' you kick the crap outta those snotty nosed kids!"

Chuck laughed out loud. "Hey! Those snotty nosed little kids are my peers now! You can't call them that!"

Simultaneously they yelled into the phone, "ONLY I CAN CALL THEM THAT!" Then they both roared with laughter at the old joke. Just two Army guys laughing at a joke that had probably been in Army circles since the first drill sergeant had recruits.

The laughing finally stopped, and the phone grew quiet. Chuck did have something to talk about with his old friend, but the phone wasn't the place to do it. "Maybe when I come over, we can take a few minutes to talk about a situation."

Hawk was slow to answer. He had known Chuck for twenty years. The tone in his voice meant something was up. A 'situation' that indicated his friend REALLY wanted to talk. "Yeah, Bubba. I think the wife needs to borrow the credit card Saturday and go to the mall."

"That would be better, Hawk," said Chuck trying not to make it sound like he was sending a coded message.

"I think we can have a couple of hours alone," said Hawk.

"Good deal, Old Man! I'll see ya' Saturday then," said Chuck.

Hawk couldn't help but add, "Do I need to get any . . . toys?"

Chuck knew exactly what Hawk meant and thought seriously about the question. Then he answered it as best he could. "Not yet."

Jeff Roberts looked at the computer screen. "Are we sure about this boss?"

Steve James looked at the information and nodded. "Last year we had twenty-nine schools under our control. Due to graduations and," he pointed to the screen, "these two have injured players that won't be able to help us, we are down to twenty-three."

"What about this one? Why is it color coded yellow?" asked Roberts.

"That's the St. Michael's University in San Antonio. The guys in Austin are sending back reports to us here in Vegas indicating they aren't too confident about the player or coach working for us this year," said James. "They need to be, I'll use the word 'watched', more closely in the first weeks to see what they are going to do. Obviously, with a yellow color code, somebody feels they are not with our program as of right now."

"And if they don't 'get with our program'?" asked Roberts.

Steve was hesitant. He rubbed his knee and looked down at his apprentice. "Only one school ever had a player decide not to come back."

Jeff looked at his boss and said, "What happened?"

"Apparently, the brakes on his car failed during the Thanksgiving break," said Steve. "He died when his car went into a bayou, where he drowned." Jeff nodded and looked back at the computer screen. Steve continued, "I think they have ways to convince the people at St. Michael's what's best for them. You just can't quit the system, ya know?"

Jeff Roberts nodded. He did know. His boss was proof of what they would do.

"One more thing I need to tell you about," getting Jeff's attention. "The boss has initiated a new payment plan. It's basically a cryptocurrency intranet."

"What the hell is that?" asked Jeff.

"It's called G-Cash," said Steve. Jeff tilted his head and frowned. "We have 12 locations of secondary physical sites. At those locations, they take in physical cash. Online we can reach anyone, anywhere and take their money. At those locations we have regular, high rollers that bet millions. The boss, in his infinite wisdom has decided we will 'allow' high rollers to, lets call it, invest, in G-Cash. They put a million dollars in G-Cash, they have that line of credit to go play everything we bet on. It's like," Steve struggled to explain. "It's like, they invest in our own cryptocurrency for the privilege of unlimited betting."

"They actually put a million dollars in a cryptocurrency to bet on our games?" Jeff is amazed.

"It is a restricted network, with minimal investors."

"How many investors?" asked Jeff.

"Last count, 124." Steve was smiling broadly. "What do you think?"

"I think the boss has set up a helluva ponzi scheme!"

Steve nodded and his smile got even bigger. "Some of them have even put in more than one million."

Jeff shakes his head and frowns. "I don't know that we can protect it. Word will get out. It screams for hackers to attack it!"

"Ah, my boy, that's all we can hope for. With every cloud, there is opportunity for wonderful rain."

"You have a something cookin', don't you?"

Steve turned and started walking away. He stopped at the door. "I will send some guidance on the G-Cash set up. See if you can find a back door in the network. I have an idea." Steve was smiling as he left Jeff scratching his head.

CHAPTER EIGHT

St. Michael's University Armadillo's first cut was a big one. Only sixteen people were left from the crowd that attended the first practice. Chuck was happy to see that Pepper, Dexter Thomas, and even Jose was still on the roster. Chuck had the opportunity to play with every one of the players left. He knew that each one of them was talented enough to play ball for the Armadillos. At this point in the process, it would take more than talent to stay on the team. It would take guts, experience and just a bit of attitude.

The team was split into two squads. The squads each had eight players on a team. Coach Round had decided to have a practice game. He coached one team; Henderson and the graduate assistant, Daymon Breyers, coached the other. There was no crowd of students to observe the game. The gym was empty except for the prospects who wanted to make the Armadillo's hoop team.

Before they started, the sides were warming up under their respective baskets. Chuck was alone by the bench saying a silent prayer and stretching. Coach Round came over and sat by him on the bench. He started the conversation off with a simple enough question. "You ready to play tonight, Hoopman?" Chuck nodded as he stretched. Something told him there was more to the question. Round continued, "I gotta tell you straight up, my assistant coach doesn't think you're worth keepin'."

The coach said it so matter of factly, the tone took Chuck by surprise. He stopped stretching and looked at Round. "I'm not gonna ask what you think, Coach Round. You're gonna do what you're gonna do." He looked at the team at the other end of the court. It was mostly kids from last year's team. A light came on in Chuck's mind and he saw what was going on. "Does this practice game decide who's really running the team?"

Coach Round nodded and said flatly, "Yeah, it does."

The team Henderson had consisted of Parnell, Holmes, a six-foot ten kid called 'OJ" who had been the backup center the previous year, two other back up forwards from the team a year ago, one heavier small forward and two speedy guards with a ton of energy.

Then he looked at Coach Round's eight. Jose, Pepper, Dexter, two guards who played pretty good defense, another forward named Lawrence Glynn, and a transfer who no one liked named Earl Frazier. Chuck looked back at Round and shook his head. "Who picked these teams?"

"I did," said the coach.

"And good old Coach Henderson let these teams go like this?" asked Chuck.

"Yeah, he did," answered the coach. He sat back, spit some chew into a soda can and crossed his legs.

Chuck got up, looked at the coach and said with a ridiculous amount of confidence, "After we're up by ten, you want me to take it easy on 'em?"

Coach Round didn't flinch. He was one helluva poker player. "Naw. I figure they need a good ass whupin' to bring 'em down a notch. Keep it up."

For the first time, Chuck smiled and said, "Is that directed at the team? Or just that assistant you got?"

Round looked at the other end of the floor. He grabbed some more chew and put it in his mouth. "He doesn't quite know how to spot a good ball player like I do."

Chuck started stretching again and said quietly, "As far as the talent you picked, is there anybody on this team that's, um . . . I guess the expression is 'on the bubble'?"

"Yeah. About half of ya'," said the coach. Then he leaned over, spit in his can, and whispered, "The big Mex kid has got to show some offense or he's gone. The off guard has got no defense. And I don't mean Dyer. That freckled kid can shoot. The other one that thinks too much is in trouble, as is that Frazier kid. He's a good player. But he's a loner. And loners ain't good for any team." He started to chew again and added, "Of course, you. You know, you're too old."

Chuck stood up and looked at his team. He thought the assessments Round had made were on the money. Chuck's advantage was not only did he know their weaknesses, but he knew what his teammates' strengths were. He also thought they could beat Henderson's bunch with no problem. "I may be old, but I'll take this team any day. I think we can take 'em. We can't run with them, but we can beat 'em." Then he thought of something else. "As long as you're the referee and not," he looked at Henderson, wanted to say, "that jerk Henderson", but stuck with "Coach Henderson, we'll win."

"Naw. I think we'll keep it neutral and let Daymon be the ref," said the Coach.

"Cool!" Chuck said with huge smile. The odds dramatically swung in favor of Chuck's team if Henderson didn't officiate. Chuck bent over and began to pretend to be stretching. "I can get the big man to show some offense, Coach. He's got the best hook shot I've seen since Abdul-Jabbar."

Round leaned over to spit again, "Well, I reckon tonight is as good as any to show it off." The coach stood up. Chuck got up and looked him in the eye. Round said quietly, "I got to have something so I can tell that young buck over there that you and those boys you want on this team are worth keepin'." He pulled his plastic cup up and looked at Henderson's team. "If you don't beat 'em, I can't justify my arguments." The coach smiled at Chuck and added, "Now I can argue really good, Hayes. But if you take these boys the direction I think you can, I shouldn't even have to raise my voice. You wouldn't want to see me mad now, would ya'?"

Chuck looked up and suppressed his smile. "No, sir!" Then he turned and started to go take a couple of shots.

The coach lightly grabbed Chuck's arm and said, "I'm serious, Chuck. I'll fight for everyone of 'em. But if you lose," the coach looked at the rest of his team under Henderson's tutelage and said, "I wanna coach a bunch of ball players. Guys that play basketball as a team. This season is very important to me."

With that statement, Chuck's smile faded. He saw something in the coach's eyes he hadn't seen in a while. It was the look of someone who wasn't going to be able to keep doing something he loved for much longer. Many commanders in the military had that look, usually when they were coming out of command or retiring. It was the look of a man who was being forced to end his career. Not because it was time to leave, but because someone else was making him do it. When the coach looked back at Chuck, the man's eyes seemed to be pleading. Pleading for help to make basketball fun again. Pleading for Chuck to win. Perhaps pleading for the return of the coach's spirit. To renew the fire that was in Darrell Round's soul.

Chuck stared back and said softly, "I understand, coach." Then he reached over and shook Round's hand. The smile appeared on his face again. It masked the pressure he was feeling inside. "I know what I need to do." Then he quickly turned away and ran on the court.

Chuck took a couple of deep breaths and started shooting. He couldn't concentrate the way he wanted. The look of desperation in Coach Round's eyes stuck in his mind. The look implied that if Chuck and the team that Round had picked were to lose, the old man was done. Not literally, but inside, where it counted. This game was about the confidence that Darrell Round had in his ability as a coach. To know a basketball player when he saw one. Chuck wasn't just playing for his spot on the team. He was playing to save Darrell Rounds' faith in himself. The spiritual life of the coach who had become his friend.

Even more than Chuck, Round needed the team he picked to win. Not only to show Henderson he was still the Coach, but to prove it to himself as well. The picture became clear. The young lion had made his play, and the old lion wasn't ready to lose the pride. That's what was happening. Henderson was forcing his picks on the old man and Round was sticking to his guns.

Knowing Henderson's gambling 'habit', Chuck guessed the two men had made a bet on the game. Henderson got to pick the team he had nurtured last year, and Round got to take the new blood or the 'ball players' as Round had called his picks. Henderson was trying to force Round out and set his mark on the team by picking the players he wanted. Round needed Chuck to prove to Henderson that the old lion still knew talent, still knew how to coach and still ran the team. If Chuck's team lost, not only would Chuck not make the team, but Henderson would literally be viewed by the players as the 'real' coach. Darrell Round would probably have to quit.

Chuck looked down the court and saw Henderson smiling. He was far too confident. Then he looked at Coach Round. He was sitting in his chair. The chair of the head coach that Darrell Round had occupied for thirty-five years. A chair that Henderson wanted, but did not have the knowledge, tact, nor ability to occupy.

With the picture clear, Chuck's mind became focused. The basketball in his hands helped him to relax. The pressure of the contest that was about to take place was more intense than any game Chuck had ever played. Yet, he was amazingly relaxed. He looked at Pepper, Jose, Dexter, Earl and the others. They had no idea of the significance of the contest. Chuck knew the players, and he knew himself. He bent down and retied his sneakers. Then he licked his hands and wiped off the soles of his sneakers. First the left foot, then the right. It was time to play some ball. It was time for Hoopman.

The first thing he had to do was talk to his team. Chuck called them all under the basket away from the bench. He noticed all of them were quiet and looking at him with anticipation in their eyes. At first, he wasn't exactly sure what to say. As he looked into their faces, the words came to him. He started slowly. "Guys. It's close to the final cuts. This little game has more on the line than any of us have played for before, or maybe ever will again. I want you to take a look over there," he said nodding toward what was essentially last year's team with some speed added. "Ain't a person in this University gonna know this game ever happened. But I guaran-damn-tee you, that the results of this game will last each one of us the rest of our lives." Chuck saw the look of shock on some of the players' faces. Even Pepper had a look of concern. "If we don't have the confidence in ourselves, that we can beat that group of guys over there, we ain't gonna make the team." He saw a couple of players nod their understanding.

Chuck continued, "I know two things. I know I can play basketball better than any of those guys. If I didn't feel that was true, I wouldn't be here. And number two, I know we are better basketball players than them." Chuck smiled and showed all the confidence he could to his teammates. "I'm fixin' to go kick some butt. You guys want to join me?" Some of them nodded. Chuck yelled, "YOU GUYS WANNA JOIN ME!?" They all yelled back "YEAH!" Chuck yelled, "LET'S GO!"

They all ran over to Coach Round's bench. They were so excited that none of them sat down. Coach Round called them all in close. He spit into his cup and said quietly, "Well, fellas. Looks like we're gonna play one for real today. I don't want any holding back. If you got an 'A' game, you better show it tonight. 'Cause there ain't gonna be no second chance." Round noticed the players all nodded in agreement and looked at each other. "Ya'll go play some ball. Dillo Defense, on three!" The players yelled the motto as directed. Round picked five players without saying their names. He merely pointed and grunted. It was Chuck who led the five players onto the floor.

From the tip-off, the game was intense. Henderson's team was focused on running. It was obvious because they took off like they were an Olympic sprint relay team headed for the gold. Jose couldn't jump with Ojayeh Nudah. "OJ" was six feet ten, but resembled a stick with arms. Nudah tapped the ball to Charles and he quickly took it to the basket for a lay-up. Back at the other end, Dexter missed a ten-footer due to heavy pressure from Parnell. The rebound came off to OJ, who passed to Charles who quickly passed to David Parnell who had sprinted the length of the floor for an easy lay-up. Then, one of the forwards Coach Round started threw an inbound pass to Frazier that was intercepted by Parnell. He immediately pulled up and popped a ten-footer. It was six to nothing and the game wasn't even a minute old.

Chuck yelled to Frazier, "TAKE IT OUT!" Frazier immediately passed the ball to Chuck. Chuck shook his head and yelled, "SETTLE DOWN!" He stopped and let the rest of the team head down the floor, then dribbled slowly to the other end. He looked at Round and smiled. The coach sat back in his chair and exhaled heavily. Chuck walked the ball up the court, he set up the offense and looked inside to Jose. He was being overplayed by OJ, so Chuck passed to Frazier and ran to the baseline. Frazier dribbled toward Hoopman's side and fired a pass to Chuck. Chuck caught it, and stopped to survey the floor again. Jose moved into position in the low post. Patiently Chuck waited for the big man to get open. Chuck hit him with a bounce pass and stepped back. OJ was tight on Jose, but it didn't matter. Jose collected himself, pivoted and shot the hook without hesitation. The shot hit the rim, bounced once and fell through the basket. There was hope.

After Parnell missed an eight-footer, Jose rebounded the ball and hit Chuck at mid court. Dexter Thomas was sprinting down the floor and Chuck saw him. He dribbled once and led Dexter with a one-handed bounce pass from half court that hit Thomas in mid-stride for a lay-up. Thomas faked getting back on defense and stole the inbound pass at his own foul line. Chuck saw the steal and ran hard to the basket. Dexter hit him on the run. Chuck dribbled twice towards the basket but was defended quickly as he headed toward the baseline. Thomas filled the lane like a freight train. Chuck saw him and threw up a lob pass. Dex caught Chuck's alley-oop and slammed it home. The score was tied.

Holmes looked at Henderson and shook his head. Henderson started pacing.

After the furious first two minutes, things started to settle down. Both teams played with abandon. With ten minutes gone in the first half, Chuck indicated to Coach Round that he wanted Pepper in the game. Pepper had been sitting next to Round patiently waiting his turn. He was more than up to the challenge.

On his first time down the floor, Chuck hit Pepper in the corner and the redhead promptly popped a three-pointer. After Holmes missed his own three-point attempt, Chuck got the long rebound and threw a pass out to a streaking Earl Frazier. Holmes sprinted back to keep Frazier from getting the lay-up to no avail. Earl Frazier drove hard then threw a neat pass to Pepper who was trailing on the break. Pepper took advantage of the beautiful pass, caught it in stride and slammed it home with two hands.

From that point last year's Dillos never recovered. Henderson tried yelling. He tried begging. Then he tried intimidation on Breyers. But Daymon Breyers was up to Henderson's wrath. Breyers called an extremely fair game, even with Henderson hollering in his ear most of the game. The younger assistant finally went to the far side of the court, so he didn't have to listen to Henderson's constant whining.

With five minutes left in the game, the pattern was clear. Chuck would get the rebound or force a steal. After he got the ball, he would slow it down. This technique not only pissed off Henderson but made Holmes and Parnell angry. They couldn't use their speed to sprint up and down the floor. By slowing down, Chuck kept Jose in the game, and the huge center outplayed Ojayeh inside. Jose took up so much space, that even when he didn't get the rebound, he freed up the lane enough for forward Larry Glynn to get rebounds.

With two minutes left, Henderson called a timeout. Round was confused. Chuck had his motley crew up by fifteen. Round set his team down for a rest.

Inside Henderson's huddle, the assistant coach's anger had reached a volcanic proportion. His voice was a whisper as he tried to vent his rage. "I can't believe you guys! This is ridiculous! Look at them! LOOK AT THEM!" The coach squatted in the player's circle. "A fat Mexican is eatin' you up, OJ! That toothpick with the red hair is totally abusing you, Charles! And that . . ." Henderson struggled to find the words. "That old . . ." He hissed, "MAN is single handedly taking you guys out of your game. You're not running, you're not hustling and you sure as hell aren't gonna beat this lame bunch!" The coach looked around. "If anyone lets that old man drive down the lane again, without so much as a scratch, I'll cut every one of you! You got that?" The players just looked at the coach. He shook his head, "Now get back in there."

Henderson grabbed Parnell before he got to the floor. "You need to take the man down, David. He's been goin' up and down your lane like he owns it. Last year, you would have punished somebody who did that to you."

"He's my teammate, coach," said David quietly. His voice betrayed the coach's wishes.

"Damn it, David! If you don't put his ass on the ground, you won't make this team," whispered Henderson. "You put him down," he pulled the large forward ear down to his mouth and said, "Or your ass is gone!"

With just over a minute left and the clock winding down, Chuck drove around his defender and down the middle of the lane just as he had been doing most of the game. He never knew what hit him.

Parnell did as he was told. Chuck put the ball up for a finger roll and Parnell fouled him hard. He never attempted to go for the ball, he merely went through Chuck. The ball and Chuck both went to the floor hard. Instantly, all hell broke loose.

Dexter Thomas tackled Parnell from behind knocking him to the ground. Jose tried to pull Dexter off, but OJ grabbed Jose from behind. This led to Pepper punching the slender OJ in the back of the head. Holmes grabbed Pepper, then Larry Glynn jumped on Charles. Each player seemed to pick someone to square off against.

Coach Round came off his bench blowing his whistle. At first it had little effect. When Daymon Breyer finally pulled Dexter off Parnell, cooler heads prevailed. Slowly the players separated, and order was restored. Round looked over to Henderson to help get control, but the coach remained in his chair, smiling as the older man tried to gain control.

Round walked over to Chuck and said, "You all right?"

Chuck looked up and winced. "Yeah." He rubbed his elbow and swung his arm to try and get feeling into his shoulder. He looked up at Parnell and said, "Did the shot go in?"

At first, David Parnell didn't say a thing. He relaxed his position and lowered his head. "Uh. No. The shot didn't go in." He slowly stuck out his hand to help Chuck up.

Chuck looked at the big hand. He shook his head, smiled and grabbed the large man's hand. "I guess I get to take two shots instead of one then!"

Round wasn't amused by Chuck's attempt at humor. "I think we've seen enough for today. You fellas head for the shower. Hayes, you stay here."

After everyone went in, Round looked closely at Chuck's eyes and looked over his arm and shoulder. "That was a pretty damn good hit you took."

"I fell off a tower from about twenty feet one time. It was on the confidence course at Ft. Dix, New Jersey." Chuck laughed, "I didn't have much confidence after that. But I didn't break anything then!"

Round smiled, "It doesn't look like you broke anything here, either." The coach stood back and looked at Chuck. "I never had any doubt you'd beat these guys." He looked at Henderson who was walking over to get the ball. "I never thought this game would drive a wedge in the team, before the team even got together."

"All we need is a little time together, Coach. We'll be fine," said Chuck.

Both men started walking toward the locker room. "You gonna be all right?" asked Round.

"This? Oh, heck, this is nothin'! I've been hurt worse than this shavin' in the mornin'," said Chuck. "I ain't even bleedin'."

Round frowned and said, "That was a cheap shot you took. Parnell will be runnin' laps for the next two weeks." Chuck nodded and smiled. Considering the situation, that seemed appropriate punishment. "As for his guidance, I don't have a solution for that yet." It was Chuck's turn to frown and Round saw it.

"In the Army, when somebody screws up, we give 'em an Article 15. It's generally used to take money and modify behavior."

"Sounds like a plan. I think I'll start with his paycheck," said Round.

Chuck changed the subject as they got to the locker room door. He hesitated a little before he asked, "So are the tryouts over?"

Round smiled and pointed at the scoreboard. "Yeah, Bubba. Tryouts are over. I think you're gonna be a college basketball player."

Chuck's shoulder and elbow didn't hurt so much anymore. "I made the team, eh?"

"Yeah, you did," said the Coach with a smile. "I guess I have to start calling you Hoopman, too!" Chuck was beaming. "I think your big Mexican amigo made it too." The coach then asked, "And that redheaded kid is only a freshman? I ain't seen a shooter like that since Pete Maravich!"

"Dyer is allegedly eighteen, Coach. Yeah, just a freshman," smiled Chuck.

"I'm not too keen on freshmen playing," said the coach. He started to walk away and said over his shoulder, "But I think we have a spot for him too. Just don't get too cocky, Hoopman. None of you are starting."

"NO SWEAT!" yelled Chuck. Then he turned and headed into the locker room. That was about as official as it could get for now. He was a college basketball player.

Round reached into his pocket and pulled out the two bottles of pills. One bottle contained the Etoposide medication to fight the bone cancer and the other was full of painkillers. He took one of the required medication pills and two of the painkillers. Not only did his body hurt, Round had a headache bigger than Dallas. He swallowed the medication and headed up to the office. He wasn't looking forward to the next encounter, but it was time to do what must be done.

"FINE ME! WHY THE HELL YOU GONNA FINE ME?" yelled Henderson. He was standing over Round's desk as if he owned the office.

Round couldn't take it anymore. He stood up and walked around to the front of the desk and said, "I know you told Parnell to drop Hayes. I know you did! I should fire your sorry ass right now!"

Henderson hissed, "I got a contract, and I'll make every dollar I'm owed! If you fire me, I get double in severance."

Round shook his head and said, "Don't think I don't regret that." He shook his head. "At one time, you were one of the best young coaches I'd ever met. You had a future here. This was gonna be your team."

"Oh, great! Head basketball coach at Podunk U.!" said Henderson. His voice was filled with hate. "I've been here for five years now! I'm ready for a head coaching job, and you know it!"

"You may be ready when it comes to your ability to do the X's and the O's. But you haven't got the patience nor the heart for the game that you need to be a head coach," said Round.

"OH, BULLSHIT! I've got the heart! I love this game and you know it," said the assistant.

Round had heard enough. He may have been 69 years old, and he may have been reserved most of the time, but Darrell Round was not a man to take any yelling in his office unless it was his own voice. He walked over, stepped right into Henderson's face and said, "Look at me, you thankless bastard. I hired you when no one else in this state would. I gave you a job when you were flat broke, working behind a bar scratching for dollars and drinking your life away. Still livin' your life like some frat punk! It's time you understood where you stand, Pete. And if you keep pushin' me, your ass will be standin' right behind that shitty little bar on a street with no name. Do I make myself clear?" Henderson bit down on his lip and knew better than to press Round when he was angry. He nodded and stepped back.

The Coach had made his point and scored a victory. Round shook his head and walked back around his desk. He regained his composure and finished with, "So accept you're the Assistant Coach and accept the fact that this is still my team." Round let the comment sink in. Then he added, "You'll get what you deserve when the time comes. As for right now, sure, you know the game, but you need to learn more about the players."

Henderson tried to say something, Round stopped him. "One more thing. You're gonna lay off Hayes, too. We're lucky he's not like you or he'd be suing the hell out the program and the school. Our deal sticks. Here's the list of the players on MY team. You can tell those four kids on your team they aren't playin' ball this year before I do. Or you can be the chicken shit I think you are, and just post the names on the wall. You see, that's how I know you don't have the heart. You didn't care that you nearly broke a player's arm tonight. And you don't care about those four kids that won't be playin' ball. But I do! So if you aren't gonna call 'em, let me know and I'll tell 'em. They need to be told why they didn't make it. Not find out on some piece of paper on the wall outside the locker room." Henderson turned and started to say something again when Round cut him off. "Just get the hell outta my office, Pete. I don't want to hear anything you have to say right now."

Henderson turned and stormed out of the office. Round sat back in his chair and grabbed some chew. Henderson had started to turn into a jerk two years ago. But now it had gotten to the point where Henderson had "suggested" who should be on the team. The ensuing argument led to the bet that the "players" Round had identified could beat the team that Henderson wanted. It was Henderson who picked his team to "test" the players Round wanted. He figured none of the "ball players" the old man wanted were worth the time they were getting in practice. Last year's players had a lot of talent and athleticism, but they didn't know how to play together. They didn't know how to win. Round had tried his best to get them together last year and it didn't work. Even Holmes, as good as he was, demonstrated inconsistency and never developed into the leader he should have been. Henderson was assuming most of the coaching in practice because Coach Round lacked the strength he needed when the cancer started. In the process, Henderson was replacing Round's role as head coach and mentor. With Henderson as their guide, last year's team was merely a bunch of undisciplined individuals that would never come together and never be a team.

The young men Round had picked for his team were a breath of fresh air for the St. Michael's program. Coach Round had watched Hayes play with them almost every evening. He'd seen their improvement over the last month, and it was amazing. Even Holmes was playing with them for a while. They weren't as athletic, but they played together. He looked at the scorer's book and the stats the team manager and trainer had taken during the practice game. The Rivera kid had 15 points and 10 rebounds. Most points on that beautiful hook shot he used. The redheaded kid, Dyer, was five of six from three-point range and had seventeen points off the bench. Thomas and Glynn each had seven rebounds and Thomas had put in ten points.

Round knew the real story was Hoopman. He finished with thirteen assists, ten points, six rebounds and five steals. He always seemed to be in the right place at the right time. Especially on defense. He covered the kid they called "Bullet" fairly well. He held the speedster to six points and three assists. Even Holmes only scored twice when Hayes covered him.

Round thought to himself, this was just his first taste of college ball for Chuck Hayes. What could he do with good players, better coaching and more experience? The only thing he needed was the opportunity. Round knew if he surrounded Hayes with good ball players on the team this year, the talent might just be enough for 'Hoopman' to complete his game. To take his game to a higher level. He looked at the calendar on his desk. He noted the circled doctor's appointment scheduled for next Wednesday. He quickly put the appointment out of his mind and went back to thinking about basketball.

The coach turned, looked outside his window and thought about his new team. He wondered how long it would be until Chuck Hayes was his starting point guard. How long would it take to turn his program into a winner? And the one major question that he hated to ask. How long did he have to live? He answered his own questions to the reflection in the window. "Not long. Not long now."

Chuck was sitting on the bench getting dressed when he saw David Parnell standing at the other end watching him. At first, Chuck wanted to walk over and punch the younger man. But he knew it would have been counterproductive. Chuck turned the other cheek. He focused his attention on his locker and reached for his shoes.

David Parnell sat on the bench ten feet away from Chuck. He coughed to clear his throat. "I want to apologize for what I did. I know it was wrong," he struggled to say the words. "I'm sorry."

Chuck looked up. "Let me tell you something, Big Guy. The next time you want to take somebody out, maybe it'd be better if you hit 'em low. Hittin' people high doesn't do enough damage. If you go low, you can cause broken arms and if that doesn't work, it may be a good way to give somebody a concussion when the head slams against the floor. You see, with your legs held up high, the head comes down first." Chuck slammed his hand on the bench loud for effect. "SLAMS ON THE FLOOR! And poof! Out cold!"

Parnell was clearly on the defensive. "Look, I didn't mean to hurt you. I was told to . . ." Parnell stopped suddenly.

"You were told to do that!?" Chuck shook his head in anger. "And you knew it was wrong too, didn't you?" Chuck bit his lip but continued, "Let me tell you something. I'm gonna be your teammate. I want to play basketball with you. But for a real long, long time," Chuck stood up and looked at Parnell. "I'm gonna remember what you did. The fact that somebody 'told you' to do that to me, tells me a lot about you. You want to know what the most obvious thing is?"

Parnell turned his head and looked up. Before he could talk, Chuck said, "It tells me you're a coward." The comment stung. Parnell turned his head and quickly looked away. "It was a decision you made, regardless of what you were told. Either you agreed with it and wanted to hurt me, which I don't believe since you just apologized. Or you just didn't have the courage to do what was right. In my book," Chuck grabbed his bag and said, "You're gutless."

Parnell jumped up and yelled, "COACH HENDERSON TOLD ME TO DO IT!"

Chuck stopped and looked at Parnell. Quietly he said, "And you did what he told you to do knowing it was wrong?" Chuck stepped back and smiled. "What was the right thing to do?" Parnell was at a loss for words. Chuck decided to let him off the hook. "Maybe you should have blocked my shot!" Parnell's eyes met Chucks. He looked back at the big man and could see his words provided no relief. Chuck shook his head and said, "You need to make decisions for yourself. You know the difference between right and wrong. Whether it's on the court, or at a party? So be right. Also, quit listening to stupid people!"

Parnell tried to speak, "But he's the coach and he . . ."

"David!" Hoopman interrupted him. "Just stop listening to stupid people. They can pull you down to the stupid level." David pursed his lips and nodded.

Chuck headed out the door. As he opened it to leave, he turned and said, "And I don't think you're a coward. I said that to hurt you. Not physically, like you hurt me. But with words. Sometimes words hurt more than getting knocked to the floor." He left without waiting for a response.

That night, Chuck met some of the players at the school snack bar. He couldn't contain the news any longer. He told Pepper how Round was proud of him.

"He said that? Really?" Pepper was on cloud nine. "I didn't even think he knew I was playing!"

"Oh, yeah! Coach Round knows everything," said Chuck. He told Pepper, Jose, and Dex Thomas that they had all made the team. They could barely contain themselves. The new teammates were overjoyed. To Chuck, it was a level of excitement he had experienced on other occasions. It was like being in an Army unit that had won a battle. The unity brought about by victory is a sweet and precious feeling, rarely duplicated. Only combatants and sportsmen can attain that feeling of camaraderie. The euphoria was a sign of things to come.

Chuck wasn't quite as caught up in the fever of his peers. In the back of his mind, the thought that Henderson had ordered Parnell to try and hurt him would not go away. Chuck held no grudge against David Parnell. Henderson had blackmailed Parnell. In the military, they knew how to take care of someone like Henderson. Chuck needed some help on this one. It was time to go back to Hawk and talk about some 'toys'. Henderson wasn't just a pain in the ass anymore. He was dangerous.

CHAPTER NINE

"Hey, Nate! Good to see you again," said Chuck.

"I guess congratulations are in order, Chuck," said the Sergeant Major with a huge smile. "I didn't think an old man like you could do it! But you've been provin' me wrong for twenty years." Hawk put out his hand to shake.

They moved into Hawk's spacious living room. Chuck had been in the house before, but he had forgotten how big it was. The college apartment was quite tiny compared to a full-fledged house.

Sandy Hawkins came in with two beers and said, "I hope that this is okay. I know you're in training, and I would hate to be a bad influence on you, Chuck."

Chuck grabbed the beer and took a drink. "You never were a bad influence before, Sandy, and I'm positive you never will be." He hugged her and gave her a little kiss on the cheek.

"I hope school isn't too tough for a guy who's been in the Army his whole life," she said.

"School is great, Sandy," answered Chuck. "Being a student is like . . . being in a different world. There is still structure and direction, but I don't have any stress. These kids don't know how good they have it."

"You keep telling them, Chuck. Someday they're gonna have to go out into the world and work for a living," said Sandy.

"They don't have a clue," laughed Chuck. "But I like them like that. They have a fresh outlook on life that you don't get from crusty old Army farts like Hawk!"

"I'll show you a crusty old fart, you sum bitch!" said Hawk as he started to grab Chuck and wrestle with him.

Sandy hit her husband with the towel she was carrying and said, "Oh, you two! I'm gonna leave now. You two knock off the crap or I'll stay here, and you won't be able to tell all those tales you tell!" Both men immediately stopped fooling around. She continued, "Now, I'm going shopping, so you'll have to get your own beer."

Hawk kissed Sandy good-bye then the two men settled into the couch. Hawk put an NBA game on the television. The old friends caught up on what had been happening in each other's life's the past two months. After an hour of casual talking, Chuck grew a little quiet. Hawk picked up on his friend's demeanor right away. Chuck never could hide a secret. Hawk said, "You havin' so much fun at college that you need me to come over there with some 'toys', eh?"

Chuck smiled. "Naw. Not yet, but maybe soon." He took a deep breath and began the saga. He told Hawkins about Charles Holmes and how he shaved points in last year's games. Then he told him about Henderson and how he was manipulating Holmes. He mentioned the fact that Henderson was turning into his nemesis in practice. But Chuck didn't tell Hawk about Henderson telling Parnell to knock him down on the drive through the lane.

Chuck knew Hawk well enough to know that he was the most lovable, trustworthy, and loyal friend on the planet. But he was also a bit uncontrollable when angered. Chuck had seen Hawk angry only once. It took four men to pull the Sergeant Major off the other man. Luckily, no charges were filed, and Hawk only had to pay for the cost of the plastic surgery for the antagonist. With his size and his temper, Nate Hawkins was not a man anyone wanted to see angry. His 26 years as a Military Policeman had put him in good graces with plenty of local law enforcement officers, not just around San Antonio, but throughout Texas.

"Anyway, this is where it's at right now," said Chuck. "I'm on the team, but every day is a struggle with Henderson."

"I could probably help get rid of that trouble for you, Chuck," said Hawk. "If this turd Henderson's into gamblers, we could probably bring him up on some kind of charges."

"I don't think it's that simple. You remember my friend Eddie, the guy in the wheelchair?" asked Chuck. Hawk nodded. "He and one of his friends are really good with computers. They have some information about Henderson and the guys he is running with, and that's how we found out about his debts." Chuck shrugged his shoulders and said, "Some of the information was gathered . . . unconventionally." Chuck saw the frown that appeared on Hawk's face. "I don't think we have anything we can go to the police with."

"No, you don't. But I can help you there," said Hawk. Chucks' eyes met Hawk's eyes, "I got a couple of listening devices. We could record what this clown is saying and doing. We can't take it to the cops, but you could screw with his head."

Chuck nodded his agreement. It didn't sound right. But he didn't have any options. He couldn't go to the police and say, 'My coach is fixing games, blackmailing my teammates and by the way, tryin' to kick my ass every practice'. Charles Holmes was no help. He hadn't said two words to Chuck since the team was announced.

Hawk could see Chucks decision wavering. Hawk took a big swig of beer and said, "Everything you have here is weak, Chuck. Now I'm sure a good ass kickin' would help Henderson get the message. But you know and I know that won't work here. We need to try and catch him saying something to somebody at the wrong time. Then you just let his sorry ass know you've got a tape. He'll come around. If he doesn't knock off the crap, I drop the tape in a lost and found box at City Police Department."

As good as kicking Henderson's butt sounded, Chuck knew that wasn't the best answer. He thought about Hawk's offer. Recording Henderson's conversations wasn't as drastic as using violence. However, it did seem like a great way to get Henderson's attention. "You really think you can get something?"

"He's a punk, Chuck. He'll be proud of his punk behavior and brag to somebody on his phone," said Hawk. "Or whoever is manipulating him will call him and we'll find out more about that connection. When he starts talking, I'll get it all." Chuck nodded. "Besides, I don't have anything to do this month except watch basketball. Sandy has been bustin' my cojones to get out of the house. This is a good thing for both of us."

Chuck smiled, "You know, I think you're right!" He got up to leave. Hawk walked with him out of the house towards the garage.

"Here, take this with you," said Hawk. Hawk walked into the garage and pulled out a trunk. Inside was Marshall Wright's new "ARMORdillo" mascot costume. Chuck smiled and opened the trunk. This ought to make your roommate a respectable mascot, and not like the roadkill that he was wearing!"

Hawk put the box in Chuck's trunk and smiled. The big man changed the subject back to Henderson. "I know what to look for and I know where to find him," said Hawk. "Are you sure you don't need anything else?" Chuck knew instantly Hawk meant 'guns'.

"No. Not . . ." he started to say 'yet'. But instead, he finished with, "No. Besides, those things you have are too big! I got smaller pistols that would work just fine! Later, Hawk."

All the way home, Chuck was nervous. He knew Henderson was garbage. He knew he couldn't prove it though. Maybe blackmailing the coach was a happy medium. Chuck just hated taking himself down to Henderson's level. He wished Eddie and Chris were back from Austin. He hadn't been able to talk to them in two weeks. Ed said he'd be back a week ago. What was he up to? Chuck thought he had a plan, and now things appeared to be falling apart. He took comfort in Hawk's words. Everything was going to be okay as long as Henderson was as loose with his tongue as he was with his wallet. Chuck need not have worried.

At next Monday's practice, Chuck decided to plant the seed for Henderson's demise. His right shoulder and elbow still hurt, but the pain just inspired Chuck. He spent most of the practice passing to teammates. He didn't shoot much and took most of his lay-ups left-handed. Every time he shot his bruised elbow made him look at Henderson. Chuck had to figure out how to shake the guy up. Every history book warns against the frontal assault. Most war stories explain how deception is a better option. At this time in the season, a flanking approach to the target seemed like a good play to Hoopman.

After practice, he was alone in the locker room with Charles Holmes. Chuck came up behind Charles and said, "Are you still gonna play clean this season?" No small talk. No side stepping, just straight to the point.

"MAN!" Charles exploded. "WHAT ARE YOU DOIN'?" He immediately started looking around to make sure they were alone. He started to talk in a near whisper. "What do you think you're doin'?"

Chuck spoke in a normal voice. "I just want to know if you're gonna shave points this year, or not?"

"That ain't none of your business!" said Charles. He started to gather his things and shoved them into his gym bag. "I got nothin' to say to you."

"I was just wondering how it works. I got a few questions I think I'd like to ask Coach Henderson," said Chuck.

"Say what?" asked Holmes. His voice no longer showed the anger he had previously demonstrated. Charles had become inquisitive.

"Just tell him the novelty act wants to know if the option is still available," said Chuck with a smile.

"The novelty act wants to know if the option was still available. You want me to ask him that?" asked Charles.

"Yup. Just ask him that for me," said Chuck. "He'll know what I want." Chuck turned to leave.

Charles yelled after Chuck, "HEY!" Chuck turned to listen. Charles walked toward him and said, "Listen, I ain't decided yet, man. I don't know what to do."

Chuck looked at him and said, "You play ball, Charles. Be a ball player. That's what you do best." Chuck turned and left without another word.

Chuck paged Hawk and let him know the seed was planted. Hawk came out to start his "observation" immediately. It didn't take long for Charles to make a phone call.

"Hey, Coach Henderson. It's Charles. I need to talk to you," said Holmes.

"What do you want?" said the coach. Hawk thought that the man already sounded a little drunk.

"I got a message for you," said Holmes.

Henderson was curious about the so-called 'message'. "All right. I'll play your little game, Charles."

"The man said, 'the novelty act wants to know if the option is still available'," said Charles. The phone was silent. "Did you hear what I said, Coach?"

"Yeah. Yeah, I heard you," came the answer. What the hell was that supposed to mean? The old fart had been difficult with his holier than thou attitude every day of practice and now he wanted to know if he could make a few bucks? Henderson was confused. "I don't get it? What else did he say?"

"That's about it. First, he said, 'he had a few questions about how it works'. And he said you'd know what he meant," said Charles. Again, the phone went silent. Henderson was thinking. Charles broke the silence, "I think he wants to get in on the shavin'."

Henderson became pissed, "I don't give a damn what you think. He's too much of a goody-two-shoes to want to be a part of our operation!"

BINGO! Hawk smiled for the first time in a week. "I got you, you scum bag!" he said to the tape machine.

"Look. You tell him he knows where to find me," said Henderson. Then he slammed the phone down. A little smile appeared on Henderson's face. Hoopman had a few questions about how it works? Maybe he could be bought?

Two days later, Pete Henderson was about to explode. Chuck had not approached him to "discuss" any option or ask any questions about the opportunities that lay before him. Henderson could wait no longer so he took matters into his own hands.

After practice, he waited outside the gym for Chuck to leave. When Chuck came out, he was ready for the coach. He'd been waiting for this chance for a week. "Hello, Coach Henderson! How are ya?"

Henderson threw his cigarette on the ground and motioned for Chuck to follow him. The two men talked as they walked toward the parking lot. "I understand you have some questions for me?" asked the coach.

Chuck smiled a broad smile. "Sure do, Coach!"

"You want to know a little about options and how things work, right?" asked Henderson. He fumbled in his pocket for his cigarettes as they walked.

"I'd really like to know exactly how everything works," said Chuck. Henderson hesitated. Hayes was tired of the word games already. Chuck saw the opening and took it. "I want to know how much you're payin' to fix games." Henderson stopped walking and looked around. Chuck asked, "I want to know what your cut is?"

Henderson cocked his head and looked at Chuck with one squinting eye. "I get enough money to take care of myself. You could too!"

Chuck smiled and said, "I want to know if you're as big a shithead as I think you are!" He reached into his bag and pulled out a recording device. He pushed the play button. On the tape, Henderson heard his conversation with Charles. Chuck turned off the recording and smiled. "Gotcha! Coach."

The coach was visibly shaken. He'd read it all wrong. Hayes didn't want in. He wanted to expose him as a critical link in a college gambling ring. This old bastard wanted to ruin his life. Henderson resorted to the only come back he could think of on short notice. He stepped back and hissed, "GO TO HELL, HAYES!"

Chuck laughed out loud. "What did you think? You think you could draw me into your crap pile!? That I'd do anything I could for some of your illegal money?" He laughed again. "Not only are you a conniving scum bag, you got jack shit where your brains are! I figured out your little deal with Holmes last year. I know the kid doesn't want to do it this year, but you're pushin' him into it again. I'm not gonna let you do it." Chuck let him think about the comment for a moment. Then continued with, "I'm not gonna do anything about it, Pete. Because the program doesn't need to have this situation discovered. But you're gonna knock it off and clean up the mess your makin'. You understand, Pete?" He said Henderson's name as if it were a dirty word.

Henderson started to lose control. He was on the defensive now. Hayes had him against the ropes in a joust for control. Henderson did exactly what slime like him would always do. He reached down into his pocket and pulled out a knife. He regained his composure and said, "I don't think you're going to do anything, Hayes!"

Now it was Chuck's turn to step back. He turned his head to look around. It seemed like a prudent thing to make sure there weren't any people watching them. Chuck turned his attention back to Henderson. "You think that's your answer?"

Henderson was wearing his Cheshire cat grin as he said, "I'm not gonna let you ruin my life! I worked too damn hard to get to this point to have you destroy it all! I'm not . . ."

Chuck didn't let him finish. His hands grabbed Henderson's wrist, and he twisted the coach's arm outward in a swift powerful move that left Henderson exposed. With the knife out of the way,

Chuck kicked him in the stomach then used his free hand to reach up and into Henderson's Adam's apple and started squeezing. The coach couldn't talk. Chuck pushed him up against the building that paralleled the sidewalk they had been walking on. It was Chuck's turn to lose his composure. "HOW LOW ARE YOU GONNA GO!" Henderson tried to catch his breath. The speed with which Chuck had struck took the coach by surprise. He stopped trying to resist and dropped the knife. Tears appeared in Pete Henderson's eyes.

It was Chuck's turn to be taken off guard. He loosened his grip. Chuck stepped back. "You are a piece of work, Pete."

"Yeah, well, I try," said Henderson. He wiped the tears off his face.

"What do you want to do?" asked Chuck. "You're obviously up to your neck in debt. You got criminals blackmailing you. Round doesn't know or you'd have been fired. Give me a reason why I shouldn't just turn you over to Round or the cops. Or better yet, why don't I just finish this now?"

"I know I'm in over my head. I don't think there is anything that you or anybody else can do to save my ass," said Pete Henderson. "If I don't give them Charles Holmes, and we don't throw some games for them . . ." Henderson rubbed at his eyes and said, "They're gonna kill us both."

Chuck picked up the knife and stepped away from Henderson. He couldn't help himself. He felt pity for the man as Henderson tried to gather his composure. "Look at me, Pete." Henderson did what he was told. "I won't let that happen. Can you trust me?"

"You don't understand!" said Henderson emphatically.

Chuck became angry again, "NO! YOU DON'T UNDERSTAND!" He stepped closer to Henderson and said, "You don't understand that I can help you. I can help Charles and I can make this problem go away. You have to trust me." He could see Pete wasn't convinced. "Do you want to get back at these guys?"

"I thought you meant going to the cops!" said Pete with surprise.

Chuck shook his head no. "With what? We can't prove anything about last year, and the cops wouldn't do anything without evidence. Charles won't say anything, and the whole deal would give the program a black eye. I can't see Coach Round staying around with his program destroyed by the scandal. Can you? Is that what you want?"

"He was never involved in this," said Henderson. For the first time, Chuck thought Henderson was climbing out of the cesspool he was in.

"Let's keep him out of it," said Chuck. "All I need is information from you. You tell me what you know with details like who, where, how much. Important information I can use about all the significant aspects of the operation and I promise you, no cops." He paused and let the statement sink in. "I promise we can get back at those bastards. The basketball program at St. Michael's needs to be clean, and with your help, we can get it back that way."

Henderson lowered his head and nodded in resignation. "I don't think you can do it, but I don't have a choice, do I?" Chuck shook his head. Pete acknowledged the truth and said, "These are bad people. I mean really bad." He inhaled deeply. "They won't take no for an answer."

"I have friends who will help us out, Pete. We won't do this alone," he said. "Any time you want to back out, you can walk."

Pete Henderson agreed. "What do I have to do?"

"Let's go make a phone call and tell them we aren't playing ball for them, we're playing for us," said Chuck. "And one more thing!" Pete Henderson looked at Hoopman. "If you ever pull a knife on me again, the gamblers will be the least of your worries." Henderson's face went white. "Any questions?" Pete Henderson merely shook his head no. "Good! Let's go make that phone call!"

"Hi, Tommy. It's me, Pete Henderson," said Pete into the phone. It was obvious to Chuck that Pete didn't want to make the call, but he was trying to sound upbeat on the phone.

"It's about time we heard from you," said Tommy Clark. "We expected to hear something two weeks ago. Mr. Grant doesn't appreciate being left in the dark like this."

Chuck looked over to Hawk to see if the recording was working. It probably wasn't necessary, but Hawk insisted that they should record everything, just in case the cops did become involved. Chuck looked at Pete and gave him a thumbs up. Henderson kept talking. "I've got some bad news. Charles Holmes is not going to play for us this year."

"What are you talkin' about, Pete?" asked Tommy with a touch of anxiety in his voice. "This is somebody we were counting on this year."

"I know! I know, Tommy. But it ain't gonna happen," said Pete.

Tommy Clark became angry. Chuck could visualize the man as he yelled into the phone. "DAMN IT, PETE! YOU SAID HE WAS GONNA COME THROUGH! YOU TOLD US HE WOULDN'T BE A PROBLEM!"

Pete stammered into the phone, "I'm . . . I'm sorry, Tommy., but he's decided not to shave points for us." Pete looked at Chuck as he said it. The conversation captured the fact Henderson was on tape revealing his involvement in illegal gambling.

Again, Tommy Clark yelled into the phone. Only this time, he sounded more afraid than angry. "YOU DON'T UNDERSTAND WHO WE'RE DEALING WITH, DO YOU? NOT ONLY ARE YOU UP SHITS CREEK, YOU'RE TRYIN' TO TAKE US WITH YOU, AREN'T YOU?!"

"You're just gonna have to explain to . . ." Pete tried to talk.

"THE HELL I WILL!" yelled Tommy. "You can expect a call! No! YOU CAN EXPECT A VISIT, PETE!" Tommy calmed down a little and finished with, "You need to think this through!"

Pete Henderson looked at Chuck. Chuck nodded his determination showing the coach his support. It was enough to keep Pete in line. Henderson said into the phone, "We've made our decision, Tommy. Look somewhere else. We're through." Henderson hung up the phone without waiting for a response.

Chuck smiled and stuck out his hand. "That's the smartest thing you've done lately, Pete!"

Pete didn't take the hand. He looked at Chuck, then over at Hawk and said, "You heard what he said. They're gonna come pay me a visit!"

Hawk said, "NO! He said you can 'expect a visit'. That's not the same thing. He just said that to scare you." Hawk tried to smile, but every time he looked at Henderson, it made him nauseous. "You aren't scared, are you?"

Pete Henderson turned and stared out his apartment window. "I'm not scared. I'm dead."

Chuck touched Henderson's shoulder and said, "Make you a deal. You keep your end of the bargain, stay away from these guys, keep them away from Charles, and I'll make sure they don't screw with you." Henderson turned and looked at Chuck. "Is it a deal?"

Henderson obviously had problems with the so-called 'deal', but he didn't have a choice and he knew it. Deep inside he knew it was the best he could get for the time being, so he reluctantly accepted the offer. "Yeah, you got a deal, Hayes."

Chuck looked into the man's eyes. Nothing with Henderson was easy. "You just need to keep your word, Pete. I'll keep mine. Hawk is gonna make sure these guys don't mess with us. I promised you no cops too, and I'll stick by that!" What Chuck didn't add was the fact that Ed Newton and Chris Crowley were collecting information on Clark and his boss too. Information that would prove to be beneficial later.

Henderson reluctantly agreed. "Good. You do that," said the coach with a forced smile. "I suppose we have nothing further to say." Henderson turned and walked away.

Chuck watched him as he left the room. He didn't believe for one minute that Henderson would agree to Chuck's plan so easily. Something else was going on in Henderson's mind. Chuck knew it would only be a matter of time until Pete Henderson broke the deal.

On the way home, Chuck and Hawk discussed what had happened. Nate Hawkins was irate. He told Chuck that Henderson couldn't be trusted, and that Chuck was a fool. Chuck said he had no options. He thanked Hawk for his help and told his friend to relax. For the time being everything was under control. As Hawk dropped Chuck off, all he could do was shake his head. He had faith in Chuck, but this idea that Henderson would stick to the plan and stay away from Clark was foolish. He tried one more time to talk to Chuck about adjusting the plan. He wanted to be on the offensive, not just with Henderson, but with Clark and even his handlers in Las Vegas. Chuck disagreed and insisted that Hawk remain calm. "It'll work out just fine, Nate. You too need to trust me, okay?"

Hawk didn't want to, but he too knew better than to argue with Chuck when he had his mind made up. "If somebody comes around and starts messin' with you guys, I'm not waitin'. You understand that Hoss?!" Chuck knew that Hawk wanted to protect him and accepted the comment as an offer for protection.

"Not a problem, Nate. If somebody messes with any of us, you're cleared hot to do what you need to do. I expect Ed and Chris will have some information for you to use too," said Chuck. He smiled at his friend and waved good-bye, "It's gonna be fine. Thanks, Hawk!"

For years Chuck had listened to his teacher and mentor. Nate Hawkins had special intuition about criminals and criminal activity. As a military man, Chuck was an analyst, a planner and a damn good soldier. On a basketball court, Chuck was the king of the world. But this area that he was entering was Hawks' world. It was a world where he should have listened to his friend.

Hawk lay awake that night. He was angry with Chuck for accepting an agreement that was really no agreement at all. Henderson would keep doing whatever he needed to do to stay alive. Chuck was the one that made the agreement with the scumbag. It didn't mean that Hawk couldn't keep on doing what he was doing. He had plenty of time on his hands now. Perhaps a little more "observation" of the target would reveal something else. Something else they could use when Henderson decided to break the deal. Nate Hawkins was certain that it would only be a matter of time until Henderson would be visited by the real leader. Hawk would be ready.

The Armadillo's first game came against a Latvian all-star team. The game went all St. Michael's way. Charles Holmes, obviously relieved to find out from Henderson they were not playing for Tommy Clark, was unstoppable. The Latvians couldn't control his speed. He ran up and down the floor like a man possessed. He was pulled five minutes into the second half with 23 points and five assists.

In the second half, St. Michael's had such a big lead that the second team players were getting some playing time. With the score becoming lop-sided, the Latvians decided to make the game physical. One of the Latvian big men elbowed Jose Rivera-Torres hard in the stomach. Jose nearly fell to the floor. The ref caught the cheap shot and gave the Latvian center a technical foul.

The player said something to one of his teammates when Chuck interrupted his conversation with a quick word in their native tongue. Clearly unnerved by the fact that one of the Americans understood Latvian cuss words, the player started talking to Chuck. In spite of the dialect, Chuck could understand enough from his familiarity with Russian to converse, Chuck talked to the Latvian center for a minute. Soon the Latvian players on the court were standing around Chuck, talking, and laughing.

With the situation under control, Chuck went over to Jose to make sure he was okay. The big guy who had thrown the elbow came over and shook Jose's hand. The potential for the game to get out of hand was gone.

Jose was fine, but he was curious about what they were talking about and why the guy had come over to shake his hand. "They told me why the big guy gave you the gut check," smiled Chuck.

"Why'd he do it?" asked Jose. He was starting to get his breath back but was also getting a little angry about the whole incident.

"He said you were stepping on his feet. And that you smelled like a goat," said Chuck.

"A goat, eh?" said Jose.

"I just informed them that you smelled more like goat shit than a goat. They thought that was funny," said Chuck.

"I smell like goat shit?" Jose said.

"Yeah. I don't know too many other words, but those were some that I remembered. Then I told him you were probably gonna average twenty points and ten boards a game. He respected that. He decided to come and shake your hand," said Chuck.

"He respects my game?" asked Jose.

"Yeah, he does," said Chuck.

"And he told you all this in his language?" asked Jose.

"Yeah. He was a little pissed at first because my accent is about the same kind of accent his enemy speaks with across the border from his home in Latvia. I said that this is just a game. It has nothing to do with the border problems in their homeland. They love their hoop in Latvia," said Chuck.

"Tell him I respect his game, too. Even if he is a cheap shot artist," said Jose.

Chuck did, and the big guy smiled. That was the end of the incident. Once again, Chuck Hayes was a peacekeeper. He was happy that he wasn't carrying a rifle this time. Shooting basketball is always better than shooting bullets.

St. Michael's went on to win by thirty, but the Dillos didn't play like a team that was together. They played like two separate teams. The first team was made up of mostly last year's players, and a second team led by Chuck. Whenever players were mixed, they ended up not synchronized on offense, and some players wouldn't help each other out on defense. On the bench, Round was frustrated by the lack of unity. He could see it was a problem.

Henderson was still Henderson. He just sat with a blank expression on his face for most of the game. He over emphasized the play of the first team and was hypercritical of the bench players. Chuck gave him a look to indicate his displeasure at the way the assistant coach was acting. After the glance, the assistant coach never looked at Chuck again.

For his part, other than becoming a peacekeeper again, Chuck tried to mend fences with the rest of his team. David Parnell had started to pick up on some of Chuck's techniques and the two were playing well together on the court. Parnell was on the receiving end of two beautiful lob passes from Chuck that resulted in scores. On one fast break Chuck delivered Parnell a bounce pass from half court that resulted in two more easy points.

Chuck still had problems with Holmes. He played hard all the time, even when Holmes would shut him out and not throw him the ball. On one fast break Chuck was wide open, yet Holmes took the ball to the basket where he was fouled. Chuck remained quiet about the play and soon after, with the game a wash, Charles Holmes was benched for the rest of the game.

Although it was an impressive win, it was still just a practice game, and the division on the team was evident to everyone. Round was at a loss and Henderson did nothing to solve the problem. The next day, Chuck had an idea to bring the team together.

"Coach Round?" said Chuck.

Round was sitting in his easy chair. He looked up and smiled at Chuck. "What can I do for you, Hayes? Shouldn't you be in class or something?"

"I'm out for the rest of the afternoon," said Chuck. He was tentative about his proposal at first. But Coach Round could tell Chuck had something on his mind.

"What is it?" asked Round as he reached for his chew.

Chuck sat down across from the coach and said, "I have an idea how we can bring the team together."

Round sat back and started chewing on his tobacco. "All right. Let me hear it."

"Back in the Army, when we wanted to build leaders and get a unit together, we would take a day, go do something that challenged everyone. We would go to the confidence course or the Leadership Reaction Course. Just the fact that everyone was required to be there, participation was always intense. No one wanted to look bad with everybody else watching!"

"I'm trackin'. But what do you have in mind, Hayes? You want to put these guys in the military?" asked Round.

"Not really, Coach. It's just a confidence course. If we have time, we could do some things on the Leadership Reaction Course as well. I don't see us coming together like we are now. Maybe if we do something different, we can become a team," said Chuck.

Round thought for a minute. Then he sat up in his chair and said, "All right. Let's try it. Hell, we can't be any worse than we are now."

Chuck nodded and smiled, "I'll set it up as soon as I can!"

Chuck finally found time to visit Grace. He had been too busy, between practice, studying and the distraction of Henderson, to get around to see her. It was late on a Thursday afternoon when he headed to her office. As he rounded the corner, he heard her voice and she sounded scared.

He quickly stepped through the door and saw a man with his hand wrapped tightly around her wrist as they stood in front of her window. The angry man turned to look at Chuck, just as Chuck caught Grace's expression of fear. She pulled her arm away and stepped back. The man turned back toward Grace and said, "We'll talk about this later."

Grace said, "No, we won't! I've got nothing to say to you!"

The man took a step toward Grace. She quickly stepped away again. Chuck walked towards the pair and said, "Is there a problem here, Miss Winters?"

Before Grace could answer, the man said, "Yes, Miss Winters, is there a problem?"

She looked away from the man and said to Chuck, "No. No, there isn't a problem."

That wasn't what Chuck saw. He could tell Grace was under duress. He looked at the man. He was probably 45 years old; he had dyed his hair brown, was about six foot two and appeared to be in pretty good shape. But the vibe that Chuck picked up was one of total arrogance. His black clothes and leather jacket projected an air of narcissism. Chuck instantly disliked the man. He took a step closer to Grace and looked at her closely.

She saw his concern and smiled a forced smile. "Everything is okay!" Then she looked at the man and said, "William was just leaving."

The man, William, grunted, "Huh! Yeah, I was just leaving!" William turned and headed towards the door. He said over his shoulder as he left the room, "I'll see you later, Grace!"

Chuck couldn't help but think the way William said 'see you later', he didn't mean it in the manner Chuck would have said it. William said 'see you later' like it was a threat.

"Who was that unpleasant person?" asked Chuck.

Grace walked over and closed the door. "That," she said with a frown, "was my ex-husband."

Chuck was stunned. He knew she had been married, but thought the guy was somewhere else, like Nepal. She had never mentioned William to him before. "I thought he was gone."

"To me, he is gone," she said. Grace walked over to her window and looked outside.

Chuck stepped over close to her. He softly took her hand and held it up to the window to look at it in the light. He could see the redness on her wrist where William had grabbed her. "He's the guy that put those bruises on your arm a couple of months ago, isn't he?" She just nodded. "Is there anything I can do?" She stared out the window. Chuck followed her gaze. "I'll help, Grace." He looked at her beautiful reflection in the glass. He could see the tear slide down her cheek.

Quietly she said, "Just hold me."

For the first time in a long time, Chuck didn't know what to say. He did know enough to do what she asked and held her. Not too tightly, but just enough to provide her comfort. Chuck put one arm softly around her shoulders, and he could sense her pain just as easily as he saw it in her face in the glass. Slowly he reached up and pulled her head towards his shoulder. He had never seen Grace Winters like this. She was totally vulnerable and genuinely afraid.

It made Chuck feel helpless. Grace's situation was the product of a bad choice and a bad person. The sadness she was feeling was not from despair, but from loss. William had taken her spirit. This was not the same Grace Winters he was falling in love with. In Chuck's mind, he viewed this shell of Grace as a product of the relationship she had with William. William had made her hurt like this. For this act, Chuck vowed to make William pay.

Chuck reached down and gently pulled Grace's chin up so that her eyes met his. Softly he said, "It's okay, Grace. He's gone. He won't hurt you. Ever."

As the tear rolled slowly down her cheek, he took one finger and carefully wiped it away. She started to say something, but

Chuck moved his finger toward her lips and just barely touched them. He shook his head no and said, "You don't need to say anything." He wiped away another tear and said softly, "It's gonna be okay." He looked out the window as Grace turned her head and quietly cried into his shoulder.

It was a quiet Saturday morning when the St. Michael's Armadillo men's basketball team showed up at Ft. Sam Houston for Army Training. "GENTLEMEN! THIS IS A U. S. ARMY OBSTACLE COURSE!" yelled Master Sergeant John Saunders. As he gave instruction to the team, he talked in an exaggeratedly loud voice. A voice that gave a person the feeling that they must listen, or they would instantly be thrust into the fires of hell. John Saunders was a man that would be heard even during a hurricane.

Round watched with a broad smile. Henderson stayed in the background. He had voiced his opinion, rather loudly, that he thought the whole thing was a joke. Henderson was quick to inform Round he would take this event to Clarence Teazin, the Athletic Director, if any players were hurt. "It might even cost you your job!" was how he ended his pitch to the coach.

Round matched the jab with, "At least we'll be doing something to make this a TEAM, instead of two squads! It can't be any worse a lesson than what you're teaching them!" For his part, Round was aware that something had changed about Henderson, but on the surface, he was still playing the part of 100 percent jerk that was trying to take Coach Rounds' job.

Saunders gave the brief then moved the team members out to the start point of the Confidence Course. Just as Chuck expected, the players were in no mood to participate. They slowly wandered to the start point. Saunders gave them another quick safety brief about the series of wooden and water obstacles that the team was about to encounter.

It was time for the natural leaders to step up, so Chuck jumped at the chance. "I've done this a few times, and it isn't easy." Then he issued the challenge to his teammates. "If you are afraid of an obstacle or can't do something, tell one of the instructors. It isn't worth getting hurt over." He noticed the younger men understood the comment as the challenge it was meant to be. "I'll go first since most of you haven't ever done anything like this before!"

Saunders yelled go and Chuck took off. He sprinted to the logs, walked across them as fast as he could, ran to the rope and jumped. He flew over the water pit and then ran to the eight-foot wall. Up, over, and on to the rope climb. He could hear a few of the players hollering back at the start. He came up to the rope climb and started up the ropes. There was even more encouragement from the team. He swung off the rope, ran through the tires and sprinted to the finish.

"DAMN, that was right up there with the best, Chuck!" said Saunders. "Forty-two point fifteen seconds. OUTSTANDING!" Saunders looked at the players. "Anybody think they can beat that?"

David Parnell stepped forward. "I'll give it a try."

"All right, young man! Let's see what you got. Ready, set, GO!" yelled Saunders. Parnell took off like a rabbit. The six-foot nine forward was surprisingly agile. He made it easily until he got to the rope climb. That's where he ran into trouble. Chuck started yelling at him to use his feet. Parnell did and soon made it to the top. He finished strong but was five seconds slower than Chuck.

Charles Homes stepped up next. Through most of the obstacles, the team was yelling encouragement for their star. Chuck noticed initially it was not just the starters cheering him on, it was not just the starters cheering him on, as if by magic, everyone on the team was rooting for Charles. The fluid movement and strength of Holmes was a joy to watch. He nearly jumped all the way over the water obstacle, then literally flew through the rest of the course. Charles Holmes beat Chuck's time by two seconds. The team hooted and hollered. Chuck smiled at Charles. Then he stuck out his hand. Charles looked at the hand, smiled broadly and smacked Chuck's open palm. After that, the rest of the team couldn't wait to try the course.

Next, the team went to the rappelling tower. Every player was encouraged to try to rappel the seventy-five-foot tower. Only Jose Rivera-Torres was exempt and that was for safety reasons. Saunders didn't feel the ropes would hold up to his 308-pound frame. Everyone else tried it at least once. Pepper and Bullet did it twice.

The final event was the Leadership Reaction Course. Each player was put in charge of his "squad" and given a mission to get his people to do a particular challenge. Some challenges were more difficult than others. Some had no solution. The LRC was merely a tool the military uses to determine the leadership qualities of its soldiers, airmen, seamen and marines.

Chuck was the leader for the first event. Taking a full five minutes to digest the task, assemble his squad, and brief his plan, with ten minutes left, he directed his team through the challenge, used the props and executed the required mission successfully with one minute to spare. After the task was completed, Saunders conducted an after-action review and asked for comments from the rest of the squad. The players seemed to understand the process and offered mostly positive input for Chuck's mission.

Every player had an opportunity to be the leader. Only Dexter Thomas and David Parnell got their squads through their mission in the allotted time. Parnell's mission was a particularly difficult one, yet he developed a solid plan. He used his people in the best possible manner at the right time and kept pushing them to accomplish the task. He used Jose Rivera-Torres as a center point for putting people over a twelve-foot wall. Then, they moved simulated fuel barrels over the wall to a designated point. The trick was not to touch any red painted areas, for that indicated a mine or an electric fence, which would have tipped any enemy to the movement of the players. Due to Jose's size and strength, he easily got his team members over the obstacle and helped steady wooden planks that allowed the barrels to roll over the "minefield". Parnell offered encouragement, was forceful when necessary and stepped in to lead when confusion became evident. By the time Pepper Dyer was pulled off the plank and standing on Jose's shoulders, the team was yelling encouragement at Pepper to finish the task. Jose caught him when he jumped down as Saunders yelled, "TIME!" The Armadillos hollered a victory howl as if they were a group of new army recruits. Chuck looked at Round. The Coach spit some chew in his cup and beamed a smile right back at Chuck.

After the last event, Saunders went over to Parnell and whispered something in his ear. Then he came over and pulled Chuck off to the side. "That Parnell kid is OUTSTANDING, Mr. Hayes! We've never had anyone accomplish that mission before! I told him, if he didn't want to play basketball anymore, he could come work for the United States Army anytime!"

Chuck smiled and said, "You want to make a soldier out of him? NO WAY!" Suddenly Chuck found himself up in the air. Jose, Thomas and Parnell had him held high and were carrying him. He started to struggle but realized what was happening. Saunders had distracted him so the players could grab him and carry him towards the water obstacle. Chuck just yelled, "SAUNDERS!!!" The sergeant was laughing too hard to respond. With Charles Holmes counting down, the three men threw Chuck into the water, much to the delight of the rest of the team and Coach Round. Chuck just happened to get a glance at Henderson. Even he was trying to suppress a smile.

Chuck got up and wiped the water from his face. He looked at Pepper and said, "Come here and give me hand, Pepper!" Pepper was still laughing but headed over to help Chuck out. Big mistake. Chuck grabbed the skinny lad and pulled Pepper into the water pit with him. Then all hell broke loose. Everyone was trying to push or pull each other into the water. It took six players, but they finally got Jose into the mud. As the group threatened to get Coach Round, he said calmly, "I think we've had about all this we need, fellas. Let's go!" The players knew enough to follow their coach's direction and did as they were told. Slowly they left the water. Chuck even noticed some of them going over to Saunders and talking to him. They shook his hand, gave thanks for his guidance and mentoring.

On the bus ride home, for the first time the Armadillos talked and acted as if they were a team. Charles Holmes was even talking to Chuck again. Chuck looked at Coach Round sitting in the front seat. He was beaming with pride. Across from him on the other front seat sat Pete Henderson. He hadn't said a word to anyone.

At the end of the bus ride, Chuck informed the coach that David Parnell had been nominated for team captain. The coach grunted and said, "That'll work!" Then he looked at Chuck and added, "By the way, that was a damn good idea, Hayes." The coach got up to get off the bus and said, "I just might have to let you play a little more this week."

It was Chuck's turn to beam. His coach liked what he'd suggested; Henderson was in his own little world not jacking with him and had not called Tommy Clark; his team was finally together; and he was gonna get to play more. College life was pretty good. Something should have told him; it couldn't last forever. There was only one thing that needed to be fixed.

"Hawk, I need another favor," said Chuck into the phone.

"Sure, Chuck. Anything," he said. What he hadn't told Chuck was that he had been spending more time watching Henderson and monitoring his phone calls. Hawk was certain Henderson would break the deal.

"I have a friend that seems to be having a problem with a guy named William Moreland," said Chuck.

Hawk wrote the name down. "Is that all you're gonna give me?"

"He's local. And my feeling is he is bad. Probably really bad," said Chuck.

"This friend of yours, got a name?" asked Hawk.

Chuck thought about not telling Hawk, but said flatly, "Gracelyn Winters."

Nate Hawkins wrote down the name and was quiet for a couple of seconds as he waited for more information. "Okay. I guess that's all you're gonna tell me, so I'm on it! You sure there isn't anything else I should know?"

"Naw. Not right now. Except she's one of my professors. Let me know what you find out soon, okay?"

Hawk wanted to tell Chuck that his focus was still on the scumbag, Pete Henderson. But he decided to reluctantly accept the new task for his friend. "I'll talk to you in a couple of days."

"Thanks, Hawk. You're the greatest!"

Hawk hung up the phone and looked at the name. He exhaled heavily and grabbed the handset to make another call.

CHAPTER TEN

It was the Sunday after the third straight road game of the season. The competition so far had been relatively easy, and St. Michael's had won all three. Chuck, Pepper, and Jose had only played a few minutes each and never enough to get into the flow of any game so far. Chuck wasn't happy with the amount of playing time he was getting, so he found other areas to keep himself focused on. He found himself thinking about Henderson and Holmes, and the gamblers who owned them. He had seen no signs that Charles was shaving points in any game they had played, but Chuck knew the prudent thing to do was to be prepared in case he did. Eddie called Chuck and said he had some information for him, but he couldn't get it unless Chuck "paid the price". Chuck laughed knowing exactly what the price was. He was sure the stop by McDonald's would be well worth anything Eddie had discovered.

Chuck showed up at Eddie's apartment just after noon. He carried a huge sack of burgers, fries, three chocolate shakes and of course, the apple pie. Eddie nearly ran Chuck over with his wheelchair as he headed into the living room. "Damn, Eddie! Give me some space!"

"Come on, Hoopman! I've been dyin' for burgers and a pie!" said Ed. Chuck thought he saw a little bit of drool coming from Eddie's mouth. He quickly put the bags on the coffee table and got out of the way. Chuck watched while Chris and Eddie literally tore up their lunch. Slowly he reached in and grabbed a shake. Chris grunted something about, "Nelp, nour shelf," but Chuck enjoyed his fingers too much to get any closer.

After five straight minutes of pure gluttony, the two men sat back and let out groans of satisfaction. Chuck sat back on the couch and flipped through channels with the remote. He settled on an NBA pre-game show and put the remote on the coffee table. "You guys won't eat that if I leave it there, will you?"

Neither man answered. They both just wore little smiles of pure satisfaction. Chuck decided it was time to get down to business. "So. You guys call me for some other reason than to satisfy your basic need for nourishment?"

Eddie sat back a little deeper into his wheelchair and said, "I guess after a feast like that, we can share some of the information we found."

Chuck laughed, "A feast, huh? You better have something after eating all that crap!"

"CRAP!?" questioned Chris. "This has all four food groups! It's got meat, grease, sugar, and chocolate. You just can't get balance like that every day."

Chuck shook his head. "And your degree is in . . . what again? Surely nothing related to health!"

"Computer Science!" said Eddie. Then he let out a loud burp.

Chuck just laughed. "Who said American youth is wasting away?" Chuck noticed that Eddie had pulled out a notebook. It was time for Chuck to find out what Eddie and Chris had discovered.

What they had gotten were details on the Big Casino Texas gambling organization. They found out that BCT had a brick and mortar site in the back of a sports bar on the northeast side of Austin. They got there by placing a couple five-hundred-dollar bets and asking for more action. They noticed the back room housed wall-to-wall computers where credit cards were used to place bets. Every "customer" would use his or her credit card and a personal identification number to drop bets on any sporting event available. Pro football, college football, golf, swimming, track and field, even dominoes was bet on at BCT. In the back of the building was a computer room that had a separate room off to the side that was secured. Eddie said he thought it was where the server or servers were. There was also an operating office with a dozen phones receiving incoming calls. They even had a fax machine. Eddie estimated this location was probably making a couple of hundred thousand dollars' worth of bets every day.

Chris said, "Plus, who knows how many thousands of people are gambling from their home computers. Throw in the fact they fix games, God only knows how many, they have the odds in their favor. They can take in huge money on parlays and only need to lose one game . . ."

Chuck interrupted Chris with a question. "Hold it! What's a parlay?"

"It's when you bet on multiple winners or a series of winners. That increases the payout due to the higher risk of the bet," said Chris. "Any single game or score not covered and the whole bet is lost. By knowing which games are fixed, parlaying multiple, highly improbable winners, they control a rigged system. . ."

Eddie finished his comment, "They making bank, Hoopman!"

Chuck stood up to walk around the room. His thoughts were so much clearer when he was moving. A plan of action started to come together. "These guys are ruining college basketball. College hoop was meant to be a game. Simple as that." He stopped and looked at his two friends. "We have to stop these guys."

Chris freaked out a little. "Man, hold on now! They have the best security available, the top-of-the-line systems, and probably online firewalls that are the most current, up-to-date online protection money can buy. These guys can afford the best!"

Eddie wasn't even listening to Chris. He was eerily calm. He had a look that Chuck had seen before. Chuck played chess against Eddie one time. They played for nearly an hour before Eddie beat Chuck. The thing was, he played Chuck without his Queen, one Rook and one Bishop, and still won. It was a look that said, "I know you've got an advantage on me, but I'll still kick your butt!"

Chris saw the look too. "OH, MAN! Eddie, what are you thinking?"

"What's the intent?" asked Eddie. "What do you want to do, Chuck?"

Chuck started walking around the room again. The plan of attack he wanted to take finally came to him. "Here we go, Ed. First, I want to send a message. I want to tell them to stop betting on college basketball."

"Just basketball?" asked Eddie.

"Just college basketball. I understand that people want to bet, and I can appreciate people across the country making money or losing money if that's their wish. But fixin' college hoop games and betting on them, that just isn't right," said Chuck. "After the message, I know they won't stop," he paused and suddenly snapped his fingers. "We need to hurt them. The way to hurt them the most," Chuck looked at Eddie and smiled. "In the wallet!"

"Better yet," said Ed. "In the virtual wallet!"

"Say what?" Chuck was confused.

Ed looked at Chris and nodded. Chris shook his head. "You tell him."

Ed smile broadly. "We found out they have a high roller option. It's called, 'G-Cash'. It's an internal cryptocurrency that only millionaires can use."

Chris added, "The G-Cash system may have dozens or even hundreds of millionaires around the globe that are in the system with a virtual account of cryptocurrency held by BCT."

"But we don't think it's just BCT! It appears they are controlled by a gambling organization in Vegas. This umbrella corporation controls a global gambling operation with a virtual bank." Ed was beaming when he finished.

Chuck walked over and gave Eddie a high five. "In the virtual wallet! I love it!" Chuck stepped back and rubbed his chin. "I have some ideas, Eddie. I think the requirements might be right up your alley!"

"If you're talking about what I think you're talking about, we have a friend in Austin who can author some experience that is right where you want to go," said Eddie.

"Oh man! You're talking about bringing him in again," said Chris with just a trace of nervousness in his voice.

For the first time that Chuck could remember, Eddie was mad. "For Christ sake, Chris! Would you grow a pair!" Chuck snickered.

"Bobby just got started on the background research, but I know you two. You are gonna get us in deep," said Chris.

Chuck was smiling outside, but confused by the addition of "Bobby" into the effort. "I thought we agreed to keep this to ourselves."

"We did," said Ed as he cleared his throat. "We have a friend that is very experienced in the….financial side of the dark web."

"Bobby is amazing, but when he and Eddie get together, hold onto your keyboard!" Chris was shaking his head.

Eddie felt he had to explain why Bobby needed to be brought into the planning. "Listen Chuck, Bobby is the best programmer we know. He was the one who found out about G-Cash and BCT's virtual bank. He can help us."

Chris interrupted, "But he always goes too far! He only tested the system last week. If he's gone too far in already, they'll change their systems before we even get in! If they figure out who and how we're footprinting them, we're hosed, man!"

"You and Bobby started footprinting their systems already?" asked Chuck.

Eddie didn't know what Chuck wanted to hear. Ed quickly decided the truth was probably the best answer. "Yes. I had a feeling you would need some more information on their networks. I know you think this thing with Henderson is over, too. He's bad news. Just like the BCT. There is undoubtedly somebody higher up that the BCT is literally linked to. These two groups or systems are linked in more ways than one. They share betting information, and they share monetary information. We think there are huge sums of money being transferred through G-CASH. Bobby is helping us map their networks. Both information and economic. By getting as much information as we can gather on all the systems, and hopefully gaining root access, we can hurt them. Right in the wallet! Bobby says he needs a little more time. Together, we can map it all. Information and Finances. We can figure out who the person at the top is."

Chuck saw the logic of Eddie's argument. He nodded in agreement. "You're absolutely right, Ed." Chuck continued to walk. "You think Bobby can help in exploiting or destroying the system they have?"

"You just tell me what you want to do. I need to know your plan. Your timeline. Bobby is the best white hat hacker I've ever met." Then he looked at Chris. "Plus, he's got the balls to go against these guys." He looked back at Chuck and said, "Both BCT and their master."

Chuck nodded. He looked over at Chris and back to Eddie. He knew that a bridge needed to be crossed. "You know. Chris isn't shabby either. He did some real good work a couple years ago for us."

"That was then. The government was behind us with lots of time and money. This is different. The repercussion from this is just on us. We might not be able to cover it up," said Eddie.

"You're gonna need to have somebody," Chuck tried to be tactful. "Perhaps not so reckless as you and your friend Bobby." He walked close to Eddie and said, "Just give Chris the defensive mission." He stepped back and said to Chris, "You need to do the operational security piece and that means more than protecting our ops. We need you to establish fake persona's and a false network. We're talking Trojan Horse, Honeypots and Spearfishing for the person at the top. I know you and Ed can do these things, Chris. Maybe you could keep an eye on the two of them and keep them from getting in trouble! Going after these guys is gonna need the best. I know you two are the best network guys I've ever met, but we don't have government support for this. If Bobby is that good, I think the three of you can take these guys down. No pun intended, but I'm betting on you guys."

Chris looked at Eddie. Eddie smiled and said, "Sorry about the nuts crack. I get edgy sometimes!"

Chris shook his head. "All right. Apology accepted! You and Bobby better listen to me sometimes!" That seemed to smooth the rough waters. Chris looked at Chuck and said, "What's your plan, Hoopman?"

Chuck picked up all the trash off the coffee table and grabbed Eddie's notebook. "You'll have to tell me a little about what you can do without sponsorship and what your friend, Bobby can do. Here are a couple of my ideas." Chuck proceeded to write down objectives, goals, and tasks. Then he wrote a timeline out for what he thought would work. He also let them know that Hawk might be available for physical security later, but he was doing some work for Chuck now that took priority. They all knew they couldn't go to the police. They had no "legal" evidence and no alternatives. If things went the way they were headed, the police might actually come after them.

Two hours later, Chuck left. A feeling of fear, anxiety, and hope ran through his mind. He didn't tell Ed to begin the operation because there were still things that needed to be done. He didn't need to look at his watch to know what time it was. It was time to prep a different kind of battlefield. A 'virtual' battlefield with different kinds of warriors.

Steve James was reviewing the spreadsheets when he noticed the red highlight by the St. Michael's University. The boys in Vegas had changed the status from yellow to red. That meant they were no longer on the payroll. That meant that somebody had decided not to play for Grant. He called Jeff and said, "I need you to do me a favor when you get in tonight. I need you to call up to

Vegas and find out what happened to the St. Michael's program. You may need to call the local fellas in Austin."

"You need me to find out anything specific?" asked Jeff.

Steve was hesitant. What was he looking for? Steve wasn't sure himself. "No. Nothing specific. Just find out what the deal was with the program going to red. Send me an email or give me a call back if you find out anything interesting."

"Boss, I know this is off track, but did you get those permissions for G-Cash from Vegas?" asked Jeff.

Steve James smiled. "As a matter of fact. I did. Let's save that for another time."

"Okay, boss!" Jeff hung up.

Steve couldn't shake his thoughts on St. Michael's University. Anything specific was what Jeff asked. That's a nice term for wanting to know if somebody in Texas had been killed. Who knows? He looked out over the waters of Paradise Island and thought how wonderful the Islands were. He was safe in the Bahamas. He enjoyed being away from Vegas. The fact that a tiny David sized basketball program in Texas was standing up to Goliath gambling syndicate in Vegas was beginning to distract Steve. He wondered, this time, would Grant let the player go? Steve thought about what he was thinking and knew he was kidding himself. Let someone go? Not Grant. Somebody in Texas was going to die.

"Bubba, when you pick 'em, you really know how to pick 'em!" said Nate Hawkins.

Chuck tried to pretend he didn't know what he was talking about. "Pick 'em?"

"Yeah, pick 'em! You didn't tell me William Moreland was married to Gracelyn Winters!" said Hawk.

"Used to be married to Grace," said Chuck.

"Is or isn't! Used to be or not, the fact is the connection is there, and you probably should have told me," said Hawk with more than a hint of anger.

Chuck was silent. He knew Hawk was right. But it was too late to apologize. He didn't try to cover up his failure to be totally up front with his friend. "I didn't think it would be that significant."

"Not significant, eh?" It was Hawk's turn to be silent.

Chuck could take no more. "All right, I'm sorry! I wanted to see if you could find a connection between the two besides the marriage."

"I'll say there's a connection. It was probably a right hook," said Hawk tersely.

Chuck was concerned. "You mean he hit her?"

"More than once. There is a history of abuse that goes back throughout their marriage. A year after they were married, William Moreland took his wife to the hospital after an apparent accident. She was admitted for broken ribs." Hawk was quiet on the line. It was apparent that he was looking up information on a notepad. "Um. Two years later she's admitted again with a concussion and a black eye."

"Damn," said Chuck.

"It gets worse, buddy," said Hawk solemnly. "You like this woman more than as a friend, don't you?"

Finally admitting the fact to someone other than himself, Chuck said, "Yes, Hawk, I do."

"Well, you better sit down," said Hawk. "Apparently, five years ago, he did a real number on her. He beat her up so badly, she was in the hospital for a week. Here's the kicker." Chuck listened intently. Hawk exhaled into the phone and said, "Chuck, she was pregnant."

"She was . . ."

"She lost the baby, Chuck," said Hawk. "As a result, she must have finally had enough evidence to get the divorce through. Plus, she got a restraining order."

Chuck was still a little stunned about the news. "A restraining order? Doesn't that mean he can't see her?"

"He's not even supposed to get anywhere near her," said Hawk. "A little further check on Moreland shows he was arrested for assault and battery of a coed in college. He must come from money because he got off. Turns out he's some kind of black belt or MMA guy or something. Probably thinks he's a bad ass. Can't whip up enough on men in the octagon, so he hits women."

"Any time served?" asked Chuck.

"No. He got probation. He's been clean since the last beating he gave Grace," said Hawk.

Chuck was thinking. "But he's still coming around her. What's his deal?"

"Some guys are like that, Chuck. It's called obsession. If he's still hangin' around Grace, it's because he still wants her. Probably to be his personal punching bag. Cops don't want to get involved in cases like this, because other things are happening in the world like fentanyl overdoses or stabbings or assaults and murders that keep them busy enough without following around some creep who is on a restraining order."

Chuck exhaled loudly into the phone. "How dangerous do you think he is?"

"If he was in her office this week, he's very dangerous," said Hawk.

Chuck said, "I need you to do me another favor."

"Let me guess! You want me to tail Grace Winters!"

"Look, Hawk. I'll even pay you for this," said Chuck. "I can't watch over her. Between . . ."

"Yeah, yeah, I know. Between hoop and school, you can't even keep track of yourself!" Hawk was smiling when he said, "I got it, Bubba!"

"I can't tell you how much this means. I'm worried about Grace and I'm sure this guy is messing with her."

"I got it, Chuck! Don't worry about a thing!" said Hawk. "And I don't want your damn money either!"

Chuck didn't know what to say. Nate Hawkins was always there when he needed him. "Thanks, Hawk. Thanks very much."

"You watch your ass too, mister! If this jerk finds out you're seeing Grace, he's liable to come after you, too. Keep your head on a swivel."

"I hope he does come after me! Then I know he's not trying to hurt Grace."

"You don't worry about Grace. I'll be watching Moreland," said Hawk. "Get some sleep. You got practice tomorrow." Hawk hung up the phone.

Get some sleep. That sounded like a good idea, but it wasn't to be. Between the plan to take down BCT and Moreland out there chasing Grace, Chuck couldn't even close his eyes. He tried to read some of his political science text, but that didn't work either. He finally got up, sat in front of the TV and watched SPORTSCENTER. With his mind numbed with scores and highlights, he drifted off to sleep on the couch.

Jeff Roberts called Steve James early the next morning. He had found a few interesting tidbits about the St. Michael's University situation. "Apparently, the player that was on the take decided not to run for us and had the guts to say no. Maybe he thinks he can get Name, Image and Likeness money at a D III school? Good luck with that! This kid told the assistant coach, who was working him for us that he wasn't gonna shave for us this year. The coach, who right up until the season starts says the kid is in, calls out of the blue and says they're both out! How do you like that for balls?"

"Does Grant know?" asked Steve.

"He found out yesterday and the word is he WENT OFF!" said Jeff. "I guess he told those guys in Austin to fix it! The quote was, nobody walks away from us! He told Tommy Clark to get them back on the payroll or get rid of both of them!"

James knew that would be the answer. Questions ran through his mind at warp speed. What had changed these men? Why was the St. Michael's program different this year? Could he do anything about it? He understood Grant's methods, he knew a contract would be coming out on one or both men at St. Michael's. It would probably be taken care of by the Austin folks, but maybe professionals. If it was Austin, that might give him a little more time to think about any changes he would need to make in his timeline, if anything. His final thought; would there be enough time for him to execute his plan?

Nate Hawkins took a different approach on the William Moreland situation. He found out where Moreland lived and began to observe him rather than wait around Grace's home for Moreland to 'visit'. He could have waited at Grace's home, but by watching Moreland, he was going straight to the source of the problem. If Moreland were to go anywhere near Grace, Hawk was going to be there. Hawk didn't want to stop his surveillance on Henderson, but Moreland had become the priority.

As for Henderson, he had seemed to be sticking to his agreement with Chuck. If Henderson chose to get with Tommy Clark and the BCT, Hawk wouldn't be there to stop him. Chuck had assured him he had help working on Clark and his operation in Austin. The BCT was out of Hawk's hands.

"Yes, Mr. Grant! Yes, sir! I'll take care of it!" said Tommy Clark into the phone. He couldn't wait to hang up, but Grant had his attention. Had Clark been in Vegas, Grant would have had a lot more than that. Tommy put the phone down like it was on fire.

"DAMN! I've heard him mad before, but never that hot!" said Tommy. He was in his office with two of his henchmen, one was an ex-University of Texas tennis star named Derrick and the other a large oaf who answered to the name of Nubbin. At one time, Derrick Monroe was the number three seed for the Texas Longhorn tennis program. With an amazing left-handed serve, he was once compared to John Lucas. His serve was once clocked at over 130 mph, but he never committed himself to improve any other facet of his game. Now he worked for Tommy Clark, finding suckers to lose money on bad bets. It was way too easy for a smooth talkin', good lookin', former sports star to set up the average Joe. He was destined to be a grifter. It was fate that Derrick ended up working for a fat, low-life like Tommy.

Nubbin, the other 'co-worker', made his name by playing some double A hockey for the local Ice Pirates team. Although Nubbin could skate, he had never scored a goal, led his team in penalty minutes, and was, without a doubt, the biggest goon in minor league hockey. Rather than work for the pittance he was paid in hockey, he took a job as Clark's lead headknocker. Nubbin's IQ was a point above the temperature of the ice he tried to skate on, and his toothless smile gave away his upstairs deficiency before he ever spoke a word.

"Whaddup, Tommy?" asked Derrick Monroe.

"I'll tell you, whaddup! That SOB Grant is out of his mind pissed!" said Tommy Clark. "He wants us to lean on Pete Henderson. If Henderson doesn't get Holmes to come around, he said 'we probably need to take out Holmes'."

Derrick looked at Nubbin, then at Clark. "You mean like . . . OUT?!"

Clark nodded, "Yeah, stupid. OUT!"

"Like in the hospital?" asked Nubbin.

Clark paused before saying, "Maybe even worse. He didn't really say it, but the implication is if he doesn't come around . . ." Clark couldn't bring himself to say, "kill them". He finished with, "Let's just see how it goes."

Nubbin said, "That's too bad, TC. Cause that kid Holmes has got a good game."

Derrick agreed. "Maybe if we lean on Henderson enough, Holmes will come around and we don't have to hurt him?"

Clark was quiet for a moment. "As much as I hate to leave, I think we need to take a little ride down to San Antonio, fellas."

Neither employee was happy at that prospect. "Get a good night's sleep, gents. We leave tomorrow."

It was what they were all waiting for. The first home game in the Armadillo Dome. The locker room was filled with the now familiar noise of players doing what they do to get ready to play. Holmes was in a corner dribbling. Parnell was listening to rap music and practicing some dance moves. Jose was in front of his locker trying not to throw up. Chuck walked by and nudged him. He stuck out his fist and the large man hit it. A smile appeared on Jose's face, and he said, "I'll be okay. Just a little nervous I guess."

Chuck smiled and mocked him. "I guess!" Then he pretended to throw up. He playfully smacked Jose and kept patrolling the locker room. He sat down next to Pepper who also looked white as a ghost.

"Hey, man. It's just like shootin' in practice. It's just that there's thousands of people screamin' at you!" Hoopman smiled and winked at Pepper.

"I ain't never played before more than a thousand people," said Pepper. "How about you?"

"Oh, yeah! I played before a crowd of over five thousand at the Armed Forces Championship. Pretty docile crowd. They had a real understanding of the game but didn't really care about who won. Everybody who plays is a winner there," Chuck said. "This is gonna be different, but it's still gonna be way cool!" He fist bumped the younger man and game him a thumbs up as he walked away.

Coach Round came into the room. It was time for the pre-game speech. Chuck looked forward to it. The team gathered around the coach and listened intently. "Fellas, it begins here. It begins tonight. You been working your butts off for most of your lives to get to this point." He looked at Chuck. "It's time to show what you got." He stuck his hand out and said, "Ya'll ready to go?"

There was a pause. Chuck looked around at the tense faces. He looked back at Round and asked, "Do you think maybe we should pray?!"

Round looked around at his team. There was some apprehension, but he saw nods of approval. "I guess it can't hurt." Everyone agreed except Henderson. "How about it, Hayes. You want to lead the prayer?"

"Um, sure." Chuck collected himself. He took Pepper and Jose's hands. The rest of the players and Round joined hands. Even Henderson reluctantly joined in.

Chuck cleared his throat and began, "Lord, first home game against a good team. Please watch over us and protect us. May you give us the guidance to make our shots true and keep us together in tough situations. We may ask you for a little bit more occasionally, but bear with us Lord. We'll get better and hope we don't need so much help. In Jesus name we pray, Amen!"

Everyone nodded and said "Amen". Round looked around. "Nicely done, Hoopman. I want to apologize for not doing that with you men before." Everyone smiled at Round. Round clapped his hands and yelled, "Now bring it in! On three, 'Dillo Defense'! One, two, three!"

The players yelled and headed out the door. Chuck waited an instant and came up to Round after the others had left. "Um. I was expecting a little more of a speech to get us psyched, you know?"

"The prayer probably works better than me giving a speech." Round laughed at his own joke, then got a bit serious. "Son, all the talkin' in the world ain't gonna get any of you guys any more psyched than you are now. You need to be ready. You're gonna get some minutes tonight. Get out there and show me somethin', Hayes!" said the coach with a grin. Chuck headed out the door with a smile. The coach waited till Chuck was out of the locker room, reached in his pocket and pulled out a painkiller. They weren't very big pills, but they made it easier to sit on the bench for an hour at a time.

Chuck ran out of locker room and was overwhelmed by the scene. The 'Dillo Dome' was out of control. The students were pumped up and every one of them was standing and stomping on the bleachers. The announcer yelled, "LADIES AND GENTLEMEN, YOUR RUNNING ARMADILLOS"!

From every speaker in the 'Hole' Van Halen was playing "Running With the Devil"! The only difference was the fans were singing 'Dillos' instead of Devil. Chuck shook his head in amazement. Warming up in his game sweats, talking with his teammates, getting pumped up all seemed new again. He stepped out of the lay-up rotation and went to half court. He took another minute to stretch and just take in the atmosphere. It was beautiful.

The moment passed as the announcer yelled, "LADIES AND GENTLEMEN! PLEASE ADDRESS YOUR ATTENTION TO THE SOUTH SIDE OF THE DOME!" The dome grew a little quieter as people looked around to figure which direction was south. Chuck noticed the cheerleaders bringing out a big mat.

The announcer came on the PA again, "LADIES AND GENTLEMEN, UP IN THE SKY! NOT A BIRD! NOT A PLANE! IT'S THE ARMOR DILLO!!!" From the support structure at the top of the gym the 'Armor Dillo', the St. Michael's mascot, jumped. He was attached to a cable that was hooked to a pulley. The Dillo came screaming out of the rooftops heading for the court! He came down the wire at twenty miles per hour, pulled a release cord, fell about ten feet and landed on the middle of the giant mat! As the mascot landed on his 'shell' and rolled along off the mat that he nearly missed. He had developed too much speed. For an instant it appeared he was roadkill that had just been hit by a truck. The Dillo rolled off the cushion that he almost missed, then lay in a motionless ball as he rolled onto the side of the court in front of the announcer's table. The crowd went quiet wondering if the mascot had injured himself in a stunt that went wrong. Chuck walked toward the crumpled pile of cloth, stuffing, and human.

In a moment of terror, Chuck realized that it was Marshall lying on the floor motionless. He took another step, and said quietly, "Marshall?"

Suddenly, the Dillo rolled over and got to his feet. The dome went berserk! Eight thousand people were on their feet cheering. The Armor Dillo lifted up his hands in a gesture of triumph. He had survived his first stunt!

Chuck walked over and said, "You knucklehead! You scared the crap outta me!"

"All part of the plan, Hoopman! I did a little rappelling with Mr. Hawkins and what can I say! I really dig rappelling!"

"You nearly killed yourself!" said Chuck.

"Pretty cool, wasn't it?" asked Marshall. Chuck couldn't see his face inside the head of the costume, but he could tell by his voice Marshall was having the time of his life.

Chuck conceded to the giant fur ball the stunt was cool. He walked over, grabbed his 'paw' and held it up. The place went nuts again. Chuck pulled the mascot around the center of the court and Marshall got a standing ovation from the crowd. Chuck said, "You better enjoy this, because you won't do that anymore!"

"Come on, Hoopman!" pleaded Marshall.

"Is your Mom gonna call me and ask me how I let her son get killed? No way!" Try as he might, he couldn't keep a straight face. "We'll talk about it later!"

"You need to finish warming up! GO KICK SOME BUTT!" yelled Marshall as he headed toward the sidelines. The Dillo Hole was still screaming its approval for the new mascot.

Chuck returned to the warm-ups with his team. He looked around the crowd in hopes that Grace Winters was there. She mentioned she was going to come to the game. He couldn't find her. The horn sounded it was game time. Chuck forgot about Grace. It was time to get serious.

The season home opener was against Lamar. It was a non-conference game against an opponent with four senior starters, two of which were over six foot eight. They were experienced, big and confident. The Dillo's started three players from last year's squad, Charles Holmes, David Parnell and Ojayeh Nudah. The next two starters were Lawrence Glynn at six foot eight and Tyrone "Bullet" DeVaugh. DeVaugh wasn't big at five ten, but his speed and jumping ability more than made up for his lack of height. In the gamblers line Lamar was supposed to have the game won in the first half. Lamar was picked to win by 18. Sometimes, the papers get it wrong.

From the opening tip, Lamar controlled everything above the shoulders. All rebounds, alley-oop passes and cross-court lobs were part of a pattern Lamar used to get St. Michael's back in a zone to prevent the two big guys from getting the ball low. When St. Michael's sat back in the zone, it freed up the two senior guards to shoot open three pointers. They moved the ball well and were very much in control of the game. With eight minutes gone in the first half, the score was Lamar 26, ST. MICHAEL'S 14. Bullet was called for a cheap reach-in foul giving him two for the game.

From somewhere on the sideline a chant started. It was only two or three people at first, but it got louder quickly as the student body picked it up.

"HOOPMAN! HOOPMAN! HOOPMAN!" Chuck sunk a little lower in his seat. He was embarrassed by the chant. Round looked down the bench, caught Chucks' eye and nodded.

Chuck looked at Pepper and said, "Here goes nothin'!"

Round smiled at Chuck and said, "Don't get too fancy out there. Don't want you to have first game jitters or anything. We gotta do somethin' different. Let's pick up a half court zone. Put Charles at the point. See if you get him fired up. It's like he's sleepwalkin'!"

"Coach, I might need some help in a couple of minutes," said Chuck as he nodded towards the bench.

Round had old habits that were hard to break. Chuck's suggestion to let some of the 'posse' play was met with a terse, "Let me be the coach, son!"

Chuck knew enough to keep his mouth shut. He nodded and trotted to the scorer's table. The fans went nuts.

Chuck went in for Bullet and ran to the lane for a defensive huddle. He called his teammates around to set the defense. Chuck said, "Coach wants a little pressure. Their guards aren't good passers so we're goin' with a 13C!" He looked at Charles and said, "He wants you on the point! I'll run the baseline and double down on the big guys! Let's go fellas! Come on!" They broke the huddle and Chuck headed to Charles. "I can't believe you only have two points! Neither of these guys is in your league. If I didn't know different, I'd say the old Charles was back." Charles gave Chuck an angry glance and bit his lip. Chuck caught the look and said, "Prove me wrong!"

The Lamar player missed the front end of his one-and-one and OJ got the ball. Chuck stepped back for the ball and took off at a full gallop. He dribbled through two players and drove hard to the basket. The center from the Lamar team tried to get in position to make a block. Chuck saw no one else from St. Michael's was running with him so he put the ball up high off the glass. The Lamar defender missed the ball and slammed into Chuck hard. Chuck went down without seeing the first shot of his college career. The roar from the crowd announced the shot went in. The ref blew the whistle, and Chuck was headed to the line for his chance at a three-point play. David Parnell was the first one there to pick him up.

"Welcome to college ball, Hoopman!" smiled Parnell.

"Thanks, Captain!" smiled Chuck right back.

He hit his foul shot and sprinted back on defense. In the one-three-one half court zone, Charles was at the point, David and Larry Glynn were at the foul extended, OJ was in the center position and Chuck was on the baseline. They applied pressure on the Lamar guards at half court. The tactic worked because the guards weren't ready to throw passes when they were contested from half court. They tried to work it around the outside, but the St. Michael's pressure was much more aggressive in the half court zone. A pass came inside to one of the Lamar big men, who then tried to make another pass across the lane. Chuck was invisible to the Lamar player as he stood behind OJ. The big man threw the pass and Chuck intercepted it in stride and headed the other way. Charles Holmes saw the steal and took off. From half court Chuck threw Charles a lob that Holmes buried with a one-handed jam! The Hole erupted again.

The next time down, Charles stole the ball and passed it to David. David hit Chuck on the run. He didn't have the numbers on the fastbreak, so he started to pull up. He dribbled outside the lane. Out of the corner of his eye he saw David Parnell running down the lane. Chuck rifled a no-look pass to David in stride. David went up strong over the Lamar center. He tried to block the shot but missed. Parnell slammed it home and held on the rim as the center bounced off him. The ref blew the whistle again as the Lamar player was called for the foul.

It was the third on the Lamar center and he headed for the bench. David got a three-point play and St. Michael's was down by four. Then the crowd began another chant, "BOOM, BOOM!" The chant was being yelled throughout the dome. Chuck looked over to the scorer's table to see Dex, Jose and Pepper coming into the game. Larry Glynn, OJ and Charles came out. Chuck called the team together for a huddle. "Welcome to the game, fellas."

"Coach Round says try a man-to-man!" said Pepper.

Chuck nodded and looked right at Jose. "All right, Big Man! This is on you. They got one big guy left on the floor and he's all yours! Pepper, you, and I have those guards. Now we're gonna overplay the jump shot and make 'em drive. When we do, David, you be the help side because Jose's on the moose! DT, hit the boards, man! Any questions?" There were none. "Let's bust it open!"

The man-to-man worked perfectly. With Pepper and Chuck overplaying the outside shots, their guards could drive around, but were always stopped by Dex and David Parnell. On defense, Lamar tried to play a zone. Chuck and Pepper destroyed it. When they came out of a timeout in man-to-man, Jose hit a hook shot that brought the house down. Round went with the flow and left the team on the floor. By half time, St. Michael's was up 42 to 34.

Lamar never recovered. St. Michael's played even with the Lamar starters for the first ten minutes of the second half. When Chuck, Pepper, Jose and Dex entered the game, they built a fifteen-point lead and finished up the game without allowing a serious threat from Lamar. The final score was Lamar 62, ST. MICHAEL'S 92. Parnell led all scorers with 22, Pepper had 16, Jose had 12 rebounds and 10 points in twenty minutes, and Charles Holmes had 10 points, 10 rebounds and six steals. For his part, Chuck finished with eight points and fifteen assists. The locker room was filled with the happiness that only comes from victory. Round gave a post-game speech that was even shorter than his pre-game one. Chuck never said a word to him after the game. He merely gave the coach a thumbs up and a nod. The coach responded with a smile and a spit of tobacco into his ever-present Coke can.

Conspicuously absent from the locker room was Pete Henderson. He was outside the Hole in an alley smoking a cigarette. The three men approached him from inside the Hole. Henderson threw the cigarette on the ground and stamped it out with his foot. He knew better than to try and run.

"Not a bad start, Pete. If I hadn't been here to see it, I would have never believed it," said Tommy Clark. "Considering you were supposed to lose by 18."

"Yeah. How 'bout that!" said Henderson feebly. "Good thing you didn't bet on the game, eh, Tommy?"

"Yeah, good thing," said Clark. "We're gonna go for a little ride, Pete. I hope you didn't have any plans for after the game?"

Pete didn't say a word. Nubbin walked up to Henderson, looked down on the man and said, "Let's go, shithead."

For just an instant, Pete thought about screaming. Perhaps if he kicked Nubbin in the groin, he could run back inside and get some help. Or maybe Chuck Hayes would pop out of the door like Superman and keep him from getting beaten up. But he couldn't scream, Nubbin probably wouldn't have felt Pete's kick, and nobody was gonna walk out the door and save him.

Henderson exhaled heavily, turned around and headed for the parking lot.

Hawk worked the zipper on the back of the 'Armordillo' costume. "That was outstanding, Mr. Hawkins! I mean outstanding! The rappel at half time was fantastic, too!"

Hawk looked at the younger man and smiled. The kid was drenched in sweat. His face was lit up like Christmas. "You were quite a show, Marshall."

"How's the robot coming?" asked Marshall as he pulled off the rest of the costume.

Hawk frowned a little. "I must admit I haven't really had time to do anything about it just yet. I've been a little bit preoccupied with something else. But I'll have something for you next month. Promise!"

"COOL!" said Marshall with a huge grin. "You gonna come to the game next week?"

Hawk was slow to respond, but finally said, "Yeah, Marshall, I wouldn't miss it for the world." Then he looked at his watch. "Oh, crap! Look, I got someplace to be! I'll see you next week, okay! Great job tonight!"

Marshall hollered as Hawk ran away, "AND I WANT TO GO RAPPELLING AGAIN!"

Hawk sat in his van and looked at the map on his cell phone. A blinking yellow light that indicated a GPS signal appeared on the map. Hawk studied the map and then looked at the light again. He looked up from the map and cried, "DAMN IT!"

Hawk thought everything would be fine and he could go to the game. Take just two hours to see the opener. He thought he could see Chuck and Marshall in the Dome for the opener. Moreland had stayed away from Grace for the last week. Moreland decided tonight was the night to visit Grace. The thought passed through Hawk's mind that Moreland may have known he was being tailed. It was too late to second-guess his actions right now. He swore out loud as he turned on the van and left a trail of burnt rubber as he sped out of the parking lot. He had to get to Grace Winter's house.

Hawk stopped across the street and one house away. He turned off his lights and looked at Grace's house. As he looked around Grace Winter's home, he saw the rear end of a car parked in the driveway. The GPS tracking device was working perfectly. Hawk knew instantly it was William Moreland's Nissan because he had put the device in the wheel well two weeks ago. The lights were off in the house.

Hawk reached into his glove compartment and pulled out his Beretta. He quietly got out of the car and walked to the side entrance of the house. He looked in the window and could see a light on in a room down the hall. That was when he heard the thump from somewhere in the bowels of the house. Twenty-five years as a military cop took over. He opened the door and slowly walked through.

The kitchen was dark, and it took a moment for his eyes to adjust. That's when he heard the noise. He couldn't make it out at first, so he moved down the hallway closer to the sound. He glanced in the dark living room and saw nothing. Then he heard the noise again. It was soft crying. Hawk turned and headed to the noise.

WHAM! The force of the blow knocked him to his knees. Hawk caught himself before he hit the ground. As he turned, he saw men's black shoes running down the hallway. Hawk shook his head as he tried to clear the stars away. When he tried to stand, he nearly blacked out. The light from the bedroom was low, but he could finally see it through the darkness. He took a couple steps and heard crying.

He staggered to the bedroom door and rested against the stoop. He heard Grace before he saw her. She was rolled up tightly in a naked ball in the corner of the bedroom. Her eyes were wide with terror.

Hawk took a step toward her, and she recoiled in fear. The whimper grew louder. Hawk stood still and whispered, "My name is Nate. Nate Hawkins. I'm a friend of Chuck's. I'm not gonna hurt you. I swear. Let me . . . let me get that blanket for you, okay?" Grace didn't move. Hawk grabbed the blanket and slowly moved toward her. Her eyes flickered a couple of times as she tried to come back to reality. She looked at Hawk cautiously. He moved slowly and tried to talk to her again. "Call me Hawk. Chucks' friend. Here. Take this blanket." He slowly covered her and then stepped back.

Hawk sat back against the wall as his head started to pound. He reached back and felt the blood. Grace saw it and recoiled again. "I'm okay. Just got hit on the head." He tried to smile to calm her, but he couldn't.

Grace took the blanket and sat up. She exhaled loudly and looked up at Nate as he sat on the bed. She wiped her face and started to stand up but couldn't. She wiped away her tears and said, "I suppose both of us need to go to the hospital." Nate stood up slowly and stuck out his hand to help Grace up. She looked at the hand, considered not taking it, then slowly reached for it. As she tried to stand, she bent over at the waist and groaned. As she stood, she looked up with tears in her eyes and said, "I think we need to hurry." She looked Hawk in the eye and said quietly, "Don't tell Chuck. Please don't tell him." Then she took a step and said, "I think something inside me is . . ." then she collapsed into Hawk's arms. He set her on the bed and called 911.

Hawk looked at the phone on the lobby wall, tossed between calling Chuck and walking back down the hall. Grace was in surgery; he'd gotten seven stitches in the back of his head, and the one thing his friend asked him to do, he had failed to accomplish the mission. William Moreland had struck at precisely the moment Hawk stopped observing him. He asked himself over and over what if this, what if that, why wasn't Grace at the game? The bottom line was, he let his friend down. What was worse, Grace Winters was having her spleen removed because he had let her down. He knew what he had to do. He picked up the phone to call Chuck.

"What the hell were you thinkin' about?" said Chuck with a huge smile. "Man, you could of killed yourself!"

"Yeah, I could have! But wasn't it great?" beamed Marshall. "Hawk is gonna teach me how to rappel from those really big towers."

The phone rang interrupting their conversation. Chuck looked at the clock. It was nearly midnight. "Who can this be?"

Marshall grabbed the phone. "Yellow!!!" He looked at Chuck and said, "Speak of the devil, it's Hawk." He turned back to the phone, "Pretty awesome tonight, eh?!" Hawk said something and Marshall got quiet. "What?" There was another pause and Marshall said, "Yeah, sure." He turned to Chuck and stuck out the phone. He was dead serious, "He needs to see you right now. He says he's at the hospital emergency room." Marshall swallowed hard. "He says Ms. Winters is in surgery, and you need to go over there."

Chuck was stunned but was immediately in motion. "Tell him I'm on my way!"

"How is she, Hawk!" said Chuck.

"Doctor says she's going to be all right. It might take a little time, but she's gonna be fine!" said Hawk.

"Can I see her?" asked Chuck.

"I don't think so. Not just yet," said Hawk.

Chuck nodded in understanding. Then he noticed the bandages on the back of Nate's head. "What the hell. . . ?"

"Got whacked," Hawk said as if he was a little kid that had been caught doing something wrong.

"Damn, Nate! What happened?"

Nate decided to give Chuck the short version. He sat on a chair and said, "I'm sorry! I screwed up, Chuck. I went to the game. Moreland hadn't done shit for two weeks. I thought he was backing off. Well, I thought wrong." He turned away.

"Don't blame yourself for this. It was Moreland? Are you sure?"

Nate Hawkins nodded and looked up at Chuck. "I had a marker on his car. After the game, when I left the Hole, I saw his car was at Grace's house. When I went in, he hit me from behind and bugged out. When I found Grace, she was on the floor. In the bedroom."

Chuck didn't want to ask the next question. He started with, "Was she. . . ?"

He didn't need to finish it. Hawk knew what he was asking. Chuck wanted to know if she had been raped. Nate Hawkins nodded and put his head down. "I'm pretty sure of it."

A feeling of anger swept over him. "What about Moreland?"

"I called the cops. They got an APB out on him," said Hawk. Then he added, "But he's as good as gone. He's probably on his way to Dallas or Houston by now. I'm sorry, Chuck."

"Not your fault, Nate. This is all on Moreland." Chuck turned and walked to look out the window. He didn't know what to do. He couldn't go to her. He couldn't go after Moreland. In the last five hours, he had gone from the greatest high in his life, to what may have been his lowest. For the first time in his life, Chuck Hayes felt helpless.

CHAPTER ELEVEN

"How'd St. Michael's do?" asked Steve.

Jeff Roberts looked at the computer screen. "Oh, man! They kicked butt. They were supposed to lose by 18, yet they won big!?"

"That doesn't sound like they're in the program to me!"

"Naw. It would have at least been close, right?" asked Jeff.

"Oh, yes. It would have been within 18 if someone was still shavin'."

Steve rubbed his aching knee. "After the systems check, let's check out their home page and see what they're doing different. Something has changed there. Maybe we can find out if it's a new coach or new players. We need to see what it is that has turned them around."

It was dawn before they let Chuck know Grace Winters' condition. She was stable and expected to recover fully. William Moreland had beaten and raped Grace. Nate Hawkins' arrival must have prevented him from continuing the ruthless attack. There were bruises on her ribs and pelvis area that indicated he used his feet on her. She had a separated shoulder, a ruptured spleen that was removed in surgery, and three cracked ribs. There was a dark spot under her right eye where Moreland had probably punched her, but for the most part that was the extent of the visual damage. The doctor informed Chuck that the emotional damage would be entirely up to Grace's mental state. Most victims of this type of "event" as he called it, would be psychologically impaired for the rest of their lives.

A nurse came to tell Chuck he could see her. She said, "Miss Winters is awake. Please don't stay too long. She needs as much rest as she can get." Chuck nodded and followed her into Grace's room. Chuck looked at her lying in bed and tried to manage a smile. It wouldn't appear. He walked over to her and slowly grabbed her hand, gently squeezing it.

Grace was the first one to speak. "I told your friend not to tell you. I didn't want you to know." She sniffed to try and keep the tears from coming. It didn't work. Grace Winters started to cry. Chuck saw her tears and he bent over to hold her. Seeing her pain and her sorrow was too much for Chuck. The tears welled up in his eyes, and he began to cry as well. Remembering all the injuries the doctor had indicated, Chuck carefully lay on the bed next to her. He got as close to her as he could. He laid his head on hers and gently rubbed her hair. One of his teardrops hit her forehead and he softly wiped it away. He held her as gently as he could while she cried. Chuck stayed there on the bed holding her. Five minutes later, she was asleep in his arms in the only place she felt safe.

Two days later, Nate Hawkins came by to check on Grace. Chuck was there sleeping next to the bed. He nudged his friend and waved him outside. Chuck got up and followed him. "I got a question for you. You ever meet Moreland before?"

Chuck nodded, "Yeah, just once in Grace's office."

"Did he get your name? Did he know you?" asked Hawk.

"I don't remember. Maybe Grace mentioned me to him. Why?"

"I think he must have known you played ball," said Hawk.

Chuck nodded, "That means he was expecting me not to be around because the game was goin' on."

Grace saw someone she thought was Chuck standing in the doorway and said, "Chuck? Is that you?"

Chuck quickly turned and came back to her on the bed. Nate followed slowly. She saw him and immediately remembered. "You're the man who . . ."

"Yes, ma'am. I brought you here," said Hawk with just a trace of a frown.

"I never got to thank you properly," said Grace.

"That's not necessary," said Hawk as he looked down at his toes.

"What were you doing there? At my house?" asked Grace.

Hawk was silent. He stubbed his foot into the ground and looked at Chuck.

"I had him watching you," said Chuck. Grace looked at Chuck confused. "Unfortunately, Nate came to see the game."

"I was supposed to be watching Moreland," said Nate uncomfortably.

Grace just looked at Hawk and nodded. "William is definitely not a basketball fan. I think he's more into boxing." She tried to laugh as she said it, but her ribs hurt too much. Chuck and Hawk found no humor in her comment.

Hawk cleared his throat and asked, "Did you tell him about Chuck? You two are seeing each other, right?"

She nodded, "I told him I was seeing somebody. I told him he was a basketball player and a student. He met Chuck in my office one afternoon, and he must have put two and two together."

Chuck and Hawk nodded. Hawk was the first to speak. "He chose that time because he knew the game was going on."

Grace said, "He asked to see me, or I would have gone to the game, too." She started to cry again. "He said it was going to be over. He said he was leaving." The tears came again.

Hawk nodded to Chuck and said, "I've . . . I've gotta go." Chuck went over to Grace and held her.

"Thanks for coming, Hawk," said Chuck.

Hawk just frowned. He wanted to say he was sorry for not being in the right place at the right time before but knew better. "Yeah, sure thing, Chuck." He didn't need to say anything else. The cops were looking all over the state for Moreland. There wasn't anything else he could do to help Grace. Hawk turned and headed out the door. It was time for him to focus on something else. Hawk had missed the boat on Moreland. He was not going to miss the boat on the BCT.

Chuck stayed with Grace until she got her composure back. They talked for a few more minutes. Grace was beginning to feel better. She said, "Don't you think it's about time you got back to school. What's it been? Two days now?"

Chuck smiled, "I have other priorities right now."

"If you mean me, this priority is gonna be just fine," said Grace. "I think it's time you got back to school and basketball."

Chuck said, "I called Coach Round and told him I needed some personal time. He understands I wouldn't miss practice unless it was important." He looked at her, kissed her hand and said softly, "And this is important." Grace smiled and laid her head on his shoulder. "I'm here for you, Grace. As long as you need me."

Grace Winters was a strong woman. Stronger than Chuck gave her credit for. As much as she loved Chuck Hayes, what she really needed was time. Time to allow herself to recover. Time to be alone and heal. It was difficult for her to say, but it was the truth and she needed to tell Chuck. "I just need some time to get over this and I'll be fine." She saw the words register in Chuck's mind. "You have things going on in your life you need to do. I know that."

Chuck's smile disappeared. She was politely asking him to leave. "Sure, but . . ."

She didn't let him finish. "You go get back to what you were doing. Give me . . . a little time." Chuck nodded and stepped away from the bed. He understood she was being truthful. "I want to thank you for being here for me, Chuck."

There was a moment of silence. Chuck didn't know what to say. He still was holding her hand. He bent over and kissed her on the cheek. It was time to go. "I'll be around." He stepped backwards toward the door and said, "Whenever you're ready, just call me." He turned and left before she could say 'Goodbye'.

When Chuck got outside the hospital, looked to the heavens and said, "Lord, you have a strange way of looking out for people. I think you missed the boat on watching over Grace. It will be hard for me to forgive you for that. I also want you to forgive me if I ever get my hands on Moreland. I will not turn the other cheek. Amen."

On the basketball court, it didn't take long for things to change. Late in the second half of the next game, Chuck had finally got a chance to play. Round had kept him on the bench for missing practice for "personal reasons". Chuck was none too talkative about why he had missed two practices, and for that, Round decided it was the best thing for team harmony to keep him on the bench for the first part of the game. Finally, with the game almost over, Chuck got in.

Jose was shooting foul shots when Chuck noticed Henderson talking to Charles. Henderson's right arm was in a sling for some reason, but Chuck never bothered to ask him why. He was pointing to Charles Holmes and then at the scoreboard with his free arm. St. Michael's was in control, up by fifteen. Chuck had a mental note that reminded him they were supposed to beat SE Louisiana by twenty. After another minute, Chuck was being pulled for Charles Holmes. Henderson had a shit-eating grin. When Chuck looked at him, the assistant coach merely looked away. Something was going on.

A large pit started to develop in Chuck's stomach. Chuck got up and knelt next to Round. "Why'd you pull me out, coach?"

"Charles needs another assist for a double-double. Don't worry, when he gets another assist, I'll have you right back in," said the coach.

Chuck checked the score. The Dillo's were up by nineteen. He sat down and did the math. As he watched Charles throw one pass away and let his man shoot a wide-open ten-footer, Chuck didn't have to watch the scoreboard anymore. Charles never got his tenth assist, and Chuck never went back in as the Armadillos won by eighteen. Southeastern Louisiana had covered the spread.

Chuck was slow to leave the bench. His anger was hidden beneath his calm exterior. But it was obviously not hidden well enough. Coach Round noticed it. He walked over to Chuck and said, "Hey, no sweat, Hoopman! I'm sorry I didn't get you back in there. That darn Holmes never did get another assist."

"No problem, coach. Next time!" Chuck tried to be cordial. Deep down, he knew exactly what had happened. He didn't know whom to approach first; Holmes to find out why he was back on the payroll, or Henderson to finally put him out of his misery.

Chuck dressed quickly and headed for the bus. Henderson was already sitting on the bus looking out the window. He tried not to look at Chuck as he stood next to him. Chuck smacked the seat and said tersely, "How much?"

The color ran from Henderson's face. The cigarette he started to light nearly fell out of his hand. "What's that?"

Chuck moved closer and said, "How much did you make off the game?"

Henderson decided he shouldn't play stupid with Chuck. He put the cigarette in his mouth and said, "Enough to make a couple of car payments."

Chuck took his hand and smashed the coach's head against the window. The unlit cigarette flew over Chuck's head. "Listen to me," hissed Chuck inches away from Henderson's ear. "IT'S OVER! You are gonna tell the coach what the hell is going on or I will! You got me?" He slowly released his grip from Henderson's face. "You tell him!"

"I don't think so, Hoopman," said Henderson. "I had to get it goin' again." Henderson shrugged his sore shoulder and tried to regain his composure. "I'm into my friends pretty good on a couple of loans. They don't see me just walkin' away." A tear appeared in his eye, and he looked at Chuck. "What do you think happened to my shoulder last week? You think I slipped on some soap?"

The light came on for Chuck. The BCT had blackmailed Henderson. Probably Holmes too. Chuck was angry again. "Damn it, Pete! Come to me. I told you I would help you," said Chuck.

Henderson shook his head in disagreement. "No. You can't help me. And you can't help Charles," said Pete Henderson. There was an awkward silence until Pete coughed to clear his throat. "I don't think you're gonna tell the coach anything either."

Chuck shook his head and said, "Why the hell shouldn't I?"

"Because they're gonna kill us if we don't play for them," said Henderson.

"They aren't going to kill you, Pete! They only want to scare you. They're into intimidation and money. Killin' people isn't good for business," said Chuck. Boldly he said, "I can stop them."

Chuck had said it so deliberately that, for a moment, Henderson had no doubt that Chuck meant every word he had said. He swallowed hard and tried to divert Chuck's anger. "There is nothing you can do," said Henderson as he pulled out another cigarette. He turned to Chuck and said, "It happened tonight, and it'll happen again." He looked straight ahead and lit the cigarette.

Chuck started to say something else when suddenly, Coach Round climbed on the bus. The coach stopped at the top of the stairs and looked at the two men. The bus was lit enough so he could see the anger in Chuck's face. "What's this?"

Henderson was the first to speak. "We were just discussing the game."

Chuck was silent. Coach Round looked at each man and frowned. He had a feeling Chuck had approached his assistant about why Chuck hadn't played more. Round knew the two men didn't like each other. But their dispute seemed to have faded since the season started. Round thought he figured it out. Hayes was just angry because Holmes had gone in for him in the last couple of minutes. Probably Hayes thought Pete had put the word in to play Charles. He eyed Chuck and said, "I decided to let Charles play, to try and get that assist. That was my decision, Hayes. Not Pete's!"

"That's not it, Coach," said Chuck. "We were just talking about . . ."

Round cut him off. For the first time a bit of anger appeared in his voice. "I don't care what you were talkin' about, Chuck! It's over. I'll get you some more playin' time next game."

Chuck was silent. He looked at Henderson. Pete turned and said to Chuck, "We don't have anything else to talk about, Coach. Do we, Chuck?"

Chuck looked at Round and started to speak. He had lost another battle to Henderson. He exhaled loudly. "No, Coach. No, we don't have anything else to say to each other." He looked down at Henderson. He couldn't leave it alone without one more jab. "We are through talkin'! It is over, isn't it, Coach Henderson?"

Henderson looked at Round and nodded. Then looked out the window and took a pull from his cigarette. Chuck turned and walked to the back of the bus. He knew it wasn't over. Chuck needed time to think.

The bus ride home wasn't exactly the place he had in mind to try and make decisions with his teammates in a great mood. Outside he was smiling. Inside, a fire was burning. For most of the ride, Chuck was quiet. Pepper and Jose wanted to joke around and talk about the good old days before the season started. But Chuck's mind was elsewhere. His friends picked up on Chuck's emotions and soon began to heckle Bullet about his shaved head.

Chuck wondered what to do next. He thought about calling Eddie when he got home to execute the first phase of the plan against BCT. Then he decided against it. He figured the best way to approach the situation was to talk with Charles Holmes. He could be a valuable ally if things headed in the wrong direction. Hawk had been correct about Henderson all along. It was just a matter of time until Henderson's fear got the better of him. The BCT had manipulated their way back into St. Michael's program and Henderson was too weak to stop them.

As the bus pulled into the parking lot, everyone was slow to get off except Charles Holmes. He was out of his seat and nearly off the bus before it stopped. Henderson must have talked to him thought Chuck. When Chuck got off the bus, he hollered for Holmes. Charles turned, looked at Chuck and continued to hustle away. He quickly disappeared behind a building and into the darkness. Chuck turned to Henderson who quickly looked away. That was enough for him. Henderson had gotten to Charles Holmes, and he wouldn't be any help at all. At that moment, the decision was made to start operations against the BCT.

When he got home, Chuck made two phone calls. The first one was to Hawk. Chuck told him how Grace was doing and that she needed time to recover. That meant he would leave her alone until she was willing to get close again. Next, he apologized to Hawk for not trusting his instincts on Henderson. He let Hawk know that BCT had gotten to Henderson, and the assistant had gotten Charles to keep the game closer than it should have been. Chuck knew Moreland was gone, so he asked Hawk to help Eddie with the operation if it wasn't too much trouble. The holidays were coming up, and he didn't want Hawk to get overly involved with the BCT situation after he had spent so much time watching Moreland. Chuck wanted to make sure he had enough time with his wife. Nate Hawkins told Chuck, "Don't you worry about us. You take care of Grace when she's ready. Keep your head into hoop because sooner or later your teammates are gonna need you."

Chuck agreed and became silent. There was nothing more for them to discuss. He cleared his throat and said one more apology. He promised he would see Nate when they got together at Eddie's place.

The next call was to Eddie. It was after three in the morning, and he could tell the man had been awake. The call was short and to the point. "Hi, Eddie. It's Chuck. As soon as you can, send the first message."

Eddie hesitated but understood. "Okay. That's done easy enough. Do you want anything else?" he asked with a serious tone in his voice.

"No. Prep the Denial of Service and be ready to start that. They will think we're bluffing. Then look at adding a couple of the other specific options we talked about. Let's see what happens when somebody visits their net. Does Chris have something in place so it can't be traced back to us?"

"Oh, yeah!" Chuck could hear the smile in Ed's voice.

"Good job. Talk to you tomorrow." Chuck hung up the phone and headed to bed. It was hard to sleep because he was angry. He took a deep breath and exhaled slowly. He closed his eyes and said a prayer. Just a quick one to ask the Lord to help him control his anger. To help him be a better man. One more deep breath and he finally calmed down. The fire was burning inside ready when Chuck needed it.

On Wednesday night, November 18th, at 1930 hours Central Standard Time, across 538 computer screens connected to the Big Casino Texas internet system, the message: "DON'T BET ON COLLEGE BASKETBALL. BIG CASINO TEXAS IS CHEATING YOU." flashed for sixty seconds.

Carl Holden was Tommy Clark's network security manager at BCT. His top net monitor, Mike Thompson, noticed the message immediately. No stranger to people attempting to interfere with their network, Holden and Thompson handled the "hack" in stride. They never ceased operations or altered their activity. They monitored the time, duration and activity of the intrusion. The event was nothing compared to other events they had taken on.

After sixty seconds, activity resumed as if nothing had happened. "Do you want to notify Mr. Clark?"

Holden shook his head no. "Naw. If we tell the boss every time we get something like this, it's just pisses him off."

"You want to notify that geek the Vegas guys got?" asked Thompson.

Holden thought for a moment. Procedure called for any network administrator to notify Steve James of any intrusion. "No, not unless it happens again."

"What about the money Clark didn't make for that minute?" asked Thompson.

"Hell, Mikey! One minute of down time isn't jack to these guys!" said Holden. "We'll let him know if and when it's gonna really cost him. A hundred thousand dollar minute is chump change to him."

"Think it'll keep anybody from bettin'?" asked Mikey.

"No way, man! It'll probably give us some advertisement!" laughed Carl. Holden made a mental note of the appearance of the message and finally got serious about his job. "Mikey, try to ID the source and let's see if we can categorize him."

It was actually closer to a quarter million dollars lost when bets couldn't be accomplished, and money wasn't transferred. In the big scheme of things, the message interruption was really a minor problem. Twenty-four hours later, the only thing they could determine was that someone in Brazil had a grudge against BCT or college hoop gambling online. The event was quietly swept under a "virtual" rug without another thought.

Chuck was walking across campus when he saw Charles Holmes. It was time for a little talk. Chuck waved him over. Reluctantly, Charles Holmes crossed the grass and walked next to Chuck. Chuck looked around and started the conversation with him, "I know Henderson's got you under his thumb again. I told you I'd help you. What's goin' on?"

Charles didn't want to say but gave in relatively quickly. "Henderson told me he was in big trouble. He just needed that one game. Just the one."

Chuck shook his head, "You know better than that! Just this one, then just the next one. Then the next! When is it gonna stop?"

"That was it! Never again," said Charles. "I did my last trick for that guy."

Chuck wanted so badly to believe it was the truth. What else could he do? He started walking slowly backwards. "I'll take your word on that, Charles." Charles was a good kid. Maybe he really believed Henderson's line about "just one game". If there were a next time, Chuck would not go so lightly on Charles. He knew it was BCT that was pulling the strings. That's where his anger needed to be directed. Not at Charles.

"Anyone stop gamblin'?" asked Chuck.

"Are you kidding? They lost over two hundred thousand dollars. And we ticked off some online gamblers for a minute, but business, as far as we can tell, didn't even slow down," said Eddie.

"Well, the fact is we sent them a message. Hopefully we got someone's attention," said Chuck.

"Losing money is what gets their attention!" said Eddie. "I've been thinking. We could prepare a couple things that will cost 'em lots of money. The Denial of Service is already in place, so I think we could do some manipulation. But that takes more in-depth involvement. Bobby can help us."

Chuck thought about the suggestion. If it would hit the BCT in the wallet, he was all for it. "All right. Turn him loose. See what he can come up with!"

The next game was a home game. The student body was into the game like never before. There was talk across campus about the new and improved mascot. Something big was supposed to happen at the game. The Armadillos mascot name was now unofficially changed to the "Armordillo". The team was an unexpected seven and zero and getting recognized for their grit. New Mexico State was visiting the 'Dillo Hole with their own six and zero record. They were a run and gun bunch, built for speed. NM State was picked to win by at least ten points.

The first half started off badly. It was all State. They were fast, athletic, and experienced. With the score, State 22, St. Michael's 8, Round called a timeout. Before Chuck joined the huddle, he happened to catch some of the excitement in the stadium. Across the court, the student body was on their feet hollering for their beloved 'Dillo's. Even with the roaring crowd, Chuck could feel the nervousness in the air.

The announcer got on the microphone and out of nowhere came, "THE ARMORDILLO"! It was Marshall in his "new" Dillo costume. It was a combination armadillo and tank. The shell was oversized and sported St. Michael's colors. The familiar Gold and Black of the 'Armordillo' matched the trimmings that adorned the Hole. The head of the costume looked like an armadillo, but with an attitude. The "beast" looked downright angry! The ears looked more like horns. The chest was covered with a camouflage shield. Marshall walked in front of the student body and started jumping around with the cheerleaders. The shell had a seam down the back that split the shell in half. Suddenly Marshall did something to his costume, and a canon appeared out of the shell on his back. The shell housed a canon made from PVC pipe which was painted to look like the canon of an M1 tank. Marshall triggered a switch that made the canon fire little "St. Michael's Dillo Basketballs" up into the stands. The Hole was going nuts.

Chuck was smiling at his roommate's antics when his train of thought was interrupted. "HAYES!" Coach Round had called his name. "I want you to go in at point. Charles, you move to shooting guard! We have got to slow this game down, or they are gonna run us to Houston! We're getting our butts kicked on offense!" Everyone was stunned to hear Coach Round shouting. No one had seen him this animated in years. "Just slow the tempo down. I guarantee you'll take them out of their game." They broke the huddle and headed onto the court.

Charles walked over to Chuck and said, "That point has got a mean cross-over! But he wants to end up going to his right. Always to his right!"

"Got it!" said Chuck. "I got you on that bank shot on the right. It's been there all night!" Charles nodded and a smile appeared. "These guys ain't nothin'!" Chuck walked over to Holmes and spoke in his ear, "If we take our time, they can't play with us, Charles."

Suddenly the crowd picked up on Marshall's chanting voice. "HOOPMAN! HOOPMAN! HOOPMAN!"

Charles stuck his hand out to Chuck. "Let's go, Hoopman!" Chuck slapped at the hand and nodded. It was his time. He was being put into the line up to try and pull his team together and win. It was what he had been doing since he was ten years old. In all the excitement, the noise of the crowd, the yelling by the coaches and cheerleaders, he was very much at peace. Chuck crossed himself, said a quick prayer, looked to the heavens and smiled broadly. He knew exactly what had to be done. Now it was time to do it.

Down by fourteen, Holmes took the ball out and hit Chuck at the top of the key. Chuck didn't hesitate. He faked with a jab step and then pulled up and fired. The ball went into the basket as if guided by a laser. SWISH! The crowd erupted. The chants of HOOPMAN began again, but with more feeling and resonance. Soon the Hole was chanting "HOOPMAN" in unison.

Without announcing it, Chuck and Charles started their own two-man press. Chuck worked hard to front the State point guard on the out of bounds pass. When the pass was lobbed over his head to avoid Chuck, Charles had anticipated the play. He intercepted the pass and started for the basket. As the defender came after

Charles, he threw a bullet pass to Chuck as he stepped to the corner. Chuck caught the ball, dribbled backwards behind the three-point line, and fired. The State point guard tried in vain to block the shot, and only got Chuck's hand. The referee blew the whistle. The shot went in, and Chuck was headed to the foul line. The Hole erupted.

As Chuck stepped to the foul line, Marshall quieted the crowd down. He kept the chant of "HOOPMAN!" going, but it was controlled, almost whispered in unison by the fans. The shot was perfect, and within ten seconds, Chuck had cut the lead to seven.

After he had gotten the State players' attention, it was easy to move the ball to open people. Scoring was no longer a problem for St. Michael's. Players who weren't open before were open in better positions for them to score as Chuck was getting the attention of both guards. Chuck kept the tempo slow, just like Round told him. He walked the ball up the floor, made at least two passes to his teammates and made sure they didn't shoot until there were five seconds or less left on the clock. This frustrated State because they could no longer run up and down the floor. With the pace of the game under control, St. Michael's was in the driver's seat.

Parnell became a one-man wrecking crew inside against the man-to-man defense. When State switched to zone, Charles fired fifteen-foot jumpers as if it were practice. When Jose came in, the skyhook was on fire. Chuck made sure he got it to him at exactly the right point. With his position established, the shot was easy money.

On defense, things were a little tougher. The State point guard was lightning quick. Chuck had to use extra energy to keep up with him. But for the most part he shut him down. The advantage went to Charles who completely stopped the State shooting guard. OJ, Jose, Parnell and Dexter Thomas took control of the lane and the backboards. With five minutes left, Round brought in the second team. The Dillo's were up by twenty. Pepper and Chuck closed out the contest playing catch at half court.

When it was over, Chuck had hit seven more free throws, had four steals, five rebounds and an amazing seventeen assists. He had only taken two jump shots. The two that started the turnaround. Charles led the team with seventeen, Parnell had fifteen, Chuck had 14, and Thomas had 13, Jose finished with ten, and Pepper closed out with eight. The final score was 83-68. The players were happy, the student body was happy, Coach Round was happy, and Chuck was in heaven. The only person not smiling was Pete Henderson.

When Chuck got home, Marshall greeted him with a huge hug and a high five. Marshall had the biggest smile that Chuck had ever seen. He was playing "Let The Good Times Roll" from the Cars CD. Five other students were in the room including two of the St. Michael's cheerleaders. Chuck was impressed at the social progress his roommate was making in college. What was even more impressive than his newfound fame, was the fact he was keeping his grades up.

"HOOPMAN!!" said Marshall. He introduced Chuck like the good host Chuck had taught him to be. Chuck nodded and talked with the visitors for about thirty minutes. The fans were extremely happy about the way the Dillo's were playing and particularly with Chuck's play. Chuck refused to have a beer with the group, claiming curfew rules. The small group understood and didn't hassle Chuck about his decision. He showed Marshall a couple of more songs that they used to play back in the "old days" of the 1970's and '80s. Chuck said his goodnights as he headed for bed. Marshall promised he would only be up another thirty minutes. Chuck nodded. He was nineteen once too.

As he lay on the bed, the chorus from the other room sang along with every note. Chuck smiled and rolled over on his stomach. To him, it was the best position for thinking. It also felt good to stretch his back out. He thought about the game and wondered what the team could have done to get better. He did the math on free throw percentages and how well they shot from the field. He and Pepper helped the team finish with over ninety percent on free throws. They hit over fifty percent on the two-pointers and forty percent on threes. Jose and Parnell worked well together inside. Chuck thought in another month Jose might replace OJ as the starter. The kid was still losing weight, and it was improving his confidence immeasurably. Scouts at the NM State game would spread the word about the hook shot. The shot would no longer be a secret.

The music got quieter, and Chuck noticed it was slower. He thought about walking out to the kitchen, just to get a drink. Not to see who had stayed, but just to make sure his roommate was staying out of trouble. He decided against it, figuring Marshall deserved his moment. The thought of Marshall in his "Armordillo" suit engaging in carnal knowledge with a willing coed came to mind, and Chuck nearly laughed out loud.

That image led to thoughts of Grace Winters. He missed her. Just talking to her. He looked at his phone. Her number was still his top favorite. He picked up the phone and started to call. But it was her desire for time to heal. Calling or texting her this late at night would not help. He put the phone on the night stand and lay back down. It was too soon. He tried to think about basketball. It was visions of the game that provided him the comfort he needed to sleep. After going through most of the game in his mind, reviewing shot selections, passes hit and missed, defensive assignments, and every other aspect of the game, he drifted off to sleep. A comfortable, deep sleep with good dreams. Dreams of Grace Winters and life after a Conference Championship.

CHAPTER TWELVE

For the next two weeks with Chuck in the starting lineup, things for the St. Michael's Armadillos kept getting better. They weren't scoring a bunch of points, but by slowing the game down, they always had enough to beat their opponents. Charles Holmes was becoming a star. The best news was he was consistent. Chuck had picked up his point guard role and that left Charles available to focus on shooting and defense. Charles was second in scoring and first in steals in the Conference. Parnell led the league in rebounding. The team was number three in the nation in free throw percentage and fifth in points allowed. Even more impressive, they were getting better every game.

Chuck also kept an eye on Henderson. His mood swings and disassociation from the team were becoming more apparent. Chuck couldn't help but think it was because the Dillo's were not only covering the point spread, but they were also crushing it. Henderson was showing no signs of connection to BCT, and Charles Holmes' play left no indication he was getting any pressure.

Marshall had taken to his new role as mascot like salmon to a stream. Somehow, he had coerced the announcer to play some "older" songs. Parliament, the Cars, and Van Halen were routinely blasted at the Dillo Hole. The whole "Runnin' with the Dillos" theme was catching on all over campus. The fans were loving every minute of the games. Marshall had gotten with Hawk on a weekend, went to the confidence course and learned how to properly rappel. Chuck stopped worrying about his roommate. Marshall was becoming a leader without even trying. He had grown two inches and gained twenty pounds in just three months. Marshall Wright was turning into a man.

The win streak couldn't last forever. St. Michael's was on the road against the University of North Texas. North Texas was favored by three. Chuck was aware of the point spread but had not paid much attention to it because all signs were Henderson and Holmes were not playing for BCT.

The game was one of unsightly errors and poor judgment. The Dillo's played cautiously, as if not to lose. They were tentative on their shots and slow to help on defense. At halftime, Coach Round tried to fire them up, but the atmosphere was one of confusion. There was no air of confidence. No air of invincibility. There was no sign of anyone enjoying what they were doing.

For his part, Chuck was frustrated. He kept getting passes to the open man in spots that normally resulted in easy baskets. They just wouldn't go in. Chuck was getting double teams at the top of the key and that kept him from shooting. Because people were consistently open, he would get them the ball. The shots just weren't falling. As for Chuck, he didn't drive the lane or go to the free throw line once.

With two minutes left in the game, it happened. For all their poor play, St. Michael's was still in the game. North Texas had just hit a three pointer and had gone up by seven. Round called a timeout. He wanted full court pressure and shots taken from inside the key unless they were down by eight with a minute left. The direction seemed clear to Chuck. Hold UNT on defense, get some steals and take the ball inside. No three pointers until it became desperate. Chuck should have known something was happening when Henderson called Charles to the side after the timeout was over. He saw the coach point to the scoreboard. Charles Holmes shook his head and walked out to the court. Probably Henderson was just reiterating they needed eight more points in two minutes. Yet Chuck sensed something just didn't seem right, but was too focused on the game for anything negative to register.

After the timeout, St. Michael's was slow to get off a shot, nearly running out of time. Parnell missed a fifteen-footer as the shot clock buzzer sounded, and UNT got the rebound. Chuck and Parnell pressed the ball defensively, but Charles Holmes' man was wide open at half court. He only applied token defense, daring his man to shoot. His man made a fake and pulled up for a ten-footer that wasn't even contested.

Down by nine with the clock showing just under a minute to play, Charles had the ball in the corner. Jose had his man pinned in the lane, but Charles wouldn't throw it in to him. Again, the clock ran down. Charles dribbled to the corner and fired a three pointer that hit nothing. As he whined to the ref about a foul, his man sprinted down the court. A long pass hit him in stride, and Chuck was forced to foul him as he tried a layup.

Chuck walked up to Holmes and hissed, "What the hell was that?!"

"Shut up, Hayes!" said Charles. Then he looked at the ref and said loudly, "And he saw the foul, but didn't call it!" The ref eyed Charles and started to call a technical. Chuck immediately stepped in between them and pushed Charles away. The crowd sensed the call and started chanting "T HIM UP", which made Charles even angrier. Chuck held him and said, "I'm not talking about the ref! I'm talkin' about the shot! We have plenty of time! We didn't need to take a three pointer. You had Jose wide open down low. Didn't you see him?" Charles was still looking at the ref. "Would you just relax!" said Chuck.

Charles stepped back and shook his head. "I'm all right! I'm cool!"

Chuck said, "If you're so cool, how come the ref is getting to you?"

Charles was quiet. Then he looked over to the bench. Henderson was waving for him to call a timeout and come over to the sideline. Charles looked at Chuck again. His facial expression gave it away. It was at the exact moment that the timeout whistle blew that Chuck knew Henderson had told Charles what to do. He was supposed to make sure St. Michael's lost by at least three. Charles started to head over to the bench. Chuck grabbed his arm. Charles turned and looked at Chuck. Chuck shook his head and said quietly, "Don't do this." For an instant, Charles started to protest. Chuck said, "We can still beat these guys."

Charles said quietly, "Sure we can." He pulled his arm away and headed over to the bench. In the huddle, Round was still upbeat and positive even though his team was playing terribly. As they broke the huddle, Henderson whispered something to Charles Holmes.

Chuck knew what he had to do. After UNT hit the free throws, they were up by eleven. Chuck got the ball, drove the length of the floor for a layup. On the inbounds, Charles Holmes was called for a foul and got into a shoving contest with his man. A technical foul was called immediately. UNT hit the shot and they took the ball out. Charles' man took the ball and dribbled right by him into the lane. He hit a layup as Parnell was slow trying to block the shot. Down by thirteen with thirty seconds to play, the game seemed over.

Chuck brought the ball down and launched a three pointer that swished. Jose tipped the inbound pass that was stolen by Parnell. He passed to Chuck. Chuck dribbled to the three-point line and scored again. On the next inbound play, Dexter Thomas picked up a charge at half court.

Chuck went up to Dexter who was set to throw the ball in bounds. He yelled, "GIVE IT TO ME!" Dexter smiled and did as he was told.

Chuck saw Charles break hard to get open for a pass but kept his dribble. He drove hard from the top of the key, then stepped out to the top of the arch and fired. Nothing but net. The shot silenced the crowd. There were nine seconds left in the game, and UNT was only up by four. They called a timeout to regroup.

The bench was going nuts. Chuck was all smiles. He hadn't felt this good about his game in a long time. Out of the corner of his eye he could see the nervousness in both Henderson and Holmes. Screw them, he thought. It was time to play to win.

On the North Texas inbound, Parnell stepped in front of a pass at half court. Unfortunately, Chuck was at his own foul line covered by his man. Charles Holmes screamed for the ball and Parnell saw him in the corner. Chuck tried to get open and get the ball before Holmes but was too late.

Holmes caught the pass and dribbled to the corner. There, he simply stopped. He moved the ball as if to pass. Chuck ran towards him and yelled for the ball, but it was no use. The clock ran out as Charles, double covered, launched a twenty-five-foot shot from the corner that hit the backboard.

North Texas had held on to win by four. Not only had Henderson and Holmes shaved points, St. Michael's had lost their first game.

Chuck didn't wait to get home. After he dressed, he headed outside towards the bus and called Eddie. "I guess you saw the game?"

Eddie said, "Only what was on social media. The highlights. Or should I say . . . lowlights!" Chuck was too angry to even chuckle at the humor. "I thought you were gonna pull that one out by yourself."

"Yeah, well. It's a team game, you know!" said Chuck tersely.

Eddie said, "Looked like Charles kind of choked."

Chuck said, "I think the best way to keep my teammate from choking in the future is if I keep my hands away from his neck. I think we," Chuck hesitated. He took a deep breath and said, "Run 'em all. Every one you guys are working on!"

Eddie was ecstatic. "EXCELLENT! We got some good stuff planned. The timeline you came up with is kind of tight, but I think we can get it done! I'll be able to let you know in about three or four days."

"Till then," said Chuck. "You guys just make sure nobody can find out the source, okay!"

"No problem! Spoofin' the source is already being worked on!" said Eddie. "Between Bobby and Chris, we'll cost them millions, and they won't even know what hit 'em!"

Chuck hung up and said to no one, "I hope you're right, Eddie."

Then he took a few minutes to figure out exactly what he was going to say to Henderson. He already had the spot figured out. It was just a matter of whether he could keep his temper in check.

Steve James said to Jeff Roberts, "How did St. Michael's do tonight? I see they are back in the green on our reference spreadsheet."

Roberts checked his screen and said, "Um, gettin' three points on the road and . . . oh, darn! Lost by four! How 'bout that?" Roberts was beaming knowing that the organization had probably made a hundred thousand dollars, if not more, off that one game.

"Looks like they really are on the payroll again," said Steve. But he wasn't smiling. Someone had gotten them to come around and 'play ball'. That was too bad. They were a sleeper team that won a couple of tough games. They didn't seem to score a lot of points, but they had been undefeated. Steve wondered who had been blackmailed or what limb had been broken to bring St. Michael's back into the fold. He started to ask Jeff to find out why they came around, but decided it was too late. If they were back into Grant's program, it didn't matter anymore.

Sandy Hawkins said, "You headed out again tonight?"

"Yeah, babe. You know how these young kids are," said Hawk with a smile. "They need as much adult supervision as they can get. They are teaching me a whole bunch of stuff about computers."

"All right then," said Sandy. She saw him to the door. "Not as late as last night, okay?"

"Sure, honey," said Hawk. He bent down to kiss her good-bye. "Don't wait up!"

Hawk made a note to himself. He'd better take her out to dinner soon. Maybe he could take her to that nice Tex-Mex place at La Cantera. These kids were keepin' him up way too late. But he had so much to learn. They were very patient at teaching him the computer terms and security issues they were trying to overcome. They had a way of making him feel involved. These 'kids' were the only real team he had been on since he had retired. Even though he was twice as old as them, they never seemed to consider his age a hindrance.

Yet, there are some things that come with age that the youngsters didn't have. Call it experience. Call it a sixth sense. It was something they were lacking. They saw the world in only a positive light. If it took experience to show them the world can be a dark place, that's what Nate was going to provide to his new team.

Henderson pulled the car key from his pocket as he walked towards his car. Chuck took one quick look around to make sure no one was watching. Quietly he walked up behind Pete Henderson. The blow to the back of Henderson's head was in the form of an elbow. Chuck had thought about a softer approach, but he wanted to make sure he had Pete's attention. If he used his fist, he might have inadvertently broken a finger or a bone in his hand. That would have been hard to explain to Coach Round. The elbow seemed like the best option.

"WHAT THE . . ." yelled Pete Henderson as he tried to gain his bearings and turn around to see his assailant.

Chuck grabbed the man's sports coat around the collar and pushed him against his car. "I could have been one your friends from Austin, Pete." Chuck looked around and said, "You need to be more careful." Then he punched him as hard as he could in the stomach. Henderson dropped to the ground and gasped to get his breath. "We need to talk."

Chuck grabbed Henderson by the collar again and pulled him to his feet. "How much? And don't give me any double speak either. Because as angry as I am right now, you could be in the hospital before I start to sweat!" He pushed Pete against the car. "HOW MUCH?"

Henderson caught his breath and said quietly, "Twenty-five thousand."

"Let me get this straight! For twenty-five thousand dollars the BCT told you to make sure we lost by four, right?" asked Chuck.

Slowly nodding, Pete said, "Yeah."

"What about Charles? Did he get paid?" asked Chuck. Pete was silent. "I ASKED YOU, DID CHARLES GET PAID?" He bounced Pete off the car one more time.

"NO!" yelled Pete. "No!" He fought back tears. "I told him the same thing they told me." His hand reached up to wipe at his face. "If we didn't pull the North Texas bet, they were gonna kill me." Chuck looked hard into the man's eyes. "I'm not lyin'! They messed me up pretty good before. They said they were 'goin' easy' on me!" Henderson relaxed in Chuck's hands. "I got a phone call two nights ago, and they told me the point spread and to make sure we lost by at least four," said Henderson as a tear trickled down his cheek. "Or I'd be dead by Friday."

Chuck released the man's collar. He wanted to tell him again that the BCT wouldn't kill him, but he wasn't sure anymore. He couldn't promise him protection either. The realism of that offer had set in. Chuck was frustrated and it showed. "You . . . scum!" was all he could say. He turned away and walked in a circle. Henderson bent over and caught his breath. "Did Charles take any money?"

Pete stood up. "He hasn't taken any money this year. He knows these guys will do what they say. The North Texas effort was for me."

"Let me tell you something!" said Chuck. "At least he's got a purpose behind what he's doin'! I'm not so sure you're worth his 'EFFORT', as you put it!" Chuck shook his head in disgust. "We could have been undefeated if he just comes up with half the effort towards winning. Instead, his effort is to keep us from scoring so somebody, somewhere, doesn't come outta the dark and WHACK YOUR SORRY ASS!"

"Do you realize the money I made from this one game is almost a third of my annual salary?" said Pete.

Chuck stepped close and said, "Do you realize; I DON'T GIVE A DAMN!?"

Pete stepped back and leaned on the car. "I don't know when or if they will even call again. They made a lot of money tonight. So that should keep 'em happy for a while," said Pete.

"Well, money isn't what college basketball is about. It's about the game," said Chuck. He let the comment hang in the air. He stepped away from Pete and said, "I'm gonna make sure your 'sugar daddy' understands that this is still a game. I'm gonna make sure that Charles Holmes doesn't have to throw a game to save you ever again." Chuck started walking backwards. "You won't be able to fix any more games! You better call your Daddy first and tell him the situation. It's over, one way or the other." He turned and yelled over his shoulder. "Do what's right and maybe you can get back some dignity!" He started to add another threat, but at that point Chuck didn't think he could back it up. It would be up to Pete Henderson to come around. Somewhere inside Henderson, he hoped there was still an ounce of courage.

Just as promised, three days later Eddie Newton called Chuck. It was eleven o'clock, and Chuck had just gotten back from the library, and sat down heavily on the couch. His cell phone rang. "Surprised you're still awake!" said Eddie.

"I've got finals to get ready for," said Chuck.

"You have a couple of minutes to talk?" asked Eddie. "I have your Christmas present ready."

"A little early for Christmas, Eddie." Chuck knew exactly what his present was. "What cha got?"

"We can play acts one and two whenever you need them," said Eddie. "We have a tool doin' some searching in the system. It will keep working through the holidays. Lots of tournaments. Lots of bets being made. But it's in position when needed."

"That is good news. And quick too," said Chuck. He felt like a spy talking in code. Eddie had gotten a "sniffer" into the BCT network, and it was collecting data, or creating a footprint of the BCT system. Literally mapping the network the gamblers were using. They used talk-around terminology because they had become paranoid that their conversations about the BCT might be used against them if things went south. It was just another form of security that Nate Hawkins and Chris Crowley insisted they use. There was just a small matter of privacy laws. Even if the BCT people were crooks, they were entitled to privacy on their networks in a court of law.

"Now for the bad news," said Eddie. "We can't get your other presents until Valentine's Day."

Chuck thought for a minute and said, "Damn, that may be too late. Another present or two may need to be delivered by the Super Bowl."

"That whole delivery thing could be a problem," said Eddie. "We'll have to talk about that face to face."

Chuck understood. "Okay. Sometime next week." He hesitated then said, "I really appreciate the work. Is your friend Bobby able to help you with protection?"

"No doubt," said Eddie. "Um . . ." Eddie struggled with the proper words while on the phone. "His father is one of the people who developed the protection for the system BCT uses. He's gonna come through with a terrific present. It just takes time."

Chuck thought about the answer. "Everybody wants presents. If he needs extra time, and we don't get the presents until after Christmas, that's not a problem! Let's shoot for opening the presents during the Super Bowl."

"Any particular reason why that time?" asked Eddie.

"About a billion reasons!" said Chuck. Over five billion dollars would be bet on the Super Bowl in Nevada alone. It was estimated that another five billion dollars more would be wagered illegally. The only event bet on more than the Super Bowl would be the March Madness of college basketball.

"Cool!" said Eddie. "That's a whole lot of reasons. I'll see you soon to talk about delivery, right?"

"Yeah! Real soon," said Chuck. Then he hung up the phone. A problem with delivery, eh. He would have to think about that. There were a couple of ways he knew of to get into a system, but they were basically primative. Eddie had been lucky to get the first options into the BCT system via the internet. If they needed to get into the system by being aggressive, so be it. The old-fashioned way was a little more exciting. He hated that high tech method anyway.

The next game produced a blow out over Prairie View A & M. Holmes had a monster game with 28 points. Chuck had thirteen assists, most of them to Holmes on back door cuts or alley-oop passes. Pepper had come off the bench for 15 and Jose had 11 points and ten rebounds. Everyone on the team scored.

Chuck didn't notice any "irregularities", but he did wait until everyone left to talk to Charles Holmes. The two teammates walked out of the locker room together.

"Nice passing tonight, old man!" said Charles with a smile.

Chuck decided to skip the small talk and cut to the chase. He was careful to make sure no one else was in earshot. "As long as I know you're focused on winning, I'll continue to throw you the ball!"

Charles stopped in his tracks. He knew better than to play dumb with Chuck. "That North Texas thing was a one-time deal!"

"Did Henderson tell you I talked to him about that?" asked Chuck.

Charles nodded, "He said you did more than talk. He also said you know I haven't taken any money this year!"

Chuck smiled, "I didn't think you had. The frustrating thing is you know we should be undefeated now!"

"I know, I know! But those guys threatened coach Henderson again. I was sure they would follow through on their threats if I hadn't thrown the game," said Charles as his voice trailed off.

Chuck stepped close to Charles. "You come to me if that happens again. Two reasons. One, I'll help you out. Two, if you try to throw another game, I'll shut you out the same way I did at North Texas, only sooner. You won't ever see the ball!" Chuck could tell Charles understood. He stuck out his hand, "Besides, I am your teammate. Plus David is dying to get more shots than you!"

"Yeah, he was pissed tonight! He only got nine points and Coach had him on the bench!" laughed Charles.

"We didn't need him tonight," said Chuck with a smile. Charles smiled. "But we need you every night, okay?"

Charles smiled faded. "No more, Hoopman! I promise!"

"That's good enough for me, Charles," said Chuck. "I'll see you tomorrow at practice!" The two men went their separate ways. Chuck was smiling as he walked away. Charles Holmes went over to a group of girls waiting to escort the superstar home.

They played one more game before their final exams and had only one loss at the end of the first semester. Marshall Wright pulled out a chart in the USAToday that had the St. Michael's Armadillos ranked as the 33rd best team in the nation. For Chuck Hayes, that wasn't good enough.

CHAPTER THIRTEEN

Finals came and Chuck did better than he expected. Grace Winters had come back to class on the 1st of December, right before finals, and she had been just as friendly to Chuck as she had been before Moreland had attacked her. Chuck wasn't sure what to expect, but on the outside, Grace seemed to have recovered quite well.

For his part, Chuck made no effort to see her anywhere other than in the classroom. As for her class, he didn't get the A he had hoped. The B+ would have to do. The week in class prior to the final exam with Grace was frustrating to Chuck because he really missed talking to her. He vowed that she would have to make the first move. He was going to wait until she was ready.

As for his other classes, he aced his Texas History, his Telecommunications in America, and of course Public Speaking. Chuck was disappointed that he only pulled a B in Anatomy and Physiology. It turned out to be a helluva lot harder than just memorizing bones and muscles. The A in Basketball was expected, but the two credit hours applied to his semester course load was a pleasant surprise.

Chuck got texts from Pepper and Jose who were both excited about their own grades. Jose surprised himself by managing a 3.1, and Pepper Dyer made Dean's List with a 3.8. Chuck stopped by the Athletic Director's office and was passing time with the secretary. After five minutes he got around to asking her if everyone on the team had passed for the semester. She let it slip out that two players would be placed on academic probation, but she wouldn't let the names out. Chuck did find out that neither was a starter.

His next stop was to Coach Round's office. Round was aware that two players had failing grades and was in the process of finding two new players. He let Chuck know that one would probably be Isaiah "Ikey" Rollins, a speedy junior college transfer. The other player getting a look would be Steve Welch. Welch was a sophomore tight end on the school football team. He was six foot five and weighed 265. Coach Round said neither player could shoot worth a darn, but "they play aggressive defense, and Welch will kill anyone that comes in the lane." He reminded Chuck that they didn't need offensive help. They needed speed against running guards and a defender that wants to "pick up the charge and claim the lane as his own". These two guys fit the bill.

Most of the campus had gone home for the holidays. Chuck didn't really have anywhere to go. His parents had died in a car accident in 2015. Chuck had to come home on emergency leave from Afghanistan. Granted he wanted to get out of Bagram, but not to come home and bury his parents. They were killed when his father lost control of the vehicle and hit a tree two weeks before Thanksgiving. The trooper informed him that their deaths were instantaneous. It was a small consolation because he never got to say goodbye. They were both in their sixties, yet were in very good health. He had always thought he would have more time with them.

It took Chuck nearly a year to get over their untimely deaths. He survived by playing basketball and running. For hours he would be at the gym, shooting and running, running and shooting. To any normal person, the monotony of the routine probably resembled abnormal behavior. For Chuck, it was a way to deal with his pain. The holiday season was bringing back those memories.

During the break, Chuck borrowed a key from Round and spent most of his time in the gym shooting. As much as he tried to block it out, the loneliness would not subside. Finally, he'd had enough. He wanted to see Grace. He didn't know if she'd be there, but it was worth a try.

Chuck saw Grace's car, guessed she was home and gave the door a try. His smile was forced, and his normal air of confidence was not there. He heard the chain on the door unlatch. Grace Winter's head popped around the door. "What? No basketball game today?"

Chuck's forced smile disappeared. "Naw. We leave for New Orleans Tuesday." He coughed and pulled something from behind his back. It was a stuffed St. Michael's "Armor-Dillo". It didn't take the marketing department long to pick up on a good thing. Chuck pointed to the camouflage shield on the animals' chest and said, "I signed it." Grace looked down and read the card. It said, "MERRY CHRISTMAS! I LOVE YOU, CHUCK."

Grace took the stuffed animal and looked at it. Then she looked at Chuck. Then she took the critter and smacked Chuck on the head with it. "I'm surprised you didn't sign it, 'HOOPMAN'!"

Chuck looked down at his toes and rubbed his shoes together. "Hoopman loves you, too!"

Grace shook her head. "You have a strange way of showing it, buddy." She grabbed his arm and said, "I've really missed being able to talk to you."

Chuck said, "I've missed you, too! It was killing me going to class. You never gave me the time of day. I thought you would never speak to me again."

"I'm sorry about that, Chuck," she said. "I didn't have a reason to be like that. You were concerned for me. But, between the incident with William and you being . . . so close." She fumbled for the words. "And you have basketball going on, too. I understand how important that is to you. I didn't want to feel like I was competition to your basketball playing."

Chuck nodded, "I'm sorry, Grace. You aren't second to basketball. You . . ."

She quickly put her hand over Chuck's mouth and said, "Don't even go there! I know where I stand. At least, I think I do. Or you wouldn't be here now."

"I missed you," said Chuck.

Grace grabbed his hand and pulled him into the house. She led him to the couch and made him sit down close to her. Slowly, she leaned over and kissed him softly, then leaned back on the couch and said, "I missed you too. Now that you're no longer in my class, I suppose I can see you legitimately and not on the sly."

Chuck snapped his head back and said, "Is that how we were before?"

"YES!" she said with a broad smile.

Chuck smiled back. "It's good to see you again."

"I'm glad you stopped by, too!" said Grace as she playfully smacked his arm with stuffed Dillo.

"Hey, now! Go easy! I don't want to get hurt," said Chuck.

"Maybe just hurt you enough so you can't go to New Orleans. You'd have to stay here. Or come home and meet my parents," she said.

Chuck was still and became serious. "You mean, you want to show me to your parents?"

Grace nodded. "You're a nice guy, Chuck. I'd be proud to have my parents meet the legendary 'HOOPMAN'." Chuck blushed. "Just because I needed some time to get myself together, doesn't mean I didn't follow the games," she said with a smile. She kissed his cheek and added, "to watch Hoopman!"

"You want to come to New Orleans?" asked Chuck with a smile.

"No. I can't. I really must go home to my parents' house," she said. She held up the stuffed animal. "I'll show them this and we'll have a talk. Maybe I can explain to them that not every man I fall in love with is a jerk."

"Maybe I can meet them next semester," said Chuck.

"Next semester should be better. Basketball will be over in March," she said. "And I'll be able to come around more often. Of course, I won't get between you and basketball."

Chuck nodded in agreement. "You can come around as much as you like. I'll be able to focus on the court, as well as concentrate in class! You were a tiny distraction for me in class. Those short dresses you wear. Another distraction."

Grace smiled again. "You don't have to go anywhere yet, do you? You think you can help me put this 'Armor-dillo' up on my shelf?"

Chuck got up off the couch and put his hand out. "Ms. Winters, it would be a pleasure. I think there is a nice spot back there!" he said pointing down the hallway. Then he added, "Maybe I can do better than a B+!"

Grace started walking backwards down the hallway. She extended her index finger and started gesturing for Chuck to follow. "Wanna try for an A in a different subject?"

He grabbed the stuffed animal and headed down the hall. He stopped at the bedroom door. Grace spoke as if she read his mind. She knew instantly what he was thinking. "William hurt me, Chuck. He hurt me physically. He hurt me emotionally. He hurt me mentally. If I am ever to get over that, I need to have someone help me," she softly grabbed his hand. "I'm asking for your help."

Chuck frowned and said quietly, "I promise, I'll . . ."

She put a finger to his lips and said, "Ssshhh! Don't talk." She looked at him and tilted her head a little. "I'm not in a hurry, Chuck. I know you would never hurt me. Let's just go slow, and see if we can get back what we had before. Maybe you can start by holding me."

Chuck finally smiled. "I'd like that, Grace." He turned to close the door, then followed her to the bed. Chuck slowly slid next to her. He put his arm around her and held her. There wasn't any reason to rush anything. It was Christmas.

"Why is the St. Michael's line red again? This is getting ridiculous!" said Steve James.

"That same kid said he wasn't playin' anymore, and this time he must mean it," said Jeff Roberts.

"It sucks to be him!" said Steve with a frown. "Did they break his legs yet?"

"No! Not yet!" laughed Jeff. "I bet he doesn't get what he wants for Christmas!" Then Jeff looked as if a light had come on. "Oh, hey! I got this report from Austin. It seems they have gotten three messages telling them and their players not to bet on college basketball."

"So?" said Steve flatly. "Don't they have an administrator to handle little crap like this?"

"They seem to think this is a little bit out of the ordinary. The first one shut down the system for one minute. The next one was for two minutes, same message. Now they get this message from some frat guys. The so called, SIGMA BROS, or something dorky like that. They gave a list of threats," said Jeff. "Specifically, they would tell the Federal online gaming commission we were fixin' games. They were gonna post messages that we weren't paying off, that our security was weak. Stuff like that. The last one covered a large chunk of the network. About 73%. That's why Vegas finally sent us the news. The Austin boys, Carl Holden I think was the guy's name, he brought it up to Vegas every time, but they're worthless. Third time is a charm. They thought you should have a look."

Steve thought about it. His first inclination was to lump the act together with the hundreds of other intrusions they got weekly. Something said these were different. It was the Austin group that was claiming to have problems. They were having difficulty with the St. Michael's program over a kid that didn't want to play for Grant. Maybe it was just a coincidence because it was Tommy Clarks' Austin guys making Grant angrier than normal. Computer network intrusions weren't things that basketball players did. Something turned on a switch in Steve James mind. He went to a computer and pulled up the schedule for the St. Michael's basketball program. He turned to Jeff Roberts and asked, "Can you pull me up copies of these messages?"

"Have 'em for you in a couple hours, depending on who's working in Austin," said Jeff.

Steve nodded. "Terrific, thanks." It would probably turn out to be like all the others. Maybe this group of "frat boys" would surprise him. Steve James had a suspicion it wasn't frat boys at all. Perhaps whoever it was would be just what he needed. First things first. "I think I'm gonna take a little vacation over the holidays." He looked at the St. Michael's schedule on his cell phone.

"I've never seen you take any kind of vacation, Steve. You goin' home for the holidays?" asked Jeff.

"No. I need to go have some good old fashion Cajun food. I think I'll go to New Orleans."

Chuck couldn't wait to get back to playing. The team had five days off and they needed to get back to practice. Charles Holmes returned from the break and was more confident than Chuck had ever seen him. He had started to be more open and friendly towards Chuck, especially since he was on the receiving end of at least five assists from Chuck in each of the last four games.

Even Henderson was starting to be more friendly. He had made it a point to let Chuck know that he had not received any phone calls from any "friends" since he had been so kind as to inform them of the new situation. He had informed them Holmes was no longer shaving points, and, therefore, Henderson couldn't help the program anymore. The BCT had apparently accepted that explanation because they had not called back. Henderson was turning into an almost normal jerk, and he even talked to Chuck now and then. There had not been any more evidence of point shaving or any other gambling activity by either the coach or the star player. As far as Chuck was concerned, things were going just great. It was time to play some serious hoop.

He would soon get his chance at the holiday tournament in New Orleans. If they made the championship, the game would be televised on ESPNU. Coach Round wanted the exposure for the program. Chuck wanted it so his daughter could see him play.

"Those bastards don't know who they're screwin' with!" yelled Tommy Clark. Derrick Monroe and Nubbin tried to be invisible. "I thought Henderson had everything under control. Then he tells me Holmes ain't playin'. After we lean on Henderson, the kid comes through for us. One freakin' game! Now they ain't playin'! Grant is ready to gut me over this! He says, 'Nobody EVER QUIT'!" He was shaking his head and pacing around the room like a caged animal.

There was a knock at the door. "Yeah!" yelled Clark.

"Hey, Boss!" said Carl Holden. He had Mike Thompson, his network security manager, in tow.

"GREAT! What the hell do you two want?" asked Clark.

"We just got another message from those fraternity brothers," said Thompson. Carl Holden hated to deliver bad news. They both could tell by Clark's mood, now was not a good time to tell him anything too bad.

Holden said, "Maybe we should come back later!"

Clark was terse. "What's the message?"

"Ummm . . ." Thompson cleared his throat and held out a copy of the message. "First, they said they would notify all their fraternity brothers across the nation to start a doxing campaign against us and any other online gambling services."

"SCREW 'EM!" said Clark. "We've had negative public messages before and nobody gives a damn. Did they talk numbers?"

Holden spoke up. "We have no idea how many people they are talking about. Probably not that many."

Then Thompson said, "Then the second part said, 'If we don't stop fixing games and betting on college basketball, they would notify the following email addresses and texts what we are doing!"

Clark looked at the addresses and cell numbers. One looked very familiar. "Is that. . . ?"

"Yes, sir!" said Holden. "That's Mr. Grant's personal home phone number."

Clark exploded again. "HOW THE HELL DID THEY GET THAT?!"

It was Thompson's turn. "We don't know."

Clark turned on the whole room. "WHAT DO I PAY YOU GUYS FOR?" It was a rhetorical question which left the employees looking at their feet. Clark balled the paper up and threw it across the room. He went to the window and was silent. The four other men in the room were perfectly still as their boss fumed.

Clark resorted to the only response he knew. "Thompson, you get that computer geek in the Caribbean or Vegas or wherever he is, here and I mean yesterday. I'll clear it with Grant. We'll pay him extra to come out here and see firsthand what's going on. I'm not gonna let a bunch drunk ass prankster college punks try and close us down."

"What if they text Mr. Grant?" asked Thompson.

Clark thought about his response. "That wouldn't be a good thing for them. I'll tell Mr. Grant about these punks, and he'll probably tell 'em to pound sand. Our profits are his profits." That seemed to satisfy Holden and Thompson.

Clark turned and looked at Derrick Monroe. "As for you, Mr. Monroe. You and Nubbin need to get some plane tickets. You're going to New Orleans." The two men looked at each other confused. "If Henderson, and that kid Holmes doesn't make sure that team loses the first game of that tournament, you take care of both of them! Holmes doesn't play again. I mean forever! You got me?" Both men nodded. "Now get the hell outta here! All of you! Go earn the money I'm overpaying you!"

After they got outside, Nubbin grabbed Derricks' arm and asked, "Did he say he wanted us to kill that Holmes kid if they don't lose?"

Derrick knew Nubbin was good for beating people up and scaring them but had never killed anyone before. Clark had not exactly said to 'kill' Charles Holmes, it was merely implied. Derrick looked at his co-worker and said, "Yeah! And that's what we'll do if we have to."

New Orleans was not known for its basketball. It was known for the Cajun cuisine and the French Quarter. Round knew the deal and even told Chuck he was worried about the younger players going out and getting drunk. Chuck pulled aside Pepper and Jose to let them know that the 'Big Easy' wasn't the place to mess up. Then he talked to Parnell.

Parnell was taking his role as team captain seriously. He called everyone into the lobby for a 'players only' meeting. David told everyone exactly what was on his mind. How he personally had great expectations for the team and where they were headed for the season. He saw the tournament as a great opportunity. He put the team on notice that anyone who messed up the opportunity would answer to him directly. Not the coach. After he was done, the players all had no doubt that David Parnell was focused for the tournament. Chuck was proud of David too. He'd gotten most of the words right. What was important was that he said them with passion and sincerity that was required of the team captain.

That first night, everyone made the bed check.

The tournament involved eight teams, and St. Michael's first opponent was Tulane. Not surprisingly, the Green Wave was favored by ten. St. Michael's was added to the tournament as fodder for other teams to pad their stats. They were added before anyone knew how good they were. The hardest thing about the game for St. Michael's was the fact that it was a home game for Tulane. It was by far the largest crowd they had ever played in front of.

At first, the Dillo's looked like they were in a different world. They started slow and got progressively worse. They dropped passes, took bad shots and weren't talking to each other on defense. The fact that they were playing at a typically slow St. Michael's pace was the only thing keeping them in the game. The halftime score was 28-20 in favor of Tulane.

Round was still composed at halftime. His speech consisted of two comments. "Ya'll need to yell at each other on defense so you can be heard. The shots are gonna fall. If you just take better shots!" He chuckled at his comment. "Just relax." Chuck expected the coach to be angry, but it just reaffirmed the respect he had for Round. He was enjoying himself.

Before they headed out of the locker room, Round pulled Chuck aside and asked, "You got something in that bag of tricks of yours to take this crowd out of the game?"

Chuck thought about it. Then said, "Sometimes if I'm watching a game, I just enjoy watching two good teams play. A lot of those fans are here for the next game and don't care if either of us win. They'd rather Tulane lose, figuring they will be the more difficult team to beat compared to us. We need to get these neutral fans to cheer for us. I got a couple of tricks up my sleeve that might wake 'em up. You don't mind if I get a little fancy do ya?"

"What? You think I'm gonna question anything you do? You only have two turnovers in twenty minutes. If nothing else, we're gonna press them more, because I think you and Charles can take their guards all over the floor, okay!" said the coach with a smile. Chuck smiled and did exactly what he was told.

As he headed for the floor, Pete Henderson was waiting for him. The coach waved to pull him over to the side so no one could hear them. Pete Henderson's face was white. "There are guys are here in this auditorium! Guys from Austin!"

Chuck looked around as if they were standing right around the corner. "I don't see anybody . . ."

"They're in the stands," said Pete. "They sent me this note." Chuck read the note. "We're supposed to lose by at least eleven points tonight."

"Shoot. The way we're playin', that might be possible!" Chuck was smiling. It was obvious he wasn't taking the note seriously.

"DAMN IT, HAYES!" yelled Pete. Then he immediately got control of himself. "These guys are really here and we are supposed to lose!"

It finally sunk in. Pete Henderson was panicking. "All right. Two questions. One, do you know what they look like?"

"I know what some of them look like, but they may have new people," said Henderson.

"If you see any of them, let me know," said Chuck. "The next question is, did you tell Charles yet?"

Henderson shook his head, "No. He doesn't know. Should we tell him?"

Chuck thought about his answer. "Yeah! I'll tell him. But let me make this clear to you right now. If he decides to blow the game, I'm not gonna throw him the ball. If he starts screwin' up with this game on the line, I won't give him the opportunity to blow it for us the way he did with UNT!"

Henderson wasn't happy with the response, but it was out of his hands.

Chuck quickly ran out to join his team in the shoot around. He grabbed a ball and pulled up next to Charles Holmes. Quietly, he told his teammate exactly what Henderson had said. He looked into Charles eyes and said, "It basically comes down to you. What are you gonna do?"

Charles dribbled the ball a couple of times and looked back at Chuck. "Hoopman, what would you do?"

Chuck started to say he would never have gotten in that position in the first place. But that would have been counter-productive, and Charles wasn't looking for a lecture. "I would play basketball."

Charles looked at him and nodded. Then a big smile appeared on his face. "That's too simple!"

"It is, isn't it! Let's just play basketball. If we lose by eleven, no one will ever know." Chuck stepped closer to Charles and said, "But you know, and I know, if you play your game, and I play my game, these guys can't beat us." Charles smiled. Chuck stuck out a clenched fist. "This crowd wants us to beat Tulane. They need us to beat Tulane! You know what? Nobody in this tournament can beat us!"

Charles was beaming. "Let's do it, Hoopman!" Charles Holmes was as pumped up as Chuck had ever seen him.

From the first possession of the second half, they were a different team. Chuck got Parnell's attention with a nod. He took the clock down to five seconds then drove the lane. Two Tulane players came after him, and he tossed a 'no look' lob up to the basket. Parnell was there and slammed it home. The Tulane fans were shocked. The rest of the crowd started to make some noise.

On defense, the Dillo's were yelling and started to help each other out. The help side defense was quick to react when Tulane tried to reverse the ball. Their lack of patience gave Charles an easy steal that he took the length of the floor for a layup.

The next two Tulane offensive trips resulted in rushed shots that Parnell rebounded. After each rebound, Chuck walked the ball up the court. The Tulane crowd was instantly becoming impatient, confused, and frustrated. Chuck hit Charles for one jumper as the shot clock expired. The "neutral" fans began to get the sense that St. Michael's could win. That was all it took. The next time down, Chuck waited. As the clock wound down, he backed up and fired a three pointer that swished. St. Michael's had the lead.

Tulane called a timeout. Chuck managed to get Round's attention away from the huddle and asked for Pepper and Dex Thomas to come in. Round agreed reluctantly.

With Pepper and Dexter in, St. Michael's was smaller but much faster on the break, more aggressive and quicker on defense. Pepper, Charles, and Chuck pressured the Tulane guards relentlessly. David Parnell played loose at half court and cut off nearly every long pass Tulane would throw. They didn't steal every pass, but they took Tulane out of their offense. When Tulane tried to run, Chuck and Charles were getting easy layups from their steals.

For ten minutes it was the St. Michael's pressure defense that ruled the court. After the steals, Chuck would take the ball to the basket and fire a pinpoint behind the back pass or 'no look' passes to Charles or Pepper that led to easy baskets. On a couple of occasions, Chuck got real fancy and put on dribbling exhibitions through the lane. Then he would take it back to the top of the key and wait for the rest of the players to show up. This infuriated the Tulane fans and recruited the rest of the crowd completely to St. Michael's side. With five minutes left, Round emptied his bench. Pepper and Jose made their foul shots down the stretch, and ST. MICHAEL'S won 68 to 56. The pressure defense had resulted in 48 second half points. Charles Holmes did not score many points, but it would be obvious to anyone that he had played his hardest the whole night. At the end of the game, Holmes was still beaming as if he had never heard what Chuck had told him at halftime.

Everyone was excited except for Pete Henderson. He was nervous, pale and chain smoking like there was no tomorrow. It was clear to Chuck that Henderson thought he might never see the sunrise again. Chuck sympathized with Henderson and understood his fear but found it amusing at the same time. Henderson was the only one responsible for his situation. He deserved to suffer. Chuck was not totally unconcerned either. Henderson certainly felt afraid that there were people from Austin that would do him harm. Chuck needed to take it seriously.

By the time they got back to the hotel, no one had appeared to beat up Henderson or Charles Holmes. Chuck relaxed and headed to bed. His mind raced back to the game and how well they had played. The St. Michael's Armordillo's could beat a lot of teams if they played everyone the way they played against Tulane. Chuck was smiling as he drifted off to sleep. Thoughts of the BCT and Henderson's fears never entered his dreams.

The next night, St. Michael's played against Georgia Southern. Southern liked to run, and they too became the victim of the St. Michael's slow down offense. Full court pressure was never used against Southern because it wasn't needed. St. Michael's won 66 to 48. Jose had a huge night scoring 19 points. Southern had no one who could cover him in the lane. Parnell only scored ten but had 21 rebounds. Charles finished with eighteen on only eight shots. He had barely worked up a sweat, and Round rested him much of the second half.

That night in the hotel, Chuck was awakened by loud voices in the hallway. For an instant, he thought the BCT was in the hallway beating up Charles Holmes. He quickly got dressed and headed out into the hallway. Once outside he found Ike Rollins and Bullet DeVaughan inebriated and about to brawl with each other. Neither man had seen Chuck come into the hallway. Behind them, Chuck saw David Parnell come out of his room. He looked as if he were ready to kill the two guards.

Parnell walked behind the two as they squared off. Without a word, he smacked each player in the back of the head. In a normal tone he said, "Just what the hell do you two think you're doing?"

Bullet spoke first. "This knucklehead says we ought to be runnin' more! I told him shut the hell up because he hasn't been here long enough to know how we play."

Parnell looked at Rollins who was still rubbing his head. "That's right! We have all kinds of speed, yet we play this screwed up, slow down, and put people to sleep ball. And that's crap, man! Hoopman is so damn slow I could run circles around him."

Parnell stepped towards Rollins and looked down at the guard. He turned his head to look at Chuck, then took a threatening step closer to Rollins. "We've only got one loss. You can't just join the team and start trying to make changes. You haven't been here long enough!" Ike had only practiced with the team twice prior to the tournament.

Rollins was not intimidated. "What you gonna do? Hit me in the head again?" At that point the alcohol took over in earnest. Rollins squared off against Parnell. Parnell started to draw back his fist when Chuck stepped in.

"Hey, fellas! Little late for a party ain't it?" said Chuck as he walked right between the two combatants.

"Old man, you need to step out da way! I'm gonna kick this boy's ass!" said Rollins. Bullet tried to step in and Parnell put a hand on Bullet's chest knocking the smaller man backward. As Parnell did that, Rollins grabbed Chuck's shoulder and started to pull him out of the way to get at Parnell.

Reflexes got the better of Chuck. He was a little tired and upset about the derogatory comment Rollins had made. The 'old man' remark had hit a nerve. It was Ike's hand on the shoulder that stirred a reaction. Chuck knocked Rollins hand up in the air, spun quickly and grabbed Rollins'shirt, pushing him against the wall. The act happened so fast that no one knew quite what to do. The flash of anger that Chuck's face displayed was still present when Parnell said softly, "Yo, Man! Ease up. It's okay!" He stepped towards Chuck slowly.

Rollins was stunned instantly sober. Chuck gained control of himself and released his grip from Ike's shirt. Chuck stepped back and said softly, "I'm not as slow as you think." Then he looked at Parnell who was frowning at Chuck. He was a good team captain. Chuck looked down and took a step back. "I guess we need to save this energy for the floor, Ike. I would hate to be so tired tomorrow that I play even slower."

Parnell looked at Rollins and DeVaughan. "You two get your asses in the sack before Coach Round finds out." The guards quickly moved to their rooms without another word. Chuck stuck his hand out to Rollins before he could get away.

"I'm sorry, Ike," said Chuck sheepishly.

Ike took the hand and said, "That's all right. I didn't mean nuthin' anyway. Besides, you ain't really that slow." He turned and followed Bullet to his room.

Parnell looked down at Chuck and said, "Hoopman, you got to get over this feeling you have that you're less of a player than everybody else. I see you do it on the court sometimes. You don't talk smack, but you get this look on your face sometimes that says you aren't getting respect. You got more game than most of the people I've ever played with." Parnell let the comment sink in. "You think because you aren't as fast or can't jump as high that you're not as good as other players. Like you always got to prove you belong." Parnell smiled. "Trust me. You belong here." He turned to walk away. Over his shoulder he said, "We wouldn't be at this point today if it wasn't for you." Then he stopped and turned around. "Now get your butt to bed before I tell the coach!"

Chuck came to attention and offered a mock salute. He smiled and said, "You're right, David. I'm sorry." Parnell went back into his room. Chuck headed back to bed. He lay there for about an hour thinking about Parnell's words. The more he thought about them, the more he knew Parnell was right. He was overly sensitive about the speed at which he played. Parnell was also right about the other things as well. He could play at the college level. The fact that he would soon be 40 was only a factor in his mind. It was time he stopped being so defensive about it. Chuck vowed to make a change. He was going to lighten up on the court. He was really enjoying himself on the floor. It was time he let everyone see that.

The next day, Chuck sat by Rollins on the bus ride to the arena. Chuck started the truce by saying, "I was told that to win the game, you only had to score one more point than your opponent. Now we could score a hundred points a game. But odds are just as good for the other team to score more points than us if they take more shots. By slowing down and taking better shots than our opponents, we improve our chances of winning. We don't need to score a lot to win. Winning is what we're about. Does that make sense?"

Ike stuck out his hand and said, "It makes a lot of sense. I'm sorry about last night. I shouldn't even have been out last night. The whole thing was my fault." He was quiet for a minute. Then he asked Chuck about the guards at Memphis St. For the rest of the ride, the teammates discussed basketball. Chuck told the team stories about Pete Maravich. How much Louisiana loved him. How he played only three years of college basketball at LSU and averaged over 40 points all three years. He scored all those points without a three-point line. Also that Maravich took nearly forty shots a game to get them. The lesson was on the value of shot selection. How teammates need to have better communication about who and what shots are working. From that point on, Rollins, DeVaughan, Parnell and Chuck acted as if the event in the hall from the previous night had never happened.

St. Michael's was more than ready for Memphis St. Memphis St. was the biggest team St. Michael's had played against so far in the season, and they were picked to win by five. The slow down offense didn't take State by surprise. They had practiced for it and were very patient. But St. Michael's had something that MSU didn't have. That was Charles Holmes.

In the first half, Holmes was unstoppable. He shot eight for ten from the floor and had eighteen points. To start the second half, MSU tried a box in one defense where one player shadowed Holmes all over the floor and the other four played a zone. It didn't matter. Chuck knew he was in a zone and just kept getting him the ball. If he wasn't passing him the ball, Chuck was setting picks for him. Charles Holmes was on a mission. Every time MSU scored, Charles would score for St. Michael's.

St. Michael's needed him to be that way. No one else was hitting anything. Sometimes MSU would switch to a very aggressive zone where they double-teamed the ball everywhere it went. They might not have been able to stop Charles, but nobody else was scoring for St. Michael's.

For his part, Chuck wasn't shooting at all. Charles was so hot he didn't feel he needed to. He merely made sure Charles got the ball in a good place to shoot. The game went down to the wire. The ironic thing was that with five minutes left, the majority of the fans were rooting for the Dillo's to win.

With fifty seconds left, Charles hit a three pointer to take a one-point lead. MSU called time out to set a play. After the time out they ran a quick shot with their forward who hit a tough ten-footer. Round called a timeout and called for a pick and roll. To Chuck's surprise, the play had Charles passing to Chuck on the roll. Charles nodded and gave Chuck a wink.

Chuck felt a bit of nervousness. He'd never been asked to hit the final shot before. He looked around at the crowd. Before the play, he just let himself feel the energy. That was what playing ball was about. To get to that moment where you can feel and enjoy the surroundings of the game. It was a good feeling to have.

All too soon it was gone. Charles broke his moment of self-actualization. Holmes said, "It's gonna be wide open, Hoopman! Take it to the hole!" Chuck smiled.

The pass came into Chuck. He dribbled the clock down to ten seconds. Charles broke to the corner and caught the pass. Chuck sprinted hard to set the pick. When he did, both defenders covered Holmes. Chuck broke to the basket as the clock went to four. Charles led him perfectly. Chuck caught the ball in stride, dribbled to the basket, and started up for the shot. The center came over to try to block the shot. Chuck put the ball up quickly in his right hand showing it to the MSU center. Then he smoothly moved the ball to his left hand away from the defender as he tried to get in position for the block. The center went by expecting Chuck to shoot with his right hand. Chuck softly put the ball high over the rim. The buzzer sounded ending the game and for an instant, the world was quiet. As the ball slipped quietly through the net, the arena erupted. From somewhere, the chant 'HOOPMAN' started. Soon the arena picked up on it. David Parnell and Jose Rivera-Torres carried Chuck off the court. Final score, MSU 68, St. Michael's 69.

Charles finished with 34 points. For his part, Chuck had thirteen assists and seven points. He had hit all five of his free throws. His only basket was the final shot to win the game. Holmes and Parnell were named to the all-tournament team, and Charles Holmes took home the MVP trophy.

The St. Michael's Armordillo's could not have been more excited if they had won the national championship. It was the first tournament victory ever for the program. Coach Round was nearly crying. Even Henderson seemed happy. Chuck spent nearly an hour just walking around the arena. He talked to complete strangers. He gave high fives to his teammates and fans. He sought out the MSU players to shake hands and encourage them for a game well played.

The one thing that was a new experience for Chuck was getting interviewed by an ESPN reporter after the game. Chuck said all the right things. They mostly wanted to talk about his age. He handled the questions in stride, being much more aware of his attitude since Parnell had made him aware of it. He even laughed at some of the comments. Plus, he got to say 'Hi' to his daughter Anna on national TV.

As he headed to the locker room, Chuck was approached by more fans searching for autographs. Most were college kids and even some children. Chuck signed every one and answered as many questions as he could. The last fan standing there was older than most of the others. He was tanned and had a friendly smile. Something about him struck Chuck as out of place. He didn't look like your typical fan that adored basketball stars. Chuck felt like he was being evaluated. Maybe even examined by a doctor.

The man stuck out his hand and said, "That was one of the best games I have ever seen. You guys have got something going on here that is really special!" He thrust out a program and a pen and said, "Can I get your autograph, please?"

Chucks RADAR went down. He was really just another fan. "Sure. Thanks for watchin'!"

Then the man said something Chuck found rather peculiar. "I heard them calling you 'Hoopman'! I saw you sign some of the other autographs that way. Could you do me a favor and sign mine with your real name, please?"

Chuck found the manners too hard to resist. "Yeah. I can do that." He signed the program and handed it back. "That's a special signature. Nobody else in the world has my autograph like that!"

The man was all smiles. "You don't know how much I appreciate it! Were you really in the Army before?"

Chuck thought the question odd but answered it truthfully. "Yes. The Army made me look this old. You know I'm only 22, right?" The man laughed at Chuck's joke.

"What did you do in the Army? Infantry?" asked the man.

"That was a long time ago. Got smart and switched to military intelligence. Use to do some analysis but spent too much time playing basketball to be any good at that!" Chuck was having fun.

"Did you ever get into computer network stuff?" asked the man.

The question made Chuck change his tone. His RADAR instantly came to life. He paused and looked the man over. After a moment he said, "I don't know anything about computers." Chuck hadn't realized it, but his smile had disappeared.

The fan must have picked up on the change. "I'm sorry! I just thought that computers are what most analysts in the military were involved in nowadays!"

Chuck tried to smile, but the questions were not typical for a normal fan. Chuck became evasive. "They're into lots of things now. I don't have anything to do with the military anymore. I'm retired."

That seemed to be enough for the 'fan'. "Okay. Well, great game! And thanks for your autograph," said the fan. "Good luck with the rest of your season." The man turned and started walking away. A bell went off in Chucks mind and he started to yell at the man to get his name. Then he noticed the cane and the pronounced limp the man was walking with. It appeared as if he had a knee that was locked up and it caused him to walk stiffly. He decided against going after him. Chuck shrugged off his feeling that he had just committed an operational security violation by revealing too much information. He had just taken his team to victory in a Holiday Tournament. He needed to revel in the moment. He quickly ran to the locker room, not giving another thought to his first encounter with Steve James.

After the team showered, they filed out of the arena towards the bus. It was parked outside the parking garage and a cold, light drizzle was coming down. Some fans were standing around yelling at the players. Some even tried to get autographs in the rain. Chuck had just slapped Charles hand as he turned to walk to the bus.

From a hundred yards away, tires squealed. Chuck turned to see what was happening. From across the parking lot, a blue car was roaring into a turn. Chuck was confused until he saw the vehicle turn towards the crowd. He looked to his left and his right. That's when his brain started working again. The vehicle wasn't out of control or headed for the crowd. It was heading directly at Charles Holmes.

Holmes stood motionless as the blue car drove straight at him. The bright lights of the car illuminated Charles as he stood in its oncoming path. His only movement was to drop his bag. Chuck finally got his body to react. He took off running. An instant before the car would have hit Charles, Chuck tackled him taking him to the pavement. The blue streak just missed both men as they tumbled to the pavement. There was a loud 'pop' as the car slammed into Charles Holmes' gym bag. The bag exploded sending clothes, sneakers, and toilet articles flying everywhere. The blue car immediately disappeared around other cars in the parking lot, down an exit ramp and out of sight. Only the roar of the engine and the squeal of burning rubber could be heard. Chuck didn't even think about looking at a license plate.

Chuck rolled over and looked up at the night sky. "Are you okay?"

"Yeah! I think so," said Charles. He slowly sat up. He rubbed his leg and started to get up. "Ow. Man, I bumped the hell outta my knee. Come on, let's get on the bus," said Charles. "Those damn Memphis fans are sore losers!"

Chuck just shook his head. "Let's go home."

On the bus, the trainer, Dianne Weston, looked at Charles' knee and determined it was only a sprain. With rest, treatment, and ibuprofen, he would be back to full strength in two weeks. It just so happened that St. Michael's didn't have another game scheduled until the tenth of January. Someone on the bus noted the streak of luck.

Chuck wasn't so optimistic about the 'luck'. There was something ominous about the vehicle. He kept running the incident over in his mind. The vehicle was headed directly for Charles, and only Charles. He wasn't walking with anyone else. Plus, the lights had the high beams glaring. They were in a fairly well-lit parking lot. He had tried to see the license plates, but the reason he didn't was because there weren't any. He asked other players and no one else saw a license plate. Was the driver trying to kill Charles, or just injure him? Surely, if someone wanted to hurt Holmes, why there and why then?

It didn't make sense. Chuck figured if someone was deliberately after Charles, they could have picked a better way or a better place to hurt him. There was a message being sent. That message wasn't intended for Charles Holmes alone.

Chuck looked at Pete Henderson sitting in the front of the bus. Henderson was nervous again. Maybe even more than before. Chuck saw Pete look back from his seat to stare at Holmes. Pete noticed Chuck looking at him then he quickly turned around to the front. Chuck just kept watching the assistant coach. The more he watched the more he began to understand what had happened. The car had been driven by the people from the BCT. That was why Henderson was nervous again. It was the BCT sending a message to Henderson. The more Chuck thought about it, the more he believed it.

He shook off his morbid thoughts and tried to be rational. Stuff like that just doesn't happen. He fought off the thoughts all the way back to San Antonio. When he got home, he quickly undressed and went to bed. Chuck tried, but he couldn't sleep. He got out of bed and went to the phone. He only needed to call one number. It was time to get his second team together for a different game. Even at two in the morning, he wasn't surprised when Eddie answered the call.

After the Holiday Tournament things were quiet on campus. The St. Michael's Armordillo's did not have any games scheduled and most students were scattered all over Texas during the holidays. Chuck tried to rest as much as he could. Chuck spent most of his time in the gym. It was the only way he could relax. As he shot and ran, he found himself thinking about two events.

The first event was the high he had from hitting the game winner at the Holiday Tournament. He found himself shooting the shot over and over, as if he could relive the feeling of elation that had swept him away in New Orleans.

The other event that kept running in his mind was the blue car that tried to run over Charles Holmes. Chuck knew without a doubt the intent was there and it was deliberately directed at Charles Holmes. The vision of the car kept coming over and over. He started missing his jumpers. After thirty minutes, he couldn't take any more. It was still three hours until the group was supposed to get together at Nate Hawkins house. Chuck decided to pack it in and go home. It was time to put his focus somewhere else.

CHAPTER FOURTEEN

They had the meeting at Hawk's house because it was the only place big enough to seat everyone comfortably. Chuck, Eddie, Chris, Hawk and Sandy, as well as Grace, were all there. Grace had returned from her parents' house and Chuck invited her to meet everyone. He made it clear to everyone that only this group and Eddie's friend, Bobby, would know what was happening. It was more people than he wanted to be involved, but they were all the people he felt he could trust. Eddie said that Bobby was going to try and stop by, but it was a two hour drive from Austin.

After introductions and eating four pizzas, the group got down to business. Eddie had set up a laptop that was plugged into Hawk's big screen TV. Eddie had put together a slide show for the group to explain what they had been working on. They all agreed the best way to affect the BCT was to hit them in the wallet. The best way to do that still seemed to be by affecting their computer network.

"We've spent nearly a month mapping the BCT network. We got in through back door access via a portal in a printer in the Caribbean. We were fairly certain it was in the Bahamas. Low and behold, the BCT's parent organization, which is in Vegas, has a casino in the Bahamas named: Big Casino Nassau."

"Let me guess. There is a 'Big Casino Vegas', too?" asked Chuck.

"Not quite. We're dealing with 'Big', pun intended, ego's here. The "Grant's Big Casino" in Vegas is owned and operated by Mr. Jackson Grant." Chris had a picture of Grant on a slide, and it popped on the screen. "Having access for any operation is key. With that access we traced all the virtual locations of the Big Casino Network, obtained email addresses, contacts and social media accounts of the top operators in the network. From there we matched them up with physical locations for the entire organization." Eddie clicked up a slide that had 15 physical locations across North America and the Caribbean. The group was impressed. Eddie nodded to Chris to continue.

"We have developed messages for the leadership of the BCT and their parent organization in Vegas. We told them we know their email addresses and their social media accounts. We did not tell them that we know the core system that operates their betting lines and Bobby is working on something else that is beyond root access," said Chris.

Eddie said, "With some luck, Bobby thinks he can get links to their financial data. Bank accounts, locations, payroll. The key things we need to hit them where it hurts. I can come up with a few more operations to screw with their business. We can do a simple denial of service for long periods of time; we can alter point spreads; we have identified the people shaving points at four schools so far. And we set up a Trojan Horse," explained Eddie.

Sandy Hawkins was confused by the term. "What the heck is a Trojan Horse? Like Roman times?"

Chris fielded the question. "Yeah! More like the Spartans than the Romans! You know that big horse they took into their castle. Then, 'BOOM'! All those dudes jumped out and destroyed the place from the inside." Sandy Hawkins nodded, but they could tell she was still a bit confused.

It was Eddie's turn to try and explain. He looked at Sandy and said, "It's somethin' like this. We planted a malicious program inside their network. Small, so hopefully they can't find it. It hasn't been recognized, so it sits on their network waiting to be activated. We can control or affect the network anytime we choose, as long as this program isn't discovered. We have additional programing we are working on so we can use the tool to do a couple different things to their network. So far, this program is undetected. Just waiting to be used."

Sandy smiled that she understood so Eddie got back on track. "We can continue to manipulate data or messages and finally, with that Trojan Horse, with a tweak, a wiper program, we think can destroy the system if we need to. We continue collecting data with a sniffer program and for defense, we continue to change the locations of where our messaging comes from. This other stuff may require us to get more specific data and Bobby is working on that aspect."

Eddie saw Sandy with another quizzical look on her face. He knew immediately what confused her. He smiled at Sandy and asked, "The Sniffer?" She nodded and smiled letting Eddie know she understood.

"A Sniffer interprets, captures, and stores packets of information that travel on the network from address to address. The tool was originally used to troubleshoot and model how a network functioned. They use one to defend their network but so far, aren't looking where we've put our packages on a server that is at an umbrella location. It's basically an eavesdropping program. It works primarily for that, and it will work for our purposes." Sandy was very appreciative that Eddie had made her feel like part of the team.

Chris looked at Chuck and added, "We have a keystroke program in place as well. No telling how many laws we've broken." Chuck was smiling as he shook his head. "Please send us Ritz Crackers to our cells in Leavenworth."

It was Hawk's turn to laugh. "We might be able to get you out of there, but…doubtful."

Some questions arose from around the room. Chuck wanted to know more about the BCT leadership. Who they were? How many managers they had? What about the network ops at the physical locations? Eddie indicated they already had most of that information. "The majority of their network is mapped. The umbrella organization is the Vegas site, led by Jackson Grant. He controls this huge online gambling system from Las Vegas. This system of networks is called, Big Online Network Entrepreneurs. To the gamblers, it's simply called; The BONE."

Chris added, "A bunch of rich sports fanatics see The BONE as the best place to online gamble. There is a reason for that. There's more."

Eddie cut in. "We also believe Grant has a side hustle with the college basketball score manipulations. Even more than the shaving. He uses an intranet within the BONE intranet to pick and choose customers for preferential treatment and fixed bets."

Chuck said, "He's picking the people he wants to win? Doesn't that hurt the business?"

Eddie smiled but quickly got back to business. "Not if he's getting a chunk of it! We think he's taking a cut from the winnings of the clients he allows to cheat. He provides them bets on the games that are fixed. It's like insider trading on Wall St."

Chuck nodded thought of another question. "Can you tell us more about the Footprint? The information you're getting."

Eddie was getting used to the group asking questions, so he went right into defining footprinting for the group. "By using tools like Cyberarmy and Dogpile, we took the BONE system, broke it down into domain names, blocks of networks and even individual IP addresses which were connected to any part of the system. We discovered info about their internet activities, their intranet, where we found special relationships via their email and text communications. Like we noted earlier, fifteen physical locations of the Big Casino brick and mortar sites. So far. They may run some that we don't know about yet or are using different names. It was only a matter of time until we gained access from that opening in the Bahamas. Now we have started mapping financial data as well."

Chris stepped in again. "We just mapped the system from top to bottom, laterally and in depth. Multiple dimensional activity, ya know?" Chris pulled up another slide that provided a 3D image of the concept. Chuck, Grace and Sandy were in awe of the work.

Eddie said, "We already sent a message to BCT that indicated that we have personal address information. What was even better was the fact that Nate has collected 132 phone numbers within the system. That includes Jackson Grants' personal addresses. The numbers included over 70 based in Vegas, 20 in New Jersey and New York, and even five in the Bahamas. With more time, we'll continue collecting information on the phone numbers of people and their locations, not just of employees, but supply companies, infrastructure support, all the bettors, and the overall structure of Grant's BONE business."

Sandy looked at Nate and said, "So that's what you've been doing all these nights?" Nate Hawkins took a sip of his beer and smiled. "I thought it was a woman." Hawk's smile instantly faded as he turned crimson red.

Eddie laughed loudly and turned to Sandy. "I can vouch that he has NOT been running around on you, because we've had him working overtime defining the organization. For which we are thankful because it's been a tedious job."

Then Grace asked about being detected. That was Chris's department. As a former military programmer who specialized in network defense, Chris focused on the security aspect of the operating system. "We've put spoofers in the programs we've used so far. The spoofer is designed to tell their systems administrator that someone else is doing the message transmissions from a different location. In this case, we created personae within groups of fraternities throughout the country." The group was a little clearer on spoofing than they were on sniffers, so Chris continued. "We've made sure they got indications that fraternity brothers were sharing BONE network information on their system. If they don't discover us, soon we will allow them to identify the fictitious sites when it becomes necessary. We are prepared to dox everyone in the system today if asked to." said Chris. Everyone was familiar with doxing.

Chuck thought of another question. "What school fraternity are you going to indicate is responsible?" asked Chuck.

"Not really a school, per se," said Chris.

Eddie jumped in. "The Ivy League."

"The PAC 10," said Chris also smiling now.

"The SEC," said Eddie. "And the . . ."

"I get the point," said Chuck smiling.

"We're spoofing a fraternity system, that doesn't exist, that goes across the country that knows all about the point shaving in the BONE. We created our own network linking multiple computers from multiple universities. That's the part I'm good at and I can assure you, nobody is gonna track the operation back to us." Then Chris said something that made Chuck perk up. "Plus, there is other stuff we can do if they really, really piss us off!" Chris caught himself. "Oops, sorry ladies!" Sandy and Grace had no issues with the slip of the tongue. "We have a logic bomb, essentially some instructions, ready to install that will set up for a time of execution to be determined by Hoopman when he needs them to be triggered. This program with additional instructions, if it works right, will destroy their network." He looked at Chuck. "That's your Christmas present. We just need to figure out the best time to execute." Eddie just smiled.

Eddie added, "I think sometime in March might be appropriate when the heavy betting occurs. But I don't think we'll have to resort to that if we can get the BCT to back off. All these other things should hurt them enough, so they leave St. Michael's, and maybe even the rest of college basketball, alone." Then Eddie asked the question Chuck had been waiting for. "We have the back door entry, but that may not allow us to put the necessary program into the BONE network. So how do we get our work into their system?"

Ed looked around the room and continued, "The problem isn't writing the program. We already have most of that done. The problem is getting the program into the system without being detected. We think we can deal with their encryption once we're inside. We need to either get a technically competent programmer from inside the gambling organization who is angry at his boss or is greedy enough to become a traitor to the business! Where are we gonna find a "technoficient" person inside the BONE willing to do that? These guys are criminals. They will probably kill anyone that tries to do something nefarious from inside the network. I could try and do it remotely, but Chris said we should do that only as a last resort. Later on, we may need to go to the BCT site and physically install something. We've shelved that idea for now. There's no sense risking getting discovered now."

Chuck thought about the comment and frowned. Then a spark popped into his mind. "If we can't get a person to turn coat, how about a machine?"

Ed thought about and said, "Yeah. Yeah, that would work. But, how are you gonna get me a machine that I can insert the program into without getting me into their shop?"

"Hawk and I have talked about that. Just show Hawk where BCT is, and he will handle that. Continue working on a program that's gonna make them want to get out of the business of betting on college basketball, okay!"

Grace Winters was smart enough to pick up on something Eddie had said earlier. "What about the encryption part? Isn't that going to be a serious problem?"

As soon as she finished the doorbell rang. "Funny you should mention that. If that's who I think it is, our visitor might be able to answer your question better than me," smiled Eddie.

"Everyone, I'd like to introduce Robert Savi Banduhar," said Eddie with a grin. "Or as we like to call him, Bobby!" Hawk and Chuck looked at each other. Bobby Banduhar looked like he could have ridden up on a bicycle because there was no way he could be old enough to drive. Bobby may have stretched to five foot-six, 135 pounds soaking wet. He had the face of a twelve-year-old and the smile of an angel. At first glance, no one would believe you were looking at a computer genius, much less one of the best in the world.

Bobby stepped forward and shook everyone's hand. As he said 'Hello' to all, Chuck was embarrassed at the stereotypical image that passed through his mind. He had expected 'Bobby' to be an Indian American man with an accent. Chuck looked to heaven and asked for forgiveness for his transgression. His prayer was answered. When Bobby spoke, he had a distinctive Texas accent and Chuck nearly giggled as he shook Bobby's hand. Bobby was sharp and picked up on Chuck's smile instantly. He immediately broke into the accent of an Asian Indian. "Let me guess. When you look at me, you expect this, right? Were you expecting dis?! You were expecting me to talk like dis, weren't you?"

Chuck's face immediately turned red. It took the group a moment to comprehend what was happening. Bobby burst out laughing. Chuck saw Bobby had a sense of humor and Chuck let go a laugh just as loud. "I'm sorry, Bobby! I really am!" Bobby provided the perfect tension breaker. Chuck gathered himself. "I want to apologize because from the second I saw you, I expected that accent you just used. I . . . I truly do apologize," said Chuck.

"That's all right, Mr. Hayes! I get that a lot. It's just you are the only one I know honest enough to say they expect me to talk like I just walked here from the 7-11 corner store," said Bobby. Bobby was still smiling as he began looking Chuck up and down. "You are a little smaller than I expected. I streamed the Holiday Tournament and you played really well."

Chuck was surprised. "Thank you. Just for that compliment, you can call me Hoopman. As for the game, my teammates were there, and they helped a little!" said Chuck with his tongue literally in his cheek. Bobby laughed and walked over to the counter for a seat. Chuck said, "Welcome to our get together. Before we get down to business, perhaps we should learn a little bit more about you."

Chris immediately jumped in, "He is the best 'cyberpunk' cracker in the business!"

"A 'cracker'?" asked Chuck.

"Yeah! Bobby's what you call a cyberpunk. Not just a hacker. Bobby is an ethical hacker. He goes into networks for a purpose. And he's the best I've ever seen," said Eddie. "Please forgive me, Robert, but I must tell them." Bobby smiled and nodded towards Eddie. "Bobby maxed the SAT's when he was twelve. His mom was smart enough to keep him out of college until he got older, so he didn't start UT until he was fifteen. Correct me if I'm wrong, but you're already in your . . . third year at UT?"

Bobby nodded. "They have an underrated Computer Science program." The Texas accent was throwing everyone off.

"This kids', I mean, this mans' dad was a mathematics professor back in India about twenty years ago. Mr. Banduhar owned a software design company and built it up in Mumbai. His mom was British. They wanted 'Robert' to get an American education, so they moved the Headquarters to the last bastion of American freedom, the grand state of Texas. He's mature enough to live in a very nice apartment in the Silicon Hills of Austin, but still goes home on weekends to Dallas. He spends most of his time online, including the Dark Web, researching computer software and hacking tools. If there is anybody who can help us keep this project together, it's this guy. On behalf of the team, Bobby, welcome!" Everyone gave a modest little golf clap for both the eloquent background introduction and Eddie's delivery. Robert Savi Banduhar was obviously embarrassed by the introduction.

Chuck said, "Just before you walked in, we were discussing encryption."

During the introduction, Bobby magically produced an ice-cold energy drink, grabbed a cold slice of pizza and some chips off the coffee table. He nearly had to climb up the barstool next to the kitchen counter that overlooked the living room. "Eddie gave me a heads up on that and I'm not too worried," said Bobby as he stuffed some chips into his mouth.

Chuck looked at Eddie who was rolling his wheelchair next to the coffee table. Eddie looked up at Chuck and grinned. "Bobby's dad invented the encryption system used by the BONE."

You could have heard a pin hit the carpeting in the Hawkins plush living room. Chuck said quietly, "He . . . invented . . ."

Bobby interrupted, "Kind of! He assisted in the design which eventually was used to encrypt packets of data that transverse the internet." Chuck looked at Eddie and shook his head in disbelief.

"If he taught you anything about it, I'd say we're in good shape," said Grace.

"He did teach me quite a bit. He made a lot of money on that design. It's used globally," said Bobby.

Hawk snapped his fingers, "Banduhar! Radji Banduhar is the Vice President of Virtuosity, Inc.!" Everyone looked at Hawk in disbelief. "Virtuosity Incorporated makes video games. Your dad's company was bought by HP about seven or eight years ago, right? Everyone expected him to be in line for the CEO position."

"He wasn't having fun. Those companies are all about money and he had enough. He's all about the fun now. He's into the Metaverse and virtual worlds. He never liked the pressure of computer systems development and mass production," said Bobby. He took a big slug of his energy drink. "Besides, they weren't gonna let anyone of Indian descent take a position like that in their company. It wasn't even racism. It was corporatism." There was a touch of resentment in the prodigy's tone.

"Glad he is doing what he wants to do now. He deserves it," said Chuck. Then he got back onto task. "This encryption process. You're saying you don't think it's gonna be a problem for us against the BONE system?"

Surprisingly, Nate Hawkins answered, "Once we gain Administrator status, we can go right to the Security Accounts Manager, or SAM status, where the encrypted data is stored."

Chuck looked at Hawk and shook his head in disbelief at what he had just heard. "You understand what these guys are doing?"

"Oh, yeah! It's not that tough. If you got out of the gym more often, even you could figure it out," said Hawk.

"Touché, Hawk!" deadpanned Chuck. He decided Hawk needed a bit of teasing. "Okay, Mister Newly Trained Computer Geek, SAM you am, after this SAM status is entered, what next? Huh?"

Hawk grabbed some chips and stood up. "Then, because of backward compatibility we use a hashing algorithm left over from the root to get the data." Hawk stuck out his tongue.

Bobby jumped off his chair for more chips and added, "He's right. It's a one-way encryption process inherent in that system." The rest of the room was stunned by Hawk's newfound knowledge.

Chuck walked over to Hawk and looked him squarely in the eyes. "Who are you and what have you done with Nate Hawkins?"

"I picked up a few things from these guys," said Hawk. He looked at Sandy and she was beaming. Hawk gave her a wink.

Chuck said, "We gotta let you get out more. You've been assimilated!" Chuck turned to the crowd and said, "It's nice to know you guys are thinking that far ahead, but the rest of us don't really get into that techno-babble, so let's get back to the mission at hand!"

Chuck looked at Eddie and said, "You say Bobby's the best and you need him." He looked at Bobby. "I guess Eddie already told you most of it. These guys we're going against showed they can be ruthless. The public doesn't know this, but they attempted to run over Charles Holmes after the tournament. So, if you're in, you're in all the way, okay?"

"I'm in all the way, Hoopman," said Bobby shoving more chips in his mouth.

"I figure it'll take us one more week to get the logic bomb ready," said Eddie. "With Chris and Bobby, maybe we can be ready earlier."

"Hawk and I discussed the computers they use in Austin. Hawks gonna need a couple days to get those machines taken down," said Chuck.

"Machines?" asked Eddie.

"You guys use multiple spoofed sights. We're gonna go after multiple machines," said Chuck.

Hawk said, "But I won't do a thing until Eddie and Chris join Bobby in Austin with a program ready to be installed. I expect two to three days before they can get the replacement machines delivered. The timing is gonna be tricky."

"All right then. I guess the four of you are headed to Austin." Then he looked at Eddie and said, "If there is anything else you want to add that would contribute to the mission, feel free to put it in the program. You have a green light to burn these guys. Please be careful. They hurt people." Eddie nodded.

Chuck continued, "Now, let's look at the calendar." Chuck put a large desk calendar on the coffee table. He had marked out a schedule over the course of three months indicating what he wanted to see done to BCT and approximate dates. Now they needed to add Grants' BONE network targets to the timeline. "Here's a timeframe of what I think we should shoot for with these guys," said Chuck. "I need the first option, the denial of service, ready in two weeks. Can you do that?"

Eddie Newton looked at the calendar and said, "That's pretty darn quick!" He thought about it, looked at Chris and Bobby. Bobby nodded it was doable. Eddie said, "We might be able to make that. Once we're deeper in the network, if everything goes as I expect, we can add some of the other 'toys' that you're looking for. But that first deadline might be tough," said Eddie.

"If anybody can do it in a crunch, it's you, Eddie!" said Chuck with a smile. "Come on. Let's go over this calendar a little bit further out." They worked over the timeline, the physical geography as well as the mapping of the system that they knew already, and the operations requirements one more time.

For just a couple hours, Chuck Hayes felt like he was back in his old operations shop working on mission planning. It felt strange to plan operations in a non-military environment, but the principles applied to civilian ops as well as military. A good military plan meant everyone survived the mission. For this plan to be successful, no one should get hurt. For even greater success, no one should even know it happened.

"What the hell went on down there? Should I have sent you guys some help?" asked Jackson Grant.

"Oh, no way, boss! Everything is fine!" lied Tom Clark. "We lost a few bucks on the tournament in New Orleans because that kid at St. Michael's screwed us. So, we sent him a little message. He'll be playin' ball with us in no time."

"I thought that idiot Henderson had everything under control," said Grant.

"We did too, Mr. Grant. But right before the tournament, Henderson called us sayin' they weren't gonna play. Said that Holmes kid wasn't gonna shave points anymore. Henderson seems to be havin' a lot more trouble with the kid than we expected," said Clark.

"You tell Henderson, from me, he gets it together at St. Michael's or he's mine," said Grant.

Clark tried to cover for his "employee". "I don't think it's anything that we can't handle here, boss."

"You got one week, Tommy," said Grant. "One week and if that school isn't under your control, it's not just him. It's you, too! So don't make me call you again." Grant hung up the phone.

Tom Clark looked at his trusted agents, Derrick, and Nubbin, and said, "You find Henderson, and you find him fast!" The two men looked at each other. Clark finished with, "You bring him here so we can have a one-way conversation! And let me tell you two something. Don't screw up the way you did in New Orleans, or we'll all be dead!"

It seemed like an eternity to Chuck until the second semester started. He decided to take an easier course load with only five classes: Anatomy and Physiology II, Introduction to Computer Science, Sports Literature, European History I and American Journalism. He would get an additional two credit hours for Basketball.

Marshall also decided to take it easy. His courses were deliberately stacked so that he could focus on other educational areas. He chose liberal life sciences and arts courses for cultural exchanges. Marshall wanted to grow in other areas, and Chuck was sure the young man needed no pointers in the proper direction to head. What surprised Chuck most was to find out that his roommate had entered the ROTC program.

Pepper and Jose both took standard eighteen credit hour workloads but were sure to take professors that were known to be hoop fans or generally sympathetic to athletes. If things weren't going well in any subject, that class could be dropped after three weeks.

The spring semester had the St. Michael's Armordillo's starting their Conference schedule. Before their first conference game, they had to get back into the routine of aggressive practice sessions. Something was missing in their first practice session on Monday afternoon. Assistant Coach Peter Henderson was conspicuously absent.

Coach Round was obviously disturbed that Pete Henderson was missing. He shifted some of the coaching responsibility to Daymon Breyers. At 23 years old, Daymon was barely older than most of the players, and he was nowhere near ready to be the assistant coach. The players received Daymon and his instruction with reservation. All except Chuck. If Daymon said to do something, Chuck would do it without hesitation. After that first practice with Breyers acting in Henderson's role, some of the players stopped Chuck after practice.

"Man, why you listening to Breyers?" asked Bullet. "He doesn't know any more about basketball than me!"

Chuck looked up from tying his shoes and said, "It's simple! Coach Round is the coach. I do whatever he says."

"Yeah, but Breyers ain't Round!" said Ike Rollins.

Chuck shook his head and smiled. "Correct. Coach Round has entrusted Breyers to be his assistant coach. If he places that kind of responsibility and trust in Daymon to lead us in practice, we need to do what he says. To run us when we need to be run. To move us to places on the court we need to be moved to. To keep our mouths shut when we are supposed to. Just as if it were Coach Round himself talking." Chuck stood up, grabbed his bag, and looked at the assembled group of players. "If it were any one of you in his shoes, I would do what you told me to do as well. So put yourself in his shoes." Chuck tossed his bag on his shoulder and headed out the door.

The next day, every one of the players did exactly what Breyers told him to do, whenever he told them to do it.

After the third practice without Henderson, Round had noticed the difference in the behavior of his players towards his young assistant. He went up to Chuck and said, "Thanks, Hayes! I heard what you said to some of the players. Daymon is gonna be a good coach someday, and what you did makes it so much easier for him to get his confidence. Again, thanks, Chuck."

Chuck knew better than to play stupid with Coach Round and accepted the compliment. "I think the young man deserves our best. We don't need any more drama than we have." Chuck quickly got quiet thinking he had already said too much.

Henderson's disappearance was definitely on Rounds' mind. "I just don't understand Pete takin' off like this."

"Has he called?" asked Chuck.

"Nothin' at all," said Round.

Chuck bit his lip. "Coach. Maybe whatever is happening with Henderson is happening for the best. Things have a way of workin' out, ya know?" That was the best Chuck could do. He was worried about Pete as a person but knowing that Pete was in deep to the BCT, he really didn't care if Henderson ever came back. It was a very un-Christian way to think, and Chuck knew it. Maybe Henderson was off somewhere on his own getting his act together. Chuck remembered that Hawk had told him Henderson was no good. Now that he had pulled this little disappearing act, Chuck was in total agreement.

Round nodded, then looked at Chuck. "I guess you're right. I probably shouldn't take him back after this stunt anyway!" He patted Chuck on the back and headed for his office.

Chuck yelled to the coach, "It's gonna work out, Coach!" The Coach just grunted and kept walking.

"Where the hell you been?" asked Tommy Clark. "The boss is ready to kick my ass over you!" Henderson looked like hell. He hadn't shaved in four days. His clothes looked as if he had been sleeping in them. Clark could tell he had been drinking too.

"We found him in a bar," said Derrick. "He came along real peacefully."

"I just came to tell you, I'm done. Holmes is out and we need to move on," said Henderson. His voice was nearly a whisper.

Clark jumped on him. "OH, NO, BABY! IT AIN'T OVER!" He started to walk around his office. "We got some money to make! You're the guy who's gonna make it for us! So don't come in here with this fiction, tellin' me you're done!" He quickly pulled some paperwork from a folder on his desk. "You still owe us over ten grand!"

"I'll work it off some other way, but I can't go back there. Holmes isn't gonna play for us. If I go back, it's all gonna come out," said Pete Henderson.

Before he was a crook, Clark was a businessman. He knew the value of investment. He had invested too much in Pete Henderson to allow him to just walk away. His mind immediately went to work. How could he take care of Henderson and still get Holmes to "play ball"?

"I know exactly what to do, Pete," said Clark. "You're gonna call your friend Mr. Holmes for me. Nubbin', get this guy a pillow and a Snickers. He's not going anywhere for a while."

"Charles! Hey, man, it's me. Pete Henderson!"

"Coach Henderson? Is that you? You sound . . . different!" said Charles.

"Yeah, it's me." Henderson struggled to breathe. The rope around his throat was a little tight. "I just wanted to let you know that . . . I need your help, man!"

Holmes was hesitant. "What do you mean help? Where are you?"

"You'd do anything you could to help me, right, Charles?" asked Pete.

Holmes knew right then something was wrong. Henderson never called anyone by his first name. "What's up?" asked Charles, certain that he didn't want to know.

Henderson said slowly, "I need you to . . ." Clark became tired of the game, ripped the phone out of Henderson's hand and hit him with it. The phone made a loud pop as it smacked against his head.

"Mr. Holmes! You don't know me, but your friend here, Mr. Henderson, does. Right about now, I'm guessing he wishes he didn't." Clark got down to business. "You need to make sure you lose tomorrow night."

"No. NO, NO, NO! I don't play for you, guys! We're gonna beat Texas Lutheran tomorrow! You should bet on us!" said Charles.

"You don't understand, Mr. Holmes. Everybody and their brother think's you're gonna win tomorrow. That's why we bet against you. And you lose! If you don't want to see your friend Mr.

Henderson in a hospital bed, you will lose the game tomorrow," said Clark.

"But I can't. We . . ."

"You can lose! Or the next time you see Henderson he'll be in a casket." Grant let the comment sink in. Then he added, "And the next time you walk down the road, we won't miss!" The phone went silent.

Charles Holmes started to put his cell phone down, but his hand was shaking so much, he couldn't do it. His mind was racing a hundred miles an hour. He didn't care about Henderson. He didn't even like the man. But he didn't want to be responsible for anything bad that might happen to him either. He surely didn't want to keep looking over his shoulder for another car to run him over. Maybe by losing against Texas Lutheran he could save Henderson, and everything could return to normal.

Charles decided that the one loss wouldn't hurt the team that much. They only had one loss. Lose the game, they'd let Henderson go and it would be over. For Charles, the decision seemed so easy. The problem was, he didn't tell Hoopman.

Chuck was getting angry. There were four minutes left in the game and Charles was playing by himself. That wouldn't be a bad thing on most nights. Only on this night, he was playing like crap. If Chuck didn't know better, he'd swear Charles was on the take again. Yet Henderson wasn't there to manipulate Holmes.

Texas Lutheran University had tied the game. Chuck brought the ball up the floor. He looked inside to Parnell who was double-teamed. He didn't want to do it, but he passed to Charles in the corner. Charles dribbled for ten seconds as Dexter Thomas positioned himself under the basket down low. He had position on his man, but Holmes waved him away. The shot clock was down to three seconds so Holmes fired a three pointer that missed everything.

On the next TLU possession, Charles' man popped an uncontested three pointer from the corner. That was enough for

Chuck. Holmes not hitting shots he could understand, but not playing defense was ridiculous. Chuck decided to keep the ball away from Charles for the rest of the game. As much as he called for the ball, Chuck never threw Holmes the ball. Instead, he worked it inside to Parnell and Thomas for a couple tough lay-ups. Jose hit two huge free throws with a minute left. After a great blocked shot by Parnell, Chuck got the ball, drove the length of the floor, and was fouled as he hit the lay-up. The Hole went nuts. Chants of "HOOPMAN" filled the air. After four more free throws, it was over. Final score; St. Michael's 58, TLU 51. Everyone was on cloud nine. Everyone except Charles Holmes.

Clark was livid. How could Holmes not do what he was told? Didn't he understand the consequences? Wasn't it clear enough? The next message would have to be even clearer.

When Holmes got home that night, there were four messages on his phone from Pete Henderson. Everyone was the sound of a phone hanging up. He was only in his room two minutes when the phone rang again.

Holmes was hesitant to pick it up. Caller ID indicated 'Coach Henderson'. He knew he had to. As he put the receiver to his ear he said, "Yes?"

"I guess you musta thought I was talkin' out my butt or somethin'?" said Clark rhetorically. "I want you to listen to something. He nodded to the two men standing by the door. The larger man pulled out set of brass knuckles and walked up behind Pete Henderson. Henderson started to beg. Clark held the phone up so Charles Holmes could hear Henderson's whimpering. The beating began with Henderson crying and yelling for it to stop. Luckily for Pete, he was unconscious when two of his lower teeth were knocked out. "I don't think you got my message, Mr. Holmes." He waited for a response that never came. "You cost me over twenty thousand dollars tonight."

"That wasn't my fault!" protested Charles.

"Don't matter. You should have done more to lose, and you didn't. So now your friend is . . . well, he's out of touch, isn't he?" Charles was silent. "Now I'm gonna call you back in a couple days, so you can talk to your friend. If he wakes up! That's when I'll tell you what you're gonna do next. You better not screw up or next time, it's you!"

Charles didn't know what else to do. It was two o'clock in the morning and he couldn't sleep. He clicked on the team roster online to get Chuck's number. Holmes did know what else to do. He picked up his cell phone and called Chuck.

Chuck was sound asleep, but could tell from the sound of Charles' voice, he was scared. Chuck listened to Holmes and said he would be right over.

When he got there, he just let Charles talk. He got everything off his chest. He talked about the man on the phone, the way Henderson was yelling and how he was going to be next. Holmes was a twenty-year-old who was suffering from a traumatic experience that he had absolutely no control over. There was no action Charles could have taken. Chuck mentioned the police, but Charles wouldn't hear of it. It would bring disgrace to the program and still wouldn't help Henderson. What was he supposed to do?

Chuck told him to sit down and relax. He explained there was a plan was in place to deal with the people that were holding Henderson. He reminded Charles that Henderson had made his choice and had gotten involved with the BCT before he knew Charles. Then he told Holmes everything he knew about the group that had been paying Charles' bills the previous year. Charles knew nothing about the organization. He simply got his money, in cash, from Henderson.

"This is what you need to do. Keep your head on straight and be observant of your surroundings. Don't get yourself in situations where you are alone. I can't be with you all the time, and the friend

I have that is good at protection is sort of pre-occupied right now. Just stay calm," said Chuck.

"I'll try, but it isn't gonna be easy," said Charles.

"Just try to relax," said Chuck with a smile. Charles nodded and a small smile appeared. "We're gonna get these guys. Just trust me, okay?" Even if Hoopman couldn't do it, the fact that he was willing to try to fight the BCT made Holmes feel better. After their talk, Charles Holmes was finally able to breathe, but he didn't fall asleep until the sun came up.

First thing in the morning, Hoopman got on the phone to Hawk. He told him about Charles' conversation with Clark. Then he told Hawk about Henderson. Hawk got quiet after that, and Chuck knew that was bad news. Hawk would get quiet when he became angry. Hawk was angry because it had taken longer to get the information he needed in Austin and develop the malware. This news wasn't helping his mood. Hawk finally said, "We need to move up the timetable. I'm gonna go play a little baseball, Chuck. If I can get that turd Henderson out, I'll try. But he isn't a priority to me." Hawk was quiet for a couple more seconds, then finished by saying, "I know what I've gotta do on this end. Let's take it to the next phase."

Chuck reluctantly agreed and said, "All right then. Good luck!"

"You guys, give 'em hell!" said Hawk. He slowly put his cell phone away and looked at Eddie.

"Does Hoopman want us to go with what we have?" asked Eddie.

"That idiot Henderson is being held by Clark," said Hawk to Eddie. "We don't have a couple of more days. We need to move now. We have to get our pieces in place."

Eddie nodded. "All right. We will be ready to go. Bobby has been great. He's got some terrific ideas, but he loses me sometimes when he gets on a roll. He's got the logic bomb program done, but it's all the follow up things he needs to work out."

"He's your man, Ed. Just help him move up the timetable," said Hawk.

Eddie looked over at Hawk and said, "We'll get him some more energy drinks and chips, and he'll be fine!"

Hawk finally smiled. "I can't believe he doesn't weigh more. The boy genius isn't exactly a health nut, is he?"

"Naw, but he is a genius. And we need him," said Eddie.

Hawk agreed, but his demeanor had changed considerably. "Excuse me, but I gotta get ready for tonight. I need to put some things in your van before we go to Austin." The game had taken on a new direction. The stakes were much higher.

The van was parked outside the Big Casino Texas office in Austin. Hawk looked at Chris in the back of the van. Eddie was strapped in behind the wheel of the modified van. Eddie and Chris had only known Nathaniel Hawkins a short while. In that time, they had never seen him display his temper. At that moment, Hawk was actually suppressing it. He was quiet, tense, and focused. Hawk finally said, "Did I ever tell you I was a big St. Louis Cardinals baseball fan?"

Chris said, "Nope. Never did."

Hawk had a baseball bat. The head of the bat was pointed towards the floorboard. He was squeezing the handle with both hands, virtually massaging the shiny wooden 38-ounce bat. "This is my Albert Pujols bat." Eddie and Chris just sat silent. Hawk turned and looked at Chris. "I'm gonna go take some batting practice." Then he opened the door and climbed out.

Chris rolled down the window. "You sure you don't want me to go with you? I could hold the door or something!"

Hawk stopped and looked over his shoulder. "Naw. It's probably better if you stay there. I'll be out as soon as I can." Nate Hawkins placed the bat under his long coat. The chilly January evening made the outfit appear normal. But under the coat, Hawk wore a flak vest and carried a 9mm pistol in a shoulder holster.

His only backup was the .38 tucked in the small of his back. He hoped he wouldn't have to use the pistols. But Hawk knew, you could never be too safe in situations like this.

"Are you all right?" asked Chuck. He slapped Charles Holmes on the back.

"Yeah. I guess I'm a little nervous," said Charles.

"Ain't anything you can do for Henderson," said Chuck. "Let's go win a ball game." The two teammates trotted out to start the game.

Though he didn't play his best game, Charles Holmes played solidly. His fifteen points weren't flashy, but they were enough. St. Michael's held on to beat Concordia 73 to 69. A win was a win, but the best part was they were on the road. Chuck made sure Parnell, Jose, Pepper, and Dexter were always involved on offense, and each man scored in double figures. Chuck finished with ten assists and five steals. As a team they hit twelve of fourteen foul shots.

Round was pleased with the game but wasn't himself without Henderson on the bench to be the bad guy. Daymon Breyers wasn't comfortable with the role as the hard ass screamer. For Henderson, it had come naturally.

In the locker room, Charles eyed Hoopman cautiously. Chuck knew exactly what was on his mind. As they walked to the bus, Chuck said quietly, "It's up to my friends in Austin, Charles. If Henderson is still there, they'll get him out. There isn't anything you could have done differently."

Charles nodded in agreement. But he didn't feel he had done enough. If Henderson died, he felt responsible for it, no matter what Hoopman said.

Chuck sat in the back of the bus, quieter than usual as he waited for his cell phone to ring. Hopefully, Hawk's part of the mission would go off without any major problems. He looked at his watch. It was past eleven o'clock. Events in Austin were about to happen. Soon it would be time for Bobby to send an email message. A message written specifically for an important recipient in Las Vegas.

CHAPTER FIFTEEN

Hawk entered the building like any other man coming in to place a bet. It was just after ten o'clock and there were over fifty people in the place playing illegal slots and playing pool. Hawk slowly walked to the back of the large room. He stopped at the bar and ordered an ice water. As he drank his water, his eyes constantly scanned the bar, watched the pool players, and determined who the employees were.

Soon enough, two men came out of a back room. One was bigger and had the face of a hockey player. The second man was black and much smaller. Probably coordinated, but not too strong. Hawk got a glimpse inside the room the two men had come from. He saw a row of computers. Business was obviously off because the room was fairly empty. Most of the bets had already been placed earlier in the evening.

The two men split up. The black man went behind the bar and joined the bartender. The large man went over to join one of the pool players. Hawk finished his water. His eyes had adjusted to the low light levels. It was time for batting practice.

Hawk walked over to the door to the computer room. With one smooth, powerful motion, he kicked the door in. He walked through the door and looked around. From under his coat came the baseball bat. Hawk drew back and let the rampage begin. He went down one side of the room swinging and flailing at the machinery. The few customers who were online immediately got up and moved to the door to get away from the man with the bat. Hawk could tell someone had shown up at the door behind him, but it was only a minor distraction. He continued with his mission without remorse, without mercy.

As he worked his way around the room, he heard a voice yell for him to stop. He did a quick count, looked at the type of laptops they used and assessed he had damaged at least thirty machines. He stopped with the bat in the cocked position and slowly turned around. The large man who had gone over to the pool player was walking towards Hawk. He carried a pool stick in his hand. His smaller friend was close behind, with some kind of metal club.

"WHAT THE HELL DO YOU THINK YOU'RE DOIN'?" yelled the hockey player.

Hawk took the bat, swung it a couple times, then flipped it in the air and caught it. Quietly, Hawk said, "Havin' a little battin' practice. Feel like pitchin'?" He couldn't resist adding, "Asshole?"

Nubbin started running at Hawk. The pool stick was high over his head. As he got close, he attempted to bring the stick down onto Hawk's head. Hawk was ready. He used both hands on the bat to stop the pool stick as it quickly came down. The bat did its job and the pool stick broke in two. Hawk swung his cowboy boot squarely into Nubbin's exposed groin. The man fell instantly to the floor. Hawk quickly hit him twice more on an exposed knee causing Nubbin to howl in pain. As he lay on the floor, Nubbin couldn't figure out whether to grab his knee or his nuts.

"That should keep you from comin' after me for a couple minutes," said Hawk. Then he turned and looked at the second man. "Now lookey here, Son. You only get a couple of chances to make real good choices in your life. I need you to make the right one now."

The man spun and started running for the door. Hawk yelled, "THAT WASN'T THE RIGHT CHOICE!" Hawk drew the bat back and threw it. He hit the man in the leg's and he too fell to the floor. Hawk ran over, picked up his bat, and stuck it against the man's chest. "Runnin' wasn't an option, Maggot!" The man was obviously concerned about Hawk's next action, and he used both hands to cover his groin. Hawk grabbed him by the throat and picked him up with one hand. He pointed with the bat. "You see that computer over there?" The man nodded. "You see your buddy on the floor?" The man nodded again. "Unless you want to end up like either of them, you tell me what I need to know!" Derrick, with the large hand on his throat, was eager to assist his new friend and quickly nodded that intent.

Hawk smiled and said, "I know you got somebody here named Henderson. You take me to him right now!" Derrick tried to say he had no idea what Hawk was talking about. Hawk provided a gentle application of the bat to Derrick's groin. A short backswing of the bat induced Derrick to come up with the right answer. Derrick couldn't speak with Hawk's hand around his throat, so he pointed down a hallway to a door. "Let's go quick, 'cause your friend is gonna need your help to get to the hospital." Hawk pushed Derrick towards the door. He smacked Nubbin hard once more with the bat as he walked by.

Derrick led Hawk to a stairway around the back of the building. He pushed open the door to a small, cramped closet. Hawk threw Derrick into the room. Off to the corner sat Henderson. He was tied to a chair. His head slumped over, apparently unconscious. Hawk pointed the bat at Derrick and said, "You better hope he ain't dead." The man started shaking his head and stepping backwards. "He was alive when we left; I swear!"

"Go get some water, Shithead! And don't get anything else or they're gonna need a second ambulance!" Hawk showed Derrick the Beretta under his coat. The man scurried off to get water.

Hawk walked over to Henderson and picked up his head. One eye was swollen shut, his lip was cut and had dried blood around his mouth. He was covered with bruises. Hawk could tell whoever had worked him over, really enjoyed his job. He knelt next to Pete Henderson and started untying him. "Hey! Hey, Henderson!" The man started to come around.

Henderson looked up and saw the outline of a man standing next to him. He mumbled something and started to beg, "Not again! Please, no more!"

Hawk said calmly, "It's okay! Don't talk. My name is Hawkins." Henderson tried to focus and comprehend what he was seeing. "Hoopman told me to get you out!"

Henderson seemed to understand. He mumbled, "Hoopman?" He cleared his good eye and said, "Hayes?"

Hawk nodded. "Yeah, Chuck Hayes." Derrick showed up with the water. Hawk gave it to Henderson who drank it down. "Easy, easy now!"

"How did you know?" asked Henderson.

"Holmes told Chuck. I had to talk this . . . gentlemen into assisting us with your location," said Hawk. "Look. We can talk about this if you want, but we need to be movin' before we get some company. Can you walk?"

"Yeah!" said Henderson. He groaned as he stood. "My ribs are killin' me."

Hawk grabbed Henderson's arm and slung it over his neck. "Come on!" Hawk headed toward the door. He had not forgotten about Derrick watching him as he carried Pete Henderson out of the room. "Hey, Shithead! You wait here for two minutes, then go call an ambulance for your friend. If you don't, I'm gonna shove this bat in your ear! You understand?" Derrick nodded, his eyes wide and unblinking.

Hawk quickly carried Henderson to the van. He laid him inside and Eddie drove away. On the way down the street, they passed an ambulance that was headed towards the BCT.

"Let's get you to the hospital," said Hawk. Henderson, lying in the back, nodded in agreement. He closed his eyes and laid his head on the floor. Hawk looked back at Eddie and said, "Then we need to get back out here and get ready for any phone calls. Clark will be ordering replacements." He was so matter of fact that

Eddie didn't quite know what to say. "How about St. Michael's? Did they win tonight?" asked Hawk.

"Yup! Won by four," said Chris.

Nate Hawkins had gone into the BCT, crushed at least thirty computers with a baseball bat, sent one bad guy to the hospital, rescued a kidnapped man, and acted as if it was just another day at the office.

All Eddie could do was nod and say, "I'll let Chuck know they can't hurt Henderson." Chris focused on driving.

For the first time in six months Hawk lit up a cigarette. He'd hoped that it would stop his hands from shaking. Hawk hadn't been that wired in years. He took a drag on the cigarette and laid his head back against the wall of the van. The first real battle had been a victory for the good guys.

"Mr. Grant?" interrupted Mike Thompson. Thompson was Grants' Chief of Operations.

"Yes!" Then Grant saw who it was. "What do you want?" answered Grant, just a little ticked off to be taken away from the game he was watching.

"We got an email you probably need to read," said Thompson. Just then Grant's cell phone buzzed. He looked at the number and didn't recognize it. He put it down on the desk.

Grant turned in his swivel chair and pulled out his keyboard. He pulled up his e-mail account and began to scroll through 126 messages. His cell phone went off again. Only thirteen had been read. As he scrolled, he saw the message Thompson was talking about.

The subject was 'Internal Dissent' Grant looked up at Thompson who said, "You probably need to read this one yourself."

Grant opened the message and started reading. His cell phone continued to go off. The email message read:

Mr. Grant,

I've been employed at the BCT for two years now. I've recently found out some employees have been ripping off your company for months. Tommy Clark is no good lying scum and he will do anything for money. If that means screwin' you, he'll do it. He has already done it. Plus, the guys he's had shaving points aren't coming through. He is still paying them! You should get rid of that idiot ASAP.

I suggest you get somebody down there and find out exactly what's going on! I will contact you again.

A Friend in Austin

"Do we know anything more about this so called 'Friend in Austin'?" asked Grant.

"We looked into employee records," said Carl Holden. "We don't have anything yet, but we're guessing he was somebody on the payroll at a satellite outlet. We have over twenty people we suspect could have written that."

Grant wasn't listening. "I could give a shit about the shavin' points money, but if Tommy Clark thinks he's rippin' me off, he's got another thing coming," said Grant. His cell phone rang again. "What the hell is going on with my phone?! I don't recognize anyone of these callers!"

"What do you want us to do?" asked Thompson.

Grant got up out of his chair and read the email once more. "Let's do our homework on the money before we go in there halfcocked. You may need to get a couple of plane tickets to go visit Austin." Grant looked at Thompson and asked, "Is there something else?"

Thompson was hesitant, but finally found the cojones to say, "St. Michael's won tonight."

"I thought we had them down as definite losers tonight?!" snapped Grant.

"Clark hosed us," said Holden.

Grant was angry. "Get those plane tickets! Clark and his bunch have no control down there! You two take a couple guys, get down there and figure this out. Nobody is rippin' me off! And find out more about the St. Michael's program. I don't want this problem to get out of hand!"

"You want us to get James on this message?" asked Thompson.

Grant thought about it. "Yeah! It couldn't hurt. My guess is he won't find out anything. He's just another overpaid computer geek!" He went back to his computer, cursed loudly, and started reading messages from Fraternity Houses as they came across his network.

Thompson disagreed with what his boss had said but didn't have the courage to question anything. James was probably one of the best computer network managers in the world, and Grant was lucky to have him. Thompson knew Jackson Grant didn't have a clue how useful Steve James could be.

Hawk and Chris were back in place outside BCT by six in the morning. Hawk set up his equipment so he could monitor any incoming or outgoing calls by the BCT. It wasn't until eight thirty when BCT made a call to order 36 new computers. Delivery was scheduled for two days later. That gave Bobby and Eddie forty-eight hours to complete their program and get it into a replacement computer. Only one computer of the same type that Clark had ordered was needed to be 'prepared' for delivery to the BCT.

Charles Holmes was relieved when he found out Henderson was alive. Chuck made sure Charles found out right away so Charles would stop worrying. Henderson was taken to an Austin hospital where Hawk told the doctor in the emergency room that he had been beaten up in a bar fight. The Doctor was upset that it had been well over 24 hours since the beating had taken place. Eddie calmed the doctor down and prevented him from calling the police. Pete Henderson had a concussion, lost two teeth, cracked three ribs, and sported over fifty bruises. His left arm was placed in a sling to keep it immobile enough so that it would keep his ribs from being any more painful.

The next day, Hawk got Pete out of the hospital. He decided not to take him back to San Antonio. Hawk took him to a military campsite on Canyon Lake. They all agreed it was best if Henderson stayed out of sight for a while.

It was at the campsite that the events of the previous week caught up with Pete Henderson. Chuck was there when the assistant coach broke down and cried. Chuck watched as the man sobbed uncontrollably on the bunk in the small cabin. He didn't feel sorry for Pete, but he was no longer as angry at him as he was before. Tommy Clark's men had done a number on Pete. No one is mentally tough enough to deal with the abuse, physical and mental, Pete had endured. But he was lucky to still be alive.

Later in the evening, Chuck was about to leave when Henderson stopped him. "I didn't tell you this before, but . . . I am sorry for what I did. And I want you to tell your friend Mr. Hawkins thanks for me. If it hadn't been for him, I'm certain I'd be . . ."

Chuck held up his hand and cut him off in mid-sentence. "Let's not dwell on that, Pete. It's time to drive on with what's right." Pete nodded. Chuck saw the opening and planted the seed. "We need to talk about Clark." Pete looked at Chuck. There was something different in Henderson's face. An appearance of resolve that Chuck had not expected to see from Henderson. "I need to know everything you can tell me about their organization, his people, his boss. We don't have to do it right now."

Pete grabbed a cigarette and said, "Now is as good a time as any. Where do you want me to start?"

"The beginning is always best," said Chuck with a grin. He took out cell phone and recorded the conversation. For the first time since he'd known Pete Henderson, Chuck found the coach to be helpful. The information Henderson provided was just what

Eddie needed to know to fill in some gaps on the BCT network operations and their intranet. Pete knew a lot more information about Clark and his boss, Jackson Grant, than Chuck had expected him to know. Chuck didn't know exactly how he was going to use it, but he knew it would be an asset eventually.

"GO! Take it over there now!" said Eddie as he sat in the van. Hawk jumped from the van with a computer box and carried it down the sidewalk. He looked around to make certain no one was watching. Hawk approached the delivery vehicle parked at the side door of the BCT building. They had timed the move so the delivery man carrying the boxes of computers was deep in the building. Hawk had about thirty seconds before he would come out. He placed the boxed computer on top of the stack of computers in the back of the delivery vehicle. Hawk quickly made certain they had the correct brand and type laptop for the switch. He quickly grabbed a different box and slowly walked away. The team had decided to switch one computer and hope they didn't catch the fact that one machine had a different serial number. The BCT would be more likely to not care about a different box as long as they had 36 machines.

The van pulled up to Hawk and he climbed into the back. The delivery man had just come out of the building and didn't even notice the van as it pulled away. The delivery driver grabbed the next stack of computers, put them on his dolly and headed into the building. He hadn't noticed any difference between the boxes. The "specially treated" computer was in the building.

"With any luck, inside they'll never notice any difference," said Eddie.

Hawk shook his head and frowned. "How long before you think they will hook them up?"

Eddie said, "I don't even think they will inventory these machines. I expect they will get plugged into the network by tonight.

"I hope you're right," said Hawk. He exhaled heavily as he climbed into the front seat. "Can we go home now?"

Eddie nodded. "Yeah. I'll check later tonight if they get them online. Once that's done, I'll run a couple of tests to see if it responds properly to commands." He looked at Hawk. "Next stop, San Antone." With their part of the plan done, Eddie Newton and Nate Hawkins were headed back home.

"Mr. Grant just wants to know what's going on here, that's all," said Carl Holden. His face was expressionless as he took a pull on his cigarette. Mike Thompson sat across the room on a couch. Not nearly as relaxed as his Vegas partner, Thompson's left foot was bouncing faster than a drummer in a heavy metal band.

Tommy Clark leaned back in his leather chair and smiled. "I know why you're here, and it's just like I told the boss. We have everything under control," said Clark as he eyed Holden.

Carl pulled a piece of paper from his coat. "Mr. Grant said I should show you this."

Clark remained calm as he read the email message on the paper. His face flushed red as the message sunk in. "This is crap! This is a bunch of bullshit, I tell ya'!" He squeezed the paper and rolled it into a ball. "First of all, I'm not rippin' the boss off! You can make sure he gets that message! I'm not payin' anybody who isn't comin' through for our program. We got one program that's havin' a little trouble, but it isn't anything we can't handle. This message is obviously from somebody who wants to get rid of me."

"Could it be someone in the St. Michael's program?" asked Holden. "The assistant coach up there, Henderson. That's his name, right? He's been one of your protégés for what, about two years now?" Clark nodded.

Clark was a little surprised that Carl Holden was aware of Pete Henderson by name. He silently wondered what else Carl Holden knew at the BCT. He hesitated before he nearly whispered, "Yes."

"Maybe this Henderson is the friend that Mr. Grant has, ya' think?" Holden asked the question rhetorically. "I think if you contact Mr. Henderson, a lot of your troubles will disappear."

Clark chuckled. "Funny you should use the term 'disappear'." He sat back down in his chair. After taking a long drink on his double Ketel One screwdriver, Clark proceeded to explain his situation with Henderson. How he had "contacted" him recently and offered him a painful lesson. Henderson couldn't have sent the message. He was under their control for the last week. He explained how he had "released" Henderson after the lesson and now he was in hiding. Henderson had not shown up at St. Michael's since he was released. Clark said their computers had been destroyed by some "nut job" but were already replaced and the operation would be fully online in 24 hours.

Holden nodded to Clark and demanded, "Tell me more about this guy, Henderson. I need information on his background and St. Michael's. Are you sure he didn't go back to the program?" Clark nodded that San Antonio was probably where he would end up, then reluctantly agreed to tell Holden and the Thompson guy everything he knew about Henderson. After all, what else could he do. He had to accept the help, or Holden would go to back to Grant and it would all be over. Clark explained it started with the gambling debt and snowballed from there. Henderson had alcoholic tendencies and used his position to blackmail a sophomore guard named Charles Holmes into shaving points. Clark even knew the bars where Henderson drank and gambled.

Holden took notes on his phone. When Clark was through, Holden said, "This is good stuff. I think I have a good picture of this clown. If it's all right with you, Henderson will be our problem now, okay?"

Clark wasn't ready to just turn over his problem completely. "How about I give you some help on this." He pointed to Nubbin and Monroe. "After all, it is my territory."

Holden said, "Sure. As long as your guys don't get in the way." Holden looked at Thompson to make sure he hadn't overstepped his lane. Thompson nodded his agreement. "All right then. How 'bout I make a call back to Mr. Grant and tell him the situation. He'll be relieved to know we have an agreement. I'll mention that I think it is something we can handle without any more help."

Clark smiled and nodded his agreement to Holden. Holden walked over to Tommy Clark and stuck his hand out to shake. Clark was eager to shake with Holden to get him out the door. Clark said, "See ya around." Holden waved to his men and walked out the door. Derrick and Nubbin dutifully followed Clark out of the office. Thompson looked at Clark. Slowly he turned and followed Holden out the door.

Once outside, Clark gave his directions to Derrick Monroe and Nubbin. "If your boss so much as thinks about talkin' to Grant, you tell me. You two boneheads think you can handle that?" Nubbin, with his cane supporting his battered knee and Monroe, with his destroyed pride after losing Henderson to Hawk, were in no position to do anything except agree to the guidance. "And don't screw anything up this time! This is big time, and we can't afford to have these guys in our business."

Thompson was on his phone to Vegas. After a quick update, he told the men, "We're a go from Vegas."

It was Holden that directed the small army. "Come on boys. I think we'll go visit the Alamo. Maybe this coach will try to make his last stand there." His guys laughed at the stupid joke. Holden was a lot of things, but comedian wasn't one. "I don't think this Henderson guy went anywhere. Heard they got the best Taco's in Texas in San Antonio. Maybe he knows a good place to eat. When we find him, it can be his last meal."

Steve James reviewed the message that Mike Thompson had sent. He checked the grammar, font, font size and style to see if there were any traits or techniques that would provide a clue as to the identity of the sender. He checked the trail of the message and, just as he had expected, the sender used an anonymizer address to protect his identity.

"I can't really tell anything from this, but it's long enough to develop some traits that we could use if this so-called friend sends another message to you, Mr. Grant," said Steve.

"Yeah. I didn't think you'd be able to figure out jack squat from it," said Grant. He was unable to hide his tone of disgust.

Steve wanted to say with more messages they could develop a pattern, but he knew Grant too well to think the bastard really cared what he had to say. He still tried. "If we get another message like it, I can tell you more."

"Sure," said Grant. "What the hell do I pay you to do, huh?" Steve was silent on the other end of the phone. "One more message like this, and you better do a helluva lot more than tell me something about it. I want you to find who's sendin' it, you got me?"

"Yes, sir," said Steve obediently. The word 'putz' was sitting on his tongue, but he couldn't spit it out. He waited for his boss in Vegas to hang up the phone. He looked at the message one more time. Something about it sent a spark off in his mind. He read it again and something clicked. The use of the acronym 'ASAP'. ASAP or as soon as possible is an acronym that started with the military but was now pretty well indoctrinated into business and general vernacular. Chuck Hayes, the 'old' man on St. Michael's basketball team, had been in the Army. He checked the message again for any sign the author was a military person. Nothing stuck out. Still, it burned in his mind. He kept the email in a special folder on his phone. James knew there would be another message, and he wanted this one close at hand. He looked at his watch and noted it was time to go back to work. Work for himself, not his boss in Vegas. He opened his encrypted file and began working on a new cryptocurrency program he was developing specifically for G-Cash, Grant's special cryptocurrency network. Steve's program was designed specifically for use with Grants' intranet. As far as

Steve James was concerned, the sooner he got it working, the better everything would be.

A week later, things seemed to be going great, so Chuck decided to take a night off. They played a Saturday afternoon game and beat UT at Tyler by 35. The starters didn't play much, but the second team, led by Pepper with 22 and Jose with 15, played nearly flawless basketball. The team only had six turnovers for the game.

Chuck went to Grace's house and took her out to the lake. First, they stopped by to check on Pete Henderson. He was looking better and obviously felt better. The coach was starting to get cabin fever. After a short discussion, he convinced Chuck he was ready to come back to the team and wanted to go back to coaching the next Monday. Chuck said he was against it, but he didn't have any reason not to let him come back. Keeping Henderson pent up would make Chuck just as bad as the BCT. Chuck agreed to take him back to his apartment the next day.

After meeting with Henderson, he drove Grace to a secluded location on the Guadalupe River where there was no public access. He started a small fire and pulled out graham crackers, chocolate bars and marshmallows. The sun was setting, and the temperature was dropping rapidly. It was time for some Smore's.

While he inflated an air mattress, he and Grace talked. She was asking him tough questions, things he had never talked about with anyone else. She wanted to know all his wants, needs and desires. What drove him and why he was really playing basketball. Chuck put her questions off as long as he could, and Grace began to get frustrated with his flippant responses. Eventually, the air mattress was full. She had heard enough diversion from Chuck and Grace Winters was tired of it.

Chuck stuffed the mattress into the bed of his pickup and grabbed a bottle of water from the cooler. He motioned for Grace to come sit by him on the tailgate. Reluctantly, she joined him.

"I guess you really want answers, eh?" asked Chuck. She nodded but was unable to suppress a frown. Chuck saw it and said flatly, "All right."

Chuck took a deep breath and began slowly. "Most guys my age are going through a 'middle-aged' crisis. A sort of, age induced insanity. Some guys buy a sports car or chase younger women. I'm trying to retain my youth in a different way, I guess," said Chuck. He looked up at the night sky and continued. "I've been playing basketball since I was six years old. I used to play in the morning before school, during school, after school and at night. My folks didn't have any money to send me to college, and I wasn't good enough to get a scholarship. I got offers to play for small schools, but nobody was willing to shell out money on a six-foot kid with a streaky jump shot. The Army gave me a chance to make a little money and keep playing ball," said Chuck.

He threw a couple of rocks out into the river and continued. "I think in my twenty years in the Army, I became a darn good basketball player. I've learned from people who have been taught by some of the best coaches in the world. I've played in all kinds of adverse situations. I've played ball with guys," he looked at Grace with a smile and continued, "and with women!" He chuckled and watched her smile. "Who could no doubt play major college basketball. And I enjoyed every minute of it. But they're serving their country." He took a deep breath.

Grace said, "And now?"

"Now, I'm taking a shot at a dream," he said. The distant look in his eyes was still visible in the moonlight. "I love this. I mean, the guys are great, the competition is great." He looked at Grace and said, "As for college, I've had a chance to meet some really great people outside basketball too." Grace blushed.

"This whole Henderson and Holmes thing hasn't ruined your perceptions of college basketball?" asked Grace.

"Oh, no! Not at all!" said Chuck. "College ball is probably the pinnacle of basketball as a game. You don't get the big money problems until you turn it into a business. As much as these programs make for their schools, I really think the players in all college sports deserve to be paid. The Name-Image-Likeness concept is a nice start. Advertisers are only going to pay excellent athletes at Division I schools real money. No one on the swim team is going to make the same money as the starting quarterback gets offered. Something, even if it is just token money, like the ROTC stipend money. You know maybe . . . five hundred dollars, one thousand dollars a month for a major money-making program. Something must be done to keep the talent coming into college sports and keep the athletes from being corrupted."

"And you're not corruptible?"

Chuck smiled. "Haven't you heard? I'm retired, Honey. I use all my big bucks to buy canes and Depends and that . . . crap that keeps my teeth in place!" They both laughed.

"As far as corruptible? I'm not corruptible on the basketball court, because in my mind, that is the last place of freedom for me. I want to keep the game pure." He was reflective again. "I don't know if I can pull that portion of it off."

Grace knew he was talking about taking on Grant and online gambling. "As long as you don't get hurt in the process."

Chuck laughed. "I am HOOPMAN! I am invincible!" He jumped off the tailgate and yelled into the night air, "I CANNOT BE DEFEATED!" Grace laughed at the act. He slowly walked over to her. "Maybe I can't be defeated on the basketball court," he said as he put his arms around her. "But if you play your cards right, I might be . . . corrupted, off it!"

Grace stood up and kissed him. "So, you admit you can be corrupted off the court, right?" Chuck nodded, no longer able to contain the grin that appeared on his face. Grace jumped off the tailgate and stepped away from him. She pulled her tank top off and stepped toward the river. She pulled down her jeans and kicked them at Chuck. "I guess it's time I corrupted you, Mr. Hoopman!" She turned and ran toward the river.

The fire was just bright enough for Chuck to follow Grace to the river. Occasionally, he would stop to drop a piece of his own clothing. The cold night air was taking his breath away, but he was being challenged. By the time he got to the water, Grace had already given out a little yell as she entered the cold water.

He shouted, "You're gonna make me do this, aren't you?"

Grace's laugh could be heard over her splashing. "You better hurry, cause I'm freezing!"

Chuck touched the water with his toe. It felt like ice. Quietly he said to himself, "What the hell! You are Hoopman. You are invincible!" Slowly he entered the water. He yelled out to Grace, "Pay no attention to Hoopmans' . . . manhood, as icy river water is Hoopmans' kryptonite!"

Grace nearly swallowed the river as she laughed. As she waited for Chuck to join her, she thought he may not be superman, but he was her man. And she really was in love with him.

The last week of January was by far the best week of basketball the St. Michael's Armordillos had enjoyed. Pete Henderson was back, but he was a different man. The anger that he usually displayed was gone. Coach Round wasn't pleased that Henderson hadn't informed him of the car accident. But the coach was happy that his protégé was back and in a much better frame of mind. The Henderson they were witnessing at practice was the Pete Henderson that Round had discovered years ago. He was teaching the players, not just hollering at them. He was excited about basketball again and it was obvious. Henderson was the first one there and the last one to leave practice. He even stayed late to work on jump shots with anyone that wanted to stay.

They played two games, winning both by over twenty. Charles Holmes was playing basketball with reckless abandon on the court and a huge smile off it. He was averaging sixteen points a game for the season after that week. Jose Rivera-Torres was becoming a rebounding machine. He had 18 in the first game and in the second pulled down twenty. The hook was becoming legendary. Jose was averaging eighty percent on the shot, but still didn't have a dunk. He was also down to 280 pounds.

David Parnell was without a doubt the team's defensive leader. He always took the other team's strongest big man and consistently shut him down. He was averaging twelve points and ten rebounds a game on the season. Pepper Dyer and Dexter Thomas had become solid role players off the bench doing whatever was asked of them. Tough defense, taking charges, hitting open long-range jumpers were some of the little things the pair was asked to do. Ask any player and you would hear their success could be attributed to one man that set the example with his 'never surrender' attitude. Chuck "Hoopman" Hayes.

For his part, Chuck Hayes accepted the part he played as "Hoopman". The fans were 100 percent behind everything he did. Even when he went out onto the court and sparred with the Armordillo, they would chant "Knock Him Out, Hoopman!" Chuck would treat the event as if he and Marshall were gladiators. The crowd would give a thumbs up or thumbs down depending on how Chuck and the Armordillo fought. Of course, Chuck would always defeat the mascot. Coach Round took on the role of Caesar. When the crowd became as loud as possible, the coach would come off the bench and issue his 'decree'. The poor mascot, of course lying on the court begging for pity, would usually get the thumbs up from Coach Round. This would naturally send the crowd into a frenzy as the mascot would be spared to go off and perform more deranged stunts for the fans.

On the court, Hoopman was more than just inspiring his teammates and the fans, he was beginning to get noticed in the press and by opponents. Chuck was leading the nation in Division III in assists averaging an unheard of eleven point five a game and was third in the nation in free throw percentage. His drive to win and 'never say never' attitude had become contagious to his team. Dropping down into the lane to fight for rebounds, taking charges and diving for loose balls were just examples of what Chuck would do to inspire his younger brothers in arms. For his efforts, he was receiving the admiration of his teammates and the respect of his adversaries. Everything a basketball player wants from the game.

What Chuck could not possibly have known was how much attention the St. Michael's Armordillo's team was drawing from Carl Holden. The Vegas boys and their new friends from Austin had gone on the road to watch an away game and stayed in San Antonio to witness a home game. They weren't watching as simple fans of the game. They were gathering information on Pete Henderson, Charles Holmes and Chuck "Hoopman" Hayes. Thompson and Holden were observing an unsuspecting enemy whose defenses were down. As the games were played, they were watching Henderson, Holmes and Hayes to determine how to attack three targets.

After watching two games, Holden had seen enough. Nubbin and Monroe would not be given the opportunity to fail again. The three "H's" as Thompson called them were Carl Holden's game now.

It was Friday night when Eddie called Chuck to tell him about a "situation." While collecting some information, they had come across some addresses that posed a problem. Chuck immediately went to Eddie's apartment.

"I have thousands of addresses that I've collected from people that place bets online," said Eddie. He was sitting at his computer terminal as he spoke. He typed as he talked. "Take a look at these addresses. Do you notice anything?"

Chuck looked at the screen and immediately saw the problem. "They have dot-mil addresses!"

"Oh, yeah! Hundreds of them." said Chris Crowley.

"How can they do that? Those guys aren't supposed to be betting using their military addresses. Knuckleheads!" said Chuck.

"The Department of Defense has thousands of people working from home because of COVID. It's probably not the troops as much as civilian employees and perhaps contractors. Football season had playoffs, basketball, both college and pro are primetime right now. Some administrators aren't as involved as others," said Eddie. "We need to stop these guys from betting online while they are at home. Or maybe even at work."

"The things we are planning could cause problems for people we don't want to cause problems for," agreed Chuck.

Eddie nodded. "Got any ideas?"

Chuck thought for a moment. "Yeah. Print me a list of these addresses. I have a friend that I think I can trust." Fortunately, the team had a home game coming up.

It was time for another message to Jackson Grant. Chuck pulled out a piece of paper and handed it to Eddie. "This is for Grant."

"When do you want to send it?" asked Chris as he reviewed the message.

"Tonight my friend," said Chuck. "We're in his head, so now let's dig around a little."

The message seemed trivial enough. Chris headed to his computer and sent the message to Grant. Perhaps they should have waited to let Hawk look at it. Maybe he would have noticed the security lapse.

"All right, geek! I got another one," said Grant into the phone. "I just forwarded it to you. I want to know how they got my credit card number?"

Steve James started to laugh, but knew his boss saw no humor in the situation. "I can't say for sure, but I'm guessing you make purchases online?"

"Sure I do, but I use a pin," explained Grant.

James didn't really care that the so-called "Friend in Austin" knew his boss' credit card number, and he certainly didn't want to take the time to explain how his PIN was collected. He pulled up the email and read the message.

"You still there, James?"

"Yes, Sir," said Steve. "Just reading the message. They just tell you they know what it is. Have you checked to see if he purchased anything with your card?"

"No, I haven't checked. Hold on a minute." Grant opened his account and checked his card. "DAMN IT! There was some kind of purchase Let me see. A purchase in Vegas for CRAP! Three thousand dollars. What the hell?"

Grant was about to say more when his secretary came through the door with a package from Amazon. She was red faced and asked, "Boss, did you make a large purchase for delivery?"

"NO! I didn't buy anything."

She set the box on his desk and showed him the contents. Grant looked inside the box and found boxes of sex toys. The secretary walked to the door. "There are twenty more boxes out here, Mr. Grant." She quickly left the room.

"DAMN IT!" yelled Grant. He went back to his cell phone for James. "I don't know who these clowns are, but you better find 'em soon! Don't let this get out of hand," said Grant.

Steve James heard what was in the boxes and did everything he could to keep from laughing. He gained his composure and said, "All right, Mr. Grant. Here's what you need to do. Close your credit card account, explain about a false order in your name. I'll keep looking to see if I can find out more about the buyers," said Steve. This time, he didn't add 'sir'. The bastard was starting to need his "geek". Steve smiled to himself.

"Just take care of this crap, James!" With that, Grant hung up.

Steve James put down the phone and re-read the message. Two more acronyms. The picture was becoming clearer. It was sophisticated stuff to get credit card numbers and his PIN, too! Steve James thought this was getting too sophisticated for some old, retired Army guy. Maybe Hayes wasn't working alone. Apparently, someone had installed a keystroke logger remotely on his bosses' personal computer. His opponents were better than he expected. Steve James decided right there that he had better not underestimate Chuck Hayes. It was time to double-check his work.

After a surprising victory against Mary Hardin-Baylor University, Chuck asked Hawk to meet him downtown on the River Walk. Chuck asked Hawk to join him to meet one of their old military buddies. Hawk was not one to miss a meal, especially if Chuck was buying.

As the two men sat next to the river at Rio Rio's, Chuck noticed Colonel Ron Taylor immediately. The men exchanged greetings and the Colonel took a seat. After drinks, appetizers and catching up, the Colonel cut to the chase.

"So, your phone call was a little mysterious. Kind of late at night for games. Why do you guys need to see an Air Force Cyber Officer?" asked the Colonel.

Chuck answered, "Sir, we have some information for you. But we hope you won't ask too many questions about it. Questions like, where we got it? How we got? Stuff like that."

The Colonel thought hard before he answered. "I'm not gonna do anything illegal, even for you guys. I mean, I appreciate all those years of hard work, and, Chuck, God knows you helped me out on more than one occasion." He looked into both men's eyes. "I'll bite. What do you got?"

Chuck started, "After we tell you this, you do with it whatever you need to. If you want to go take it to the CID, or civilian police, go ahead, Sir." Hawk gave Chuck a glance that indicated he was not too thrilled with Chuck's response.

The Colonel agreed. "All right, Chuck. That seems simple enough."

Chuck knew a lot of people still in the military intelligence and cyber community, and Ron Taylor was the one person who would know what to do with the list. He reached into his pocket and handed him the list of 137 dot-gov email addresses that had been collected by Eddie Newton and Chris Crowley.

The Colonel looked at the list. "What's the significance of these?"

"These addresses are government employees who are using government computers to gamble online," said Chuck.

The Colonel started to ask something, and his jaw was visibly lower. "I don't think I want to know how you got this list, but I am a little curious why you're giving it to me," said Taylor.

It was Hawk's turn to speak. "We need . . . Well, we would like for you to insure these people stop gambling online." He didn't expound any further.

Taylor looked from Hawk to Chuck. "I don't suppose you want to tell me why I would do that?"

"Ah, no, Sir," said Chuck. The Colonel was quiet as he pondered what he was holding. "Sir, what these people are doing is against every policy the Department of Defense and every other organization in the U. S. Government has established. These are just the ones we know about. We're not asking for any kind of legal action. We're not takin' it to the press or doxing them. But we are asking you to pull some strings and get these people stopped. It would really look bad if this got out."

Hawk added, "We know they are doing it. We know they are using military computers, but we can't tell you how or why. We really don't want to see these folks hurt for their poor judgement. That's not our purpose."

Taylor was convinced. "Okay, guys. I've heard enough. I can't make you any promises, but I will see what I can do."

"That's all we can ask for," said Hawk with a smile.

Chuck handed the Colonel a card. "Please give me a call when you find something out. And thank you, Sir!"

Taylor stood up and shook his head. "By the way, nice game. Hoopman!!"

Chuck smiled sheepishly, "I miss running with you, Sir. You may be older than me, but you come out and drain those threes!" The colonel laughed and shook Chuck's hand. "See ya' later, Sir!"

"I hope I see you in the D III championship game," said Taylor.

"Me too!" laughed Chuck.

Taylor tucked the list into his pocket, turned and waved goodbye. Hawk shrugged his shoulders. "Hey, we did what we could."

Chuck nodded solemnly. "I hope it's enough."

Chuck didn't think much when he saw Pepper Dyer running towards him. Maybe he wasn't getting enough running in practice or something. He smiled at the thought. Chuck was definitely getting enough. His toes hurt and his knees were killing him. The thought reminded him to get more Motrin. "What's up, Pep?"

The redhead was flush and could hardly breathe. "Chuck . . . Chuck, it's Charles!"

"What?" Chuck was confused. "What do you mean?"

Pepper Dyer exhaled loudly and said, "You haven't heard, have you? It's Charles! He's in the hospital!"

It was Chuck's turn to go pale. "In the hospital?" Chuck couldn't think. "Wha . . . What happened?"

Pepper grabbed Chuck's arm and said, "Come on!"

"Stop a second, Pepper," said Chuck. "Talk to me."

Pepper wiped his brow and said, "Somebody beat him up, Chuck! I mean beat him up bad!"

Chuck was stunned. His emotions went from fear to instantaneous anger. He needed to see Charles. To talk to him. Then the realization of what Pepper said hit him. Charles was in the hospital. Everything else would have to wait. "Come on, Pep! I'll drive!"

CHAPTER SIXTEEN

Chuck and Pepper made it to the hospital without a speeding ticket. They got directions to Charles' room. At first, they weren't allowed in. Only members of the immediate family could see people who were in the intensive care unit. The players soon found Coach Round pacing in the waiting room. His eyes were red, and his face was flush. When he saw Chuck and Pepper, he quickly wiped his nose and put his handkerchief in his pocket.

Chuck went up and hugged the man. He didn't know what made him do it. It just seemed like the thing to do. Round accepted the hug then turned and pulled his hanky out again. The coach walked to the window and looked outside. He recalled what made Charles Holmes so special to him and shared it with Chuck and Pepper. "I started recruiting Charles Holmes in the ninth grade. He wasn't as fast as a lot of kids. He couldn't jump as high. Just another C student." The coach inhaled loudly and stared up at the ceiling. "I knew he was gonna be a late bloomer. I could tell. He waited and waited for the big schools to offer him a scholarship that never came. After he realized the offer was never gonna come from one of those schools, I was there. I kept a position open for him because I knew," he said. He turned to Chuck and Pepper with a tear in his eye. "I knew how special he was. Now he's in here," sniffed the Coach. "What happened, Chuck? This kind of thing just doesn't happen without a reason?"

Chuck swallowed hard. "I don't know, Coach. But if there is any way possible to find out what happened, I will." He put his arm around the coach's shoulder. Chuck had a very good idea what happened to Charles but wasn't going to tell Coach Round.

A doctor came into the waiting room and introduced himself as Jonathan Trumble. Surprisingly, Darrell Round and Dr. Trumble were on a first name basis. Chuck got the impression the coach had met the doctor prior to coming to the emergency room for Charles. Chuck put the thought away and listened as Dr. Trumble spoke. "He's in pretty bad shape. It looks like whoever did it mostly focused on his face and ribs. As for his legs, especially his knees, they probably had steel tipped boots. I'm just assuming it was more than one individual. I already gave the police as much information as I could. He's in critical condition right now. I'm hoping by morning we can upgrade him. Has his family been notified?"

Coach Round answered, "Yes. His mother is on the way. She should be here by morning."

"I hope for her sake he is responsive by then. Gentlemen, I'd like to tell you some better news, but I don't have any. I don't think I'll be able to give you anything new for a few more hours," said the doctor.

Round nodded in agreement and tried to smile. He said, "Thanks, John. I appreciate you taking the time to come down here and look at him for me."

Trumble said, "It's nothing, Darrell. How are you doing these days?"

Round looked at Chuck and Pepper and said, "Could you excuse us for minute, fellas?" Chuck and Pepper nodded and walked away.

As Pepper spoke, Chuck looked over his shoulder and watched as the doctor put his hand around Coach Round's shoulders as they walked down the hallway. Round pulled a bottle from his pocket, and the doctor nodded.

"Chuck?" asked Pepper. "Did you hear what I said?"

Chuck looked at Pepper and said, "I'm sorry, Pepper, I was somewhere else for moment."

"I said, 'Do you have any idea who could have done this?'" repeated Pepper.

Chuck looked at his friend and lied. "No, Pepper. I surely don't." He turned his attention back to Round and watched as he shook hands with the doctor and came back to the waiting room to join his players.

Round gave Pepper the task of notifying the rest of the team. Chuck volunteered to stay around with the coach until the prognosis got better. Then he asked the coach if he wanted some coffee and took off down the hall. He thought about what he had just seen and made a mental note to ask the coach about it. It was not the time or the place to bring it up. Charles Holmes was the priority right now.

Chuck stopped at the first phone he came to. He dialed Eddie's number from memory. The phone rang four times. Chuck grew impatient. After what seemed like an eternity Eddie answered, "Hello?" Chuck could tell his friend had been sleeping.

"Eddie, it's Chuck. I need you to run whatever you got in the hopper that's ready to go, right now," said Chuck.

"Right this very minute?" asked Eddie.

"Right now!" Chuck realized he hadn't told Eddie what had happened. He took a deep breath and said, "They beat up Charles Holmes." The phone was quiet for an instant. Then Chuck added, "They hurt him bad." He let the words sink in. "Whatever you can do to those bastards, you run it."

"Okay, Chuck," said Eddie. "We got the DDOS ready to go. I'm all over it. It'll be on the way by morning."

"And Eddie," added Chuck. "You hurt 'em. Hurt 'em bad!"

Two messages were sent. One to all the gamblers who used Grant's service telling them not to gamble on the upcoming Super Bowl and a second message directly to Grant explaining why he was being targeted. It was up to him to get out of betting on college basketball. Chuck didn't really care if they bet on football, but it made a great target to hurt Grant's profit. The Super Bowl would be the most bet on event of the year. BONE stood to lose millions.

Eddie, Chris and Bobby had prepared a Dedicated Denial of Service that would prevent Grant's organization from conducting any online business potentially for hours. They deliberately bypassed the BCT and went after the bigger fish in Vegas. The program only targeted those specific addresses that bet using BONE online. The DDOS would keep the company from receiving any bets or sending out any responses. They still needed some more time to prepare their "cyber battlespace" for the future attacks. With any luck, the DDOS would do enough financial damage to get Grant's attention. It was hoped he would stop interfering with St. Michael's operations or maybe even all of college basketball. It didn't matter what Eddie and the crew did to Chuck, as long as they hit Grant quick and hard. If Grant had a heart attack from all the money he lost, Chuck's only wish was that he would be there to watch.

Two days later, Charles Holmes was sitting up in bed and could see visitors. His mother stayed with him constantly. Chuck talked to her a couple times and tried to comfort her. She couldn't understand what had happened to her son. Who would do such a thing to Charles?

Chuck had answers, but he didn't tell her. When Chuck visited with Charles, he let him do the talking. Charles had over fifty stitches in various places on his body. Fortunately, he remembered nothing about the actual attack.

When Chuck left, he managed to bend over and whisper a message he felt Charles needed to hear. "I'm sorry we weren't there to help you or be with you to prevent this. We will get the men that did this to you." Charles was quiet but nodded and squeezed Chuck's hand. Chuck reached up and wiped the tear from Holmes' battered cheek. "I promise you that, Charles." Holmes silently turned away and looked out the window.

Dr. Trumble told Chuck that Charles' most difficult time would be the first time he got out of bed. Yes, he was hurt badly, but emotionally, inside he was just as battered as Grace Winters had been. Chuck thought about what the doctor said. Charles Holmes would need something positive to motivate him once he got out of bed to get him over his trauma. Physically, he would recover in two or three weeks. Mentally, something else would have to be done to make him strong again. Chuck's first response was to put a bible on the night stand next to Charles' bed. Maybe he could find comfort there. It couldn't hurt. Chuck's prayers could only do so much. The event had left Chuck feeling things that were very un-Christian in manner. He was angry. He channeled that anger and decided to focus his off-court efforts on revenge. It was not time to turn the other cheek. Chuck started working on a plan to take care of his friend.

For the next week, the morale in the Armordillo locker room had never been lower. They had probably been playing as well as any team in the country. Charles Holmes was doing much better, but he remained in the hospital out of precaution. Chuck could sense what Charles meant to the team when he looked at his teammates. Charles' absence was visible in every player.

The coaching staff was down as well. Pete Henderson, understandably to Chuck, walked around as if he was a zombie. The competitiveness that he had demonstrated just days earlier was gone. Coach Round seemed lost without the player he viewed more like a son. He spoke without the experience and passion that he normally brought to the locker room.

It was an atmosphere that Chuck was familiar with. In the military, when a solider or sailor, marine or airman is killed, either in combat or by accident, a mourning period takes place that is necessary to heal the loss. Charles Holmes' absence was eerily like the death of a loved one. Though he wasn't dead, the effect of simply not having him with the team was enough to bring back those feelings Chuck had experienced when he was on active duty.

Unfortunately for the Dillo's there was no time to grieve over Charles. They had a game to play against Schreiner. The only good thing was the game was on the road. The bus ride would be miserable, but at least the Dillo fans would not see their team play in a catatonic state.

Before tipoff, Chuck called all the players out on the floor. "Look, fellas, this one is gonna be tough. Without Charles, the rest of us are gonna have to pick it up a whole bunch if we're gonna pull this off. Let's play hard, okay. I know we'll all be thinking about him not being here, but he'd want us to give it our best shot. Let's do that!" The faces brightened somewhat. For an instant, Chuck thought they could pull it together. They almost did.

Schreiner played their best game of the year. They were a group possessed. Even if Holmes had played, Schreiner would have given the Dillo's a tough game. As it was, the Dillo's seemed to be a seven-cylinder engine. They would get open shots, but they wouldn't fall. Rebounds would bounce off hands and out of bounds. Tip-ins would roll off the rim. Every little thing that usually went St. Michael's way, went awry.

As bad as things were going, they still had a chance to win. Hoopman had put on his cape in the second half and brought the team back. The score was tied with thirty-two seconds left. Schreiner had the ball after a timeout. On the inbounds pass they pounded the ball in low, but OJ and Jose were packed in to prevent an easy lay-up. The Schreiner center threw the pass out to a guard that launched a two-pointer as Chuck jumped to block it. The shot hit nothin' but net and the home team's gym erupted. Schreiner—73, St. Michael's—71.

St. Michael's called a timeout as the gym chanted "Runnin' on the DILDOS"! The profanity was not lost on the players, and some started to use hand gestures to show their disgust with the chant. Chuck quickly went over and said, "KNOCK IT OFF,

GUYS! Let's focus over here!" He pulled them into the huddle and said, "They paid their money and if they want to show they have no class, LET 'EM! We need to rise above that kind of crap, GOT IT!?"

Then he looked at Round who was obviously running options through his mind. Chuck asked the question that was on every one's mind. "You want to go for the win right now or play for the tie?"

Round looked at Henderson and said, "This crowd is gonna crap themselves if we hit a three pointer!"

Henderson nodded. "We don't need to stay here any longer than we have to. I say we take the three!"

Round agreed. He thought about his lineup and realized he needed another three-point shooter. He looked at Chuck. Round said honestly, "They are gonna double team you, Hayes. Anybody you want on the floor that can put the ball in the hole?" Chuck looked at Pepper.

"Let's see. We got Parnell, OJ, Earl, Hayes and . . . Dyer," said the Coach. Chuck could see the lump appear in the Pepper's throat. "They're probably gonna leave you wide open, son!" Round looked around his huddle and said, "Let's do it, fellas! If you got the three-pointer, take it! Let's beat these guys!!"

They broke the huddle and headed out to the floor. Chuck pulled Earl and Pepper aside. "If they double team me, one of you guys is gonna be wide open for the three. I'm gonna drive and make 'em think we're goin' for the tie, so set up for the three and you'll be wide open!" He patted Pepper on the shoulder and said, "They are more likely to cover Earl, so be ready. Just like back at the farm, Pep! Bust it!"

Schreiner did think St. Michael's was going for the tie. After pressuring the inbounds pass, they set back tightly into the lane. With five seconds left, Chuck drove hard down the middle of the lane. Their defense took away Earl's three-pointer. Two players converged on him and just as predicted, left Pepper wide open. Chuck threw a hard pass out to Pepper in the corner as he set himself behind the three-point line. The crowd collectively gasped in horror as Pepper caught the ball and set for the shot. A Schreiner player from inside the lane saw what was happening too late. He sprinted to the corner and leapt uncontrollably as Pepper launched.

The ball had perfect rotation as it sailed over the oncoming players outstretched fingertips. As it reached its pinnacle, a hush fell over the crowd. Pepper tried to watch the rim, as the Schreiner player collided with him and knocked him to the ground. The buzzer rang indicating time had expired. The ball came down and made a resounding thud as it hit the rim and bounced away.

The crowd went crazy. Schreiner had just defeated the fifth ranked D III team in the nation. Pepper had been knocked to the ground and was looking at the ref. Round and Henderson went ballistic that no call had been made. Their protest was to no avail. Chuck quickly went over and stuck out a hand to Pepper as he sat on the floor. Pepper was nearly in tears. "Hey, man! That was a damn good shot!"

"It didn't go in," said Pepper as he got up.

"No biggie, Pep! That which doesn't kill us, makes us stronger!" He grabbed his friend and said, "Come on, let's find the rest of the guys and go home."

As they started to leave, Chuck noticed two of his teammates squaring off with some Schreiner fans who were a little too exuberant in their victory celebration. Chuck grabbed Pepper as they headed to the face off. "HEY, NOW!" Chuck said as he approached the group. He had his hand extended to the biggest of the Schreiner fans. "Nice game, ya'll! Ya'll played a good game tonight! We'll get you next time!"

The fans were unnerved by Hoopman's reaction. They weren't sure what to do. Chuck looked at Bullet and Steve Welch and said, "Come on, guys, coach wants us in the locker room!" Bullet started to protest, but Steve Welch understood the situation. "Good game, fellas! We'll see you next time!" said Chuck as he grabbed Bullet.

As they were heading to the locker room, Chuck said to Bullet and Steve, "We need to have as much class in defeat as we have in victory!" Bullet started to say something and stopped in his tracks. Chuck looked at him and said calmly, "Bullet, it's called class. They're not disrespecting us or trashing us out. They just won a big game. Maybe we see them in the playoffs. We'll get 'em next time. Okay?"

Bullet wanted to protest, but Steve Welch helped move him along. In the locker room things were nearly as hectic. Marvin Earl was yelling about how St. Michael's was "ripped off". His comments were fueling the fire of discontent. Then something was said that caught Chuck's ear.

Bullet walked over to Pepper and said, "How could you miss that shot? Man, you were wide open!"

Chuck came unglued. "WHAT THE HELL DID YOU SAY?" He ran over and got in Bullet's face. Bullet was unprepared for the charge and backed up quickly. Chuck looked around the locker room. "ANY BODY ELSE FEEL LIKE THAT? HUH?!" The room was quiet. Chuck tried to control himself, but all the frustration he felt; Charles in the hospital, taking on Grant and the BONE, and the frustration from losing came out. "Let me tell you guys something! I applaud the shot!" Chuck started clapping his hands and looked at Pepper. "I applaud the shot because of a couple things! First of all, he put us in a position to win the dang game. WE PLAYED LIKE CRAP! If we play halfway worth a damn, it doesn't come down to a final shot. Yet we were still in position to win because of that shot! And secondly, he had the COURAGE to take it! That's right! It's called courage in the old school! He had the courage to fire that sucker up on the enemy's turf and try to stick it! He nearly hit it! In any other gym, he's shootin' three foul shots and if we don't win, we're probably in overtime. But there's a helluva lot of guys who wouldn't be able to be in the right spot, much less take that shot" then he stepped toward Bullet and hissed loudly, "OR HAD THE COURAGE TO SHOOT IT!"

Round and Henderson entered the room, but Chuck wasn't quite finished. "I don't want hear anybody speakin' any garbage about could've! The fact is, DIDN'T is what happened! Show some class, get your heads up and understand that the next time Pepper Dyer will bust a hole in the net with that shot! The next time, we kick these guys tails so bad for forty minutes that they aren't around in the last minute!" The room was quiet.

David Parnell, leader that he was, broke the tension. He walked over to Pepper and stuck out his hand. "I thought it was a damn nice shot, Pep!" Pepper tried to smile, stood up and took the larger man's hand. Chuck threw his towel at his locker, sat down, and started getting undressed. Gradually the tension in the room faded as the players hit the shower and got ready for the long bus ride home.

On the way out, Chuck saw Coach Round putting his pill bottle into his pocket and threw away an empty cup of water. Chuck decided not to ask Coach Round about the pills. If he wanted to say what they were, Chuck would listen. At that moment, he wasn't concerned with his coach's medical condition. His mind was on the loss. The coach put a dip in his mouth and said, "I didn't hear all of it, but I heard enough of it." He looked at Chuck and said with a huge smile, "I couldn't have said it any better myself." For the first time that night, Chuck smiled.

"We'll see Schreiner again. Losses like this are remembered, Coach," said Chuck. "We won't lose again. If we can play here, like that, without Charles, we're goin' places." Chuck said it so matter of factly Round almost believed it himself.

The Saturday night before the Super Bowl, St. Michael's had a home game against Sam Houston State. Chuck had received reports from Eddie that betting at the BONE had been totally shut down. The group was offline by the DDOS that Bobby had engineered. That fact was little consolation for the loss of Charles Holmes, but it was partial retribution that allowed Chuck to concentrate on basketball. He took on a new demeanor since Charles had been hospitalized. He was more aggressive, more focused, and ready to do whatever he needed to do to win. Both on and off the court.

Holmes was easy to play with because he was talented. Now, Chuck had to come up with other ways to get the best from a team that was visibly less talented. He was up to the challenge.

Chuck did think of one way to help his team emotionally. In fact, it was taking care of two birds with one stone. For that, he asked Hawk to do him another favor.

It had been a week since Charles Holmes was attacked. Chuck heard he was getting better but spent most of his time sitting in a wheelchair. Physically, he was more than capable of walking, but he wasn't even trying to participate in physical therapy. Chuck would send his friends to see if they could help.

Meanwhile in Vegas, "WHAT THE HELL IS GOING ON?" screamed Grant into his cell phone.

"We are having what's called a Denial of Service," answered Steve James flatly. "It prevents us from performing transactions. Our systems are all under attack."

"This is costing me millions! You need to get this fixed! We got the Super Bowl tomorrow! This is . . . This is ridiculous! Is it ransomware? What are we supposed to do?"

Steve James smiled to himself. Now it was what are "we" supposed to do. A week ago, he was just another "geek". Oh, how he hated Grant. What a two-faced bastard the man was! "No it's not ransomware. No one has asked us for money or anything else. It's just gonna take some time. I've done what I can from here. I have a plane scheduled to depart this evening. I'll be there before midnight." He didn't add that he knew they couldn't do anything to fix the problem before the game.

"Great! The sooner you get here, the better off we'll be. You gotta fix this!" said Grant before he hung up.

Steve James put the phone down and looked at his computer. He glanced at the email message he was writing on his screen. No. It wasn't time to send it just yet. He needed to be sure Chuck Hayes was not acting alone. Hayes and whoever was helping had done a job on the BONE with this attack. It was Steve's responsibility to prevent this type of attack. He was certain they were prepared, yet the organization was in full stop mode. It would take hours for the computer forensics to sort out the attack.

Inside, Steve was smiling at the timing and how well the attackers had done with the attack. Outside, Steve was developing tremendous respect for his adversaries. They were good. It was time for him to show them he was better.

"How are you feeling?" asked Hawk.

Charles was sitting in his wheelchair by the window next to his mother who was sitting in a chair looking outside. He turned to see one man inside his room and another in a wheelchair coming through the door. "A heck of a lot better than I was a couple days ago," said Charles. "Who are you guys?"

"We're friends of Chuck Hayes," said Hawk. He pointed to the man in the wheelchair rolling up to Charles. "This is Eddie Newton." They exchanged hellos.

"Did you hear about the game last Tuesday?" asked Hawk.

"Yeah, I heard," said Charles. "I wish I could have been there."

"How long you gonna be laid up?" asked Eddie.

"Doctor says I can be released when I feel like it. He said most of the damage on the surface is healed. Need some stitches removed soon. Said it was up to me to heal what's goin' on inside."

"He told us that you could be runnin' in two weeks," Hawk said. "That's great news!"

"That's just his opinion," said Charles. "I don't think I can make it back this season."

Charles Holmes' mother spoke for the first time. "He thinks he's got me to push him around in that wheelchair all day. Doctor says he can walk. He just don't want to."

It was Eddie's turn to talk. "Man, do you know how much I'd give to get out of this chair. And you can?" Eddie grunted. "I'd be up and around. Hell, I'd be out working on my dunk." The comment brought smiles from everyone except Charles. "I'd at least go to a game and walk around with my teammates."

"I don't know," he said. "I just don't feel like it. I don't feel strong enough to do it."

Hawk walked closer to Charles and asked, "Are you strong enough to go to the game with us?"

Charles saw the pitch coming. He really did want to see the game. He smiled, "How we gonna do that?"

"The question isn't how, the question is, do you want to?" said Hawk. Charles smiled.

"Dillo's are at the Hole tonight," said Eddie. Charles' smile broadened and he looked at his mother.

"We have room in my van," said Eddie.

Then Hawk applied the finishing touch. He reached into a gym bag and pulled out Charles Holmes' jersey.

As sore as he was, Charles Holmes found a smile. He said to his mother, "You want to go to the game with us, Momma?"

The Dillo Hole was buzzing with anticipation. The atmosphere was one of nervous tension because of the team's last second loss to Schreiner. The crowd exacerbated the tension with social media. Rumors and theories were being expressed that were just speculation, particularly with thoughts of Charles Holmes' disappearance. Some texts were claiming he was dead. Some speculated someone attempted to murder Charles and he was in hiding. There was a full court press to get pictures of Charles Holmes.

The team was aware of Charles Holmes' hospitalization, and they had done their best to placate the student body that Holmes was well. Yet as dedicated fans, they were worried not just about their star, but about their team. The internet loves to fuel fires, no matter how much truth is applied. The Hole was screaming for answers to their questions. Chuck had an idea how to satisfy them. That was what he tasked Eddie and Hawk to do.

The teams came out and went through their warmups. Chuck did his gladiator routine with Marshall the "Armor Dillo". Things were going as well as could be expected. Just before the national anthem, the singing was interrupted by cell phones and fans talking excitedly. When the Anthem was finished, the Hole started to churn with emotion. Something was happening at one end of the arena.

As everyone on the bench stood up to see what was happening, Chuck grabbed a towel and sat down. Hawk sent him a text before game time. He knew exactly what the commotion was. He gladly gave spotlight to someone else for a few minutes. Chuck went under the towel and said a prayer of thanks to God Almighty for Charles Holmes' return to his fans.

Hawk was pushing Charles Holmes in the wheelchair through the access way towards the gym floor. He leaned over and said to Charles, "Are you ready to watch some hoop?"

Charles exhaled loudly and said, "This isn't as easy as I thought it would be. I thought we'd just come here and watch the game." He could see some of the fans waving at him. He raised his hand and waved back. The noise level in the Dome started to raise a notch. He looked at Hawk and said, "It's a different perspective, ya' know?" The cell phones lit up as the crowd took pictures and shared proof that Charles Holmes was alive. He wasn't ready to play, but he was there with them. Charles Holmes was trending on the internet in minutes.

"They didn't know how bad you were hurt. The fact that you are even here at all gives every one of them hope. Hope for you. Hope for the team. Hope for the season. They want to know that you're okay," said Hawk.

Eddie rolled up next to Charles. "I still don't think this is right." Together they wheeled toward the court.

"What do you mean?" asked Charles.

"I mean, if all these people wanted to see me, and I was in your situation instead of mine," said Eddie. "I'd walk out there on that court. I'd show 'em I was okay." Eddie wasn't finished. "I know I'm a dynamic guy, and you want to hang with me in the handicapped section because we get the best seats," said Eddie.

Eddie became serious. He stopped and grabbed Charles arm. "You don't belong here. You can get out of that chair. You belong over there," he nodded toward the Dillo bench. "With those guys. They need you."

Charles Holmes understood what Eddie meant. Eddie Newton had hit the mark. Charles nodded at Eddie and said, "You're right." He took a deep breath, looked at Eddie and said, "I belong over there." Tears appeared in Charles' eyes. "Thank you, Eddie. For everything."

Charles pushed his chair towards the edge of the court. The crowd was clapping and cheering wildly. With a little help from Hawk, Charles stood up and walked out onto the court. The Hole roared their approval and gave him a standing ovation. It didn't matter how badly he had been hurt. Just his presence in the arena, the fact that he was up and walking toward the bench gave the fans new hope. It would be a while till he was totally back, but by being there he was providing inspiration not just to the fans, but to his team. A team that needed him any way he could help.

As he got to the bench, he pointed to the seat next to Chuck. He said, "Got room for me here?"

Chuck stood up and said, "Not really there. I got room for you out there." Chuck pointed over his shoulder to the court.

Charles smiled. "Maybe next week, okay?"

Chuck said, "That'll work." He started to head out to the floor. He stopped and looked back at Charles. "By the way. Nice entrance!"

Charles beamed. "LET'S BEAT THESE GUYS!"

Sam Houston State didn't have a chance. Final score, St. Michael's—94, SHSU—58. Jose was a man possessed against Sam Houston. It was the first time any Dillo player had scored 20 points and had 20 rebounds. Round pulled him with five minutes to play to a huge standing ovation. Chuck stood next to him with his thumb up for the crowd to see. In true Roman fashion, the crowd returned with the thumbs up for the hero of the game.

St. Michael's basketball was back on a roll.

CHAPTER SEVENTEEN

"HOLY CRAP!" exclaimed Jeff Roberts. He was analyzing the data on his screen. Steve James cocked his head to try and better interpret the data they were seeing.

"You say you don't have any email on your local area network or the external networks?" asked Steve. Grant grunted his affirmation. "For the last two days?"

"Yeah, at least two days," said Grant.

Jeff Roberts was impressed. He whispered to Steve, "Wow! I can't say I've ever seen anything like this." He pointed to the screen and said, "Is this typical for bandwidth-consumption attacks?"

"For the local network, yes. But the other stuff is more than email bombs. It's not real sophisticated, but it's damn effective," said Steve. For an instant, a smile seemed to appear on his face. Grant's anger quickly made the smile disappear.

"What the hell is goin' on?" asked Grant.

Steve stood up and said, "You had your domain name servers attacked. What the perpetrators did was redirect your packets to different sites. Probably a virtual black hole or to a network that doesn't even exist."

"All our online business disappeared into the Metaverse?" asked Grant in disgust.

"Not just your business," said Steve. "They added a little insult by rerouting all the email sent to you too. Most of it was email bombs. What the perpetrators did was SMURF you." Steve James was having a hard time suppressing a smile.

"You're telling me some kind of little blue cartoon is in my internet?" asked Grant.

Steve James coughed to cover his laugh. "No. What I'm telling you is you had a Denial of Service that used email traffic to perform bandwidth-consumption on your network. The SMURF attack used an amplification effect to send forged packets of message traffic through the servers," said Steve. He wanted so badly to add "you stupid, stupid man". He continued but slowed down so his "boss" could comprehend what had happened. "This amplification network probably had a 100 to one ratio. With that ratio, he saturated your network with forged packets which were accepted by the network."

"In English," said Grant.

"The perpetrator used a fire hose of information to fill up a thimble which was your network," said Jeff Roberts, smiling at his own analogy.

Steve corrected him. "More like a water cannon."

"WHATEVER!" exploded Grant. "Can you two twenty-pound heads fix it?"

"Yes. But it's going to take some time," said Steve. Steve ran the numbers in his mind and smiled at the thought. He estimated his boss had lost at least twenty million dollars each day his system was down prior to the Super Bowl. Now came this attack. Steve estimated two weeks before he could get all Grants networks online. On the conservative side, Grant was going to lose two hundred and fifty million dollars' worth of business.

"Just get to it. There's no tellin' how much money I'm losing," said Grant. He turned, yelled something into his cell phone and stormed out the room.

The two men sat in silence until Grant was out of the room. "He didn't take that very well," said Jeff.

"Would you take the fact that the most bet on sporting event of all time happened, and your entire network was down. And you didn't make a dollar?" asked Steve rhetorically.

"It sucks to be our boss," said Jeff with a chuckle. Jeff smiled at how much money Grant was losing. "Those guys on the intranet are ticked at him. They were expecting to get tips on both the Super Bowl and college basketball. They got nada!"

Steve looked down at the screen. He smiled broadly. Jeff saw it and said, "You didn't tell him everything."

Steve stood up again. "He wouldn't understand."

"What do you think of all this?" asked Jeff.

"You mean these attacks?" replied Steve with a smile.

"How many do you think there are?" asked Jeff.

"I think there are at least three separate events going on. They hit the LAN, the intranet, the routers, the servers and who knows what else!" He thought about the attack and smiled. "Not real impressive DOS by itself, but to synchronize the event at specific targets." He whistled. "I think that's pretty damn good work," said Steve with a huge smile. "With impeccable timing! When we get control back, run another system evaluation to see if we have spyware hiding in our bowels," said Steve.

Jeff looked up. "You think we got something in our network? You think we have some sort of 'cyberterrorists' or something coming after BONE?" asked Jeff.

Steve grunted and looked at Jeff. "I was expecting ransomware to be honest. We've had no messages with blackmail or asking for millions. That Grant would have paid!" Steve exhaled heavily. "That's funny to me. They aren't looking to make money. Cyberterrorists that aren't even trying to bankrupt an online gambling organization. I don't think it's a cyberterrorists. No. I think it is someone much more dangerous."

Steve stood up and walked behind Jeff. He looked back at the computer and said, "This is someone who wants to take revenge against our boss. And they are succeeding. If we don't get it fixed, Grant won't need us. Understand?" His adversaries had just gained newfound respect from Steve James.

Steve knew things were headed south. He needed to check his new program and make sure he was ready to go before it was too late. BONE was compromised. He couldn't prove it, but he could feel it. These guys were good. If the adversary had tools hidden in the system, Steve didn't think he could find them. Unless they could get BONE online quickly, and keep whoever it was attacking the net away, their lives meant nothing to Grant. Steve was having doubt's that he could protect the system. It was time to either up his game or get out. He would plan for either option.

Hawk was the calm voice in the crowd. Chuck, Eddie, Chris and Bobby were giddy over the way things were going. BONE was getting spanked, Charles Holmes was back on his feet, and the St. Michael's Armordillos were back in the top ten in Division III. As the small group celebrated, Nate Hawkins sat at the kitchen counter quietly.

Chuck finally noticed Hawk's subdued demeanor. "All right! What is it?" Ed, Chris and Bobby became quiet.

"I think it's too soon to get excited," said Hawk.

"Okay! I'll bite," said Eddie. "We kicked their ass!"

Chris spoke next. "They don't have a clue who did it or we would have some feedback by now. I'm sure of that!"

Hawk stood up and started walking around the room. "That's great. For now. But you better not get too cocky. Because these bastards we're going against aren't gonna quit easily." He stopped and looked at each of the younger men. "Do you know how much money you cost them?" The men smiled at the thought. "If you lost that much money, would you just let it go? Give up?" He looked at Chuck. "I know you. You wouldn't give up on a dollar bet! You guys cost them potentially five hundred . . . million . . . dollars!" He let the comment sink in.

"I suggest you pull the plan out again and get ready for the next fight. All you did was take this cyber war to the next level.

Trust me when I say this, you did just declare war. If we don't watch our asses, we'll be the ones getting kicked."

The speech was on the mark. Eddie pulled out his ever-present laptop and set it up on the coffee table. Chuck walked over to Hawk and said, "How come you're always so right?"

Hawk just shrugged. "Not always. I missed the mark on that maggot William Moreland." He didn't have to add Grace Winters paid dearly for that, because the younger guys were not aware of the details. He sat down and said, "I just want to make sure you guys don't get a bat shoved up your ass by these guys we're goin' against. We're talkin' huge dollars here, and guys like this don't roll over when they're smacked this hard!"

Chuck nodded. After a moment of quiet, Chuck said, "Thanks, Hawk."

"For what?" asked Hawk.

"For keepin' us on that even keel I always harp about," said Chuck. "You know, not too high . . ." They both finished the comment together. "NOT TOO LOW!" Hawk was smiling again.

"I better go see what the wonder boys are up to," said Chuck. He smiled at Hawk, shook his head, and walked over to the coffee table.

Hawk's comments sank in. The team got their heads back into the fight. Chuck joined them. Hawk smiled because he knew they were doing the right thing now. They had taken the fight to a new level, and next time, Grant wouldn't be caught with his pants down. Hawk poured himself some more coffee. They needed to execute another attack, just to keep the pressure on. It was going to be another long night.

"Did you find Henderson yet?" Grant spoke into the phone quickly.

"Yup. He's back on the bench trying to coach that second-rate team," said Holden.

"That second-rate team you're talkin' about is back in the top ten. That second-rate team you're watchin' is havin' a helluva a lot of fun while I'm losin' millions!" hissed Grant. He gathered himself. "How much longer are you two gonna be on vacation?"

"We're just waiting for the right time to execute," said Holden.

"Don't wait too much longer. I need you back here. They're gonna have the system up in another week. I want it done by then. You got me?!" said Grant.

Holden didn't like to be put to a deadline. "I'll need more time than that. Two, maybe even three weeks." That should be enough time to get Henderson alone.

Grant wasn't happy about it, but he conceded to the extension. "Just get it done." Holden hung up the phone. He knew his boss was having plenty of problems. Soon enough, Henderson would not be one of them.

According to ESPN, the St. Michael's Armordillos needed to be buttered, "because they were on a roll". It was mid-February when Sportscenter announcers mentioned the tiny program from Texas to the rest of the nation. Cell phones were lighting up throughout Texas, and the team was trending. Fans everywhere were streaming St. Michael's games.

Charles Holmes was back, but not quite himself. He finally worked his way back into the starting lineup the week before the conference tournament. His statistics were down, but his play was inspiring. His teammates rallied around their star. Everyone's level of play improved. Pepper, Dex Thomas, and Jose improved their play while Charles recovered. Coach Round had developed a bench that went eight deep. The team was playing well enough to keep the starters on the bench for that last five minutes of most games. Going into the Conference tournament, St. Michael's had an 18-2 record. They were tied with Schreiner for first in the conference. Only the conference champion would receive a shot at the Division III Championship and an automatic bid in the National Tournament.

Pete Henderson had been feeling pretty good about himself. It had been a long time since coaching had been this fun. As he pulled into his parking spot behind his apartment, he didn't notice the rental car parked across the street. He whistled as he headed up the stairs and tossed his keys in the air as if he was shooting a jump shot.

As he got to the door, he noticed the light above the door was out. He made a mental note to tell the apartment manager to have it fixed. Finally, he got the door open and started to walk in. He thought he heard something and tried to turn around. A man with a black ski mask pushed him into the apartment and closed the door.

"HEY! What the hell. . . ?"

"SHUT UP!!" The man pushed Henderson further into the room. He looked around the apartment to make sure they were alone. "Come with me," said the masked man.

Henderson did as he was told. "If you want money, all I have is what's in my wallet," said Henderson. The masked man grunted.

They walked into the bathroom. "Stand against the wall."

Henderson started to protest, "I don't have any. . . !"

"JUST STAND AGAINST THE WALL!" yelled the man. Henderson did as he was told. The man went through the cabinet over the sink. He didn't find whatever he was looking for. "A turd for brains like you, and you don't take any kind of medication?" Henderson shook his head 'no'. The man hissed, "GET OUT OF HERE! Do you have an office? Take me there."

Again, Henderson did as he was told. Nervously, he walked down the hallway. The fact that he was not being robbed began to sink in. Why had the man gone through his medicine cabinet?

"Just stand there," said the man.

"Why?" asked Henderson.

"JUST DO WHAT I SAY!!" yelled the man again. "I figured you for a Prozac suckin' pill popper. I guess you won't be a pretty boy when they find you, eh?"

Henderson started to get the picture. "Now wait a minute! I don't understand. I can get you money!"

The masked man held back the fact that he was holding a.45 caliber pistol and was fighting the urge to use it as a club against Henderson's head. That wasn't part of the plan though. "Shut the hell up!" The man grabbed a chair from the computer desk. "Sit here!" he ordered.

Henderson did as he was told and sat next to the computer. The masked man slowly paced behind Pete as he sat there. Henderson said, "I . . . I don't understand what you want?"

The man said, "Tommy Clark asked me to say 'Hello'!" Henderson's face immediately went white. The fear of what was about to happen set in, he started to get up. "No! NO, you don't! Sit down!" Once again, Henderson did as he was told. The masked man pulled out a piece of paper and handed it to Henderson. "Read this into your phone!"

It was then that Henderson understood exactly what was happening. Pete grabbed his phone and began to read. The masked man had his cell phone and was recording Pete as he read.

When Pete finished, he slowly looked up from the piece of paper and in a quiet voice said, "I would have told my mother how much I loved her."

"Maybe I'll give her a call, AFTER YOUR FUNERAL!" The masked man put the gun to Pete Henderson's temple and pulled the trigger.

Hawk was the first one to call Chuck with the news. He was able to get some information from some friends at the police station. They were officially calling Pete Henderson's death a suicide. After asking some more questions Hawk found out one item that told him it was no suicide. Henderson had apparently been sitting at his computer when he shot himself, but the suicide note wasn't written on his computer.

Chuck didn't buy the suicide either. Chuck told Hawk how Henderson was a different man since Hawk had saved him. He was showing absolutely no signs of depression or anxiety. He didn't think Henderson even owned a gun. Hawk said he thought the deal was way too professional to be accomplished by Tommy Clark's bunch of goons. Hawk felt it was probably a professional hit. Maybe even someone from the home base in Vegas. Hawk said he would continue to lightly press his buddies in the Police Department to look for signs of a struggle and continue to hint that he thought the man was murdered. Hawk knew there was a point where his friends in the SAPD would become suspicious if he dug too deep. Chuck agreed that they couldn't afford to press the police. Henderson was not what he would call a real friend, more like an acquaintance who by circumstance he was obligated to associate with. Whatever their relationship had been, Chuck was sorry for the way it had ended. He picked up the phone and called Eddie.

Chuck was subdued on the phone. "Hawk was absolutely right. I can't prove it, but I think they murdered Pete Henderson."

Eddie was stunned. "Murdered?!"

"He was found dead in his apartment, apparently from a self-inflicted gunshot wound," said Chuck.

"Man, oh, man, Chuck! I'm sorry!" said Eddie.

Chuck dismissed the comment and got down to business. "I'm going to send a personal message to Grant!"

"You better let Chris or Hawk look at it first!" said Eddie.

"The gloves are off, Eddie. It's gotten personal," said Chuck. "We need to go to Phase III."

"I don't know if we're ready for that yet," said Eddie. They had planned Phase III for the Championship Tournament if needed, not Conference tournaments.

"Phase III, Eddie," said Chuck. "Get the spreads for every game in every tournament and run Phase III."

"We don't want to do every game!" said Eddie.

A voice of reason calmed Chuck down. He listened to Eddie and let the comment sink in. "You're right, Eddie. Sorry about that. Focus on the intranet. Those insiders should literally have to pay for the insider information." Chuck thought about the best way to approach the situation. A plan of attack came to mind. "Start slow and escalate the set up unless they figure it out. Just do one game the first night, then two games the next and so on. By the time the Championships are played, they'll either turn off their systems again or be bankrupt."

"Now you're thinking like 'Hoopman' again! We're on it," said Eddie. "I think Bobby has got the G-Cash cryptocurrency figured out."

"Sweet!" said Chuck.

"One more time, I'm sorry about Henderson. He was comin' around," said Eddie.

Chuck hung up the phone. "He was comin' around" rang out over and over in his head. Henderson should still be around. Chuck went to his computer and typed up an email. For just an instant, he hesitated before he hit enter. The thought that it could have been Charles Holmes or some other player or coach on some other team was not lost on Chuck. He was sure Henderson was murdered. Someone was going to answer for it. For an instant, he wished he hadn't felt so angry. He tried to pray. He looked up to heaven and said, "I don't think you can help me with this. I know I should let it go. Turn the other cheek." He looked at his keyboard and said, "If not me, who." Chuck hit the enter key and sat back in his chair. To no one in the room he said, "You want to take it up a notch? I'll play your game, Grant. You changed the rules. Now the gloves are off!"

Steve James was about to leave when Jeff Roberts knocked on his door. "Did you hear?"

Steve put his suitcase back on the bed. "Did I hear what, Jeff?"

Jeff Roberts quickly made sure the door was closed. He looked around the room nervously. "They found that assistant coach from St. Michael's dead! Apparently, he shot himself!"

Steve James sat down on the bed. He didn't have to ask, "Are you sure?" He knew the information was sound.

"I knew they were serious and there were always rumors. But I never heard of them killing anybody before," said Jeff.

"They lost a lot of money. Somebody had to answer for that," said Steve.

"Do you honestly think this coach was the dude messing with the BONE?" asked Jeff.

"Oh no! He's just a secondary effect. Collateral damage," said Steve. His cell phone rang.

Steve picked it up, listened for a moment then said, "I'm on my way." He looked at Jeff and said, "Cancel our flights. Grant just got another email message."

"WHO THE HELL DOES THIS GUY THINK HE IS?" screamed Grant. He stormed across the room and handed the printed copy of the email message to Steve James. James took the paper and started to read.

> Jackson Grant,
>
> You had your chance to help us out. You and those clowns you sent only got you in deeper. You could have let me handle it for you. You took it too far this time and for that, you will pay dearly. I thought last month I taught you a lesson, but you obviously need more training. Sure, you got somebody down here like I asked, but they put you in a situation you can't recover from. You jeopardized my situation. If you thought you were in a bad way before, you will really be FUBAR next time. Sleep tight if you can. Just let me know if you want to shoot yourself. I've got your bullet.
>
> BTW, I never was your,
> Friend in Austin

Steve read the note again. He cued in on two words. To him, they stuck out. "More training" had military all over it. Grant interrupted his concentration.

"What the hell is that . . . FUBUR?" asked Grant.

"It's actually, FUBAR. It stands for, Fucked Up Beyond All Repair." Steve omitted the fact that it was a military acronym.

Grant started ranting again. He thought he had it all figured out. "It's that dirtbag Clark! I know it is!" Grant started walking around the room. Jeff looked at Steve, not knowing exactly who sent the message, but knowing it wasn't Tommy Clark. Tommy needed one of his goons to send his emails for him. Steve shook his head and put his index finger to his lips.

"It's gotta be that bastard Clark!" ranted Grant. He looked at Steve and said, "He knows I sent Holden and Thompson there!" Steve wanted to say the message didn't say that. It merely said, "You got somebody down here". This was probably a guess by the "friend".

Steve asked a question that he already knew the answer to. "What does he mean by 'Just let me know if you want to shoot yourself'?"

Grant was hesitant. "I have no idea what that comment is for. Maybe Clark thinks I'll stick a .45 to my head because he took all my money with that damn SMURF he used!"

Steve knew right then that Grant was involved in the death of Pete Henderson. He implicated himself when he implied the coach died with a .45 caliber pistol. On top of that, he was stupid enough to believe that Tommy Clark had taken his money with the DDOS.

Then a light came on for Steve. It was too good to be true. His boss was headed down the wrong train track. Steve decided he might as well be the conductor. He snapped his fingers. "You know what? I think you're right, Mr. Grant!" He looked at Jeff Roberts who started to protest. He waved his hand and winked at Jeff without Grant noticing. "I think Clark probably has the most to gain out of all of this!" Jeff Roberts walked over to the couch and plopped down heavily. He wasn't exactly sure where Steve James was headed. Even Jeff was smart enough to know Clark didn't have a thing to do with the DDOS. "Hell, he probably thought he could take over your organization!" Steve continued to pile it on.

Grant smiled at the fact that his computer geek had finally seen the light. "Yeah, that's it! He probably wanted to take over my business! But we got him, don't we?" Steve nodded in agreement. Then Grant had a really good idea. "Hey! How about this? Maybe you guys work up some kind computer crap to use on that shithead?! Huh?!"

Steve jumped at the offer. It was all too good to be true. "We could definitely do that!" He looked over at Jeff for support. "Couldn't we?!"

Jeff had no idea what his boss was doing. But he played along anyway. "Yeah, sure! We can screw him just as much as he screwed you, Mr. Grant!" Steve nodded approvingly at his protégé.

"How long would it take you to get something to take him down?" asked Grant.

"Probably two weeks, boss," said Steve. That was all the time Steve needed.

"Can you do something to take all his money and put it in our account?" asked Grant. "I've read about computer guys doing stuff like that. That's the same shit he pulled on us, right?"

Steve nearly jumped for joy. "Yeah! He did start it, didn't he?" Steve saw an opening and decided to take it. "I'll need to get some permissions. Specific permissions from you, Boss. We can get everything he has in his G-Cash account!"

"You got it! Just tell me what you need!" Grant was positively beaming. Steve waved to Jeff, and they headed out the door.

"We'll get that bastard for you, Mr. Grant," said Steve. "Don't you worry about a thing." They left the office and quickly closed the door.

Jeff spoke first. "I have no idea what just happened in there. He doesn't understand anything you told him about the DOS, and there is no way Clark sent those messages. I'd bet your paycheck on it!"

Steve stopped walking after they got far enough away from Grant's office. "You need to trust me on this, Jeff. Things couldn't have worked out better." He looked around to make sure no one was listening. "We need to let him think he's right about Clark. And you need to let me run with this one, okay?" Jeff frowned but relented.

"Right now, I have to get busy on the computer. The best place for you is over at the casino, monitoring the systems for Grant," said Steve. "Make sure we don't get surprised again, okay?"

"What about takin' care of Clark? You gonna make a program to take care of him?"

"I'm gonna take care of everybody, Jeff," said Steve. It was the first time in a long time Jeff had seen his mentor smile.

Sandy Hawkins was surprised when she saw her husband cleaning his 9mm Beretta at the kitchen table. She couldn't help but ask, "What are you doing with that, Nate?" Nate married Sandy not just because she was beautiful, but also because she was intelligent and caring. She was once again demonstrating those traits.

Hawk stopped cleaning the pistol and walked over to her. After twenty-three years, now was no time to start lying to the woman he loved. "Things are getting a little rough. I can't prove it, but I think the guys we're after are responsible for Pete Henderson's death."

"You decided to start wearing that gun again?" There was more concern in her voice than anger.

Hawk held her in his arms. "It's just a precautionary measure. I'm not gonna pull the trigger."

Sandy knew her husband better than that. She also knew how deep he was involved in a situation with some very bad people. She understood there was no way to stop what her husband wanted to do. "If you're gonna wear it, you better be ready to use! Get your body armor out, too." She smiled at him. "Don't make promises you can't keep, Nate Hawkins!"

Nate hugged her tightly. "No promises I can't keep! Roger that, ma'am!" He let her loose and looked at her. "It's not me I'm worried about. It's Chuck and those knuckleheads he's runnin' with. Somebody has got to take care of them. Considering this situation, I'm probably suited to do that better than anyone else."

Sandy nodded. "Yes, you are, Nate." She couldn't help but make sure he had his priorities right. "We all need you!" Nate knew exactly what she meant. She was telling him to take care of himself and remember how much she still loved him. He hugged her again. After a tender moment, Sandy pulled away and said, "Now get back to cleaning your gun. I don't want the damn thing to jam if you have to shoot a bad guy."

Hawk burst out laughing. He playfully patted his wife on the butt and walked back to the table. He sat down and called her one more time to ease her nerves. "Sandy," he looked at her with a smile. "After all this is over, you want to go on a vacation?"

Sandy smiled and turned away. "As long as you leave your gun here," then she looked back and added with a grin, "and you promise to watch me and not Sportscenter!"

Hawk burst out laughing again. "Easy enough! You got a deal, Baby!"

"Hey, Hoopman!" It was Daymon Breyers and he was holding a message. "I have a message that came to the team twitter account for you." Chuck walked over to the assistant coach. Breyers had taken on a greater role since Henderson's death. One of those tasks was monitoring and putting out information to fans via the social media accounts. "It looks pretty cryptic to me. Thought you might be able to make something out of it."

Chuck grabbed the note and said, "Thanks, Daymon." He quickly read it.

> hoopman: i know what you are doing.
> don't worry, i have not told grant. i've got
> your six! You're a go for the fubar. Hoopfan

Chuck was nervous at first. He had sent the last message to Grant without letting Hawk or Chris review it. It was obvious his message had compromised the operation and it was his fault. He stuffed the message into his pocket and headed into the gym for practice.

As hard as Chuck tried to compartmentalize the note, nothing was working. The content of the message wouldn't go away. As he was shooting jumpers, he couldn't think clearly about basketball. His shots were clanking off the rim. He just didn't feel right as he shot.

Then it hit him. Whoever sent it was not compromising the operation at all. Sure, the sender knew Hoopman was involved. He knew about Grant and obviously had read the last message Chuck had sent to Grant because he referenced the 'FUBAR' comment. This so called 'Hoopfan' also said he was covering his six. That meant he was going to make sure nobody figuratively got behind Chuck. Hoopfan was inside Grants organization and apparently on Chuck's side. This could only be a good thing. He launched a twenty-footer. Nothin' but net!

St. Michael's swept through the conference tournament like a wildfire. Chuck was a man possessed. He had over ten assists in each of the first three games and hit twenty-eight straight free throws. He was second in the nation in assists, assist to turnover ratio and number three in the nation in free throw percentage. David Parnell and Jose Rivera-Torres were unstoppable on the boards, and the role players all stepped up. The best news of all was the fact that the old Charles Holmes was returning. His quickness was back, and the old jump shot that was so beautiful, not only looked good, but it was also starting to go in the basket again.

They easily made it to the Conference Championship blowing out their opponents by over twenty points in all three games. The championship would not be as easy. They had to face their nemesis from earlier in the year, Schreiner.

Meanwhile, BCT was getting hammered by an unknown cyber attack. There was no message or threat. It seemed as if a bomb had gone off on their network. By Friday afternoon before the championship game, BCT posted a message that indicated they were suspending operations until further notice. That evening, the site was no longer operating.

The teams were familiar with each other having already played each other twice in conference games. The championship would be played in Austin on a neutral court. From the opening tipoff, Chuck knew it was going to be a battle.

Schreiner came out on fire. They hit their first twelve shots and used full court pressure to rattle the Dillo's. Round had seen enough and called a timeout to rally his troops. He put Pepper in the game, and they went to a three-guard set. The Schreiner full court press was never an issue after that. Chuck set picks for Pepper and Holmes, who started off slow, but were getting their rhythm. Holmes' shooting got St. Michael's back into the game.

With eight seconds left in the first half, Chuck drove the length of the floor, threw a behind the back pass to Parnell, who dunked the ball as the clock expired. The score at half time was Schreiner—39, ST. MICHAEL'S—39.

As Chuck sat in the locker room, he realized how tired he was. He hadn't noticed anything before, but his legs were weak, and his two big toes always troubled him. Round gave a calming, reserved, fatherly type speech at halftime. He told the team how proud he was that they had made it that far. How this St. Michael's team was the best team he had ever coached, and he emphasized the fact that it was a privilege to be their coach. He brought up Pete Henderson and said he would have been proud to see the first half comeback. The assistant coach would have chewed them out and said, "they weren't done yet"! Although it didn't fire them up any more than they already were, the speech was tactful, honest and downright brilliant. When they left the locker room, any player would have walked through a wall for Coach Round.

Just before they went on the court, the coach pulled Chuck aside. "I just wanted to make sure you knew one thing, Hayes." The coach spit some chew into his plastic cup. "We would've never gotten this far without you." He stuck out his hand for Chuck to shake.

Chuck looked at the hand and said simply, "I can't take that yet, coach. We're not done! Excuse me, I have a game to win!"

Round took the hand away and smacked Chuck on the back. His smile was from ear to ear. "That's what I wanted to hear, Son! Get out there and win us a championship!"

It seems like victory is always easier to say than to do. This game would be no different. Chuck could tell his hot was off. Of all the times for it to be off, why was it during the conference championship. It was causing his shot to come up short. He was hitting the front of the rim on his foul shots, and that was a perfect indicator to Chuck that his legs were fading. Perhaps the long season was starting to wear on him, or perhaps he had just used too much energy breaking the press in the first half. He was struggling with himself to stay in the game. If it had been any other game, he would have taken himself out. But not this game. He would have to find another way to win.

The dogfight continued throughout the second half. Every time St. Michael's made a run, Schreiner would recover. They were the only team that had effectively shut down Jose's hook by double-teaming him. Schreiner made a terrific adjustment on defense by tightening up on Charles Holmes' jumper. With under a minute left, Chuck knew where the game was heading. Whoever made the last shot would be the Conference Champion.

Disaster struck with twenty seconds left and Schreiner up by two. Schreiner stole Parnell's inbounds pass. The Schreiner guard thought he could hold the ball and run out the clock. As the player dribbled at the top of the key, Chuck motioned for Charles and Pepper to play tighter. When the guard was reaching up to call a timeout, Chuck dove at the ball. He tipped just enough of it knock it away. As he laid out on the floor, Chuck pushed the ball as hard as he could towards Charles. Charles saw the ball coming and dove for it. The ball skidded back towards Chuck. Schreiner players and St. Michael's players sprawled all over the court to try to gain control of the basketball. Somewhere on the bottom of the pile was Chuck Hayes. The referee blew the whistle. The stadium was hushed until the ref raised his hand and pointed at a Schreiner player for a foul. Schreiner fans moaned, and St. Michael's fans roared.

Schreiner was not in the penalty, so the Dillo's gained possession at half court. Chuck popped up and looked at his elbow. It was bloody from the scrap. He held it as he quickly walked to the bench for a towel. The trainer helped as he cleaned the wound during the timeout.

Round called the team together. "Well, boys, I think we've been here before!" They all nodded as visions of the last second loss to Schreiner surely played in every one's mind. "We're down two, and. . ." he checked the clock. "Eight seconds." The coach spit into his cup. "Any open shot. Got it! Any open shot, with three seconds left. Maybe we'll have enough time for a tip in!"

As the huddle broke, Round pulled Chuck aside. "If you got the three, feel free to get this over!"

Chuck smiled and said, "I haven't hit squat the whole second half. But I know who's hot. We got this, Coach!"

Chuck walked over to his teammates on the floor. "All right, guys. They think we're gonna try to tie it up. Just like the last time. I know we'll get an open three. Don't think about the clock and don't hesitate if you're open!"

As they headed out to the court Chuck pulled Pepper and Charles close and said, "Just like last time. Only this time, Pepper, come set the pick and stay at the top of the key. Charles, head to the corner and take your man away. You guys both want the shot, right?" The players looked at each other and smiled. "You want to win a championship, right? Be ready!" Both players smiled. As they walked away, Chuck yelled to both, "SQUARE UP AND FIRE!"

The ball came into Chuck, and he quickly dribbled to the top of the key. He noticed Schreiner had packed down into the lane and had one man on Charles. They were basically playing a box in one defense to take away Charles Holmes' shot and shut down the two-pointer inside. They were going to give up the three. Charles ran to the corner for a three taking his man away. Pepper came over for the pick on Chucks' defender. Chuck drove hard to the lane. Two Schreiner players went with Chuck toward the lane. Chuck threw a lightning pass out to Pepper at the top of the key.

This time, no one from Schreiner came out to contest the shot. This time Pepper had a wide open three from the top of the key. This time... he buried it!

Pepper Dyer was mobbed by delirious St. Michael's fans. It was sweet revenge after he missed the last shot against Schreiner just three weeks prior. Chuck went over to Coach Round and said, "Sorry about him taking the three, but I thought you would rather get it over now!" Coach Round was speechless.

Chuck ran over to Marshall and hugged the big mascot. Marshall and a large group of fans started chanting "Hoopman! Hoopman!" Soon the gym had picked it up. The auditorium joined in. For thirty minutes, the scene was pandemonium. Chuck loved every minute of it. St. Michael's University had won the Conference Championship. Along with it came the number four seed in the NCAA Division III Championship Tournament.

By Sunday morning, Tommy Clark had left Austin. The BCT was offline because they could no longer operate and they were bankrupt. The online business had lost over 25 million dollars in 48 hours. Thousands of online gamblers were never paid. Chat rooms filled with complaints about the company that failed to payout. Gamblers began to question the security of online betting. The timing was critical because the NCAA tournament was scheduled to start the next week.

The event did not escape Steve James. Fortune had smiled on him once more. Before Tommy Clark stopped taking calls and disappeared, Tommy had called Steve to ask if there was anything Steve could do. Steve assumed Tommy's network was hit by a sophisticated and targeted Dedicated Denial of Service and there was nothing he could do.

Steve had his suspicions about what was done to BCT and he provided Jeff a template to prevent it from happening to the BONE. Steve explained to Grant he knew what had happened to BCT, how it was done and made sure they were protected. Grant was impressed that James knew what happened and made an assumption that it was Steve that had done the job on BCT. It was accomplished so fast and now Grant had gained back the confidence he had lost in James. Grant also assured James that Clark would be found. Grant was so ecstatic that Tommy Clark was gone, he didn't even care about the millions Clark had cost the business. Jackson Grant may have been rich, but he wasn't smart.

CHAPTER EIGHTEEN

The "Doctors", as the young trio; Eddie, Chris and Bobby had started to call themselves, were busy prepping for the next phase of the operation. Hawk continued to remind them to prepare as if Grant and his minions were going to fight them to the end. BONE would be better prepared than BCT, so they needed to come up with something special. The computer they had put into the system in Austin made alterations easy on the BCT network. They needed to make sure the Trojan Horse they planted still had access to the Vegas network. The Austin program had allowed root access which provided the Doctors all the authority they needed to execute any number of programs to a connected network, which now was no longer viable. Bobby had been working for nearly two months on an exploitation program and another surprise that he had kept to himself, but it needed access to work.

Chuck was going over the tournament bracket and listening to the "Doctors" discuss their situation. He got up and showed them the bracket to take their minds off their work. "Did you guys see our bracket? We pulled a number one seed in our region. We're gonna play right up the road in Dallas! This is so cool. I thought we'd have to play in New York or California, but we're gonna play right here in Texas!"

Eddie rolled over and grabbed the paper. "But look at this number three seed. Mitchell! They got guys that can shoot from half court. I hope you all come up with a good game plan," said Eddie.

"It only takes one more point than the other guys have to win," said Chuck.

Bobby jumped up. "That's what we'll do."

The others looked at him in confusion. "What?" asked Eddie.

"We do just one game," said Bobby. "We don't need to alter multiple games this time. Just one game to see if we still have access with the Trojan Horse. If we get one game on the first night, we know we can use our access until..." he stopped.

"Until what?" asked Eddie.

Chris Crowley knew what Bobby was thinking. "We get caught."

Bobby nodded. "If we get root access with one machine, I don't think they'll catch us because they won't have enough time to clear our program. We'll still be in the BONE before they can find out what we did." After a moment he added, "We need to be prepared to whack the whole system and every machine that's associated with it based on what Mr. Hawkins believes."

"What do we do to whack the system?" asked Chris.

Bobby had the answer. "We go Godzilla!"

"What?" asked Chuck.

"We'll run my Godzilla program," said Bobby.

Chuck walked over to Bobby and said, "You don't look old enough to know about Godzilla."

"My dad is a huge Godzilla fan!" He stood up and became animated as he talked. "Remember how Godzilla would walk through town and step on everything in his path. He would just destroy anything that got in his way!" Chuck remembered, but Eddie and Chris were clueless. Bobby continued, "That's exactly what my surprise program will do! It will go through the system looking for hard drives and memory to crush. I know that I can take everything, servers, routers and hard drives! I can take all of it down!" Bobby looked like a kid who had just gotten a new toy. "I've always wanted to do this!"

Eddie and Chris looked at each other and nodded. Eddie said, "I guess Godzilla it is then!"

"When?" asked Chris.

Chuck said, "The night of the Championship." The 'doctors' looked at Hoopman and smiled. "That's the only night you can turn Godzilla loose, Bobby. More people will bet on the Championship than any other game. We're not gonna wait until the Division I National Championship. We run the other options until we get caught. We set Godzilla loose on BONE, here," Hoopman pointed to the calendar. "If we're still in their network, if Grant is still betting on D III games, you can turn Godzilla loose here. The night of the D III Championship game."

"Godzilla will take care of everything after that," said Bobby. "I know it will!"

Bobby was so confident, he even had Chuck believing they could pull it off.

The week of the Conference Championships provided some of the best betting opportunities a gambler could hope to find. With hundreds of games to choose from, only the savviest of gamblers noticed point spread discrepancies. The gamblers that usually checked multiple sites would find where the best bets were, or the sites where a point here or there mattered. The ones who went to the BONE smiled at the point spreads and immediately emailed or texted their friends with the best options. Especially if they noticed something wasn't right.

Eddie, Bobby and Chris worked around the clock to research the spreads, find the best games to alter, and get changes into the BONE network without being discovered. They started with the smaller conferences, finding just one game to alter the first night of the playoffs. With 8 hours until the game started, they decided to change a positive point spread to a negative spread. They used a cyber tool to freeze the betting lines in Vegas. What was posted on the internet for BONE bettors was one game with an altered point spread from +8 to -8. Such a small change that could have been an input mistake. No one at the BONE caught it as their site was locked in at the Game time minus ten-hour time frame.

By game time, the observant bettors used the internet chat rooms to share that one game, creating ten times normal activity. The internet did the work they needed to have done. Gamblers shared the altered game and heavy money was being bet on a Division III game that no one would have even noticed without a 16 point flip.

On top of this, Steve also got a consolation prize from his boss. Grant had already provided the G-Cash accounts. Out of the blue, he provided Steve access to a folder of e-wallet information. Steve was to take not just Tommy Clarks' funds, but his customers money as well. Grant's reasoning, if his customer got ripped off, they would assume it was Tommy Clark and they would go after him instead of the BONE. The intranet customers of Tommy would not get any special considerations or betting privileges during the basketball championships. The anger would grow, and Jackson Grant would say there was nothing the BONE could do about it. Tommy Clarks' customers would need to direct their anger at the Austin site, the BCT. Grant finished by saying, once Steve and Jeff re-checked the network, they could come to Vegas. Steve could barely contain his smile as he wholeheartedly agreed with his bosses' fantastic plans.

Jeff Roberts thought that his mentor, who had been working incredibly long hours, had actually been the one that had taken BCT down. It was one thing to do it; it was another not to tell his subordinate how he did it. The events of the last two weeks had nearly ruined their teacher-student relationship. They were fortunate that Grant gave them a pass after they failed to protect the Super Bowl betting attack, but now the issues in Austin were making Jeff's job very precarious. Jeff knew Steve was planning something big. Between Grant's ranting and Steve's long hours in his office, Jeff was close to packing up and running.

While the BONE was getting attacked, Steve James was busy working on his own program. Now he had information on the cryptocurrency accounts of dozens, perhaps hundreds, of millionaires. He was very close to being able to execute the culmination of two years planning. He had everything he needed except time.

Things seemed to be going along just fine for Chuck and his off-court team. It didn't take long for a ghost from the past to change the atmosphere in San Antonio.

"Mr. Nate Hawkins, please?" said the voice into the phone.

"Yes, this is he," answered Hawk.

"This is Detective Gary Darden at the SAPD," said the voice. "One of our officer's pulled a guy over last night. He didn't have enough information to hold him. But he does have a file with us. When I was going through it, I found your name as someone that was interested in this individual in question."

Hawk was momentarily confused. "Could you help me out a little bit here, Detective. Who are we talking about?"

"An individual named . . . William Stephen Moreland. That name ring a bell?" asked the detective.

"Oh, yeah! Mr. Moreland and I had an encounter. The shitbird hit me over the head with something hard, so I owe him," said Hawk.

"The note says you're a retired MP, and you wanted any information on this clown," said Darden.

Hawk answered, "Definitely, Gary! What do you have?"

"We pulled him over for running a red light. He passed a sobriety test. Just thought I would pass along, your friend is back in town."

"Could you do me another favor? Tell your guys to watch out for him. I think he has some unfinished business here."

"You got it, Mr. Hawkins. You wouldn't want to tell me why he's come back, would you?" asked the detective.

Hawk thought about keeping the information to himself, but it was Grace Winters' life that was at stake this time. Hawk stated flatly, "He's going to attack a woman named Grace Winters."

As soon as he was off the phone, he went to Sandy and told her that something had come up. He put his Beretta in the holster under his coat and jumped in his car. He'd be ready for Moreland this time.

Steve James said to Jeff Roberts, "We have reviewed all the firewalls and router security again. I haven't seen anything keeping us here. I just told Grant his system was well protected from anything like the BCT got hit with. The good news is, he believes me. He said we can come to Vegas."

It was the best news Jeff had heard lately. "I've been ready to go for a week now. I never thought I'd miss that little stinking apartment with the ten-million-dollar view. Some cheap buffets and a couple of umbrella drinks would really hit home right now."

"I have to admit I'm ready for a Vegas buffet myself," smiled Steve.

Seeing his mentor was in a good mood for the first time in weeks, Jeff had to ask a question that had been bothering him. "Did you take down the BCT?"

Steve stopped in his tracks and looked at Jeff. It was probably okay to be honest with him. Jeff didn't like Grant either. "No. No, I didn't."

The answer just confused Jeff Roberts more. "You didn't do it? But you've been working around the clock for a month. Are you gonna tell me what's going on?" asked Jeff.

"I didn't bankrupt the BCT," Steve said with a smile. "But I have an idea who did."

"The same person or group of people that sent Grant the messages, right?" asked Jeff.

Steve nodded, "You got it! You have nothing to worry about."

"Okay. You're the boss."

"That's right. I am your boss. You need to trust me," said Steve with a smile. "We need to get on that plane and head back to Vegas! We'll be there before next weekend's bets are placed." He grabbed his suitcase and headed out the door. Jeff quickly joined him. He wasn't happy with the way their time had been spent in the Bahamas, but at least they were leaving without Grant having a contract on their head.

"Hey there, beautiful!" yelled Chuck. He jogged quickly across the grass to join Grace as she walked.

"Well, hey there yourself, Mr. Hoopman!" she smiled. "I'm getting requests from some of my freshman students to see if I can get them tickets for Dallas."

"How many you need, Baby! I got about ten thousand right here in my pocket!" cracked Chuck. Chuck bumped lightly into her shoulder and said, "I'm sorry I haven't been around much. I just haven't . . ."

Grace stopped walking and looked at him. She shook her head. "You don't have to say anything, Chuck. I know what you're doing. Everyone on campus knows what you're doing!" She bumped lightly back into him and started walking again.

Chuck reached into his pocket. "I know you were kidding before, but here you go." He held out a ticket. "Sandy and Nate are gonna come up to Dallas on Friday. Unfortunately, we leave on Thursday night."

Grace smiled as she took the ticket and said, "I'll give Sandy a call." She started walking slowly and said, "I've heard Mitchell is pretty good. Do you think you guys have a chance?"

Chuck was quick to answer, "ALWAYS!"

"I want to see you guys go deep in this tournament. Not just for the school or your teammates." She stopped again. "But for you."

Chuck looked into her eyes. "If it ends on Friday night, it ends. It's been a great ride. But I'm gonna do everything I can to take it all the way. I mean, we've come this far, we might as well win it!"

"Yeah, you might as well."

Chuck kissed her on the cheek. "Gotta get to class. You know how those professors are!" She laughed as he waved goodbye and headed off to his next class. She looked at her ticket. It had been a while since she'd gone to Dallas. Getting away for the weekend sounded like fun.

Moreland was sitting in the driver's seat of the car. He put the binoculars on the passenger seat and picked up a picture of Grace. From a bag on the floor, he pulled out a knife. He set the picture on the seat of the car, then drove the knife into the picture so deeply that it stuck. He knew he shouldn't be there. But she was making him crazy. Why was she still with that basketball player? It would've been nice to have them both together when he "took care of business". Too bad the basketball player would be out of town on Friday. He decided to up his timetable. He started the car and slowly drove away.

"It's about time you guys got back. It's a shame about that Henderson guy shooting himself," chuckled Grant. Holden headed straight over to the bar. He poured two Scotches. One for himself and one for Thompson.

"I have to admit," said Holden. "It's good to be out of that two-bit city and back in Vegas."

Grant was in a surprisingly jovial mood. "While you were off on your vacation, James came and took care of that bastard Clark. He did something to Clark's network and basically bankrupted the organization."

Thompson became inquisitive about what James had done. "Did he say what he did to Clark's network?"

"I don't know exactly. He used some of that computer crap to put that bastard Tommy Clark out of business. Now Clark skipped town. He's not gonna cost me another dime," said Grant. He sauntered over to the bar and poured himself a drink. "James also checked us out to make sure we're protected from any of the same crap that happened to BCT. I mean, James must know what was done and how it can be used by someone else, right?"

The answer seemed to satisfy Holden for the moment. He didn't like James and the story didn't sound right. He certainly didn't like anyone else checking out the Vegas network without his approval, especially James. Holden made a note to find out what had happened to the BCT network. Thompson was responsible for the Vegas network with his own IT people before James had weaseled his way into the position. He knew Grant wasn't up to speed on computer protection. Thompson decided to have his people go through the system before next week's betting.

Grant interrupted his thoughts. "I'm wondering if you should've taken care of that Holmes kid permanently, too?"

Holden swirled his drink around in his glass. "I think we did enough to send the right message to anyone that wants to screw with us, Boss." He threw back the drink and poured another. "Holmes still isn't one hundred percent. I don't know how they keep winning."

Thompson, who was really a basketball fan, broke in. "I'll tell ya' how. That guy they call Hoopman!"

"Hoopman?" asked Grant. "Who the hell is Hoopman?"

Thompson said, "He's this fifty-year-old guy St. Michael's got playin' for them" He chuckled at his own joke. He was much more relaxed now that he was back in Vegas. He continued, "Actually, he's a retired Army guy. The deal is he's pretty good. I think he's leading the nation in assists. We might look at puttin' some money on them. Anybody who hasn't seen them play is bound to pick the other team."

Grant grabbed the paper to look at the bracket. "They did pull a four seed. That's pretty good for an unknown team. But they got Mitchell! No chance!"

"I'll take St. Michael's," said Thompson.

"You gotta be shittin' me!" said Grant. "You got it! How about a grand?"

Thompson nodded and took another drink, "A grand on St. Michael's."

"No points!" said Grant. Not only was he a ruthless jerk, but he was also a tightwad.

Thompson didn't hesitate. "Deal. We watched 'em play." He looked at Holden and said, "You didn't hurt the Holmes kid enough. He'll pick it up for the tournament. I bet they make the finals." It was a bold statement, but Thompson knew his basketball.

"We didn't want to kill the Holmes kid, or the word would get out on the street, and we wouldn't be able to get anyone to shave for us," said Grant. "I'm all for messages sent to players, but it's bad for business if we have to hurt them." Then he said, "Coaches are a different story." He and Holden laughed at the comment. Thompson poured himself another drink. He found absolutely no humor in the comment.

Grant said, "I think you've done enough for the time being. Why don't you two take a couple of days off. I expect we'll make a killin' from the tournament this year." He moved to the door to show them out.

Mike Thompson didn't hear the last comment. He was thinking about the BONE computer operation. He knew Grant had hired James as the computer "geek extraordinaire". He also knew that Steve James actually "volunteered" for the position after having his knee dismantled by a power drill. It was for that reason alone that Thompson didn't trust James. He was one slimy guy when he was in debt years ago, and he was still slimy. Plus, revenge is a great motivator.

Holden said, "You want to get a beer?"

Thompson, suffering from a mental itch he couldn't scratch said, "I don't think so. I'm gonna go to my office. There are a couple things I want to check." It would be more than a couple things. He was going to have his IT guys do multiple systems checks from every mouse to all the servers.

The BONE betting service used the standard Vegas point spreads that every online group used. The unique thing about their line was one game was different than every other line in the country and they never noticed. In the western bracket, a regional ten seed had somehow become an 8-point favorite. That in itself was not unheard of, but when the team was getting eight points by BONE and other betting sites saw them as an 8-point underdog, some people noticed. Real money was laid down and the Vegas personnel didn't catch it as their betting board was frozen. The betting spread change was posted at 11 o'clock on that Friday morning. With 10 hours to tip off, the gamblers who noticed the spread were quickly back in the chat rooms to their friends. Like an internet wildfire, the word was out.

Mike Thompson was not looking at point spreads. He was checking equipment, trons, and traffic. There was nothing out of the ordinary as far as his team could tell. On Thursday morning, an assistant told him everything was fine. They had greater volume of betting in the western bracket, but nothing out of the ordinary. No one at BONE noticed why.

Ed Newton called Chuck and told him confidently, "we're still in." Chuck hung up the phone. He thought the news would help relax. Faced with the fact that he was about to play the biggest game of his life, the good news didn't matter. He was a bundle of nerves.

Grace Winters left her office at noon. She was in a hurry when she got to her home. She clumsily struggled with her keys as she got to her door. She shuffled through the door, dropping her bag as she entered. She put everything else on the couch, turned and headed back to get her handbag and close the door. She let out a little 'gasp' when she saw the man standing behind her in the doorway.

As her eyes focused to the light, she relaxed just a bit when she saw it was Nate Hawkins. Strangely enough, he had his index finger to his lip. In his other hand, Grace noticed the gun. Grace started to ask him what he was doing, when Hawk moved quietly into the house and up against a wall in the foyer.

Grace walked over and closed the door. She gave Hawk a querying look, then she heard the yell from down the hallway. William Moreland shouted and came running down the hallway heading straight for Grace. High over his head he was holding a large butcher knife as he came.

Nate Hawkins stepped in front of Grace with his pistol drawn. "FREEZE!" Moreland, totally focused on his heinous act, showed no reaction. It was as if he didn't even see the man standing in front of Grace Winters. He kept coming. Hawk's reflexes got the better of him and he squeezed the trigger.

The bullet hit the oncoming man in the shoulder, slowing him down. He staggered, shocked to see the man standing in front of Grace, took one more step and raised the knife again. Hawk didn't warn him the second time. The next shot hit Moreland in the upper thigh. Moreland screamed as he hit the floor.

Hawk walked over with the gun pointing at the man's head. He stepped on the wrist that held the knife. He said over his shoulder to Grace, "You okay?" He noticed her nod and saw her shuffle to the couch to steady herself.

Hawk addressed Moreland as he lay on the floor. "You hit me in the head, you maggot, so I owed you. You also owe this woman an apology. Now you have a choice. You can tell her you're sorry," he pointed the gun towards Moreland's groin. "Or you can let me take some more target practice!"

The man's eyes grew wide, and he screamed, "NO! NO! Don't shoot again!" He looked at Grace and started to say something.

Hawk said, "Make sure it's an apology!" He put both hands on the pistol to emphasize his point.

Moreland exhaled, looked at Grace and said, "I'm sorry." Then he turned to Hawk and snapped, "I should've killed you!" Hawk took the pistol and smacked Moreland on the forehead hard with a baseball bat that had appeared out of nowhere. Moreland's head went limp on the floor.

"Yeah, but you didn't," said Hawk. He tossed the bat down, grabbed his phone and waved it at Grace. "I called 911. You could probably go to that door and tell those cops that are coming not to shoot!" Grace quickly did as Hawk ordered. To her surprise, sirens indicated the police were working their way towards her house with pistols drawn.

A minute later she came back inside, she went to Hawk who was watching Moreland as he lay in agony on the floor.

Hawk turned to Grace and said, "He's not so tough." The whole thing had happened so fast, that it hadn't sunk in until right then. She glanced at the pistol in Hawk's hand and for just a moment, she wanted Hawk's gun. Hawk saw her expression change and her anger flashed. He promptly put the pistol in his holster. Then it hit her. Hawk watched as the tears appeared in her eyes. He stuck out his arm and pulled her to him. "It's okay! It's over, Grace!"

The police came in, followed by paramedics. Hawk took Grace Winters with him as they walked to the couch. He tried to comfort her. "You know, the really tough part comes now." She gave him a confused look. "You're going to have to testify in court."

"I don't have any reservations about that, Hawk," she said.

"I . . . I think we might be a little late getting to Dallas tonight. That is, if you still want to go?" asked Nate Hawkins.

She thought about the statement and smiled, "How soon can we get out of here?! We need to be there for Chuck."

"We need to answer some questions for the police first, then we can leave," said Hawk. "You want a drink of water or something?"

"Yes, I'll help you!" she said. They both headed for the kitchen. Grace said, "How did you know he was here?"

Hawk got two clean glasses from the dishwasher and said, "I got a tip a couple of days ago, and I've been following you ever since." Grace nodded. "I knew you were coming home so I headed here. I saw him walking around to the back when you were driving up. Before you say anything else, I apologize for not telling you he was here, but if you would have done anything to spook him, he would have just disappeared again. I'm sorry, but I wasn't going to let him get away this time."

Grace walked over and kissed Hawk on the cheek. The big man blushed. "One thing I will ask of you," said Grace.

Hawk said, "Sure. Anything I can do."

"I don't think we should tell Chuck about this tonight. He probably doesn't need to know about this until after the tournament, okay?" she said.

Hawk laughed. "I wasn't gonna tell him!" Hawk took a big drink of water and said, "Let me get Detective Darden in here. We got a game to catch!"

The St. Michael's vs. Mitchell game had a seven PM tip off. It was 6:50 and Chuck had something else to be nervous about. Not just the game, but because Grace, Sandy and Hawk had not shown up. Pepper Dyer noticed his friend's demeanor. "Hey, Hoopman, they're gonna be here. It's still early. They're probably getting a taco or something!"

Chuck smiled. "That obvious, huh?" Pepper nodded at his friend. "You look like you're ready to play. You've been on cloud nine since last week!"

"Hoopman, when I'm your age, I'll still be smilin' about that game!" said Pepper with a huge grin.

Chuck laughed at Pepper's comment. He decided to get down to business. He got a ball and started to dribble around half court looking at his teammates. "How's everybody else!?" Chuck yelled. "ANYBODY ELSE READY TO PLAY SOME BALL!" He got high fives and hoots from all his teammates. Charles Holmes simply winked at Chuck as he drained a fifteen-footer. Jose was the only one that looked nervous about the game. Chuck went up to him and said, "Hey! You need me to kick your butt or what?" He smiled broadly.

Jose just shook his head. "Look at all the people, Hoopman! I've never played in front of so many people!"

"It's a Championship Tournament, big man!" Chuck got serious. "Fifty years from now you can tell your grandkids about this, Jose. You played college basketball and competed for a National Championship!" Jose just nodded in awe. "Come on, big guy! Time for the anthem."

After the player introductions, Chuck wiped off with a towel. He went over to Charles and just looked at him. He couldn't help but smile. "Are you ready for this?"

Chuck started to fist bump Charles. Charles moved his hand and gave Chuck a hug. "Because of you, Hoopman!" Charles stepped back and said, "Let's do this!"

After the Anthem and player introductions, Chuck said a quick prayer. Finally, the players took the court. Chuck looked at Mitchell. They were big and they were fast. Chuck was matched up against a nineteen-year-old rocket named Tyrus Donnelly. He was a first team Division III All-American and within the first minute, Chuck knew why. The kid was lightning in a uniform. It didn't take Chuck long to figure out he was going to need help. He played way off Donnelly and dared him to shoot threes. Donnelly did not want to shoot from the outside when he knew anytime he wanted to, he could drive by Chuck to the basket.

Charles Holmes volunteered to switch and offer help defense, but Chuck refused the offer. With the score 22 to 15, Mitchell on top, Chuck finally found Donnelly's weakness. He was very weak dribbling to his left. Chuck started to force the guard to go left every time he touched the ball. After two times down the floor pushing Donnelly to his left, Chuck started to scoot up on him. The change in tactics rattled the younger player and it showed. He threw one left-handed pass straight to David Parnell, then followed that up by dribbling off his foot out of bounds.

On the offensive end, Chuck slowed the game down. The team had seemed anxious early, but they responded well to the change in tempo. By halftime, the St. Michael's was only down by one.

In the locker room Coach Round let his players do the talking. David Parnell reminded his teammates that while they were there, they might as well win it! "IT AIN'T TIME TO GO HOME YET!" The team rallied around their captain and exploded out of the locker room. Their confidence was back.

The feeling carried over to the court and the Dillo's hit their first five shots to go up by six. Mitchell made a surge that was shut down when Parnell dove across the lane and gathered in a loose ball. When he got up, he held his arm up so the Dillo fans could see the floor burn. Marshall in his mascot costume started a "Floor Burn" chant. The crowd joined in, and the St. Michael's students went nuts. At that moment, the neutral fans got the sense that St. Michael's was worth rooting for. The majority of the crowd started rooting for Armordillo's. The crowd put Mitchell on the defensive and they never recovered. As Donnelly continued to struggle with his left hand, the crowd began to verbally challenge the nineteen-year-old. With three minutes left in the game, he was benched.

Chuck Hayes came out of the game a minute later. The Dillo's, even as the higher seed, had shut down a fan favorite and walked off the court with a 68 to 56 upset. The crowded arena was buzzing not only at the score, but how well the boys from Texas had played. Some fans called it a fluke, some fans called it luck, but others had problems finding a weakness with the group of unknowns. They were now 22-2, and you don't win that many college games by having weaknesses.

Later that night, the first seeded Babson rolled over the University of the Pacific. On Saturday evening, St. Michael's would take on Babson, the number one seed in the west. For St. Michael's to get by Babson, they would have to shoot much better than they had against Mitchell.

The BONE had a problem. The western bracket of the D III Tournament cost them nearly ten million dollars due to one upset and the number ten team point spread which "had a glitch". Rather than lose all those customers, the BONE decided just after midnight to honor the bets and accepted they were responsible for an error in the betting line. The 'Doctors' were still in business.

It did not prevent the BONE from continuing operations.

At dinner that night, Chuck sat with Grace, Sandy and Hawk, Jose, Charles, and Pepper. Over dinner they talked about how great they had played against Mitchell and what they needed to do to beat Babson. Chuck pulled out the ever-present bracket that he carried with him. "Look at all these upsets! This is great for the game." Then he made a bold statement. "I don't see anyone left that can beat us."

Pepper laughed out loud, and Jose nearly choked on some bread. "Dang, Hoopman! Don't jinx us like that! Don't you know you're not supposed to say stuff like that. That's bad luck!" said Jose with a huge frown.

"I'm serious! Look at this." He pointed at the paper. "All the other top seeds except Babson went down. All these other teams are perimeter playing teams. We play the outside game as good as anybody in the nation! We can win this region. Easy!" said Chuck.

"Wait! Are you saying we don't have an inside game?" asked Jose. The frown on his face had grown larger.

"Not at all, mi amigo grande!" Chuck teased. "I think you guys can hold your own against anybody. But some of the teams rely on their inside games to win. When we get against those teams, you and OJ and David are gonna step it up for us to win!"

"All right, I'll buy that, Senor Hoopman!" said Jose. The frown disappeared. "I suggest you little guys step up your game to get us there!"

"That sounds like a challenge," said Chuck.

Jose shrugged, "Whatever."

Chuck said, "Challenge accepted!"

The waiter came to the table. "Would anyone care for anything else?"

Jose said loudly, "Nothing more for me! I'm watching my weight for another two weeks!!" The waiter looked down at the huge man and just shook his head.

Suddenly Hawk sank down in his chair and got Chuck's attention. Chuck was confused but moved his seat a little closer to his friend. Hawk whispered, "Don't look directly at the guy, but do you see the black man in the corner of the room?"

Chuck said, "I'll check in a minute. What about him?

"He's one of the scum bags who was holding Henderson in Austin!" said Hawk. Chuck was shocked, yet still managed to hide it. Hawk nodded and said, "I'm positive!" Chuck leaned back and took a glance at the man. He was alone, drinking a beer and eating. The man had positioned himself so that he could observe the diners in the restaurant.

"I need to get that guy alone and find out what he's doing here," said Hawk.

Chuck thought about the comment. "I got it!" He called the waiter over.

The waiter came over to Derrick Monroe and said, "The woman at the bar bought you a beer. Would you like another one?" he asked.

Monroe looked over the waiter's shoulder. He put on his best smile as he tried to see the lovely lady who had bought him the beer. He was quickly disappointed. "I don't see no lady at the bar."

The waiter looked and shrugged. "She must've gone to the restroom." He turned and walked away. Every two minutes, the waiter would return and fill Monroe's glass of water and ask him if he would like another beer.

Ten minutes later, the plan was working. Hawk saw Monroe get up from the table to go to the rest room and got up to follow him but waited for Chuck.

The waiter was quick to return to Chuck's table. The waiter said, "Sir, I believe the gentlemen in question is headed to the location you desired."

Chuck gave the waiter a twenty and said, "Don't bet on college basketball with this!" The waiter was totally confused by the comment, but quite happy with the tip.

Hawk slapped Chuck on the shoulder and said, "I just need two minutes alone with him. If you could get Charles to join us, that might help." Chuck agreed and nodded at Charles's to follow him.

Derrick Monroe thought nothing about the man at the sink in the restroom. He shuffled over to the toilet and began his business. Hawk walked in and quickly assessed the surroundings. He walked over to the man at the sink and opened his coat. The man saw the Beretta, quickly dried his hands, and hurriedly left the bathroom.

Nate made sure no one else was in the rest room. He walked up behind Monroe and stood there. Monroe became a little uncomfortable as he realized there was a large man standing behind him as he was peeing. "Yo, man! There's another toilet right over there!" Hawk lifted his foot and slowly pushed Monroe into the toilet. "YO, MAN! WHAT THE F. . . ?"

The barrel of the Beretta slowly appeared from behind Derrick Monroe's head. "I AIN"T GOT NO MONEY, MAN!"

"When you're done, turn around slowly, shithead! Get your hands up," said Hawk. Derrick Monroe did what he was told. "Do you remember me?" Derrick Monroe was afraid, but after a couple seconds, he knew the man who was holding the pistol.

"Yeah! You're the dude that beat the hell out of the computers and beat up . . ."

"That's right. Beat up your fat friend!" said Hawk. "You remember Pete Henderson? The guy I took away from your place!" Monroe nodded. "Do you know what happened to him?"

"Man, I don't know nothing!" said Monroe.

Chuck and Charles Holmes entered the rest room. Chuck walked over to Hawk and said quietly, "I think I know what you're doin' here, but you might want to relax for just a second and let him take care of that!" Chuck pointed to Monroe's groin.

"Good idea!" Hawk pointed the gun down at Monroe's groin. "Put the horse back in the barn!" Monroe did exactly as he was told and quickly put his hands back up.

Chuck whispered into Hawk's ear, "Is there something going on in your life you're not telling me about? A lifestyle change maybe?" Chuck nearly burst out laughing.

"NO! Would you stay focused?" said Hawk tersely.

Chuck pulled Charles over to look at Monroe. "Do you recognize this guy?"

Charles looked at the man. "I don't remember. I can't say that I've ever seen him before."

Hawk leaned in towards Derrick. "Did you beat this man up, shithead?" He cocked the pistol.

"NO WAY! I didn't have a thing to do with that!" cried Derrick.

"Who did?" Monroe didn't want to answer. Hawk stepped closer. He tapped the barrel of the pistol on Monroe's head, then pointed it at his shoulder. "You need to think about this. I'm not gonna kill you. But a limb at a time would eventually cause you to lose a lot of blood. You know I'll do it, don't you?"

Monroe frowned and nodded his understanding. "The dude's name is Holden. Carl Holden. He's the guy who beat that dude up!"

Hawk didn't ease up. "And Henderson? Did he kill Henderson?" Monroe didn't want to answer. Hawk smacked him lightly on top of the head with the pistol again. "DON'T MAKE ME MAD!"

Monroe finally broke. "That was Holden too! He killed that man and made it look like he shot himself."

Hawk stepped back but didn't put the gun away. "That still doesn't explain what you're doin' here, Buttboy!"

Monroe explained, "Tommy Clark, the dude we work for, lost his ass and then some 'cause somebody screwed up the online gambling portion of his business. There are people from all over the state who are lookin' for his ass."

"That still doesn't explain what you're doing following us," said Chuck.

Monroe looked at Charles. "Clark thinks that if we can get Holmes," then he looked at Chuck and said, "or the legendary Hoopman, here. Mr. Grant, the head guy in Vegas would bail him out. Let him back into the operation. Maybe set him up another operation in a different area."

Chuck was a little unnerved by the fact that Clark was targeting specific players, but one thing Monroe said was comforting. Chuck needed to confirm the information. It was a test question. "What happened to the online portion of his business?"

"I don't know! Only person who knows is some computer geek Grant has workin' for him. Apparently, he made sure that Grant's system won't get taken down the way ours was," said Monroe.

Chuck needed more information. "The computer geek, does he have a name?"

Monroe shook his head no. Then he added, "I don't know his name. But Holden's got a network Nazi that he runs with. His name is Thompson. Mike Thompson. He isn't the guy that Grant went to. Grant's got somethin' on this geek who works the whole network from the Carribean. Whoever that guy is, the dude from the islands. That's the dude who knows how Clarks' network got screwed up."

Chucks first reaction was to call the 'Carribean Dude' by what he thought he knew him as. "HoopFan." But he couldn't be sure. Monroe had a good story, but was it reliable?

He looked at Hawk and pulled him aside. "It fits. What do you think?"

"This guy is small fish. I don't think he had anything to do with Charles getting beaten or Henderson's death. He's probably telling the truth about Clark and this guy 'Holden'," said Hawk.

"What now?" asked Chuck.

Hawk exhaled loudly. "It's getting deep, Chuck. We probably need to call in the reinforcements before it gets out of hand. If Clark is targeting guys, that could be dangerous." He thought a little more. "I'm gonna take this guy to the cops. He'll squeal on Clark, and the cops will pick him and the other fat guy up too. They won't be a problem. They don't know anything about why their net was hosed up, so we're still clear there. Maybe Clark can spill enough dirt on Grant and his group to shut 'em down before we do. More importantly, maybe I can convince my brothers with badges to pick up Carl Holden." Chuck nodded in agreement. "I'll see you at the game. Tell Sandy I've gone to the police station."

Hawk looked at Charles Holmes. He was standing off to the side looking at Derrick Monroe. "You want me to leave you alone with this guy for a couple minutes, Charles."

Charles looked at Hawk and then at Monroe. "No. I'm above all that now. I got a game I have to get ready for. Wouldn't want to hurt my hands."

Chuck smiled and patted his teammate on the shoulder. "Come on, Charles. Let's go finish eating."

The game against Babson had an eight o'clock tip-off. In the locker room, Parnell gave the team a quick captain's speech. This was the big time and they needed to act like the class act they were. Of course, Parnell smiled at Chuck after delivering the speech. Seems he had heard those words a few minutes earlier in a private setting.

As the Armordillo's were leaving the locker room, Chuck noticed Coach Round coming away from the water fountain and putting his pill bottle back into his pocket. It seemed the coach was walking with a slight limp that Chuck had never noticed before. He walked up and said, "Are you okay, Coach? I noticed your leg or hip doesn't seem to be working as smooth as before?"

Round smiled broadly and said, "We're in the tournament, Hayes! I couldn't be better!" Chuck nodded and smiled back at his mentor. "You get ready for Babson." Chuck was slow to move, and his smile faded a bit. Coach Round picked up on it and said, "Hayes, there's nothing you can do about it except play ball, okay."

Chuck didn't like the answer but understood he wouldn't get any more than that from his coach. "Guess I better get ready to play then, eh?"

The coach grunted, "Uh-huh. Bring it tonight, Chuck." Chuck quickly turned and headed to the floor. He put the exchange behind him and tried to stay focused on playing ball. It was what the coach wanted him to do. Yet deep down, he knew something wasn't right.

The Runnin' Dillos as the papers were callin' them, were as ready to play as Chuck had ever seen them. There were no more pep talks or speeches, just shared confidence, and enthusiasm.

Babson was a program that relied on long range shooting. St. Michael's had shown they could shut down the long shot against Mitchell. Babson decided to try a different game plan. After the tipoff, they took the ball inside to try a power game. The tactic didn't suit them at all. David Parnell and OJ repeatedly swatted away shots or intimidated the Mitchell shooters into mistakes.

Chuck noticed Charles was into a rhythm early. He was hitting jump shots from two feet behind the three-point line. He had never demonstrated that kind of range before. The fact that he was hitting from there was not lost on Coach Round. He told Chuck to keep feeding him. Babson didn't bother to contest Holmes from that distance, because they didn't have anyone to stop him if he decided to penetrate. With Holmes hitting open

25 footers and the Babson big men trying to play an unfamiliar game, the first half was a wash. St. Michael's went into the locker room up 44 to 25.

Marshall Wright, as the 'ArmorDillo', had the crowd roaring for more Dillo basketball. At one point, he performed a flip off a trampoline and ended it with a dunk. He brought little kids out of the stands during timeouts and helped them to shoot and show their dribbling prowess. He would tease the officials. Best of all, he gave away tons of free St. Michael's merchandise. Marshall had learned from Chuck to go after the neutral fans. The "Armordillo" would go to the neutral fans and give the kids St. Michael's merchandise. By the start of the second half, most of the arena was cheering for St. Michael's.

Babson came out in the second half and played the game that got them there. There was a reason they were the number one seed in the region. They could shoot long range jumpers like layups. They hustled for loose balls and played aggressive defense. What was a laugher in the first half, turned into a surprisingly good game.

Chuck began to feel the toll the game was taking but didn't want to come out. He stopped driving to the basket and slowed the tempo of the game to a crawl. Babson became impatient and started to foul. The new tactic backfired as Chuck, Charles, and Jose buried Babson with free-throws. The free throws won it for St. Michael's, and the final score was 82 to 75.

As a team, the St. Michael's was 30 out of 35 from the charity stripe. Chuck was an unbelievable 13 for 13 from the line. He also finished with 15 assists that were primarily passes to Charles Holmes on the wing for open three pointers.

In the locker room after the game, the mood was one of unbridled joy. The team was going to the Regional Championships the next weekend. They were at an emotional and physical peak.

Some reporters tried to talk to him, but Chuck stayed low key. He complimented Babson on a good comeback and a tremendous effort but deflected most of the attention to his teammates. He would be described by one reporter on Twitter as "distant" and "aloof". One of the Sportscenter reporters said he was "merely more focused" than his teammates. The reason for his restrained attitude was Hawk's advice, "not too high and not too low", kept playing over and over in his mind. The Babson game was a great victory, but the war was not won. Chuck wanted to stay on mission. Let the rest of the team enjoy the limelight.

After answering as many questions as he could stand, Chuck moved quickly to the bus. Alone in his seat, Chuck had the time to reflect how lucky he had been, off the court as well as on. He couldn't help but smile at his fortune. He said a prayer of thanks for the fortune that he had been blessed with. For a moment, all was right with the world.

If the cops showed up tomorrow, or "the doctors" were discovered by Thompson, or another team stepped up and really played well enough to beat them, those were things he could live with. The fact that the St. Michael's Dillo's team, his team, had come so far brought a huge smile to his face. The fact that they were on the cusp of something much bigger was not lost on Chuck. If they lost the next week, that would constitute a true crime. They didn't have another game until the next Friday against the University of Massachusetts at Dartmouth. It couldn't come fast enough.

CHAPTER NINETEEN

Steve James was drinking a coffee as he looked over Jeff Robert's shoulder. "St. Michael's won, eh?"

"Sure did," said Jeff. "Looks like it was a pretty good game too. Let's see," he looked at the point spreads. "They got Dartmouth next. No chance. Looks like 'Lady Luck' is gonna run out for those guys on Friday."

Steve said, "I wouldn't count that bunch out. They got a long way to go yet." He smacked his protégé on the arm. "I gotta check somethin'."

"What are you checkin'?" asked Jeff.

"We only had the one game with the whacky point spread, right?" asked Steve.

"As far as we could tell. It was still about an eight-million-dollar loss on that one game. Made that region a loser, too. But, no. We didn't see any other problems."

Steve smiled to himself. They were still in the network. Thompsons' team hadn't found the problem or he surely would have mentioned it to Grant. "I just want to see what kind of point spreads our boss is giving these guys," said Steve. "Then I want to finish up that program I've been building. You could help me out a bunch if you covered for me here. I only need two more days, maybe three at the most."

"You want to tell me what it is?" asked Jeff.

"No, no, no! Not yet! I'll let you know what happens if it works," said Steve. "Just let me know if anything . . . unusual happens or if Grant calls, okay? I don't think anything will happen this week. But next weekend things could get interesting!" The comment confused Jeff, but it didn't matter. James was much more relaxed since they were back in Vegas.

Tuesday night Chuck and Grace went over to Hawk and Sandy's house to eat. Most of the conversation involved basketball, but Sandy and Grace were getting used to that. The knock at the door came as a surprise. Hawk answered the door and let the visitor in.

"Everyone, this is Detective Gary Darden. He's with SAPD," said Hawk as he led the Detective to a seat in the living room. "I think you know everybody here, except Mr. Hayes. What can we do for you, Gary?"

"Mr. Hayes! Nice game against Babson!" Chuck nodded and shook the detective's hand. For an instant, Chuck wondered how the detective had known Grace, but he let it go. "Well, I'll be brief because I see you have company," said the detective. "We have some good news for you. Derrick Monroe took the Dallas Police right to Thomas Clark in a hotel in Fort Worth. They also arrested an individual named Winston Carmichael, also known as 'Nubbin'."

"That's terrific news," said Nate.

"We've gathered a lot of information from them about a gambling organization in Las Vegas and a man named Jackson Grant. Do you know anything about this organization?"

Hawk looked at Chuck and said, "I don't think that I've heard of him? Have you, Chuck?"

Chuck shook his head, "Jackson Grant? No. Can't say that I have."

"I doubted you had. The guys at the office said that Monroe was singing like a bird about this Grant guy. He said that Carl Holden, the guy you told the Dallas cops about, Mr. Hawkins, worked for Jackson Grant." Gary Darden was a good cop. He wouldn't have been a detective if he wasn't. He looked at Hawk for a reaction.

Hawk remained calm. "When Mr. Monroe and I talked, we discussed Mr. Henderson's death. He was an assistant coach with St. Michael's. I was aware that Monroe had been following the St. Michael's basketball team to try and get some of the players involved with his former organization, the Big Casino Texas. I asked him if he knew about Pete Henderson's so-called 'suicide'. He told me he thought Carl Holden probably killed Henderson. I thought that was information the Dallas cops might want to know about."

The answer seemed to put Gary Darden at ease. "Okay. I needed to ask so I can tell the guys downtown. I figured Monroe had told you about Holden. We have a warrant out for Mr. Holden, and I expect the police will want to talk to this Mr. Grant, too!" Darden got up and started for the door.

In the foyer, he stopped when he noticed all the plaques for service on Hawk's wall. "How many years were you a military policeman?"

"I retired with twenty-six years of duty," said Hawk.

"My dad was an MP," said Darden. "Tough duty." He headed to the door. "If I hear anything more on Jackson Grant, I'll let you know." He turned to leave then stopped.

"One other thing," said the detective. "I thought you might want to know that a couple of FBI agents have been asking questions about Clark's online gambling service. You mentioned it before. The Big Casino Texas or BCT. Seems Clark's organization went bankrupt, and Monroe said Henderson was somehow involved. They didn't fill me in on any details, but you can rest assured I'll let you know if I hear anything. Good to see you under better circumstances, Miss Winters." Grace nodded and blushed a little.

Nate stuck out his hand and gave a smile to his friend. He held the hand a little longer than normal and said, "Thank you, Gary. Thanks very much!"

Gary Darden had just provided Nate and Chuck a heads up about the FBI investigation that was going on. Chuck was confused about how Darden had known Grace and under what "circumstances" that had been, but he needed to take care of first things first.

"Thank God, he's on our side!" said Chuck. "It was good to hear they are gonna try to arrest Holden, too. Maybe if they put enough pressure on Grant, he'll shut down before this weekend."

"Don't count on it," said Hawk. "Those guys always have great lawyers. He'll be able to run for another year before anything happens. By then, he can take his money, run to Costa Rica, and be untouchable."

"What about the FBI?" asked Grace.

"They can't do much without evidence. Even if they knew all the ins and outs of what was going on, they still need evidence," said Hawk. "Right now, they don't have any, or it would be them asking us questions instead of Gary Darden." Hawk added, "Maybe we should run Godzilla right now and get it all over with?" Sandy and Grace looked at each other confused but knew better than to ask.

Chuck said, "Naw. Not yet. I think one more week ought to be enough to drive BONE out of business. It worked on BCT. Besides, if BONE didn't notice last weekend, maybe we can stick 'em one more time."

"All right! I guess there isn't anything we can do so let's eat some dessert!" said Hawk.

They started for the kitchen when Chuck looked at Grace and said, "You gonna tell me how you and Detective Darden know each other?"

"Why, Mr. Hayes! Are you jealous?" she asked.

"Yes, usually I am. But not this time," he said. He stopped at the doorway. Chuck noticed the conversation had suddenly stopped. "Tell me. How do you know Gary Darden?"

"We thought it best not to tell you," said Hawk.

"You had the game, and we didn't want you to be upset," said Grace.

"I tried to convince them to tell you all the way to Dallas," said Sandy.

"WHOA! TOO FAST!" Chuck looked at Grace. "You first!" She told him about Moreland and how Hawk had been there. Then Hawk explained that Moreland had come after Grace, but Hawk was ready for him. The police now had him in custody and Grace was going to testify against him. Chuck started to get mad because Hawk had used her for bait, but Grace defended Hawk and agreed it was the best way to capture Moreland. Chuck wasn't happy about it, but it was over. Moreland was locked up and Grace hadn't been hurt.

"NO MORE OF THAT CRAP, HAWK!" said Chuck. "You start using those cop friends of yours."

"Next time, I will. I swear it!" said Nate.

Chuck walked over and lightly smacked him on the arm. "And by the way, you dirtball! THANKS!"

Chuck changed the subject and said, "I hate to break this up. No desert for me. I am not as young as I used to be. I need to get home and take my Motrin and hit the sack."

"You are getting old!" said Grace.

Chuck tried to laugh it off. "Nag, nag, nag! Come on beautiful! I'll give you a ride home. I need to get some sleep."

Grace walked up next to Chuck and they said their good-byes. Chuck felt good hearing Moreland was locked up. Knowing Grace was safe was a blessing. It was also good that Nate Hawkins was there. It was nice to know his prayer for her protection worked.

On Wednesday night, Chuck received an email on the team website from 'Hoopfan'. The message said all was well, and he wished Hoopman and the Dillo's good luck against Dartmouth. The fact that he had said, "all was well" in the message meant that as far as Hoopfan knew, Grant had not discovered the alterations in the point spread at BONE.

Everything else was as good as could be expected going into the Semi-Final Championship weekend. The 'Doctors' had not been caught, and the police were looking for Carl Holden. Between Hoopfan and Gary Darden, Chuck felt like their backs were being well covered. To top it all off, the St. Michael's Armordillo's looked sharp in practice. They would be ready for Bucknell.

Yet, Jackson Grant had not stopped betting on college basketball. Chuck thought hard about the fact the objective had not been achieved. They had cost Grant millions, but he was still operational. Chuck called Eddie and asked a simple question. "The money doesn't seem to hurt him, maybe his own employees can get his attention. Do you have anything you can run against the BONE employees?"

Chuck could feel Eddie's smile through the phone. "We just happen to have separated the employees, from the Intranet bettors, from the venders. Would you like me to take care of all those?"

Chuck laughed. "It would be just what a doctor ordered!"

"I'm on it," was all Eddie needed to say.

In Vegas, Grant was getting edgy. Thompson still had not discovered the subtle alteration Eddie and Bobby had made to their network nor the Trojan Horse, but Carl Holden had received word that there was an all-points bulletin out on him for the murder of Pete Henderson. After the Vegas cops came by asking questions about Henderson and the BCT, Grant banished Holden to a cabin near Reno. He told the cops nothing and said the next time they came back to bring a warrant, and he'd have his lawyer present.

Thompson had talked to Jeff Roberts about the anomaly in the system at BCT. Jeff told Thompson that Steve James had taken care of the problem. When Jeff asked if Mike Thompson wanted Steve to look into the Vegas network, Thompson got angry and said he'd do it himself.

When Mike Thompson told Grant the "anomaly" in the BCT computer system may have been done by Steve James, Grant wanted specifics that Thompson didn't have. Thompson "recommended" shutting down the system, just for a couple days.

Grant blew a gasket and said Thompson was nuts. "We have one of the biggest weekends in gambling coming up, and you want to shut down? Unless you can give me something more than 'anomalies', we aren't shutting down a single bet!" But when Thompson went back to check the point spreads, they were the same as the original Vegas line.

Something was wrong, but he sure as hell couldn't figure it out. Thompson had no good answer for his boss. He had numbers. Millions in lost payouts from a previous Regional game should have been all Grant needed.

To top it all off, the fraternity boys were back sending emails all over social media. Not only that, they were in the intranet and messaging employees and vendors about betting practices that played favorites. They threatened to prevent payments to workers and other businesses. Thompsons' phone was constantly ringing as he tried to calm everyone down. The same theme was sent to the bettors: All the BONE customers were not to bet on college basketball. Thompson got another cup of coffee and sat down at his keyboard. It was going to be another long night of looking for virtual ghosts.

The fans in Ft. Wayne, Indiana were surprisingly kind to the St. Michael's Armordillos. The Dillo's were the Cinderella of the tournament. Dartmouth was cocky from the opening tip-off. They had a reason to be.

Dartmouth played a different style of basketball than St. Michael's was used to playing. They were small, quick and smart. It would have been easy for the Dillo's to fold early, but sheer guts kept them in the game. They spent most of the first half chasing smaller track stars as they ran the Dillo's ragged. Dartmouth substituted every 3 minutes with fresh legs. The majority of points came on drives to the basket after running two to three picks on every defender.

Chuck wasn't much help on defense. Dartmouth was very good at setting picks. While defending the three-point shot on his man, Dartmouth players would set up multiple picks that Chuck couldn't get around. Just before halftime, Chuck's man decided to run Chuck off a pick and take him to the hole. Chuck knew it was coming but was too slow to get around the defender making the pick. His right foot kicked into the picking player's set foot causing Chuck's toe to jam against the other player's shoe. He went down on the floor hard, writhing in pain.

Round called a timeout and helped Chuck off the floor. Chuck knew immediately what he had to do. "I gotta go to the locker room, Coach! Just let me go to the locker room; I know what happened!"

Round looked at the score. It was 29 to 23 Dartmouth. He didn't want to let Chuck go to the locker room, but he could tell Chuck needed it. "All right, go ahead! But whatever it is, get it done quick." Everyone in Allen County War Memorial Coliseum thought it was Chuck's ankle. Even Round thought it was a twisted ankle. The Coach hollered for the trainer, Dianne Weston, to go with Chuck and re-tape him.

In the locker room, Chuck slowly took off his right sneaker. He knew he had a serious problem when he saw the blood had soaked through his socks. "This is gonna suck," he said. He pulled off the first sock and looked at the blood.

Marshall Wright in his 'ArmorDillo' costume came in with his 'Armordillo' head held under his arm. "Are you all right?!" That's when he noticed Chuck's toe. "DANG! That is so gross!"

"That's an understatement," said Chuck. Dianne Weston had to help him take off the second sock. "You're pre-med, right?"

Dianne mustered a smile and said, "Nope. English!"

"Guess what, Dianne? You're pre-med now!" said Chuck. "This is an ingrown toenail and it's dug into the skin. I've had these before, and I know what you need to do. I'd do it myself, but I can't get the right angle." Dianne was confused, but she did what Chuck told her to do.

"First, find the sharpest pair of scissors you have in your bag." She reached into her trainer's bag and pulled out a pair of scissors. "Nope. They need to be the ones with the pointed end." She reached in and pulled out a second set of scissors. Chuck nodded approvingly. "Those will do."

"What you need to do is wash the toe off first, so you can look at the nail," said Chuck. She washed it off with water, then with alcohol, and once more with water. "Now you need to take those scissors and get under the nail about one third of the way across on the bloody side. You gotta cut that part of the nail off that is getting into the skin."

"I'm no doctor, Mr. Hayes, but I'd say this thing needs someone that is," said Dianne.

"The best way to cure pain is to get rid of what's causin' it. The nail diggin' into the skin tissue is the cause of the blood," said Chuck. "Marshall, come over here, buddy!" Marshall stepped closer. "I'm gonna need some of your claw to chew on, cause this is gonna hurt!"

Chuck adjusted his butt on the bench and let out a deep breath. "All right, Dr. Weston. I'm not gonna flinch, but if you could do it quickly, that would definitely be better."

"Are you sure you don't want a doctor?" asked the trainer.

"We don't have time. Tonight, you are the doctor, Dianne. After you get down in there a way, you need to twist the scissors out to about forty-five degrees and trim away the nail from the infected area. Okay?" The girl was frightened but nodded. "Now we need to get this done, cause we got a game to win." He exhaled again. "Go ahead, Doc. You can do this!" Chuck grabbed Marshall's extended Armordillo claw and took a bite.

Dianne Weston bent over and examined her target carefully. She put the scissors up to the nail slowly and put it in position. Chuck mumbled, "nittle more!" She slid the scissors closer to halfway across the nail. Chuck nodded and braced himself.

Dianne smoothly inserted the scissors into Chuck's toe, applied steady pressure down into the nail and started cutting. Chuck bit down hard on Marshall's costume and groaned loudly. Dianne pushed the scissors a little deeper and cut down again. Chuck held his foot as still as he could. Somehow, he managed the strength to say. "Forty-five degrees! Quick!" Dianne did what she was told and made the cut. She pulled the bloody piece of toenail away from Chuck's toe and held it up to examine.

Chuck spit out Marshall's claw and said, "Now get some gauze and squeeze the toe as tightly as you can to get all the nastiness out!" Dianne Weston did what she was told and held the cloth in place tightly.

"Hoopman! That is the about the grossest thing I've ever seen!" said Marshall.

"Maybe it's gross, but it feels a helluva lot better after the nail is outta there than when it's in there!" He looked at Dianne Weston and said, "OUTSTANDING WORK, DOC!" She cleaned it out one more time. He examined the work in earnest. "Now if you have peroxide, we need to put some of that on it, then some of that anti-bacterial cream you have in there on it, too. Then find me a band-aid! Marshall, get in my bag and pull me out another pair of socks. If I have two pair of clean ones left, toss 'em both over here." He looked at the TV screen to check the score and the time left in the half. "Take your time, Marshall. It's almost halftime."

With Chuck in the locker room, Dartmouth made a small run just before halftime. When their starting guard hit a three-pointer at the buzzer, the score at halftime was 39 to 25 in Dartmouth's favor. It was the lowest point total for a half that St. Michael's had put on the scoreboard all year.

St. Michael's came slowly into the locker room. Chuck was quickly lacing up his high-tops. Dianne Weston said something to Coach Round and Chuck could tell by his facial expression, she told him what she'd done. Round came over and glared at Chuck. "You should have told me, Hayes!"

Chuck nodded in agreement. "I wasn't sure it was the toenail. You probably wouldn't have let me play."

"Dang it, Chuck! You don't always know what I'm thinking," said the coach. It was the first time he had ever been mad at Chuck, and it showed. The coach moved into the locker room and held up an imaginary trophy for the "WORST PERFORMANCE FOR ACTING LIKE BASKETBALL PLAYERS" that he had ever seen. He had enough class not to point out any individual player's deficiency, because as a team they were all playing badly. It would have been counterproductive to pick out just one or two guys. There was enough suck to go around for everyone.

Then Round hit below the belt. "I'm glad Pete Henderson isn't here to see the way you're playin'!" The comment immediately struck a chord with every team member.

The coach kept digging into their hearts. "Are you afraid? Do you think you don't belong here?" He paused for effect. "I've coached for over thirty years, and I've NEVER, EVER, had a team play so well together as ya'll last week. And play like SUCH CRAP, the next time outta the chute!"

He walked around the room and calmed down a bit. "Now if ya wanna pack it up and go home now, just let me know! 'Cause if the same team shows up out there in the next half as was out there in the first, I'm gonna walk out. I won't watch you embarrass yourselves! You've come too far to go out like a bunch of . . ." He had trouble saying the word, but it finally came out; "Losers."

He looked at Parnell and said, "You're the captain of this bunch. You figure 'em out! I don't know where the team went that won 23 games this year, but this bunch ain't them!" The coach turned and walked out of the locker room.

Parnell was particularly upset with his own play. He knew he wasn't having his best game either, but he had to do something. He waited till the door closed then stood up. He walked slowly around the room, looking at his teammates. "I've been here for four years now. That's the first time I've ever heard him say a negative word about us. First time ever! A couple of years ago we weren't very good, but he ALWAYS talked us up! For him to say what he just said tells me how bad it really is!"

Parnell paused to catch his breath. He exhaled heavily and continued, "I know what it's doin' to him. But I don't know what it's doin' to you guys." He stopped in the center of the room. "I don't know how this one's gonna turn out, but I do know I'm not givin' up on him. Coach Round stuck with each and every one of us when we stunk! I'm not playin' my best game, but I'm gonna leave whatever game I got out on that floor! Ya'll can come out there with me and make that man proud of us. Or you can pack your bags and head for the bus. So, what's it gonna be?!"

Chuck stood up and walked to the center of the room. "That's easy. We win this sucker!" Chuck put his hand out for Parnell to grab. Charles Holmes was next to come to the center of the locker room and they were quickly joined by Jose and Pepper. Soon enough the whole team was together in the center of the room and holding hands.

Parnell was bent over in the huddle nodding his head, and he yelled, "ALL RIGHT, Y'ALL! THIS IS THE RUNNIN' DILLOS I KNOW!" Every player started to holler and bounce up and down. The emotion that had been lacking in the first half had finally appeared. Parnell yelled, "YEAH! THIS IS THE DILLOS I KNOW!! LETTTT'SSS ROOLLLL!"

They practically sprinted out of the locker room. This was the St. Michael's team that had won twenty-three games. This was the team that Round was looking for.

Just before the second half started the coach came up to Chuck and asked, "You sure that toe of yours is good enough to go?"

"Doctor Weston could've cut it off, and I'd be ready to play now!" said Chuck with a huge grin. It still hurt like hell, but it wasn't nearly as bad as it was before the trainer fixed it.

"I'm tempted to sit your butt, Hayes," said the coach. Then he walked over close to Chuck and said quietly, "But I need you to win this game!"

Chuck nodded. "Consider it done, coach!"

It was a different team that hit the court against Dartmouth in the second half. David Parnell called for the ball the first time down the floor. After getting it, he banked home a ten-footer. It was the leadership by example the team had come to expect from their captain.

On defense, Parnell planted himself in the lane and took away a lay-up from a Dartmouth player by taking a charge. When he got up, his elbow was bloody, and Marshall got the crowd involved. The chant of "FLOOR BURN! FLOOR BURN!" filled the gym.

Jose got into the act by hitting a hook shot. The crowd started to buzz with anticipation. This was the St. Michael's team that had been the Cinderella story of the tournament. After Holmes hit a three pointer, Chuck made a lay-up that got the fans on their feet. After a quick steal, Chuck hit Charles with a behind the back pass for an easy lay-up. The gym became full of 'Runnin' Dillo' believers. St. Michael's was back in a big way.

Dartmouth tried to call timeouts. Then they tried to run. After everything else failed they tried to get physical. Jose and David weren't ready for the aggressive tactics, but Chuck was there to remind them to keep their cool. The Dillo's hit thirteen foul shots in the last two minutes. That's all it took. The Dillo's held on to win, 79 to 75.

After the game, Chuck realized he had forgotten all about his toe. The pain was still there but winning had taken most of the pain away. Playing well had taken away the rest.

On Saturday morning Chuck went to a doctor's office and got precautionary antibiotics. Round let him shoot at the shoot around, but he didn't let him do any running. Chuck was thankful for that. Not so much for the toe, but his legs needed the rest. He could tell the season was catching up to him.

Ft. Wayne was a long way from San Antonio, but some of the diehard fans made it to Indiana to watch the game. Hawk, Sandy, and Grace made the trip and joined the players for dinner. This time, Hawk didn't notice anyone following them.

Later in the evening, Chuck called Eddie from the hotel room to see what was going on with Phase III, if anything. Eddie wanted to talk about the game and Chuck answered every question he could. Finally, he cut Eddie off and asked him about BONE. He hated to cut off Eddie's enthusiasm, but he had to know if they had been discovered. Eddie seemed surprised, but there was still no sign that Mike Thompson had discovered the alterations that had been made in the BONE system.

Then Eddie let Chuck know the PHASE III social media attacks had taken on a virtual life of their own. Plus, there were complaints about employees not getting paid and vendors were not providing supplies to Jackson Grant establishments. PHASE III was working across the board.

After Chuck hung up the phone, he had time to think. He wasn't sure if Eddie and Bobby's skills were that good, or if 'Hoopfan' was covering for them. There was really no way to tell. It didn't matter, as long as Jackson Grant's operations were being impacted.

Chuck laid on the bed and watched the ceiling fan. Because he was 'older', Chuck got his own room. Grace came over and laid beside him. He was glad she was there. His toe hurt, his knees ached, and he was giving himself a headache worrying about things he had no control over. With Eddie apparently in control back in San Antonio, Chuck focused on the future. He kissed Grace goodnight, rolled over, and tried to sleep. Both on and off the court, things just seemed to be going well. Chuck wondered how much longer it could last.

With the biggest game of his life only eighteen hours away, sleep didn't come for a long time.

Chucks' toe was feeling better, but he took an extra ten minutes to stretch his legs out. As Dianne Weston pushed against his leg, Chuck watched the Worcester Polytechnical Institute team run through their warm-ups. If they were to defeat this team, they needed to go inside. WPI was big, but their conference had a reputation for softness. If they could get WPI's two big men in foul trouble, they would have problems inside. They didn't have the bench to cover Jose, OJ and David. Chuck had his game plan; now came the problem of execution.

Chuck pulled Charles Holmes and Pepper Dyer over to Coach Round to discuss his plan of attack. Chuck proposed they hold off on the long shots and attack the basket. If they could get to the WPI big men, WPI might have to go to a zone or sag back into the lane to stop Jose's hook. Round nodded in approval. Charles wasn't happy that he wouldn't get the ball early, but Chuck assured the shooters the plan would help them get better shots later in the game. Holmes understood and said, "We've come this far listening to the 'Hoopman', why stop now." Coach Round was the first one to agree.

WPI won the opening tap, got the ball inside and went right after Jose. The big man held his ground on the first play, refusing to back down against one of the best big men in Division III basketball, Erik 'the Red' Barth. The WPI center tried to hit a bank shot, but Jose was too tight on him. The shot went long, and David Parnell ripped down the rebound.

Chuck walked the ball upcourt. He passed out to Charles then sprinted to set a pick. Charles went hard off the pick and pulled up as if to take the jumper. As Chuck broke to the basket, Charles led him perfectly. Chuck caught the ball in stride and went straight to the goal. Barth was a step late to help. Chuck went up as high as he could and launched a shot high off the backboard over the seven footer's outstretched hand. The center slammed into Chuck and missed the shot completely. The ball came down off the glass and into the basket. The whistle blew and Chuck was headed to the line. The fans started to chant "HOOPMAN! HOOPMAN!," as the 'ArmorDillo' led the chant. The tone of the game had been established in the first minute.

Charles Holmes, Pepper Dyer and Chuck drove the lane constantly. In the first ten minutes, they only took three jump shots. With seven minutes left in the half, the two WPI big men each had two fouls, and WPI switched to a zone. Chuck would let the clock go down to five seconds, then drive hard to the basket. As WPI sunk in to protect their big men, Chuck would pass out to Charles Holmes or Pepper Dyer for wide open threes. The plan was working.

St. Michael's went in at halftime up 38 to 28.

Round managed to keep his players on an even keel. They seemed too excited with another half of ball to play. He reminded them they were playing a team that was the Third ranked team in D III for a reason. If St. Michael's were to win, they needed to maintain the intensity for another half. Too quickly they were out of the locker room, anxious to play. It was a tactical error that St. Michael's would pay for.

WPI came out of the locker room with newfound determination. They switched to an up-tempo style that had the St. Michael's team wheezing after five minutes. The WPI point guard made it a point to run all over the floor, making sure Chuck stayed with him. Chuck was up to the challenge, but it was taking its toll.

On offense he continued to keep it slow and pounded the ball down low. Eventually, the referees saw the WPI center with his hand on Jose's back. It was his fourth foul. The call could not have come at a better time. WPI had come back to tie the score with ten minutes left.

With Barth on the bench and their power forward playing with four fouls, St. Michael's continued to put the ball inside to Parnell and Rivera-Torres. Parnell was playing like a man possessed on the defensive end, and Jose was hitting his hook shot like a pro. Soon, St. Michael's was back up by eight.

After a WPI timeout, Barth returned, and their plan was obvious. Get him the ball and let him shoot. The center was hitting every shot he took. Jose and Parnell were double teaming him, and he still was making every shot.

The break St. Michael's needed came with just under five minutes to play. It started with Pepper Dyer throwing an ill-advised pass across the lane to Charles. The WPI center stepped in front of the pass and headed the other way on the break. Chuck saw what had happened and sprinted back on defense. He saw the center pass to his guard and started sprinting to fill a passing lane. WPI had a two on one break.

Chuck could have gone to the guard and tried to stop the ball but knew exactly what UNC wanted to do. A slam-dunk by the center off an alley-oop pass would have provided the emotional lift that would have probably turned the momentum to WPI. Chuck faked like he was going to stop the guard, then ran to the dotted white line in the lane to prevent the center from getting in position for the dunk. The guard lobbed the ball up, but he was too short on the pass. The WPI center saw the ball but did not see Chuck. Before he could get the pass, he ran over Hoopman who had set his feet just outside the defensive line. The ref blew the whistle, and an anxious crowd came to their feet. The call could have gone either way.

The referee put his hand behind his head and pointed at the center. Barth fouled out. Chuck hit the free throws and St. Michael's had the momentum. WPI was not the same team the rest of the way. They fouled to try put St. Michael's on the foul line, but the Armordillos again shot well at the foul line and put

Dartmouth away with 2 minutes left to play. The final score was St. Michael's 72, UNC 62.

Cinderella was headed to the Division III College Championship to be played in Ft. Wayne the next weekend. The contest pitted the Cortland St. University of New York against Elmhurst, and Marietta College against a previously unknown program from San Antonio named St. Michael's University.

CHAPTER TWENTY

Monday morning all the phone calls that Mike Thompson was getting told him that BONE had a problem. He had expected a huge payoff from the volume of betting the company had processed. Betting was down 62%. Then he saw the gambling revenue report of the weekend's college basketball games. The report indicated a 68 percent loss rate in games bet on. Then he checked the payout numbers. A total of over five million, two hundred sixty-five thousand dollars was sent out to the intranet bettors that received "special updates". The intake from all bets was less than two million. Thompson knew enough about the BCT losses to start by looking at the point spreads. As he compared BONE's spreads to the spreads in the previous weeks USA Today, he didn't find any discrepancies.

Then the employees calls showed up. Not just to him, but to Jackson Grant. The payroll failed to pay anyone. Some employees were unable to pay for groceries or gas. Thompson checked with the banks and the money was in the business account, but for some reason was not dispersed.

Grant called Thompson to his office and after a barrage of profanities, screamed about an email message he got from "some frat boy" saying they prevented his employees from getting paid. All the while, their cell phones continued to ring. After five minutes, Grant went to a window and threw his phone away.

Grant finally gained his composure. He yelled at Thompson, "What the hell happened this weekend?"

"In a nutshell, we got screwed because someone knows all our communications and business accounting processes," said Thompson flatly. He held out a computer print out and a folded copy of the sports page.

Grant stood up and grabbed the papers. "What do you mean, Mike?"

"None of our employees got paid. Neither did our vendors since Thursday." Thompson nervously walked over to the bar and grabbed the scotch. "The money is in the bank, but our business operations have been compromised."

"Compromised? What do you mean compromised?" asked Grant. He was pissed again.

"I mean, it appears those frat boys have our personnel accounts under their control. Everything from email, to texts, to bank accounts," said Thompson as he took a drink. He continued to explain everything he had found that morning. "So we're getting calls from hundreds of broke workers and hundreds of pissed businesses that want their money!" He took another drink.

Grant was in shock. "How many? How many people?"

"I have to check the numbers," said Thompson. "Probably over 800 employees for the last two weeks pay period and close to three million dollars in payments to our vendors."

Grant was walking around the room. "It was Clark! He's behind this. He's trying to take me down. I'm not gonna let him do it!"

Thompson said, "Did you say Clark did this?"

"Yeah, it's that bastard Clark! Here! Let me show you the note he sent me." Grant pulled the email message from his desk drawer.

Thompson quickly read it. "I don't know how to tell you this boss, but it ain't Clark! Clark can barely send an email," said Thompson.

Grant went to his desk and pulled out a piece of paper. He held the note up and said, "Clark used to be in the military right? James told me this last note has some military language in it."

"Clark went to basic training for like a day. They kicked his butt out. He doesn't know anything about the military," said Thompson. He slowed down as the picture started to become clearer. He grabbed the note from Grant and read it. "Military acronym. Texas problems. That old guy at St. Michael's. What do they call him? Hoopman!" The light came on for Thompson. "It was that damn HOOPMAN!" said Thompson. "He's the one that sent this note! He's a freakin' boy scout, Boss! He's the one telling our customers not to bet on college basketball!"

Grant stuttered, "But James said . . ."

"It doesn't matter what James said that note was written by Hoopman Hayes from the St. Michael's program!" said Thompson. "All the problems for the season started when that program didn't get on board. Remember?" Grant began walking slowly and listening to Mike Thompson. "The Holmes kid didn't want to play. We got emails, supposedly from a bunch of fraternity kids. The problems started with St. Michael's and Clark in Austin. I'm tellin' you, it was Hayes!"

Grant still had a question. "What about James? Did he lie to me about taking down the BCT?"

Thompson thought for a minute. "He was here for over two weeks while I was in Texas. You had him reviewing our network, right?" Grant nodded. "His purpose was to prevent the same thing that happened to Clark from happening to us." Thompson swirled the scotch in his glass. "He probably figured out what was done to Clark and . . ." He stopped in mid-sentence. Thompson started to get angry. "James! That's it! Hayes doesn't know enough about computers to do this kind of shit. Army guys don't do shit like this with computers! This has James written all over it! I know what he did, I just don't know how he did it."

Grant interrupted and said, "SHIT!"

"What is it?" asked Thompson.

"I authorized him to have special permission for administration privileges that he didn't have before," said Grant. "You weren't here, and I needed to allow him all the access he needed."

Thompson shook his head. "He can do serious, serious damage to our network! The crap Hoopman was doing is nothing compared to what James can do. And now that he has authorization," Thompson hesitated, "we're screwed!" He finished his drink and poured another.

Grant sat down behind his desk. Thompson was a little unnerved by his boss' reaction. He expected another explosion, but saw his boss started to think. "You've already shut the net down, right?" Thompson nodded. "I want you to go back and completely check our systems. I want the system back online by Thursday!"

"That's not enough time!" said Thompson emphatically. "We need to take it offline and completely . . ."

"In case you didn't notice, we got Championships going on this weekend!" came the reply. "Do you know how much money we could lose if we aren't up by then? Huh?"

Thompson went numb. He wanted to say losing money was nothing compared to what could happen with James running lose in the system. Instead of trying to explain it all, Thompson poured himself another drink. He made a mental note to pull all his personal funds out of his two bank accounts. That's if there was any money in them.

"All right," said Thompson. "I'll get back over there. The systems will be back up on Thursday." He got up to go back to the control room. "What are you gonna do about James and Hayes?"

"Hayes started all my problems. He's my priority right now, and I know just how to take care of him. I might need you to take care of James, so get our network clean and find him. I know it's not your line of work, but you may have to bring Mr. James here to see me," said Grant. He sat back in his chair. "We'll start with his good knee, then his hands. We'll make sure he can never touch a keyboard again."

Thompson wanted to tell his boss that it was already too late, but it didn't matter. Chances were slim that James could be found. James could do whatever he needed to do from anywhere in the world with the access he had gained. Grant was in a different world, so there was no reason to even try to talk to him. Thompson left the room to get back to work.

Grant reached into his desk and pulled out a sheet of paper and read the phone number on it. He dialed the number and waited for Carl Holden to answer. Holden would take care of Hayes.

Eddie called Chuck with the news. "They shut down their operations!"

"That's the best thing I've heard lately!" said Chuck.

"They put a message out at their website that says they are temporarily suspending operations," said Eddie.

Chuck thought about the statement. "It didn't say they had terminated operations, so that means to me they intend to come back online as soon as possible!"

Eddie hadn't thought about that part of it. "Yeah, but they probably won't be back online by this weekend!"

"We don't know that for sure, do we?" said Chuck.

"You're right," answered Eddie with a touch of conciliation in his voice.

Chuck thought about what to do. "How about you check on them every once in a while, and see if they come back up. How about Godzilla?"

"Godzilla is already set. If they come online, Godzilla is locked and cocked!"

"Good deal, Eddie," said Chuck. "You can still send out a couple of messages to other sites and warn people in their intranet not to bet this weekend."

"We tried that, but the site managers are removing anything we post and blocking our messages," said Eddie.

Chuck said, "Well. We tried to warn 'em. Thanks for the news, Eddie. Let me know if they come back up. See ya'."

Chuck hung up the phone and thought about what had transpired. With any luck, Hoopfan would send him a note and let him know what was going on. He tried to read from his textbook, but there were too many things going on. He knew his grades were going to drop this semester. Studying hadn't really been a priority. His focus was divided between two missions. For one thing, he had a murdering crook and his organization to take down. Then there was this small item of winning a National Championship. Of the two, he didn't know which was more important.

It was Monday evening when Steve walked into the computer control room at the Nassau site. "They've shut down the Vegas operation! Completely!" reported Jeff Roberts. "Do you know what's going on?"

Steve had been expecting it. "Must be my buddy Mikey Thompson got to Grant. I was hoping he wouldn't be able to figure out what was going on. He and Grant must have gotten together and talked for a change. That's okay, though. I was expecting that."

Jeff just looked at his boss confused. Steve seemed almost giddy. "You okay?"

"Yes, I'm very well, Jeffrey," said Steve. "I think we still have some time. I've got a couple of things to do here tonight, but you need to meet me here at eleven o'clock tomorrow. Okay?" Jeff nodded. "Now get out of here! I have work to do."

Jeff shook his head, grabbed his St. Louis Cardinals baseball hat and headed to his apartment.

Chuck exhaled heavily into the phone. "I was just feeling a little down. I needed to talk to you."

Grace Winters lay back on her couch and said, "Shouldn't you be studying?"

"I can't study! Are you kiddin'?" said Chuck.

"Even though you are the legendary 'Hoopman', you still need to keep your grades up," said Grace.

"Yeah, I know. That's the same thing I keep tellin' all the guys on the team," said Chuck. "It seems I have a bunch of other things on my mind," said Chuck.

"I hope that one of those things would be how you're gonna stop Darrin Jones," said Grace. Darrin Jones was Marietta's six foot-three All-American point guard for the number two-ranked team in the nation.

"OH, PLEASE!" laughed Chuck into the phone. "That's still three days away! That guy is putty in my hands!"

"That putty in your hands as you say has a thirty-eight-inch vertical jump and is averaging 23 points a game," said Grace.

"When did you become such an expert on college basketball players?" asked Chuck.

"Since I started dating you!" she said matter of factly.

Chuck smiled. Three months ago she didn't even know who Darrin Jones was. Now she knew his statistics. Chuck changed the subject. "The real reason I called was to tell you I've been thinking about something."

"What would that be?" said Grace.

"After this is all over, the tournament, the school year, everything, would you like to go away for a vacation somewhere?" asked Chuck.

Grace thought before she answered, "Somewhere?"

"Yeah, somewhere! I don't know where, I have no clue! I just know I want to get away from everything," He hesitated before adding, "except you."

Grace hesitated just to make Chuck nervous. Finally, she said, "I'd love to."

"Phew! That's one less thing for me to worry about," said Chuck. "Now if I can just stop thinking about my tests, Marietta and Darrin Jones, and . . ." he hesitated before he said, "a couple of other things."

Grace knew what those other things were. "You can't control those other things, Chuck." She tried to add some levity, "If

Godzilla goes to town and doesn't work, there isn't anything you can do about it, right?"

Chuck laughed. She was right again. "Okay! I'll get focused on my books and maybe think a little bit about Darrin Jones. But none of the other stuff!" said Chuck.

"Good! Now," she said playfully. "One last thing!"

"What, Grace?"

She started to tell him she loved him but didn't want to add that to his already too full mind. "He can't shoot free throws."

"WHAT?!"

"He's only hitting 55 percent from the line! If you have to, make him shoot foul shots! See ya'!" Grace hung up.

Chuck looked at the phone in disbelief. What a woman! Patient, understanding and a hoop fan! He made a mental note to get off his butt and tell her how much he loved her.

At eleven o'clock sharp, Jeffrey Roberts walked into his boss' office. Steve James was sitting behind his desk looking at his computer. Upon seeing his subordinate enter the room, Steve sat back with a big grin on his face. "That's what I always liked about you, Jeff. You're disciplined. You always did what you were told when you were told to do it!"

The fact that his boss was talking in past tense was not lost on Jeff Roberts. "What do mean "did"? You sound like you're firing me? Did I do something?"

Steve got up, grabbed his cane and walked around to the front of his desk. Jeff did not notice the envelope in his hand. "Relax, Jeffrey. You're not being fired. But I am quitting my current position. Without giving our boss, the fat bastard, notice!" He giggled at his own comment. Jeff couldn't help but notice his mentor had been acting really strange.

Steve continued, "SO! I'm sure you don't want to work for him anymore, and I figure you need a severance check to get you through to your new job."

Jeff was confused. "I don't want a new job! I get paid just fine working with you. You teach me, and that's something other bosses I've had couldn't do!"

Steve held out the envelope. "I am terminating my duty with BONE and trust me, you are terminating your employment there too." Jeff took the envelope and opened it. Inside was a cashier's check. His face went white. "You'll notice the bank on the check is in London."

"I could give a crap about the bank! IS THAT POUNDS?" asked Jeff with a huge smile.

"Yes, that's pounds! I figured that would be enough to tide you over. I don't want to tell you what to do, but there are a lot of online gambling houses in the United Kingdom, and they may need your services. You should learn more about soccer. Er, football there. I thought a million pounds might be enough to get you started," said Steve.

"I don't know what to say," said Jeff.

"You say thank you! Then you say goodbye and pretend you never met me! Do you understand?" It was definitely a directive. The younger man nodded. "Things are going to happen, and you know the organization. You know what they did to Pete Henderson in Texas. The odds are damn good they will try to do the same thing to me. And it's best if you don't know any more."

The young man nodded. "I don't want to . . ." He tried to protest but Steve had expected it. He held out another envelope. It was a plane ticket.

"London's calling," said Steve. "Your flight leaves in an hour and a half. That gives you just enough time to go to your apartment and get the things that are important to you. Then you leave, and you don't look back. Got it?"

Jeff nodded. Steve stuck out his hand and said, "I might come over and check on you, but you need to drive on with your own life. Everything will be fine for me. I've got plans." He giggled again. "Goodbye, friend!" The younger man dropped the hand and gave his 'former' boss a hug. He turned and quickly left the room.

Steve James went back to his desktop computer. He pulled out a thumb drive and placed it into his laptop bag. It was time for him to leave too. He hoped that Hoopman would read the message and heed his advice. Even if he didn't, Steve could live comfortably in his present financial state. He checked his watch nervously. His flight to Ft. Wayne was only two hours away.

Just before practice Daymon Breyers handed Chuck a printout of an email. "It's your number one admirer again!" said the assistant coach with a grin.

"Thanks! I've been waiting for this," said Chuck.

"It was posted yesterday. I just got around to reading them today," said the coach. He didn't pick up on Chuck's look of concern.

Chuck quickly read the note.

> hoopman,
>
> they have turned it off temporarily. when it comes back, and it will, do not continue! I will take care of them. they know about me, so i'm sure they know about you too. watch your back. good luck with Marietta. see you soon.
>
> hoopfan

Hoopfan seemed confident that BONE would be back up and running. He needed to call Eddie and tell him about the recommendation not to do anything else for now. There was just one decision to make. The only thing Chuck wanted Eddie to do was run Godzilla and get it all over with.

As for the 'watch your back' part, he decided to make a second phone call. If anyone was to cover his back, he wanted it to be Nate Hawkins.

Thompson walked over to his assistant and announced it was time to turn the system back on. "Are you sure you want to do that? We haven't completed the backup drives' review."

Thompson smiled and said, "Just put it online again. Mr. Grant said we had until today, so let's put it back online." The assistant did as he was told. "Anything else that goes wrong is on Mr. Grant. Now if you'll excuse me," said Thompson. He shoved a stack of computer printouts into his laptop bag. "I've got a plane to catch."

"You headed to the Bahamas, Boss?" asked the assistant.

Mike Thompson answered as honestly as he dared. "As far as you know."

St. Michael's got another break. The basketball team waited until Thursday morning to fly back to Ft. Wayne. Grace and Sandy followed on Friday at Hawk's urging. He was taking his role as Chuck's protector very seriously. On Friday morning, while the St. Michael's Armordillos were at the shoot around, Hawk met with security people and went through the arena.

Grant heard the knock at the door and quickly opened it. "Where the hell have you been?"

Carl Holden walked through the door and said, "I've been busy. They got cops all over the arena. I don't think we're gonna be able to do it there!"

"You're not going to get any other chances!" hissed Grant.

Holden reached into his coat pocket and pulled out his gun. The move startled Grant and he stepped back. Holden held the gun out and said, "You want to do this?" Grant shook his head no and turned away. "Then you let me worry about Hoopman." He walked over to the bar and made himself a drink.

"What's going on with the system? Mikey get it fixed?" asked Holden.

"He said he fixed what he could. The good news is we're back up and taking bets. Initial reports are we recovered from the debacle of the last two weeks, and we've got record setting bets coming in for today's games," said Grant with a smile.

"What about that gimp James?" asked Holden.

"Mike said he didn't find him. He showed up at Paradise Island and both James and Roberts had left the day before. But the guys in the control room said everything was online and functioning properly. He found a note from James that said he was coming to Ft. Wayne."

Holden shrugged, "Maybe I can take care of that cripple for you too!"

"You just take care of Hoopman! I'm not worried about James. I think Mike is just jealous because James is a better computer geek than he is! Those twenty-pound heads are like that. They're temperamental. Like actors or politicians!" said Grant.

Carl Holden had his own problem to work through. How was he going to get close enough to Hoopman to kill him? He hoped St. Michael's lost so the team would get out of Ft. Wayne and back to San Antonio. His chances of killing Hoopman there and getting away with it was much better than in an arena filled with people. But if he needed to kill him in front of thirty thousand people, so be it.

Cortland St. and Elmhurst played one of the most exciting D III final four games ever played. Cortland St. hit a shot at the buzzer to tie it at regulation. Even better, in overtime Cortland hit a halfcourt shot as the clock expired to win by one. Cortland St. was headed to the Division III National Championship.

As Chuck watched the game from the tunnel behind the Cortland bench. His eyes sought out Darrin Jones. He was easy to find in the bleachers. He was a magnet for teammates, coaches and fans. He wore an ever-present smile that exuded confidence and strength. As Chuck watched his opponent, he could see he had no fear about the upcoming contest. The fact that Darrin Jones was always like that didn't matter. Chuck was taking Jones' lack of apprehension personally. For the first time in a long time, he wished he were younger.

Soon enough, the St. Michael's Armordillos took the floor to warm up. Just being on the floor shooting helped Chuck to feel like himself. It felt good to be out on the floor with a ball moving around. He gently prodded his teammates to test their demeanor. He couldn't help but egg on Jose who had already thrown up twice in the locker room. He started speaking Spanish to the big man, got a smile out of him and that seemed to help calm him down. But Jose was not alone. Half the team was nervous. Their jump shots clanked off the rim like trying to skip round rocks on a flat lake. The bookies watching in sports bars must have been licking their chops. The line had Marietta picked as a twelve-point favorite. After watching St. Michael's warm up, money said twelve points was not enough. You could have gotten St. Michael's and thirty.

As St. Michael's took the floor, Chuck hurried over to shake hands with his opponents. Darrin Jones had his ever present, way too cocky smile out there for Chuck to see. For the first time all season, Chuck's smile stayed off the court. Even before the game started, Darrin Jones made him feel old. After the tipoff, it got worse.

Marietta won the tip, got the ball down the floor fast where Jones was hit in stride for an alley oop dunk. The Marietta side of the Coliseum erupted. On the inbounds pass, Jones hounded Chuck all the way down the floor. When he finally got the ball across half court, it took an extra five seconds for St. Michael's to get into position to run their offense. The first St. Michael's shot was a twenty-foot airball by Charles Holmes. No one would have blamed any of the Dillo fans if they picked up their belongings and left.

Ten minutes into the game, Round had already used up two timeouts. St. Michael's was tight emotionally, and it showed on the court. He was out of ideas, so he did something he hadn't done in seventeen years. David Parnell was called for traveling under the basket, and the coach became unglued.

Round stomped down the sideline and used curse words for the first time all season. The last straw was when he threw his towel onto the court. The referee quickly blew the whistle and gave the coach his first technical of the year. Marietta's shooting guard dropped the technical, and they went up 28 to 11.

Chuck had been getting burned by Jones because he was not being aggressive. He was tentative and looked for help from his big men too soon. Jones' smile was becoming broader, and Chuck didn't appreciate it. With five minutes left in the first half, it was Chuck's turn to explode.

Chuck tried to get in position to take a charge on Darrin Jones as he was driving the lane. Jones slammed into Chuck as he tried to take the lay-up. Jones' knee came up and just missed hitting Chuck in the groin. Chuck saw it coming and moved enough to avoid catching the knee. He went under the All-American, and both men fell in a heap on the floor. Chuck rolled over quickly and pushed Jones on the back of the head as he got up.

"WHAT WAS THAT CRAP?" yelled Chuck.

Jones looked up in disbelief. A forty-year-old man had just smacked him in the back of the head on national television. Chuck bent over and got in the younger man's face and said, "THAT'S THE BIGGEST CHICKEN SHIT I'VE SEEN ALL YEAR!" David Parnell immediately stepped in and pulled Chuck away. He was a second away from getting kicked out of the game. As he was pushed backward, he kept yelling, "NO CLASS, JONES! NO CLASS!"

It was Jones' turn to lose his composure. He broke away from his teammates and headed toward Chuck. A referee and Jose Rivera-Torres got between the two combatants. The St. Michael's fans rallied around their warrior and started chanting, "HOOPMAN! HOOPMAN!"

Parnell quickly pulled him aside and said, "HEY! LOOK AT ME!" Chuck walked backwards to try and get away, but Parnell wouldn't stop. He stayed close to Chuck and continued to try and calm him down. Meanwhile, Jose and Charles Holmes got into a pushing contest with two Marietta players.

Parnell stayed with Chuck and got through to him. "You need to look at me, Chuck," said David Parnell.

The use of his name worked. "You called me Chuck!"

"Yeah, I did! Because you ain't Hoopman right now!" said Parnell. The comment hit home as Chuck realized exactly what David meant. All season long he had been Hoopman Hayes. Right until that moment. David Parnell knew if St. Michael's stood any chance at all, they needed Hoopman, not Chuck. "If you're gonna play up tight and angry, like some forty-year-old man with a chip on your shoulder, you ain't gonna be able to play here! You did this once before, remember? In the hotel in New Orleans," said Parnell looking hard into Chuck's eyes. "We can't have you do it here! I don't know what you have to do to get Hoopman back on the floor, but one way is to start having fun. Remember?"

Chuck relaxed and straightened up. It wasn't Jones that was getting to him. It was Chuck getting to himself. He saw all the youth and enthusiasm that Darrin Jones had, and Chuck didn't see it in himself. Chuck was looking in the wrong direction. He was looking outside, when he should have been looking inside. Was he having fun? No. Should he be having fun? Hell, yeah! Anybody who loved basketball would love to have the opportunity he was getting. He was getting a chance to play against the best in the world. Could he play at that level? Yes. He wouldn't be there if he couldn't. David Parnell was absolutely right, and Chuck knew it. He gathered himself, walked to the bench. Parnell followed him closely. He grabbed a towel and said a prayer. He exhaled and asked for peace and strength. It worked.

A smile appeared on his face. He nodded at David. "Yeah. Yeah, I remember. And you were just as right then as you are now, captain!" He smacked his teammates hand and said, "I was missing the point again, David. Thank you!"

"Don't mention it!" said David with a broad grin. The two men looked around the arena as they listened to the chanting. "You certainly got the crowd back into the game! Think you can get us back into it?" asked Parnell.

"Yeah! I can do that. I'm gonna shoot a little bit to get Jones thinking. That'll open things up inside," said Chuck.

"That's the Hoopman I know and love! You're thinking about the game again," said David with a grin.

The referees called for a double technical against Darrin Jones and Chuck. Chuck immediately walked over to Jones with his hand out. Quietly he said, "I was out of line. I'm sorry!"

Jones took the hand but didn't quite know what to say. Finally, his smile reappeared, and he said, "No problem, old man!"

Parnell overheard the comment and started to step in again expecting Chuck to be offended. There was no need to. Chuck said, "Not old man, Darrin! It's HOOPMAN!" He smiled and headed up court.

The incident must have incited more than Chuck, because the Dillo's held their own the rest of the half. They went into halftime down 42 to 33. The fans were actually buzzing because St. Michael's had shown some spark. They had cut an eighteen-point lead in half and were starting to play together. Hope was alive for the fans and their team.

Round was relatively calm at halftime. He apologized for his outburst and smiled at Chuck. "I damn near felt like I was fifty again!" The players all laughed at their coach's stab at humor. "If we're gonna go down, let's make sure they know who they played. Let's play Runnin' Dillo basketball."

The coach stopped walking and introduced a new attack. "Fellas. We're gonna do something we haven't done all year. We're gonna run. Chuck, I know I'm askin' a lot from those old legs, but they're a big bunch. If we can run 'em for fifteen minutes, I don't think they'll have anything left the last five."

Chuck nodded, "I got all the legs I need! I can run all night now and all night tomorrow!" His teammates knew exactly what Chuck meant. They had to do something, or they wouldn't be around for the Championship.

David Parnell yelled, "LET'S RUN!" That was all it took.

All the Dillo's jumped up and released the pent up emotion that had been lacking in the first half. Round looked at Breyers and said, "It's a dangerous tactic, but we don't have any reason to save anything for tomorrow if we ain't playin'!"

Round turned to his players and said, "LET'S GO WIN THIS THING!"

The second half offered the fans a completely different game. It wasn't a one-sided affair anymore. The Runnin' Dillos were aggressive, competitive, and played with intensity. They pushed the ball up the court at every chance. The tactic caught Marietta off guard. Marietta was back on their heels trying to recover the rest of the game.

Chuck could tell the tactic was working because Darrin Jones' smile disappeared. When play would stop, the younger man would slump over and grab his shorts, a sure indication that fatigue was setting in. Chuck made it a point to stand up next to the younger man, smile broadly and conceal the fact that he was out of breath. The physical battle was taking a back seat to the mental one. Only in the huddles during timeouts would Chuck rest his legs or breathe heavily. He made the game his personal mission. If this was to be his last game, he was going to have fun.

With five minutes left St. Michael's had scratched its way into a tie. Jones was beginning to tire, and Chuck decided to take advantage of the taller man. He had been setting him up by driving to the basket and dishing passes off to Charles and Jose the entire second half. It was time to give the younger man Chuck's version of an education.

The next time down the floor, Chuck drove hard to the right. At the foul line, he quickly stopped, pulled up and popped a fifteen-footer. The next time down the court, he did the same thing to the left side of the foul line. He could see the younger man starting to show his frustration.

Knowing he would play tighter defense the next time, Chuck pulled an old shot from his years of experience. He drove hard to the right again, but this time he took it a step farther. With Jones playing tight against him, Chuck stopped hard then stepped backward and fired a fade away. Had the shot been a straight jumper, Darrin Jones would have blocked it. As Chuck fired, Jones hand just missed the ball. It floated gently toward the basket and swished. The St. Michael's fans were on fire now as Chuck had taken control of the game.

Marietta didn't get to the Final Four just to collapse against a tiny no-name school. Their pride started to show. Darrin Jones stepped up the way a team leader was supposed to. He slowly drove Chuck back into the lane, then did an amazing crossover dribble, went around Chuck and over David Parnell for a game tying lay-up.

Going down the court, Chuck took Grace Winters' advice and shared it. "David, next time he does that, put him on the foul line! He's tired and he won't hit the shots!" David nodded and spread the word to Jose.

Then it was Chuck's turn. He backed Jones back down into the lane and pretended to use the fade away again. This time, Chuck held the ball for an instant. Jones jumped but Chuck didn't shoot. Jones bounced into Chuck as he fired the jumper. The ball went in and the ref blew the whistle. Jones' frustration was showing, and he nearly got a technical for arguing the call. With the fans chanting "HOOPMAN!", Chuck stepped to the line and neatly put his team up by three.

The game had become a one-on-one contest for four minutes, with Chuck and Darrin Jones matching each other basket for basket. With a minute to go, Jones drove the lane and was promptly hammered by Jose.

As the All-American picked himself up, Chuck noticed Round wanted to call a timeout. Chuck waved to the coach with a frown, indicating it was okay. Round bit his lip and went back to the bench. Jones was tired and the speed of play was taking its toll. As he stood at the line, he was bent over and breathing heavily. The guard stepped to the line and missed the first shot. Seeing his fatigue, the Marietta coach called a timeout.

Jones was in better shape for the next foul shot and hit it. As Chuck brought the ball up the floor, the speed of the game began to take effect on his legs as well. He could feel the fatigue, but he wasn't going to let Darrin Jones see it. He set the play and drove hard to the basket. Jones and two other defenders blocked Chuck's path. As they came towards him, Chuck saw his opportunity and dropped a bounce pass to Parnell under the basket. He was immediately fouled before he could get the shot off.

The intensity of the game had taken its toll on everyone. David Parnell wasn't immune to fatigue and missed the front end of his one and one foul shot. Marietta got the rebound, and Jones slowly brought the ball up the court. With time running out on the shooting clock, he drove the lane again. Chuck reached for the ball as Jones shot and thought he had a clean steal. The ref blew the whistle and said Jones was in the act of shooting.

The St. Michael's fans were hot about the call, but Chuck just smiled. Darrin Jones was headed to the free throw line. From somewhere deep inside, Jones gathered the strength to hit not just one, but both free throws and tie the game up. The fans were truly getting their money's worth. The game was tied with eight seconds left.

During the timeout, Round set a play for Chuck. Chuck appreciated what the coach was doing, but he knew his body and he knew his legs were feeling fatigue. The only way he would score would be from the foul line, and the chances of getting a call from the refs on a final shot were slim and none.

He walked over to Charles Holmes. "I've been settin' this up the last five minutes. I saw your man come to help out Jones last time I drove, so I'm gonna do the same thing. Only this time, you're gonna be wide open. We don't need a three either, so you can step in. The best thing is, it doesn't matter if you miss 'cause we go to overtime." Charles smiled and nodded. "But I would surely appreciate it if you'd get it over with now!"

"I've been waitin' for this all night. Just hit me, Hoopman!" said Charles.

Chuck had it figured out perfectly. As he backed Darrin Jones down, he waved Charles Holmes away as if he was going to try and take the All-American one on one. Charles' defender was not going to let that happen. As Chuck drove hard to the right, Charles' man slid down to try and stop Chuck's penetration. He came down just a step too far.

With three seconds left Chuck fired a hard pass to Charles as he slid to the corner. His defender was in no man's land and could only watch as Holmes perfect jump shot headed to the basket. The ball went through the net, and the horn sounded. Ball game! St. Michael's 78, Marietta 76.

St. Michael's fans poured onto the court. Charles Holmes was picked up and carried off the floor. Chuck walked over to Darrin Jones who had collapsed on the floor after the shot. The All-American had put up 32 points against Chuck, but they weren't enough. Chuck extended his hand and said, "Nice game, Mr. Jones! You used me up!"

Darrin Jones, as heartbroken as he was, knew he was part of history. Holmes' shot was one for the ages. At any other time, in any other place, Marietta would have won. He took the extended hand and said, "I didn't do enough, did I?"

Chuck gave the younger man a hug and said, "You put your team in a position to win and played your heart out, Darrin. All we did was score more points than you. You guys didn't lose," said Chuck honestly.

Jones nodded and said, "You know tomorrow we would beat you guys by twenty points. Unfortunately, today's the day that counts." Chuck nodded because he knew Jones was probably correct. Then the All-American showed his class and said, "You guys beat the best tonight, so you better whip Cortland."

Chuck nodded and headed to join the celebration. The realization finally sunk in as he jumped into Jose's arms. They were going to play for the National Championship. All the fatigue that Chuck had felt in his legs was gone. He was just one win away from achieving his dream.

In the upper deck of the arena, Carl Holden watched the joyous celebration. Somewhere in the stands, Jackson Grant was probably cursing like a pirate. The idiot had bet on Marietta and lost one hundred thousand dollars of his own money. Holden chuckled at the thought of his boss sitting alone in a crowd of jubilant St. Michael's fans. Grant would pay twice the price to see Hoopman dead now. He smiled at his good fortune. Now came the question of how to get close enough to do it?

As Holden watched the celebration, he saw something that set off a spark in his mind. The St. Michael's mascot was jumping up and down with Chuck Hayes like some kind of cartoon character. The image was frozen in his mind like a portrait. A plan began to form in Holdens' mind. He smiled and said to no one, "It just might work!"

In spite of his personal loss, Jackson Grant immediately called back to Las Vegas to check the status of the system. The fact that Mike Thompson was not available should have triggered some kind of warning. Thompson was supposed to have returned from the Bahamas. Thompson's assistant informed Grant that the systems all seemed to be working normally and they had received no new messages. The betting had been heavy for Elmhurst and Marietta. The volume had remained high based on previous years. Grant hung up the phone and smiled. It sounded like fifty million dollars was headed into the BONE coffers.

Steve James sat alone in the hotel room. He was watching highlights of the St. Michael's victory and smiling. His joy had nothing to do with the St. Michael's win. It had to do with a different kind of win. He turned his attention to the laptop computer that was set up on the desk. His message to Hoopman must have worked, because the BONE gambling system was working fine.

Steve stretched out his crippled knee and leaned back against the chair. He casually took a drink from his Diet Coke and watched the screen. He looked at the clock again. Banks were closed, but it just seemed too early to execute the plan. After all, the banks were only half of the plan. He giggled to himself. What the hell.

Steve James stuck his index finger in the air, made the sound of a bomb dropping and hit the enter key. Within seconds, electronic funds transfer commenced that sent money from the BONE gambling system to three separate accounts. One each in the Bahamas, the United Kingdom and Belize.

Steve began typing feverishly into his laptop again. He stopped to look at a piece of paper and read it. Back to his laptop he cut and pasted a link into his browser. Steve clicked on the link which opened up a spreadsheet of 187 electronic wallets. Wallets that held the account numbers of global millionaires that had received special betting advice via a secret intranet coordinated through Jackson Grant's gambling service based in Las Vegas, Nevada.

Steve scrolled through the intranet accounts. Accounts that had been in place for at least four years. Years of cheating fellow gamblers out of God only knew how many millions. It was time to see what real payback was like. He rubbed his knee and said out loud. "Say goodbye, Mr. Grant." He hit the enter key once again and waited.

Revenge had never been so sweet or so simple. There was nothing anyone could do to stop it. Not that murderer Holden, nor the incompetent administrator Mike Thompson. There wasn't a damn thing Grant could do to stop Steve James now.

As they left dinner that night, Chuck couldn't help but jab at Grace and say, "I thought you said he was gonna miss his foul shots?"

Grace said, "SO! I was wrong!" she said. "He did miss one, didn't he?"

"Yeah, but Darrin Jones was the best player on the court today," said Chuck.

"At least you won," said Grace. She quickly changed the subject and made Chuck think about the future. "What about Cortland?"

Chuck thought about it. He hadn't really paid much attention to Cortland. He knew about their big men, but not much else. "I guess we'll have to look at the game film tomorrow. Tonight, I just want to go back and get in the hottest tub I can stand."

"I'd join you, but . . ." said Grace with a devious smile.

"HEY, NOW, WOMAN!" said Chuck with a smile. "I gotta stay focused here. You know they say that sex takes away a man's strength!"

"You are the Hoopman!" she giggled at him. "Indestructible and all that!"

Chuck looked over his shoulder and saw Jose and Pepper smiling at the couple. "I better take a rain check. My teammates are watching!"

Grace said, "I was just teasing. I know you need to 'stay focused'!" She kissed him on the cheek and said, "Goodnight, Hoopman!" She turned and headed to the elevator.

Chuck smiled and walked over to Jose and Pepper. "You two jerks got anything to say?"

Both players together said, "Um! Ah! No! No!"

"Good!" said Chuck. "See you tomorrow!" Then he noticed Hawk standing by the wall, watching people as they walked by. Chuck walked over to his friend and leaned against the wall next to him.

"You come here often, sailor?" said Chuck.

Hawk exhaled loudly and said, "I can't help it if you aren't worried about anything! I still think those assholes are gonna try something. I don't know where and I don't know when, but they are gonna come after you, Chuck! So excuse me if I give a shit!"

Chuck instantly felt lousy. "I'm sorry, Hawk. I apologize! I just feel pretty good about today, ya' know?"

Hawk was trying to stay focused, but a crack showed. "Yeah, well, you almost blew it with that foul!"

"Now that was a bad call! I got that ball cleanly!" said Chuck. Hawk finally cracked a smile.

The two men were quiet for a second. Chuck exhaled loudly and said, "I guess I'll go up now."

"How 'bout I go with you?" asked Hawk.

Chuck nodded. His friend just wanted to protect him, and he understood why. The threat was still out there. "Yeah! I appreciate that, Hawk. Come on!" It would be a tough night until the Championship game. Deep down, Chuck knew what Hawk was doing was right. Grant had already killed Henderson, and Hoopfan had given him the heads up.

Chuck had purchased a suite and offered the second bedroom to Pepper Dyer. Pepper had never stayed in a room as nice as the one Chuck rented.

As Chuck entered his room, he saw Pepper Dyer and knew how lucky he was to be surrounded by people who really cared for him. He knew how lucky he was to be on a team that was playing great basketball at just the right time.

What Chuck didn't know was less than a mile away Carl Holden was finalizing his plan to kill the legendary Hoopman.

It was the next morning when a "little problem" appeared.

Chuck was obviously annoyed. "Now let me see if I understand you?" said Chuck. He looked across the breakfast table at Eddie, Bobby and Chris. "Something happened, you guys didn't do it, and you don't know what it was?"

Eddie was the first spokesperson for the group. "Exactly." Chuck shook his head.

Bobby was subdued when he followed up. "Godzilla is just sitting there, hidden on a server waiting for the client to accomplish a given task. I haven't touched it as I was waiting to see if you still wanted me to use it."

Eddie jumped in, "The problem is, their intranet, the employees, their business partners. Even the ones that are legit, are all pissed off."

"Which means," Chuck started to think out loud. "The activity from last weekend is still not fixed, right?"

"It was. But something else happened in the last 24 hours. We didn't do anything, but the company bank accounts that we know of, have been emptied," said Eddie.

"So what happened?" asked Chuck.

"Someone, with access to BONE money has taken it all. BONE is no longer financially viable. We think we have succeeded. But we don't know how!" said Eddie.

"All right guys!" Chuck shook his head. "Let me get this straight! We got them to stop betting?"

"Essentially, yes!" said Eddie. "Because there is no money anymore. The organization is still there, but has no money to function."

"They may be able to go back and reconstruct some activity, which may or may not find out what happened. If they do really, really good forensics, they will probably be able to figure out what was done, how it was done and worst of all," said Chris, "who did it."

Chuck was visibly upset. Hawk stepped in with the voice of reason. He didn't like the situation any more than Chuck. But he defended the 'Doctors'. "Look, Chuck. We know the FBI is already checking into the computer activities of BCT. They have Clark and he's gonna sing like a bird, if he hasn't already. It's just a matter of time until they check into BONE activity. We need to destroy any and all records of what we did that might be used by law enforcement agencies."

"When Godzilla goes off, it's gonna do that." said Bobby.

"But whatever happened wasn't even us?" asked Chuck.

"It seems someone may have beat us to the punch to destroy BONE financially, but left the operation still capable," said Bobby. "Unless we can destroy it as an online business, we may still be discovered."

Chuck exhaled heavily. "Sounds like the answer is Godzilla, right?" said Chuck.

"That would be the best thing for us," said Eddie.

Chuck nodded. "Do it. Run Godzilla and make it all go away." The doctors and Hawk looked at each other and nodded. Chuck added, "When will we know if the program was successful?"

The group all looked at Bobby. "To the maximum level of success, perhaps an hour? Maybe later."

"OK. I've got a film session this morning," said Chuck with the trace of a smile. "Bobby, we're putting our trust in you," said Chuck. "Please send me a text if it works"

Hawk said, "What if it doesn't work?"

Chuck stood up and looked around the table. "If it doesn't work, do I leave my friends who may or may not get caught, open to a criminal investigation by the FBI? No. I've got your back the same way you've had mine during this whole thing. What we're doing is the right thing. We set out to prove a point about gambling on college basketball. To make Jackson Grant stop. It was the right thing to do, and it sounds like we've done it." Chuck became solemn and nodded at his friends. "If Godzilla doesn't work, so be it. Now if you'll excuse me, Fella's, I've got a Championship to win!"

CHAPTER TWENTY-ONE

The text message alarm on Chucks' phone went off at 1:15 PM. It was from Eddie and it was two words. "It worked." Chuck laid back on the bed and smiled inside. At least one problem seemed to be over. He closed his eyes to try and get a nap in. It was pointless to try and sleep. Visions of Cortland State players danced in his head. The thoughts of losing after coming so far prevented him from relaxing. Chuck was still awake when Pepper knocked on his door.

"It's time to go," said Pepper.

Sitting alone in a Buffalo Wild Wings was Steve James. He sat quietly watching the warmups for the St. Michael's University Armordillo's and the Cortland State University Red Dragons. The waitress came up and asked if he needed a refill on his Amaretto Sour. Steve smiled politely, handed her a hundred-dollar bill and said, "Yes, please. And keep them coming."

St. Michael's Armordillos roared in unison "DILLO DEFENSE!", then headed out to take the floor to play for the National Championship. Everyone ran out of the locker room except Chuck and Coach Darrell Round. Round had nodded for Chuck to stay behind. Slowly the coach walked over to Chuck and sat next to him. Chuck noticed the man's limp seemed a bit more pronounced but said nothing. Chuck fought the urge to ask him about the hip and the medication the Coach was taking.

Coach Round said to Chuck, "In our lives, we've both been involved in games that have meant more than this one." The duality of the statement was not lost on Chuck. He smiled and nodded in agreement. "Remember that first one against Henderson's bunch? If you'd lost that one, none of this would have been possible."

Chuck said, "The fact that we made it this far is a minor miracle. God is good." It was Round's turn to nod.

"I guess I should have given some kind of speech or somethin' to these guys," said Round.

Chuck shook his head no. "Every one of them knows this is it. This is what we worked for all season. There isn't anything you can say that will make a difference, Coach." Chuck got up from the bench and headed out to join his teammates.

Round gently grabbed Chuck's hand and said, "If Hoopman's got one more win in him, this would be as good a game as any to use it!"

Chuck said, "One way or the other it's the last one, right?"

The coach looked at Chuck and smiled. "It is for me, Chuck."

Chuck knew from the way Round had said it that the coach didn't mean he was simply retiring. The look on his face, the pills, the way his limp had gotten so much worse in such a short time. Chuck turned to face his coach and said flatly, "Prostate or bone?"

Round pushed up from the bench and managed a smile. "Bone cancer, Chuck." He moved his hand to Chuck's shoulder and said, "Yes, it's terminal, but I've got nothing to complain about. This has been the best season of my career by far. So, if I'm goin' out," the coach sniffed back a tear and finished, "I'm goin' out a winner, right, Chuck?"

Chuck smiled and moved beside his coach. "Coach Round, you were a winner before this season. Winning isn't always measured in numbers of wins or losses. Sometimes, making a tough decision that seemed wrong by so many people is still a win. You knew that when you put me on this team. Winners are measured by greatness of the heart and stature of character. Coach, you have conducted your life with honesty and integrity. For that you have memories you should treasure. There are hundreds of players and people whom you have had a positive impact on." Chuck smiled and saw the man wipe a tear from his eye. "But if I can give you one more memory," Chuck swallowed hard. "One more memory before you go out, I'll try to get you that Championship, Coach. I owe you that much. Just for giving me this chance." Chuck wiped away his own tear.

The coach wiped his nose with his handkerchief and coughed. "Chuck, you don't owe me a thing." He stuck out his hand. "Win or lose, Hoopman, it has been one hell of a ride. I'm glad I didn't miss it," said the coach.

"I think we both have one more ride left, Coach," said Chuck. His familiar smile was present only because he knew it made the coach comfortable. He didn't know how bad off his coach was. Round had hid his pain so well for so long. Now Chuck had one more reason to win it all.

The coach smiled and got out his can of chew. "One more ride with Hoopman." The coach nodded and put the chew in his lip. His composure regained and Round put his game face on. He looked at Chuck and said, "Let's roll!"

When Chuck came out of the tunnel, he walked over to Eddie who was sitting on the sideline in his wheelchair. Eddie looked at Chuck with a huge grin. Chris and Bobby walked over toward the bench and Chuck waved for the Security Guard to let them pass. Eddie held up his iPad and showed the message to Chuck as if it were priceless. The screen indicated, 'SITE COULD NOT BE FOUND'. Chuck looked at Bobby and asked, "Godzilla?"

"Yeah, man! Godzilla!!" said Bobby with a huge smile.

Chuck stuck out his hand to shake with Bobby and said, "I never doubted you for a minute." Bobby was beaming.

Jackson Grant was sitting ten rows up behind the announcers when his phone rang. It was one of Mike Thompsons' underlings that had drawn the short straw to inform Jackson Grant he no longer had a gambling network.

Grants' face was a shade of crimson red that would have made any Alabama fan proud. Except it wasn't paint. "What do mean 'off line'?" There was stuttering on the other end of the cell phone. "GONE?!" More stuttering. Grant hung up, searched in his phone for his bank account information. He checked three accounts. All were empty. Grant fidgeted in his seat as he searched for any site in the BONE. No results. Then reality set in. He had nothing. No Network. No organization. And no money.

Grant slammed his program against the seat and got a dirty look from the man in front of him. He hissed, "WHAT?!" The man turned around and continued to watch the warmups. Grant looked around. Where the hell was Holden? What was he waiting for? It was bad enough that he jacked up the price to kill Hoopman, but he still had not done the job. The thought that Holden would probably kill him during halftime popped into Grant's head. He sat back in his seat and relaxed. Halftime was the perfect time to do it.

Chuck was alone in the world on the floor as he stretched. Godzilla worked so now he could focus on basketball. Yet, there was still the memory of Hawks' message ringing in his ear. Grant would not give up easily. Chuck took in the sights of the arena. He saw Marshall in the 'Runnin' Dillo' costume doing all the things he did best, keeping St. Michael's fans happy and gaining new fans everywhere he went. He saw Hawk, not actually hiding, but setting himself in an overwatch position at the front of the tunnel closest to the St. Michael's locker room.

Chuck found Grace and Sandy in the stands and gave them a wave. In the handicapped section sat Eddie with Bobby and Chris sitting right next to him.

Chuck turned and watched his opponents. It was easy to spot Tekema "T-Bone" Washington and Anthony Potter. T-Bone was a six foot ten forward who could play guard for most folks. Tony Potter was a six-foot eight sharp shooting guard or forward, wherever the coach felt like playing him. Then there was Kenyon

Taylor, the Red Dragon point guard. He wasn't as big or as fast as Jones, but he was a senior. He was responsible for hitting the shot that put Cortland into the Championship. Kenyon Taylor was going to be Chuck's best friend for the next forty minutes.

Down in the bowels of the Allen County War Memorial Coliseum sat Carl Holden. There were no other people around him. He stood alone looking at the pistol in his hand. Above him he could hear the crowd singing the Star-Spangled Banner. When he heard the roar from the thousands of fans above, he knew it was time for him to earn his pay.

Just before tip-off, Chuck walked slowly around the center court circle and shook the Wildcat players' hands. They were confident, lean and by far the tallest team in Division III basketball. He walked by Jose and said quietly, "You let me know if you need any help, okay!"

Jose smiled and said, "I don't need any help, Hoopman! I'm a lean machine!"

"You better be, Amigo!" He yelled to Holmes. "YOU READY, CHARLES?!"

Charles had his game face on and just nodded. Chuck smacked Parnell's butt then fist bumped with OJ and it was time to play.

Fans knew immediately that this Championship was going to be a war. From the tip off, players were diving on the floor for loose balls, fighting for position under the boards, picking up charges and flying into the stands. Chuck played as tight as he could on Taylor and managed to contain him for the most part. Taylor hit only two shots in the first ten minutes.

T-Bone Washington was posting either OJ or Jose Rivera-Torres every chance he could. Surprisingly, Jose was having more success than OJ. Jose's weight was a problem for T-Bone, but tough defense was wearing Jose down as well. Coach Round saw what was happening, pulled Jose, and went to a three-guard offense with eight minutes left in the half.

St. Michael's was small, but much faster than Cortland State. The problem was the tactic did not work. Pepper and Charles' three pointers were not falling, and St. Michael's was slowly losing ground. Cortland was not only big but they were smart and they were tenacious. Taylor would work the ball around until he found which Cortland big man had the mismatch and put the ball in low. At that point, T-Bone or Tony Potter would get the ball, back down the smaller St. Michael's player and get a relatively easy shot.

With five minutes left in the first half, and the score Cortland 35, St. Michael's 27, Chuck had seen enough. He called a timeout and quickly went to Round. He grabbed a towel and said, "I need to come down and double on the big guys, or we gotta get Jose and OJ both in there!"

Round pulled Chuck and Daymon Breyers aside, "If we go with our big guys too much, I don't think they'll have enough gas for the second half."

"If we're down by 10 at halftime, we ain't coming back against these guys," said Chuck. Round thought about the comment and finally agreed. "Taylor can handle our pressure, but I don't think the big guys can deal with a big double team." Chuck hollered at Parnell. "David, can you come over and double on T-Bone?" David nodded.

Chuck said, "Let's get him stopped first, put Charles on Potter, and I've seen enough of Taylor to take away his game."

Round nodded. "We'll try it your way. Just try to slow it down more. We need to have something left in the tank for the second half!" Chuck nodded and slowly walked back out onto the court.

Holden walked around the mezzanine of the coliseum until he found a place where he could watch the St. Michael's fans. The game was of no interest to him. Soon enough, he found the damned "Armordillo" mascot. Then all he had to do was wait to make his move.

The new defensive tactics worked much better. T-Bone had problems when OJ and Parnell double-teamed him. He lost one ball out of bounds and threw an errant pass the next time down the floor. Chuck was patient on offense. He and Charles worked the pick and roll to perfection, and Chuck made a mental note that they would be able to use that again if they needed it.

Holmes was running Potter back and forth around picks, and it was taking a toll on the taller player. With two minutes left in the half, Potter had missed his last three shots. Cortland was starting to show signs of fatigue.

On the other side of the ball, St. Michael's got stronger. Chuck started to drive on Taylor, and the tactic was paying off. He was drawing fouls on T-Bone or Carter, the Cortland center, with every penetration.

With a minute before the half, Round changed the defense to a full court press. He replaced Jose with Dexter Thomas. UK was unprepared for the pressure, and Taylor threw a weak pass to half court where Thomas intercepted it. He quickly found Chuck who didn't hesitate. He drove hard to the basket. Taylor cut him off, but Chuck was ready. He threw a no-look behind the back pass to Dexter as he cut to the basket. The super-sub took the pass cleanly and dunked over Taylor.

Taylor took the next inbounds pass and tried to slowly dribble the ball up court. Chuck pushed him to the corner, where Taylor stopped before crossing half court. Holmes joined Chuck and they double-teamed the Cortland guard who got no help from his teammates. The ref blew his whistle. Taylor had failed to get the ball across half court within ten seconds.

With eight seconds left in the half, Chuck set up the offense again. He ran the pick and roll with Charles. After setting the pick and dropping a no look pass to Charles, Chuck headed to the basket. Charles hit him in stride with a beautiful bounce pass. Chuck knew he had only two seconds left, so he drove hard to the hoop. T-Bone came out to stop him, so Chuck took one more dribble, went under the big man and hit a left-handed reverse lay-up. The buzzer sounded and St. Michael's had pulled within one, Cortland—39, St. Michael's —38. The Armordillo faithful were delirious.

Carl Holden was the only person in the arena who didn't know the score. He posted himself outside the St. Michael's locker room. Players and coaches came and went. But that wasn't what he was waiting for. Soon enough the St. Michael's cheerleaders, trainers and mascot came into the tunnel. As they walked by, Carl Holden stepped in front of the mascot and nearly ran him over. "Oh, I'm sorry," said Carl in an overly friendly gesture. He looked around nervously and made sure the cheerleaders kept moving. Then he looked down on the ground and said, "Oops! I untied your shoe! Step over here and I'll tie it up for you!"

The 'Killer Dillo', who could barely see out of his costume, much less tie his shoe, quickly stepped out of the way and into a doorway. Carl Holden timed his move perfectly. With no one watching, he opened the door and shoved the mascot into the empty room. He glanced around to make sure no one saw what he had done, quickly entered the room and closed the door.

Chuck wiped off his face with a towel. He had Dianne Weston check his toe. After he had taken care of himself, Chuck checked on his teammates. He walked around and talked calmly to everyone in the locker room. "That's a darn good come back, fellas! Darn good! We got another half against these guys. They aren't invincible! The way we're playin', I know we can beat 'em!"

Coach Round watched his players. He saw their confidence. The Coach walked to the center of the locker room and said,

"Take about five minutes and just relax. We got these guys!" Round was saying it to convince himself just as much as his team.

Jose came over and sat down next to Chuck. Chuck stuck out his fist and tapped knuckles with the huge man. "You're kickin' T-Bone's butt down low!"

Jose nodded with a smile. He bent over to Chuck like he was going to tell him a secret. "I want to do something."

Chuck looked around and acted like he was getting classified information. "What's that, big man?"

Jose looked around again. "I wanna dunk the ball."

Chuck struggled to hold back a laugh. "You . . . want to . . . dunk?!"

Jose nodded. "You know how you throw those lob passes to David?" Chuck nodded. "I want you to throw me one of those!"

Chuck thought about it and smiled. "All right, Jose! You know how to get T-Bone on your hip, right?" The big man nodded. "You take him up to the foul line and get him on your hip away from the basket when I go to the top of the key. As I start to drive away, break to the basket and I'll put it up there."

Jose smiled broadly. "I might only be able to get up with one hand, but I want to dunk one."

Chuck said, "I know you want to do this, but if you time it right and turn your head to see the ball, your adrenaline will help you get up there. Go up with two hands," Chuck stood up. "And you TEAR THE RIM OFF THE SUCKER!" Just the thought had Jose fired up.

"Let me hit the john, and I'll be right behind you," said Chuck. There was no need to worry about Jose's state of mind. Chuck went into the rest room and for just a moment, enjoyed the solitude. As he washed up, he looked in the mirror. He stared at the man looking back at him. With no one around Chuck prayed, "Father please give me the strength I need to finish this mission. I just need twenty minutes."

Chuck looked to the heavens and nodded. "Give me wings! Amen." A smile came to his face, he nodded to the mirror, turned and joined his team.

As they came out on the floor for the second half, everything seemed to move in slow motion. The St. Michael's faithful were on their feet for the start. Chuck took his normal scan at the surrounding sights. The fans were up, Round had his spit cup, Eddie and the 'Doctors' were cheering.

Everything Chuck saw seemed right except one constant. Usually before they took the court in the second half, the 'ArmorDillo' would come out to shake his hand. Where was Marshall? Chuck chalked it up to nerves. Marshall was probably just in the rest room. That costume had to take forever to take off and put back on. Chuck didn't have time to worry about Marshall. It was time to play the most significant hoop of his life.

Whatever momentum St. Michael's had in the first half was erased by an emotionally fired up Red Dragon team. Any fatigue Cortland State had at the end of the first half had disappeared. Taylor had his team energized to run, and that was what they did.

With every rebound, Cortland pushed the ball up the floor. Chuck and Charles were forced to stay back on defense, and that kept them from attacking the boards. This put additional pressure to rebound on OJ, Parnell and Jose. Cortland was too fundamentally sound at rebounding to be outplayed on the boards.

Chuck saw what was happening and hollered at Charles, "You gotta get on the boards with them, and I got your back!" Charles saw it too and started to attack the boards on both ends.

The improvised tactic worked. As Cortland was boxing out the big men, Charles used his athletic ability to slip between the big guys and get rebounds. On the offensive end, when he did not get the put back points, he was getting fouled.

Cortland was forced to make an adjustment that kept their guards from breaking down court for fast breaks. That allowed Chuck to start driving to the basket again. He hit two lay-ups in a row and dropped a neat no-look dish to Parnell for a dunk.

Cortland answered with a pair of long-range bombs from Potter and Taylor. ESPN needed some money and thankfully there was a television timeout. St. Michael's was showing signs of fatigue. Chuck was the first one to the bench where he nearly drank an entire water bottle by himself.

After a television timeout, St. Michael's came out of the break ready to run their set offense. It seemed like the crowd wasn't as into it as usual. That's when Chuck noticed Marshall sitting on one knee in front of the cheerleaders. Chuck thought that was odd since Marshall was always on the floor working the fans, especially during timeouts.

Chuck walked over to Eddie with a towel. He bent down and said, "Can you do me a favor, please?" Eddie nodded. Chuck looked over at Hawk standing by the tunnel. "Can you text Hawk and have him check on Marshall? He usually comes over and says something to me, or engages with me, but he hasn't since the first half. I hope he's not sick or something!"

"I'm on it, Chuck!" Eddie bumped knuckles with Chuck, pulled out his phone and called Hawk.

The ever-watchful Nate Hawkins was watching Chuck as he talked to Eddie. He noticed Chuck glance his way. When Chuck walked away, he saw Eddie pull out his cellphone. Nate Hawkins the military policeman went into immediate action. Hawk already had his phone out when it rang.

Chuck waved his hands to try and get the crowd into it. They quickly responded and some chants of 'HOOPMAN' came from the crowd. Still Marshall sat there. What the hell was wrong with Marshall? The question was interrupted by a nudge from Jose.

"Is now a good time?" asked Jose.

Chuck looked around and saw the crowd was a little lifeless and nodded his head. "Now would be a perfect time, Jose. Just remember, make him think you're going up to the foul line, roll hard and sky, Brother!"

Chuck took the inbounds pass and set the play. T-Bone was really overplaying Jose. After Chuck nodded, Jose moved up to the foul line. T-Bone tried to come up and overplay Jose. Jose spun off T-Bone, rolled hard and ran to the basket. Chuck threw the lob pass perfectly to the far side of the basket. Cortland was caught totally off guard. Jose went up higher than he had ever jumped before, caught the pass with both hands just above the rim and slammed it home!

The arena exploded with a roar! Chuck couldn't help but notice the look Taylor gave to T-Bone. It said what the entire Coliseum was thinking. How could you let that happen? Jose literally sprinted back on defense. The fans were on their feet. The momentum had returned to the Armordillos.

With eight minutes to play, Hawk saw the two security guards across the gym run towards the opposite tunnel. He quickly looked out on the floor and noticed the teams were coming out on the floor from the timeout. He quickly walked over to the tunnel where the guards had gone. He followed them a short way down the tunnel. They met with another security guard who was pulling a tied-up and nearly naked kid behind him. Hawk thought he saw something familiar about the kid but couldn't quite see his face. He stepped closer as he watched the guard pull tape off the young man's mouth.

Marshall jumped and got Hawk's attention yelling, "HE'S IN MY COSTUME, HAWK!" It took a moment for Hawk to realize the tied-up kid was Marshall Wright! "MY COSTUME! HAWK, HE'S IN MY COSTUME!" The message sank in, and Hawk sprinted back to the floor.

The teams were coming out onto the floor. Hawk had his hand on his Beretta as he found the 'ArmorDillo'. The mascot was sitting on the sideline watching the players as they came onto the floor. Hawk moved closer to the floor and kept his hand on the pistol under his coat. As long as the "mascot" didn't go out on the floor, Hawk would stay fifteen feet away and just watch him. He knew Holden was waiting for the right time to make his move. The question was, when?

Chuck checked the scoreboard that read, Cortland - 75, St. Michael's – 74 with four minutes left. He wiped his face with the towel, exhaled heavily and headed back out onto the court. The game had become a battle of wills. The will of Kenyon Taylor to keep his team ahead of a team they should have already put away. Chuck didn't need to look at the clock to know what time it was. It was time to put away how tired he was and turn up the intensity.

Chuck brought the ball down court and passed to Charles. Chuck broke to the basket, came hard off a Parnell pick and received a return pass from Charles. He set his feet at the three-point line, squared up to the basket and fired. The shot was pure and drew nothing but net. The fans roared their approval. St. Michael's was up by two.

Cortland brought the ball down quickly. Taylor dumped a pass into T-Bone, but Jose and David forced him to pass it out. Potter took the pass and banked a beautiful shot from fifteen feet.

Chuck walked the ball up the court and called a play for Charles. OJ and Jose set a double pick in the lane, and Charles ran hard off of it. He popped around the double pick wide open. Charles took Chuck's pass and pulled up for a two pointer that swished. St. Michael's was up by two again.

Down the floor came Cortland. T-Bone Washington took Taylor's pass in the post. Parnell was too slow to get there, and T-Bone dribbled around Jose for a dunk. Cortland tied the score at 79 with forty-eight seconds left.

Round called a timeout. As Chuck sat on the bench, he wiped his face with a towel and dried his hands. Round called for Chuck to take a shot off a low screen similar to the play Charles had just run. On the way out, Chuck told Jose to be ready for a pass because Taylor would be all over Chuck.

Chuck was right. As he came around the pick, Taylor was set in front. Chuck had to go out past the three-point line to get the ball. As soon as he got the ball, Chuck bounced it into Jose who did not hesitate. He set his feet and shot the skyhook. T-Bone stretched but couldn't reach it. St. Michael's was up by two, 81-79.

Back down at the Cortland end, Kenyon Taylor was in total control. He set up the offense, checked the clock and waited. With ten seconds left, he drove hard to the basket pushing Chuck deep into the lane. Chuck expected the senior to go for the tie. He dropped down a step too far. Taylor saw Chuck deep, backed out to the three-point line and fired. The ball swished, and the Cortland fans went crazy. Chuck immediately called a timeout. Cortland was up 82 to 81, with only seven seconds left.

During the timeout, Round called for Holmes to set a pick for Chuck. If he had the shot, he was supposed to take it. If not, look for David underneath. Chuck wiped off his face and looked at the scoreboard. He saw Pepper Dyers' smile, and Round nodded at him. At that point, the decision was easy enough to make. It was time to put Cortland away.

Jackson Grant was losing his mind. He had left his seat and moved up to the second floor and was standing across from an usher. He was smacking his program into his hand as the usher gave him a questioning glance. Not wanting to catch anymore attention, Grant mustered a smile and put the program behind his back. Where the hell was Holden?

Mike Thompson was puffing on a cigarette. One FBI agent across from him was stretching and trying to stay awake. He had given as much information as he could to the agency and was now about to enter a witness protection program.

The second agent turned up the volume on the game and said, "I can't believe this Podunk little school is even in this game, much less about to win it!"

Thompson said calmly, "Agent Harper, I'll bet you a thousand dollars that Podunk school wins this game!" The FBI agent just blew him off. What did Thompson know about basketball? He was just another crook.

As he headed out to the floor, Chuck refused to look at Eddie. He ran over to Charles Holmes and said, "All right, man! We've been here before so it's you and me, okay?"

Holmes smiled and he wiped the dust from the bottom of his shoes. "Let's do this!"

Parnell inbounded the pass to Chuck who immediately set up at the top of the key. Taylor was overplaying him to the left, probably expecting help from the right. Charles was being overplayed and couldn't get close enough for the pick. Chuck knew the time was running out and couldn't wait any longer.

He drove hard to his right, with Taylor matching him step for step. With two seconds left he pretended to pass to Charles Holmes who was covered in the corner. Taylor tried to block it, so Chuck pulled back, double pumped the ball, then shot it. Taylor's leg inadvertently hit Chuck's right leg, and he fell to the floor hard. Taylor jumped to avoid falling on Chuck as the buzzer sounded. The ball hit the rim and bounced harmlessly away.

But the referee blew the whistle and pointed at Kenyon Taylor. Taylor quickly stepped away with his hands up in the air and carried a look of disbelief on his face. Chuck was going to the foul line with no time on the clock.

Cortland fans hissed and the St. Michael's faithful prayed. The only thing going through Chuck's mind was the foul shot. It was time to get the game over. He looked over at Coach Round and nodded. The ref tossed Chuck the ball. Hoopman toed the line, exhaled slowly, and got ready to shoot.

As expected, the Cortland coach called a timeout to try and ice Chuck. As the players moved to the bench no one sat next to Chuck. Chuck had St. Michael's in position to win, and that's what he was going to do. For his teammates, for Darrell Round and for himself.

Chuck wiped his face one last time and headed onto the floor. The St. Michael's faithful began chanting, "HOOPMAN! HOOPMAN!" Chuck moved to the free throw line and took his position. The referee blew the whistle and threw him the ball.

Carl Holden wasn't going to wait anymore. He knew as soon as the game was over, all the noise and confusion would keep him from killing Hayes when the fans rushed onto the floor. He would never be able to escape. As he moved the large head of the Armordillo costume to get a better view, he could see around the arena. St. Michael's had come out of the timeout, and Hayes was heading to the foul line. As he continued to look around, something got his attention. Two security guards were standing over by the tunnel with the kid that was in the mascot costume! The kid was pointing at him. The guards were starting to come towards Holden. Too late! Holden put the mascot head back on, stood up and started walking toward Chuck as he stood at the foul line.

Nate Hawkins was watching Holden's every move in the Armordillo suit. He wasn't watching Chuck. When he saw the head go back on, he pulled his Baretta and put it behind his back. He started walking quickly towards the mascot. Hawk glanced at the opening of the tunnel and saw Marshall pointing out the 'Killer Dillo' to the guards. Hawk looked back at the mascot and saw him stand up.

Hawk felt as if his feet were in mud. He began walking faster towards the Dillo but wasn't gaining any ground. He hollered

"CHUCK!" as loud as he could, but the chanting just drowned out his yell.

Chuck dribbled once and started to look at the basket. Out of the corner of his eye, he saw movement. He turned to see the 'ArmorDillo' headed his way. Right behind him was Hawk, and he was yelling something. He looked back at the 'Dillo and wondered what the hell Marshall was doing with a gun. That's when he knew it wasn't Marshall headed towards him. Chuck did the first thing that came into his mind. Out of reflex, Chuck threw the ball as hard as he could at the mascots face.

With a perfect chest pass that seemed like it was shot from a cannon, the ball hit Holden squarely in the face of the Armadillo head and spun it sideways. Holden couldn't see his target anymore! From behind, Hawk grabbed the gun with his free hand and shoved his gun up under the costume head. The move served two purposes. It got Holden's attention and hid the pistol from the crowd. Hawk yelled into Holdens' ear, "Make the wrong move and you'll be known as the man who died dressed in an armadillo costume in front of 25,000 people!"

Holden was confused. He started to put his hands up. "Don't put your hands up, Shithead! Wave one hand as we walk off the court! I want to see the other one too. Now move out slowly," said Hawk. He quickly placed Holden's gun in his pocket then pressed his gun into the back of Holdens' neck as they walked off the court. "Wave your hand!" He smacked Holden on the head.

From his elevated position, Jackson Grant watched as Holden was captured and taken off the court. He threw his program to the ground. The usher gave him another dirty look, and Grant hissed, "WHAT? Turn around and watch the game!"

As they walked off the court, Holden said, "Who the hell are you?"

"I'm the ghost of Pete Henderson, Maggot, and you're going to prison!" He moved Holden into the tunnel and handed him over to waiting security team. He saw Marshall there standing in his underwear and said, "Guys, can we get that costume off that asshole so this kid can do his job!" Hawk turned around and looked at Chuck out on the floor. He smiled broadly and sent out a thumbs up sign to let Chuck know everything was okay. Chuck saw Marshall half naked next to the 'Killer Dillo', and everything became clear. Hawk mouthed 'Carl Holden' and pointed at the mascot. Chuck nodded at Hawk and gave him a thumbs up back.

The Coliseum was in a state of confusion. Between mascot's being taken off the court and security people with handcuffs out, it seemed things would get out of hand. The ref called a timeout to get order restored. Chuck went to the bench shaking his head. The reality of what had happened began to set in. Holden had been in Marshall's costume and was coming out on the floor to kill him. The thought kept running through his mind. The strange thing was, he wasn't afraid. He was pissed! Right in the middle of the game, Holden would have killed him!

Chuck looked over at Eddie and nodded. Eddie smiled back with a huge grin, gave Chuck a thumbs up and smacked Bobby on the arm.

A referee came over to the St. Michael's bench and said, "Coach, number 10 needs to come out and shoot the foul shot! We can't wait anymore!" Everyone looked at Chuck. He took a deep breath and headed out to the line again.

All the Cortland fans in the world were trying to put a hex on Hoopman as he stood at the foul line. The Cortland fans booed, and the St. Michael's players prayed. Through it all, Hoopman was focused. His mind was fixed. Chuck addressed the foul line and took the ball from the referee. The arena was roaring with fans trying to be heard. For some reason, Chuck didn't hear anything.

Suddenly, he was fifteen years old again, shooting foul shots in the park all by himself. Pretending to be Walt Frazier or Pete Maravich. Copying their styles and the form from the videos he had watched so many times.

Chuck put Hoopman away for a moment. He moved his left foot back from the line three inches, placed the ball lower in his hand and flicked the ball without a follow through. The ball hit the rim, bounced once, and rolled into the basket.

The gym erupted with Cortland groans and Armordillo joy. The game was tied at 82 each. Chuck stepped back from the line, inhaled deeply and caught the pass from the ref. He walked up to the foul line, dribbled twice, and exhaled slowly. He didn't hear a sound, his vision was clear and he set. The shot was straight as an arrow, but short. The ball hit the rim and bounced straight back at Chuck. The basketball Gods were unkind. Chuck bent over at the waste and looked at the ground. Charles Holmes quickly walked from the bench and placed his hand around Chuck. The reason he had missed didn't matter. Jackson Grant, Carl Holden, Godzilla, or old age. The fact was, he missed. Charles nearly had to drag him off the court. Chuck couldn't look his teammates in the eyes. He went to the bench, sat down, and put his head in a towel. The only saving grace was Chuck would get five minutes to put the miss out of his mind and win a championship or be haunted for the rest of his life by what could have been.

CHAPTER TWENTY-TWO

Chuck didn't even hear what was being said on the bench. Then he looked down the bench to see Eddie, Chris and Bobby. Eddie waved at Chuck to come over. Chuck looked at Coach Round and said, "Excuse me, Coach. I need a minute. Chuck stood up and walked over to where Eddie was sitting.

"Man, I screwed that up," said Chuck softly.

"What?! That shot? Listen to me, Chuck. Everything is going fine!" said Eddie. "We're got the bad guys! BONE is gone. Hawk stopped a guy from killing you. Marshall is OK! AND…you can still win the National Championship!"

Chuck stared in disbelief at his friend. "First of all, the dude in Marshall's suit was Carl Holden and we think we were successful in taking them down, the FBI is going to be investing this whole mess," then he slowly added as he turned to his teammates out on the court, "And I may have screwed those guys out of winning the National Championship because I missed a foul shot. I never miss foul shots!"

Chris reached up, grabbed Chuck's arm and said, "Listen! You can't change what you just happened. It isn't over. You need to get the Hoopman cape out, strap it on, and buckle up! Chuck, you gotta put all that behind you. You gotta do that RIGHT NOW! Anything we did to take them down was the right thing to do! But that's all over." Chuck nodded. Eddie's comments started to sink in. He pointed at all the fans in the stands. "You should prove to them that Hoopman is real!"

Eddie's tone changed and he rolled backwards away from the bench. "If I wasn't in this chair right now . . ."

Chuck interrupted him and said, "You'd go out and win the National Championship?!"

Eddie gave Chuck a wry smile. "Damn right!"

Chuck bent down, grabbed Eddie and hugged him. Eddie squeezed Chuck for a moment then pushed him away and said, "Get out of here or I'll go do it!"

Eddie's comments hit the mark. The best thing to do was to go back and do what had always been his savior. What had always given him peace of mind in the past? The answer was to play basketball. It was time to be Hoopman again.

Steve James was watched as fans from Cortland and St. Michael's cheered on their respective teams. The waitress brought him another Amaretto Sour. He watched the screen as the camera focused on Chuck "Hoopman" Hayes as his every move was broadcast across the nation. He saw Chuck go over to a man in the wheelchair. He saw the man put away his tablet and share an embrace with Hoopman. Steve wasn't 100% certain, but he would have bet all the money he had stolen from Grant that his revenge would not have been possible without the man in the wheelchair.

Chuck shook the Cortland players' hands again and winked at Charles. For some unknown reason, probably adrenaline, Chuck wasn't even tired. He felt like he could run all night. He took his place next to Kenyan Taylor without a word. The Cortland guard said quietly, "Too bad you had to choke, old man! Now I'm gonna have to school ya!"

As much as Chuck was against talking smack, he couldn't let the comment go. Chuck looked him straight in the eye and said, "I am old enough to be your daddy, so don't make me spank you in front of 25,000 people."

Taylor became furious. "BRING IT, OLD MAN!"

Chuck nodded slowly, "Okay. If you insist!"

An official showed up and separated them. Chuck just smiled and nodded. If Taylor wanted it to be personal, so be it.

The tap was controlled by Cortland. Every player for St. Michael's played tight defense against his man. It was obvious within the first thirty seconds the refs were going to let the two teams play. There would be no more last second whistles. Taylor tried to drive on Chuck. Chuck cut him off and turned him into Jose. Jose held his ground and the guard ran into him. When Taylor picked up his dribble, Chuck was there to double-team him. Hoopman reached in and smacked the ball away. Cortland fans roared for a foul that never came.

The ball rolled out to Charles who scooped it up in stride. He took it the length of the court for a dunk. St. Michael's 84, Cortland 82.

Cortland brought the ball back down and ran a play for T-Bone. Parnell came over too late, and the big man shot over Jose for two. On the inbounds pass, Taylor made a great read and stole a long pass from Jose to Charles. The senior guard quickly brought the ball up court. Chuck pressed him to take away a three-point shot, so Taylor dribbled by him and drove the lane. He went up and over Jose for a dunk. Cortland was up 86 to 84.

Chuck became deliberate on offense. He slowly brought the ball up court. He made a safe quick pass on the wing to Parnell. Then he sprinted across the floor and set a pick on Holmes man. Charles came off the pick wide open and drilled a two pointer to tie it again.

Both teams began to feel the pressure and the fatigue and missed their next two shots. St.Michael's had one more open shot that Charles Holmes barely hit from the foul line. Round could see the trajectory of the ball wasn't there. They were a tired bunch of ball players. With only a minute and forty seconds left, Round called a timeout so his team could catch their breath.

"All right, fellas, we got a tie! You're doin' fine, but we need to apply pressure on Taylor. Double team him if he has the ball, and Hayes," the coach looked at Chuck. "You know where they're goin', so get on Taylor! Play some D!" They broke the huddle and came out onto the floor.

As had become his custom, Chuck grabbed Charles after the huddle. "I'm gonna lay off him on the far side. I wanna see if I can sucker T-Bone into a bad pass!" Charles nodded and ran over to Jose and OJ to relay the message. Chuck repeated his plan to David Parnell who nodded.

As Cortland set up their offense, it took about twenty seconds for Taylor to realize St. Michael's was now basically playing a box-in-one on him. He knew T-Bone would be open so as soon as he got the ball, he dropped it inside and moved to the other side of the court. His mistake was not telling T-Bone. Chuck quickly ran through the lane while Parnell and OJ double-teamed T-Bone. Jose was on the far side of the lane and Chuck literally hid behind him. Chuck saw T-Bone look across court at Taylor who had stepped out to the three-point line. Taylor knew the pass was coming and tried to yell for T-Bone not to throw it, but it was too late. The center threw a direct pass towards Taylor when Chuck stepped out and knocked the pass down. The ball headed out of bounds, Hoopman and Taylor both dove into the stands to retrieve it. Chuck reached the ball an instant before Taylor got there, and with one smooth motion, threw the ball back in bounds towards half court. The momentum of his body kept both he and Taylor flying out of bounds and into the stands.

Charles Holmes raced to pick up the loose ball, saw Cortland was already back on defense and decided to wait for Chuck. As Chuck and Taylor pulled themselves from the crowd, Taylor said, "That was some chicken shit you just pulled! If you're gonna cover me, why don't you cover me?!"

Chuck smiled and said, "If I can't beat you, I'll beat your team!" He turned and sprinted to Charles to get the ball. The fans were still in awe from the diving save, and the chants of "HOOPMAN! HOOPMAN!" were filling the Coliseum once more.

Chuck knew it was time to set up Taylor on defense. For some magical moment Chuck realized he wasn't even breathing hard. He wasn't tired. There was no sound other than the ball dribbling on the court. The only thing moving at full speed was Taylor. Chuck knew he couldn't take him to the hole. Taylor's legs were as strong as they had been at the start of the game. As he dribbled the shot clock down, he called for Jose to come and set a pick. With Taylor 100% focused on Chuck, Taylor had not seen Jose set the pick. Taylors' teammate didn't switch and wouldn't let him slide through the pick.

With two seconds left on the shot clock, Chuck dribbled hard off Jose's pick. Jose and his defender were so big that Kenyon Taylor had to drop behind them both and that gave Chuck just enough room to shoot. He set his feet, jumped and fired from eighteen feet. Nothing but net! St. Michael's 88, Cortland 86.

The arena exploded yet again. Cortland called a timeout to set a play. During the timeout, Round preached for good, solid man-to-man defense. Chuck told everyone, "NO SWITCH! NO SWITCH!" He was sure Taylor wanted to take any shot.

When they came out of the timeout, Marshall Wright came over as the 'ArmorDillo' to slap Chuck's hand. Chuck smacked his hand then playfully pretended to kick his 'Dillo butt to get him off the court. The crowd still loved the antics.

Then it was time to get serious. There were thirty-eight seconds left on the clock as Kenyon Taylor crossed half court. Chuck tried to pressure him, but the kid had a fire burning in his eyes. He was the hero who had carried his team to this point. Chuck knew he still wanted the ball. The only question was what shot would he take?

Taylor dribbled the clock down to five seconds left on the shooting clock. He worked Chuck from the top of the key down to the foul line. At that point, Chuck was sure he was going for the drive. Taylor stepped hard to the right, and Chuck collapsed to head down the lane. The guard stopped instantly, then dribbled back to the three-point line! Chuck was too late to recover. Taylor pulled up with a wide-open twenty-five-footer. BAM! Cortland was up by one, 89-88. The St. Michael's faithful moaned as the Armordillos used their last timeout.

Chuck was upset with himself. How could he have let him get such an open shot! Round patted his knee on the bench. "Listen to me now! Live for the moment!" It was as if he had directed the comment to Chuck alone. "Don't none of ya' live in the past! We still got," he looked at the clock. "Eleven seconds." He turned and spit into his cup.

"Chuck, you want another pick?" asked the coach.

Chuck shook his head no. "He'll be a little better prepared for it this time. I got something else for him though!"

"You got us this far! Let's go! Get a good shot, fellas!" yelled Round.

As the huddle broke, Charles Holmes came over and said, "I'm sure I can get you a good pick!"

Chuck smacked him a high five. "I don't think I'm gonna need it, Charles. But this is what I need you to do. As you go by Taylor, tell him I'm gonna hit a three pointer right in his face, just like he did to me. Tell him there isn't a damn thing he can do about it!"

"All right, Hoopman! I'll tell him," said Charles with a smile.

Chuck took in all the sights and sounds of the game. Some fans were cheering and some fans were booing. Cheerleaders were cheering. He couldn't help but notice Marshall again. He was having a ball. He checked the scoreboard and tried to think about what he was going to do. He tried to visualize the move. It was going to be a shame, but one way or the other, it was going to be over.

Charles threw the ball in to Chuck. He dribbled to his favorite spot about five feet from the top of the key. With eight seconds left, he threw out to the side where Charles caught the ball. Chuck broke for the basket as Charles took one dribble. Taylor was right with Chuck until he ran him into the lane. Quickly Chuck jumped back out to the three-point line, and Charles threw him the ball. Chuck caught it at the three-point line, turned and set his body for the jumper.

Kenyon Taylor was all over Chuck. He was positive Chuck was going to try a three pointer. Taylor let Chuck go at the three-point line then raced at him to block the shot. Chuck crouched, cocked the ball just as Taylor leaped to block the shot.

Chuck pulled the ball down and dribbled to his left and back towards the lane. Taylor flew by Chuck and completely missed him. Taylor was left in no man's land.

Chuck counted down the time left on the clock as he headed towards the foul line. Four seconds left, one more dribble and he was on the foul line. A Cortland player was coming towards him, but he was too late. Chuck set, jumped and fired.

For just one instant time stood still. Chuck tried to watch the rim, but the Kentucky player was blocking his view. He heard no sound and only felt the pureness of the shot. There was no anger at Jackson Grant. There was no sorrow for Pete Henderson. There was only the basketball . . . the perfectly round sphere reaching its peak as it headed for the rim. Chuck's gaze went upward as his feet hit the floor, and he stepped sideways to watch his shot. The ball in flight was a thing of beauty. It looked as if it had a chance. Chuck leaned to the right to give it some body English. It was just enough.

The horn went off as the ball barely ripped the net. This time, the basketball Gods were kind. The shot was pure, and all was right with the world. The final score was, Cortland State – 89, St. Michael's – 90. The Armordillos were the Division III Champions of College basketball.

Jackson Grant looked down, shook his head and exhaled loudly. The Coliseum was pure chaos. He looked at the usher and said, "I didn't see that coming." He turned and headed out of the Coliseum avoiding any eye contact with security personnel. He made it to the escalator when his cell phone rang. He pulled out the phone and said, "This is Grant!" Whoever was on the other end had the unenviable task of telling the boss he had just been put out of business. Grant got off the escalator and started to scream profanities into the phone.

Two Ft. Wayne Policemen noticed the irate man and became interested in his behavior. Without hanging up, Grant turned and threw the phone against the wall. One officer was on the radio for backup as the other approached the red-faced man. "Excuse me, sir. Is everything all right?"

Grant noticed the officer and froze. His first impulse was to run. It was the wrong thing to do. He made it about fifty feet before four other officers cornered him. A crowd of interested people showed up and started videotaping the man as the officers arrested him. Unable to answer any questions to the satisfaction of the police, the man broke down and started babbling about how "Hoopman took my money!" Jackson Grant was handcuffed and taken away. The video went viral.

Somewhere in the frenzy, someone handed Chuck a t-shirt that had "St. Michael's, National Champions" and Chuck slipped it on. Someone else put a ball cap on his head with the same message. He was mobbed by fans and reporters stuck microphones in his face. He was slapping high five's with Jose, Charles, David and Pepper and anyone else that was celebrating. In forty years of life, Chuck had never experienced anything that compared to the sheer pleasure he was enjoying at that moment. It was the kind of moment one dreams about. Yet, it was real. The team with no chance had won it all.

As he climbed the ladder to cut down the net, he found Marshall, Eddie, Chris, Bobby, and Nate in the crowd and gave them a big wave. As he cut the net, he took a couple of extra seconds to reflect at the accomplishment. He cut a small one-inch piece of the twine, just for himself. The small piece of net was a big piece of history that he would always carry with him as a token of the achievement. Then he cut off a larger five-inch piece of the net and held it up for the crowd to see. The fans roared their approval. If there truly was a heaven on earth, Chuck Hayes had just entered it.

Eventually, he had to come down both literally and figuratively. He found Coach Round. He quickly went over to his coach and embraced him. "WE DID IT, COACH!" Chuck hugged him again and whispered. "You got a darn good eye for talent!"

Round said, "Yeah! I do, don't I?!"

Chuck took his hat off and put it on his coach's head. "Thanks for having faith in me, Darrell," said Chuck with broad smile.

"I never doubted you for a minute, Hoopman!" The coach put a finger up under his eye to wipe a tear and said, "maybe for a second after that foul shot that ended regulation. I think you need to work on that for next year!"

"You gonna be there to help me work on it?" asked Chuck with a smile.

Coach Round was honest with his answer. "I think I'll leave while I'm on top, Chuck." He didn't say any more. He just smiled and said, "Thank you for this."

Chuck smiled, "Okay, Coach!" The older man turned away to answer a reporter's question, and Chuck didn't talk to him for the rest of the night.

Behind Coach Round, over on the Cortland bench sat Kenyon Taylor with a stunned look of disbelief on his face. Chuck walked over, stuck out his hand and said, "Nice game, Mr. Taylor. That was a helluva three pointer you popped."

Taylor wasn't thinking about his own shot. "You suckered me on that last one! I thought you were gonna try and bust me on the three!"

Chuck shook his head, "Only needed the deuce!"

Taylor nodded sadly. "You play good ball." Then he added with a smile, "For someone . . . as mature as you are!"

Chuck smiled and said, "You're gonna see a lot of guys my age next year where you'll be playin'. Bigger, faster, stronger, and yeah, lots of 'em . . . older." The two men chuckled. "Mind if I offer you one bit of advice, Kenyon?"

"Naw, man! Anything you got, I'll take. You're a champion!" said Taylor.

"When you're playing those . . . older guys next year, listen to them. Soak up everything they tell you because they been doin' it for years! I wish you this kind of happiness." said Chuck.

Taylor nodded and said, "I'll do that. And I'll tell 'em, Hoopman told me to learn from you guys." Chuck nodded, turned and started to walk away. Taylor hollered, "I already got my first lesson from one of the best tonight!"

Chuck didn't say anything. Kenyon Taylor was a great basketball player, and would go on to be get a tryout with the Knicks. Chuck had a feeling that he had earned Taylors' respect. Which by itself was a great feeling, but not nearly as good as the feeling of being on the best team in the nation.

EPILOGUE

Chuck was sitting alone at the dinner table when the man walked up to him. The first thing he noticed was the cane and the awkward limp. It seemed as if he knew the man from somewhere in his past, but just couldn't recognize him.

"Mind if I join you?" said the man. He stood patiently next to the chair and waited for Chuck's response.

"Uh, I'm kind of waiting for a lady friend of mine," said Chuck honestly.

"I won't be too long, Mr. Hayes," said the man.

Chuck couldn't help but feel at a loss. The man knew his name, but he had no clue as to who the man with the cane was. Chuck extended his hand to shake, and gestured for the man to take a seat. "Please," said Chuck.

The man looked at the hand, smiled and shook it. "You can call me Steve. I will call you, Mr. Hayes, if that's OK. I'm a big . . . 'Hoopfan'," exclaimed the man with a coy smile.

Chuck nodded his head and sat back in his chair. "It's always nice to meet a Hoopfan."

There was a strange silence as the two men sized each other up. Finally, Steve said, "I met you once before . . . in December."

Chuck thought back and remembered the Holiday Tournament. "New Orleans, right?"

Steve nodded. "My congratulations on your fine play during the tournament. If I were still a betting man, I would probably NOT have bet on you!"

Chuck said, "Me neither!"

Then Steve asked, "Do you have a lot of experience with computers, Hoopman?"

Chuck shook his head no, unable to hide his frown. "Not as far as you know, Steve. Send and receive emails. I've been known to Google. That kind of stuff."

"You mean you don't know how to do a Denial of Service?" asked Steve. Chuck shook his head no and took a drink of his Dos XX beer. "You mean to tell me, you don't know how to 'Spoof' an address?" Chuck shook his head again. "How about install a Trojan horse?"

Chuck shrugged his shoulders. "I don't even know how to ride a horse!"

Steve leaned forward in his chair. "Then whose ass was I covering?"

Chuck leaned forward and whispered, "It wasn't mine!"

Steve sat back and thought for a moment. "You don't know this. But you and your 'friends', whoever they are, helped me make a lot of money." He sat forward again. "A lot of money, Mr. Hayes." Chuck sat back and took a pull on his beer, unimpressed.

"All right! I'll tell you!" said Steve.

"I figured you were here for a reason, Steve," said Chuck.

"I got it all!" Steve leaned closer. "I took every penny from that bastard Grant!" He sat back for a second and could no longer hide his pride. "I planned to steal every cent from Jackson Grant for almost three years. I was . . . limited in my . . . early attempts. But when you, or your friends, it matters not to me, came along. You afforded me an opportunity to make certain acquisitions!"

Chuck took in the comment. "Those acquisitions," Chuck sat forward and looked at the man's eyes and said, "It isn't your money. Is it, Steve?"

The man slammed his hand on the table. "I EARNED IT!" He quickly looked around the restaurant and regained his composure. "I earned every last cent of it!"

"I figure that money belongs to the idiots who were stupid enough to bet on the BONE and got ripped off. Who knows how many games Grant had fixed? To take a slice of winnings from gamblers that received insider betting information is probably the lowest thing I've ever heard of. How many millions of dollars did he steal from people? And you just stole it from him," argued Chuck.

Steve shook his head in disagreement. "You don't understand!" He smacked his knee with the cane. "They did this to me!" He looked at Chuck and said, "Grant did this to me!!" He sat up and said, "That bastard," he swallowed hard as he remembered, "took a drill. And he put it in my knee! Not once. He couldn't stop with one, NO! Five times he shoved that thing into my knee! In and out, in and out!" He tried hard to regain his composure. "Didn't stop until I begged . . ." He started to tear up. "Until I begged for my life."

Chuck sat silently. He didn't know what to say.

Steve James wiped at his eyes. He cleared his throat and continued, "So don't tell me I didn't earn it! I sold my soul to that bastard and worked my way up to be the administrator of his entire network!"

Chuck sat back and said, "All right. Let's just say for giggles in your opinion, you earned it. I just don't see it that way. Are you braggin' or complainin', Steve?"

Steve laughed off the comment. "Neither Mr. Hayes. I just thought that your friends, the ones you are covering for, deserve a little . . . something for their effort!"

"They don't need any of that kind of 'something' that you have to offer," said Chuck.

"It's quite a lot of 'something', Mr. Hayes. Do you want to ask them?"

Chuck thought about the offer. "I don't need to ask them. They're probably in deep enough doo-doo without adding large sums of money showing up in their accounts." Chuck thought of what would be appropriate. He took out a pen and started writing on a napkin. "I'll tell you what, Steve. You're feeling so . . . generous. How about putting something into these?"

Steve took the napkin and read the lists. He nodded approvingly. "The San Antonio Animal Shelter? My goodness, you are a Boy Scout! I think I can do that, Mr. Hayes." The man stood up and said, "By the way, is the young man in the wheelchair the person responsible for destroying the BONE?"

Chuck was hesitant to answer. He looked around, then sat up and quietly said, "I can't say. What I will tell you is, it was a team. It was my team. That man in the wheelchair is a very good friend of mine. I would appreciate it if you just moved on and left my team alone," said Chuck as he finished his beer.

Steve James smiled. Then he reached into his pocket and pulled out a little black notebook. He tossed it on the table. "If I fail to give enough money to any of your organizations, or you think of a couple more. Perhaps you could use that to cover it."

Chuck picked up the book and read the cover. It was a bankbook from the *Internationale Banc de la Bahamas*. "What the hell is this?"

"I got your signature in New Orleans, Mr. Hayes. I just thought you might need a savings account after your basketball playing days were over," said Steve. "And don't worry. It isn't that much compared to what I got from Grant. Goodbye, Hoopman." He turned and said over his shoulder, "Nice game!" He tipped his hat as he passed Grace Winters.

Grace sat down and said, "Was that guy sitting with you?"

Chuck nodded and opened up the bankbook. He saw the handwritten amount of $25 million dollars. He looked up and must have gone white in the face. Grace said, "Are you okay? Did that man say something to you?"

Chuck handed her the bankbook and said, "We talked a little, then he gave me this."

Grace looked into the book and was stunned. "Do you think this is real?"

Chuck thought about what she asked. "It could be. That was 'Hoopfan'. The guy that was working over Grant from the other side. He stole all Grants' money."

"More than $25 million? How much did he get?" asked Grace.

"He didn't say exactly. I told him what I thought and that it wasn't his. He offered to give some to 'my friends', and I told him they definitely didn't need money to compound their potential problems. I gave him a list of some charities I thought he should give it to, then he tossed that at me," said Chuck.

"What are you gonna do, Chuck?" asked Grace.

Chuck thought about and waved at the waiter. "I think I'll have dinner with a very beautiful lady. Whatever comes of this," he tucked the bank book into his pocket, "we'll deal with it later."

For a very long week, the St. Michael's Armadillos story was played and replayed on every sports television show, sports radio show and sports chat line in the country. The City of San Antonio had a small parade down the River Walk as the City took the day off. People called from across the country and around the globe to get interviews with Coach Round, Charles Holmes, David Parnell, Jose Rivera-Torres and of course, Chuck "Hoopman" Hayes. Charles and David were contacted by agents as they were the latest NIL commodities on the college scene.

Chuck did break down for two interviews. One with USAA insurance company that focuses on support to Veterans and the other to the American Legion.

Coach Round had everyone over for a Bar-b-que where he announced he was retiring effective at the end of the school year. Between the recognition, the fanfare, Coach Round's announcement, the team knew there was not going to be a repeat next season.

The players started to get drained from the experience and found themselves taking more and more time away from each other just to collect their thoughts. It would be a while until everything they had achieved would be fully understood.

Two weeks after the Championship, Chuck was sitting on the couch at Grace's home, drinking an iced tea and flipping the channels with the remote. Grace walked in and watched him in silence as he sat there. Chuck glanced up and said, "What?"

She laughed at him. "You are LOST!"

"WHAT?" said Chuck with a smile.

"Your season is over, there's only garbage on TV and you," she came over and sat next to him, "ARE LOST!" Then she grabbed his head and gave him a big kiss.

Chuck smiled at her and nodded up and down. "Just like a woman! Always right!" She smiled at him. "I'm . . . I'm in such a weird state. I feel happy, but I'm apathetic about almost everything."

"Um, not everything," she said as she rubbed his thigh.

"I said 'almost' everything," said Chuck. "I feel this tremendous sense of accomplishment, but it took so much effort and so much focus . . ." His voice trailed off. "It all seems like a dream." He looked into Grace's eyes and said, "A really, really good dream."

"I'm very happy for you," said Grace. "For the whole team. It's a great way to put the school on the map." Chuck nodded in agreement. He was silent for a moment as he rubbed her knee.

"We're still going over to Hawk's tonight for dinner, aren't we?" asked Grace.

"Six o'clock, and don't be late!" said Chuck as he tried to sound like Nate Hawkins. "I can't believe the way he came out on the court and took Holden away!" Chuck sat up and snapped his fingers, "DAMN!"

Grace gave him a confused look and said, "What?"

"I never told him 'Thanks' for savin' my life! Remind me to do that!"

"You are way too focused, Chuck Hayes!" said Grace. She sat back and asked, "Have you gotten any more emails from 'Hoopfan'?"

Chuck said, "Nope! Steve, if that's his name, is long gone. Hawk said he heard through his sources that a guy named Mike Thompson had turned himself in to the FBI and was telling everything he knew about BONE to them. I'm sure it's just a matter of time until they come and ask us a few questions."

"I thought the 'Godzilla' program took care of everything," said Grace.

"We think so, but the FBI may have some way of recovering the data," said Chuck. "Who knows? I'm beyond even worrying about it."

Suddenly Chuck turned up the sound on the TV and said, "OH! Did you hear this?"

The reporter said as many as three online gambling organizations had apparently been robbed electronically. The thefts had occurred over the last month, and no one knew the source of the thief or thieves, but many unnamed sources had indicated the Russian mafia was involved. The same sources said that losses may have totaled over seven hundred million dollars.

Immediately after that story, a local San Antonio reporter stated five "anonymous" donations to various charitable organizations ranging in amounts between ten and twenty million dollars were being announced. Some of the organizations receiving large donations included the Army Combined Federal Campaign, The Houston Institute for Spinal Research, and Gamblers Anonymous.

Grace smiled and asked, "Your buddy Steve?"

"I don't know for sure, but those were some ideas that I gave him as suggestions," said Chuck. "At least something good can come from the money."

"Speaking of money, did you call the bank in the Bahamas?" asked Grace.

"Yeah, I did," Chuck said with a grin. "Apparently I have twenty million dollars sitting in a savings account there."

Grace couldn't believe it. "What are you going to do with all that?"

"I've thought about it some, but I have to check into some things first. Plus, I need to talk to Hawk and Eddie and make sure they are okay with my ideas of what to do with it. We might need it for lawyers," said Chuck.

"Lawyers?" said Grace.

Chuck nodded and looked into her eyes and said, "Lawyers. One thing Mr. Hawkins has taught me is to be prepared for the unexpected."

"You're not going to do anything else with all that money?"

"I believe we are taking a vacation next month, right?" Chuck teased.

She stood up and walked towards the hallway. "I think I need to see if I can get an advance on that vacation, Mr. Hayes," said Grace. She momentarily stood in the hallway and unbuttoned her shirt. A devious smile appeared on her face as the shirt came off. She threw it at him and said, "Do I have your attention, Mr. Hayes?"

Chuck turned off the TV with the remote, stood up, and walked slowly down the hall. He said with a laugh, "You're only doing this cause I'm rich, right?" She pulled him into the bedroom and slammed the door closed.

The St. Michael's University Sports Award banquet was a combination of emotions for all the athletes. On one hand, they were thrilled with the opportunity to shine and be with friends in a venue other than the playing field or the court. The Athletic Director, Clarence Teazin, was eloquent in his speech to the assembled crowd and immediately began presenting awards to the student athletes. The largest ovation was saved for the St. Michael's Armordillo basketball team. When the coveted award of St. Michael's Athlete of the Year Award was announced, Junior Charlton Hayes was announced at the winner. The 40-year-old basketball player for the National Champions was honored by the entire crowd with a standing ovation.

As Chuck took the podium, he was slow to start his speech. He looked around the crowd and waited for the cheering to stop. He said, "Thank you all very much," and the noise finally died down.

"Thank you, Dr. Teazin," he said to the Director, then he coughed and began a short speech. He didn't have any notes prepared, but he had taken a class that had helped him prepare for moments like this.

"I'd like to thank you all for your support this year. I just want to make sure that everyone knows that this award should be chopped up and spread around to about fifteen other people. Basketball is a team game, and anything I receive personally is just an extension of my teammates' effort to play with me. The trophy that really counts is the one over there," he said as he pointed to the National Championship Trophy across the room. The crowd looked at the beautiful ornament, and someone started another clap. The room came to its feet again to honor the achievement.

When order was restored, Chuck said, "To my teammates," he sought the familiar faces in the crowd and said, "Every one of you is a part of that Trophy. It is something that can never be taken away from us." There was more clapping from the audience.

"I only have one more thing to say." Chuck stepped away from the podium and got some water. He looked over to the head table and saw the empty seat where Coach Round would have been sitting. "Last weekend, we lost a teammate." The crowd grew silent. "Coach Darrell Haywood Round was a warrior right up to the end. He was a mentor, a leader and a father figure to everyone on our team. We were very fortunate to have him as our coach during our season of triumph." Some in the audience talked softly as they agreed with Chuck's comments. "I'm just happy that we were able to let him leave this world a winner. I'm certain he is on a bench somewhere up in heaven telling Pete Maravich how to follow through on his jump shot. Coaching up Heaven's Team."

Chuck reached down for some more water and wiped his nose with a napkin.

Chuck changed his tone and started again, "As you heard Dr. Teazin say tonight, through an anonymous donation of ten million dollars," Chuck looked over at Sandy, Grace and Hawk and contained his smile, "St. Michael's is proud to announce the start of a brand-new arena for all St. Michael's athletes to be completed within two years!" The crowd clapped and cheered once again.

Chuck held up his hands for quiet and said, "I don't know how I'll be able to play anywhere other than the 'Hole', but if I get a fifth year, maybe I can play in the new facility! They'd be giving me Geritol and Ensure instead of Gatorade!" The crowd chuckled at their star's stab at humor.

Chuck waited for the laughter to end and said, "I also want you to know that I prayed. I prayed hard for this. Somehow, the Lord has granted us this blessing. It is through Him that we are given opportunity here on earth to achieve great things. I know many of you do not believe. It is not my place to convert you, but I will say that faith allows a trouble heart Peace." Chuck listened and actually a few "Amen's". Chuck exhaled quickly and got serious once more. "The Lord works in mysterious ways and if He can work through me, I'm OK with that."

Chuck paused and looked at the crowd. "One more thing before I step down. I would like to propose to Dr. Teazin and to you all out there, maybe we should name the new 'Dillo Dome, the Darrell H. Round Memorial Auditorium!" With a resounding ovation, the suggestion was accepted by the audience. Chuck quickly stepped to the microphone and said, "I thought you'd agree with me. THANK YOU ALL VERY MUCH, AND WE'LL SEE YOU NEXT YEAR!"

As he stepped down Marshall started the chant, "HOOPMAN"! They didn't stop until he took one last bow. With a tear in his eye, he stepped to the stage and yelled, "WHO'S NUMBER ONE!"

The room erupted again with the familiar chant. He held the trophy up and stepped off the stage to Grace Winters' waiting arms.

As the nurse rolled the wheelchair down the ramp, the man in the chair was in surprisingly good spirits. The nurse said, "I still think you should stay a while longer and get therapy on your knee, Mr. Jones."

Steve looked at the waiting cab and said, "I'd love to stay here and let you torture me some more, Nurse Fineman, but I need to get to some sunshine. New York City is all right for a short time but stay here too long and the city will swallow you up." He reached behind the wheelchair and made a playful grab at her leg.

The nurse gasped and stepped away from his reach, "Stop that!" She giggled like a schoolgirl. She stopped pushing as they reached the cab. The nurse reached down to try to help him from the chair.

Steve said, "No. No, thank you, Jenny. I don't need any help!" He picked his cane up and took one last look at it. "Here, you can have this. I won't be needing it anymore."

"Are you sure you don't want to use it for just a while longer? You're not strong enough yet to get around," said the nurse.

Steve pushed himself out of the chair and said, "I'm just fine, Jenny." He stood slowly and added weight to his leg. A small smile appeared on his face. "Just like new." The nurse smiled at her patient.

Steve reached into his coat pocket and pulled out an envelope. "I cannot fully express my thanks for your weeks of effort and care Jennifer. I hope this little token of my appreciation is accepted." He handed her the envelope, grabbed her hand and softly kissed it. The woman blushed. "I wish I could stay, but I have some living to do."

The nurse was still blushing as she said, "I can't accept this if it's what I think it is!"

Steve said, "You're a single mother with two daughters, Jenny. You deserve every break you get. What you have in that envelope is a break. Use it to put those beautiful girls of yours through college."

She looked at the envelope and smiled back at the man. She shoved the envelope into her pocket. "If you ever get back to New York, Mr. Jones, you know where to find me."

Steve smiled and released her hand. He took a deep breath and said, "Yes. Yes, I do." He gently touched her face. If he wasn't such an ass, he would probably stay with this woman. Perhaps it was just because she was the first woman he had been with since his new life had begun. It just wasn't time to settle down. He was rich, he was free, and the million dollar surgery to his knee made him a whole man again. There were other things he needed to do and other places to go. He had not seen enough of the world. The first thing he wanted to do was walk on the beach without a cane.

Steve exhaled heavily and said, "Time to see how good that surgeon really was." He slowly picked up his leg and took a step towards the cab. After years of agony, there was only relief. He walked over to the door and pulled it open. The nurse handed him his bag and he threw it in the car.

"It's too bad your family couldn't come here to get you, Mr. Jones," said the nurse.

"I don't have any family, Jenny. I have a friend in the Bahamas," said Steve. "I'm going to the airport now to catch a plane and join him there."

"That sounds wonderful, Steve," said the nurse. "I hope you have a great time down there and you recover completely."

Steve slid into the back of the cab and smiled. The knee felt wonderful. He looked at the nurse and said, "Physically, I'll have plenty of time to get my knee strong again." He closed the door and put his head out the window to add, "Mentally, I already have, Jennifer." He blew her a kiss goodbye then turned to the cab driver and said, "LaGuardia, please. I have a plane to catch."

Steve James, or Stephen Jones as his new passport identified him, pulled the New York Times off the seat and read the headline: *DEFENSE DEPARTMENT COMPUTERS ATTACKED BY UNKOWN GROUP*. Steve folded the paper and put it in his travel bag to read on the plane. As he headed to the airport, the headline wouldn't leave his thoughts. He quickly dismissed the thought and dreamed of his future. What would he do with all his free time?

"The sunsets on this beach are spectacular," said Grace Hayes. "I could stay here for about a year. That would be enough."

Chuck got the waiter's attention and signaled for two more drinks. "You two want anything?"

"No, thanks," said Sandy. Nate shook his head no. Chuck told the waiter just two and laid back in his beach chair. He sucked in a big breath of the salty air and said, "One more week to chill."

"Do you know why Eddie and Chris had to leave? I thought they were going to stay with us the whole two weeks," asked Grace.

Chuck wiped his sunglasses clear and said, "I don't know exactly. They were out of here so fast, they didn't really say."

"I hope it wasn't work related. They said Colonel Taylor didn't want to let them go," said Grace. "I'm glad you made the call."

"I'm glad they made it here, too. Those guys are nuts," said Chuck. He was thinking about Eddie racing his motorized wheelchair around the pool. A couple more 'Bahama Mamas' and he probably would have driven into the water. Chuck picked up the newspaper and started to glance at the cover story. It was two days old. In the corner was a small article that read *PENTAGON ORDERS SOME RETIREES TO ACTIVE DUTY*. A fleeting thought raced through his mind that made him want to know what was happening. Then he looked at Grace. He put his sunglasses on and lay back in the chair again.

Suddenly, Hawk smacked at his iPad as he was reading. It was the sports section and Chuck was instantly curious about what could make his friend so animated. "What's up? The Rangers finally win a game?"

"Hardly!" laughed Hawk. "Check this out!" He handed the paper to Chuck.

Hawk said, "Seems some other 'anonymous' donor sent ten million more dollars to the Darrell Round Memorial Auditorium fund! The fund is up to nearly thirty million now."

Grace lifted up her sunglasses and said, "Your buddy Steve?"

Chuck read the article and said with a grin, "I don't know for sure, but if I was a betting man." He looked at Hawk with a squint and said, "I'd say it was him."

"Maybe he's not such a maggot after all?" said Hawk with a grin.

Chuck didn't say anything at first. He sat up in his chair and started to tell Hawk what he really thought when a waiter showed up with a cell phone. "Excuse me, Mr. Hayes, phone call for you!"

Chuck looked at the waiter and frowned as he put down the newspaper. He took the phone call as Grace looked at him with a puzzled expression. Chuck shrugged his shoulders and said into the phone, "Chuck Hayes."

"Hello, Hoopman," said Steve.

Chuck knew instantly who was on the line. He lay back against the chair and put his sunglasses back on. "We were just talking about you." The statement caught Grace, Hawk and Sandy by surprise. Chuck continued, "Yeah, we were talking about a maggot!" Hawk laughed out loud and sat back in his chair and began surfing his iPad again.

"Very funny, Mr. Hayes," said Steve. "I have a favor to ask."

"Wait a second now," said Chuck. The comment made him sit up in the chair. "I don't owe your sorry ass anything. If I'm not mistaken, you are set for life!"

"Just hear me out," said Steve.

"We just read about the money for the Round Auditorium and seriously that was very generous of you. But if you think I owe you something for that, you are mistaken," said Chuck with a scowl.

"I didn't think you'd find out about that until you got home," said Steve.

Chuck was confused. "You did do that, right?"

"Yes," said Steve flatly. "He was a good man, and I'm probably the only person on the planet that knows where the first ten million came from. Very nice gesture yourself, Hoopman. But that's not what I'm calling about."

"So why are you calling?" asked Chuck. Hawk and Grace noticed the hostility was gone from his voice.

"Like I said, I need a favor," said Steve.

Chuck mouthed the statement to Grace and shrugged. "What is it?"

"I need you to see if you can get me a job with your friends," said Steve.

Chuck was stunned. "What?" He stood up and started walking around. Hawk was trying to ask him something, but Chuck held up his hand to tell him to hold on. He put his finger in his ear and turned away. "Did you say you want a job with my friends?"

Hawk said, "WHAT?" Chuck waved at him and put his finger to his lips.

"Yes, Mr. Hayes. I would like to see if I can . . . assist your friends again," said Steve.

"What kind of assist do they need?" asked Chuck.

Steve said quickly, "You really need to stay in the loop, Hoopman. I know you're on your honeymoon, but the world is falling apart around you! Haven't you heard any of the news?"

Chuck turned around facing the group and said, "What are you talking about?"

"We're at war, Hoopman," said Steve. "Your friends are dealing with a special problem. I think I can help them. I need . . ."

Chuck cut him off. "Hold on now! Did you say we're at war?"

Steve exhaled loudly into the phone. "I already said that. Listen. Perhaps Mr. Hawkins can use the iPad for something other than the sports news."

Chuck pulled the cell phone down and looked around. Steve was watching them.

Steve continued, "I need to help your friends. You know my work is sound."

Chuck put his hand over the phone and yelled to a waiter, "Can you turn on that TV behind the bar to US News please!"

He turned to the phone, "All right! I'll play your game. What makes you think I can or even will help you? How can we trust you?"

Steve said, "You can trust me. The question is can I trust you? You are the only one that knows the truth. In a way, anything I do only happens if you let me do it."

Chuck let the comment sink in. Steve was right. "I never cared about the money."

Chuck walked around the chairs and looked out at the sunset. "I don't know, Steve."

"I just need a chance, Mr. Hayes," said Steve.

Chuck noticed he didn't say 'Hoopman'. Hawk stood up and pointed to the iPad. "Hawk just showed me the news. What do you want?"

"I want to go work for the U. S. Government," said Steve. "I'm serious when I say I can help."

"I don't know," said Chuck honestly. "I have to think about it." As he sat down in the lounge chair he said, "They might not even want you."

"If you tell them I'm okay, they'll take me," said Steve.

Hawk was reading the article. He pointed at a part in the article and said, "It's computers, Chuck. Whoever it is, they're raising hell with our networks."

Chuck got back on the phone. "Let me make a call. I can't promise you anything. I probably won't even be able to get through. How can I call you?"

Steve was hesitant to respond. He was still a man in hiding. "I will send a message to the front desk."

Chuck said, "That works."

"Give me a couple hours," said Steve as he hung up the phone.

Chuck put the phone down on the stand next to the chair and said, "He wants to help." He looked at Hawk and said, "Do you think I can trust this guy?"

Hawk smiled. "Did he put that money in the Memorial Fund for the Round Auditorium?" Chuck nodded. "I'd trust him."

Chuck tried for hours to get a call to Texas. When he got through to Eddie's cell phone, it went to voicemail. He left a message to call him back. Just after midnight, the phone rang. It was Eddie, and he filled Chuck in as best he could on an open phone line, and they were on the defensive. Whoever was behind the attack was doing a number on America. Chuck asked if Eddie wanted help.

Eddie jumped at the offer. "How soon can you get here?"

Chuck said loudly, "WHOA, big guy! Not me! I got a call from our old friend Steve. You remember Steve, don't you?"

Eddie said flatly, "Yeah. I remember your friend Steve. What's he want?"

"He wants to come and work with you," said Chuck. "He wants to help."

"Like last time," said Eddie. "Even if he did help, he only helped himself. Do you trust him?"

Chuck was ready for the question. "Yes, I do, Eddie." There was silence on the other end. "If you are in the situation, you say you're in, you can use all the help you can get."

It was Eddie's turn. "If you say so. I'll ask Colonel Taylor. You can expect a call one way or the other tomorrow. I don't think you can get through to me, so we'll call you." Eddie hung up the phone.

Chuck lay on the bed next to Grace and stared at the ceiling. She rolled over and hugged him. "What's my Hoopman thinking about?" Chuck smiled down and looked at her.

"I love the way you say that," he kissed her on the forehead. Then he exhaled and stared up at the ceiling again. After a long moment he said, "What would you say if I was to go back in the Army again?"

Grace sat up quickly and looked at her husband. "You're not going off to fight are you?"

Chuck smiled at her. "There is one advantage to being old. I mean being older than those young kids who will go fight. I'll probably be stuck behind a desk somewhere." She lay next to him and was quiet. "I don't know if they'll even want me, but if they call, you know I'll go, right?"

She squeezed him tightly and said, "I know you'll do what you have to do." She reached up and kissed him. Chuck pulled away and turned out the light. The light from the full moon lit up the room enough so he could still make out every curve of her beautiful face. He had done the right thing when he married Grace. Even if the world was falling apart, to Chuck, she was the best thing in it.

Chuck woke up about five o'clock and slowly got out of bed. He picked up his laptop and went out to the kitchen. After fifteen minutes and two cups of coffee, he was online. He opened his email and saw 12 spam messages. Cursing to himself, "Jesus help us! There's a war on and they still get through the filters?" Finally, he saw the mail he was looking for.

hoopman,
what was the word from your friends?
provide answer to concierge
hoopfan

Chuck powered down and was headed back to bed when the phone rang. His first impulse was to run and get it so as not to wake Grace.

"Hello?" he answered.

"Mr. Hayes? Mr. Charlton Hayes?" said the voice.

Chuck noticed the static on the line which led him to believe the caller was on a cell. "Yes, can I help you?"

"Hold on please, sir," said the voice. The voice said something and obviously handed the phone over to another person. Chuck turned to see Grace come walking around the corner. She walked over and snuggled into his chest.

"Mr. Hayes, this is Brigadier General Mickey Shelton from Crestview Air Force Base. I need to ask you a couple questions if that's okay?"

Chuck said, "Uh, um sure, General. What can I do for you?"

"I have some young men working for me, and they said they would appreciate it if I got you to come give them a hand on a little project. Are you available?" asked the General.

Chuck looked down at Grace. It was obvious that she heard the General's question. She smiled up at him and nodded. "Yes, Sir!"

"Good! Good deal, Mr. Hayes! I also understand you have another friend or two that you need to come and work with you on this project. Is that correct?" asked the General. It was clear that Eddie had told the general about Steve and Nate Hawkins.

"From what I hear General you can use all the friends I have," said Chuck.

The General was quick to answer, "If your friends can do half what I've been told they can do, I needed you here yesterday. Can you get here tomorrow?"

"The airport is a mess, sir, but we'll get there as soon as we can," said Chuck.

"Good. Bring your friend . . . Steve, no last name, and . . . Mr. Nathaniel Hawkins, too," said the General. "See you soon." The phone went dead.

Chuck looked at the receiver and said, "Yes, sir!" He looked at Grace and said, "I think the General is busy!"

Grace said, "You're really gonna do this, aren't you?"

"If the country calls, Grace, I'm there," said Chuck.

"Before Hoopman goes off taking care of the country," she grabbed his hand and pulled him back toward the bedroom. "Come take care of your wife. Can you show me that behind the back little move that you do? I like that one!"

Chuck was trying to recall the 'behind the back' move she liked as she dragged him down the hall.

Chuck handed the concierge a note before they checked out at noon. The message told Steve to fly to Crestview AFB tomorrow and he would have another message waiting for him at the front gate.

At three o'clock the foursome was sitting at the airport with two thousand other people waiting to get back to the United States. Chuck finally got next to an electrical outlet and fired up his laptop.

Chuck surfed the net for the latest information from the states. Things weren't looking good for the home team. Transportation and electrical power were intermittent across the country. If they could just get to Miami, they could rent a car and drive to Crestview. As he stared at the screen, he was unaware that Hawk was reading over his shoulder until he heard his friend's deep voice say, "Looks like they need some help."

Grace popped up over his other shoulder and added, "They need Hoopman!" She rubbed his shoulder and bent over to peck his cheek with a little kiss.

"It looks like Hoopman may be going away for a little while," said Hawk. "Your hoop days are gonna be on the back burner, Buddy."

Chuck started to power down his computer, looked at his friends and said, "If we get there and get to work, we can be back on campus by January!" Hawk laughed out loud at the boldness in Chuck's statement. Chuck continued, "I'm not gonna let these guys mess up my season. I have a championship to defend! We take care of this little War and I should be in the starting line up by February! Never count me out when it comes to hoop."

"I hate to say this, but I bet we won't be done by Christmas," exclaimed Hawk.

Chuck stood up and looked at his friend and said, "I know you know better than to bet against Hoopman! We stopped all the betting, remember?" To anyone else it would have seemed a brash statement, but to the people who knew Chuck best, he was just telling the truth.

Chuck smacked his friend lightly on the shoulder and walked over to look out the window at the planes. He reached into his pocket and pulled out the piece of basketball net that had become a part of him since the championship. He rolled the twine slowly between his thumb and fingers. As he looked out the window, he noticed a group of baggage handler's shooting a beat-up basketball at a rim with no net. For just an instant, Chuck had the urge to join the men as they battled on the playground. In spite of his inner desire to play ball, whether it was with baggage handlers or the best college team in the nation, he knew there was something he had to do first.

Chuck took one last look at the twine and shoved it back into his pocket. Hoopman would have to suit up for a different type of game. Another National Championship would have to wait.

www.ingramcontent.com/pod-product-compliance
Lightning Source LLC
Chambersburg PA
CBHW070624010826
48976CB00023B/116